"Moorcock writes with the dynamism of a nineteenth-century master operating with all the darts and shuffles of our electronic, amnesiac, fast-twitch culture."

Iain Sinclair
The Spectator

"If one purpose of fiction is to lead us into different worlds and, as Virginia Woolf says, to make of them 'some kind of whole,' then Michael Moorcock succeeds brilliantly."

The Guardian

"What is extraordinary about Moorcock's fiction is the largeness of the design. Moorcock has the bravura of the nineteenth-century novelists; he takes risks, he uses fiction as if it were a divining rod for the age's most significant concerns."

Peter Ackroyd
The Times

"Moorcock can be funny, his irony is blissful. . . . When we read him we want more and have no appetite, at least for a while, for anyone else's fiction. He casts a heady, enslaving spell."

Ruth Rendell

"A great English novelist."

The Independent

"A blast of energy and pleasure."

The Times

"One unstoppable, spellbinding, brilliant voice."

Times Literary Supplement

"A dazzlingly esoteric cultural rumpus."

The Spectator

The Metatemporal Detective

Michael Moorcock

The Metatemporal Detective

Newmarket Public Library

an imprint of **Prometheus Books**
Amherst, NY

Published 2007 by Pyr®, an imprint of Prometheus Books

Inquiries should be addressed to
Pyr
59 John Glenn Drive
Amherst, New York 14228–2119
VOICE: 716–691–0133, ext. 210
FAX: 716–691–0137
WWW.PYRSF.COM

11 10 09 08 07   5 4 3 2 1

Library of Congress Cataloging-in-Publication Data

Moorcock, Michael, 1939–
    The metatemporal detective / Michael Moorcock ; [edited by Linda Moorcock].
        p. cm.
    ISBN 978–1–59102–596–2
    1. Detective and mystery stories, English. 2. Fantasy fiction, English. I. Moorcock, Linda. II. Title.

PR6063.O59M47 2007
823'.914—dc22

                                                                            2007028501

Printed in the United States on acid-free paper

Acknowledgments

As a boy one of my favourite magazines, found in secondhand shops because it was at its hey-day during the 1920s, was *Union Jack*. It ran the adventures of perhaps the world's longest-running detective hero, Sexton Blake. One of Blake's greatest adversaries was Zenith the Albino written by Anthony Skene, a government surveyor whose real name was G. N. Phillips. These stories are in homage to my boyhood hero and are dedicated to Anthony Skene. He only published one hardcover novel featuring Zenith— *Monsieur Zenith*—published in 1936 and recently reprinted in a gloriously lavish illustrated edition, with all kinds of "extras," by Savoy Books of Manchester, England.

The Metatemporal Detective is also therefore dedicated to Messrs Britton, Butterworth, and Coulthart, the backbone of Savoy Books. Thanks are also due to my wife, Linda, for her professional copyediting of this book. Further details of Sexton Blake and his opponents, together with a selection of reprinted stories, can be found at the Blakiana Web site, which I heartily recommend.

Michael Moorcock

FOR WALTER MOSLEY

Contents

The Affair of the Seven Virgins

Black it stood as night,
Fierce as ten Furies, terrible as hell,
And shook a dreadful dart; what seem'd his head
The likeness of a kingly crown had on.
Satan was now at hand, and from his seat
The monster moving onward, came as fast
With horrid strides; hell trembled as he strode.

Milton
Paradise Lost

CHAPTER ONE

A Queer Visitor

In all his long career as a consulting detective, Mr Seaton Begg had never received a stranger visitor to his Sporting Club Square rooms. Though it was not yet noon the personage now languidly seated across the desk from him was clad in full evening dress, complete with cloak and silk hat. This alone was remarkable, but what was truly striking about the creature, who spoke with the faintest of educated Middle European accents, was that he was a pure albino!

From the visitor's bone-white skin stared eyes as crimson as the lining of his hat and cloak. Upon his long, delicate fingers he wore two rings, one of plain gold and the other some black, mysterious metal, engraved with the crest of a family which had been old and civilised before the Romans ever attempted—and failed—to conquer its land.

Seaton Begg felt himself in the presence of a great power—able to command the wealth of Europe, who smoked, after polite enquiry of his host, an oddly smelling little brown cigarette which Begg, long familiar with Limehouse, recognised as opium. This doubtless explained the man's languor, his slightly hooded, if sardonically amused, eyes which regarded Begg with a certain understanding. The albino introduced himself, handing his card to the famous investigator.

The ivory pasteboard bore a simple inscription:

Monsieur Zenith
The Albany

The hint of a smile crossed Begg's lips as he read the name. "You prefer to be incognito, your highness?"

"You are discreet, Mr Begg. I can see that your reputation is not baseless."

"I hope not, sir. By the way, as a fellow fiddle player, would I be right in thinking you are at present having trouble with your E-flat? A trifle sharp?"

The albino examined his little finger. "Just so, Mr Begg." He raised his right eyebrow a fraction. "I am impressed."

"No need to be, sir. An easily learned and very simple observation. The calluses on your hands are not, after all, dissimilar to my own! The rest was schoolboy logic. You are presumably here to seek my professional advice?"

"Exactly, sir." Whereupon, "Monsieur Zenith" dispensed with further formalities and launched, in precise, economical English, into his explanation for making this appointment.

Sir Seaton Begg's success was legendary. On more than one occasion he had been employed by the government of which M Zenith had until lately been a member. Blackshirt revolutionists had, with finance from a certain Great Power, succeeded in ousting the elected government and sending the king into exile. Now a puppet sat on the throne of Monsieur Zenith's mountainous land and a dictator, supported by foreign gold and arms, tyrannised a pleasant, if backward, nation, enslaving and destroying, creating dissension amongst people once living in easy harmony. Dr Papadakia had divided in order to rule. And rule he did—in a land drowning in its own blood and shrieking in its death agonies.

This, said Monsieur Zenith, was what any intelligent reader could deduce from the newspapers. What was not generally understood was how, to make further capital from his country's suffering, the Dictator and his bullies were in essence kidnapping prominent people and ransoming them to relatives abroad. On more than one occasion tortured, ruined corpses had been delivered to those unable or unwilling to pay.

"That alone is an horrific trade, Sir Seaton, I think you'll agree. There is a streak of ancient blood in our people which occasionally reemerges. When it does, such cruelties become commonplace. What Papadakia and his gang are doing is offensive to all we civilised men hold holy." The queer looking creature paused, lowering his eyes and drawing deeply on his little cigarette.

After a while he continued. "But now, Sir Seaton, they have devised a varia-tion on their vile theme.

"They are blackmailing the king!"

Their puppet, a distant cousin of the legitimate monarch, had rebelled and died. But having succeeded so well in their obscene enterprise, these bandits-in-uniform had sent a message to King Jhargon the Fourth (with his family in Paris): "Unless he returns to my country and gives his blessing to the present dictatorship, so that the world might think them reformed, Dr Papadakia and his bully-boys would painfully and brutally dispose of a young woman every day. Virgin blood, they declared, would be upon the king's hands."

Long familiar with the world's infamies, Begg felt his own blood chill in his veins as Monsieur Zenith described the fate of the women, all members of his country's oldest families, who would die foully if the king did not return. It was a scheme of almost unimaginable fiendishness and Begg's loathing for the "fascisti" rabble informed the set of his lips and the hard-ening of his cool, grey eyes.

"You have my help in whatever form you desire, sir." The detective's tone had grown singularly grave. "Though I do not have the resources to start a counterrevolution in your country, if that is what you are proposing."

"Those ideas are being debated elsewhere," Monsieur Zenith told the detective. "And moves are afoot to oust the dictator. But meanwhile there are seven young women, two of whom are directly related to me, who will die dreadfully if we do not help them. Dictator Papadakia already has the seven under lock and key. They are imprisoned in the Martyrs' Tower, from which in olden times the famous Ziniski monks jumped to their deaths rather than submit to the Injinkskya Heresy. Well, if you know that story you know that the tower is impregnable. Protected, they say, by Hell and History." The albino casually extinguished the remains of his drugged cigarette in Begg's ashtray.

"You are telling me that the position of these young women is hopeless, Monsieur?" Begg's eyes narrowed.

"Unless the king capitulates."

"Which he must not do—for the sake of his people and his honour."

"Precisely, Sir Seaton."

Begg mused upon his caller's appalling position. "Rescuing those seven maidens would be one thing," he murmured. "Ensuring that this foul dictator was ousted from his unearned eminence and foiled from committing any further evil—that would be another!"

Monsieur Zenith's expression did not change, but his posture appeared more relaxed and there was a certain amused alertness in his strange, crimson eyes. "You are a man after my own heart, Sir Seaton. I came to you for advice, as I said. What would you suggest?"

Begg placed his elbows on his desk. He put his fingertips together and regarded the albino over hands that seemed poised to pray. "I have the glimmerings of an idea. But to explore it I must take a little time. And then, my dear sir, I shall require you to put me in your confidence on certain delicate matters. If convenient, I should be obliged if you could meet me again in twenty-four hours. Then we might discuss our plot . . ."

The albino rose, picked up his hat, and bowed. "I am obliged to you, Sir Seaton. Until I came through your door I had no hope at all. Now I have a little."

"Your opinion is flattering, sir. I sincerely hope I deserve it." With a quick, almost clumsy movement, Begg reached to shake the albino's hand.

⟿ CHAPTER TWO ⟾

To Spin a Web

Less than four hours after his meeting with the strange aristocrat, Seaton Begg would have been unrecognisable as the clean-cut gentleman who had interviewed Monsieur Zenith. Not that his appearance was inappropriate to his surroundings, which were slovenly, the foulest kind of thieves' den, and stank of a thick mixture combining opium, nicotine, alcohol, and fried food. The vast maze of underground chambers, some of which connected directly with sewers and other routes which formed the secret roads of London's criminal intercourse, was known by the title of Smith's Kitchen. Smith himself, a seedy, corpulent individual who kept control of his premises by a mixture of blackmail and brute violence, was a kind of aristocrat. Although the police had sought to catch him over and over again, he had never been arrested. It was rumoured he had a hand in almost every kind of crime in London. He barred nobody from his premises, so long, he said, as they kept their noses clean. Deadly rivals met at Smith's, but they had sense enough to keep their grudges to themselves.

Begg's reason for adopting the disguise of a petty sneak-thief and coming to Smith's was to meet a particular creature who went by the name of William Duck but was generally known as "Dirty." Duck was considered disgusting even by Smith's regulars, yet for some reason he was party to the kind of information about the "upstairs" world of power, parliament and people in high places denied the most assiduous of modern journalists. Although suspected of it more than once, he was not an informer. But he knew the name of almost every prominent person staying on any particular night at any one of twenty London hotels.

Through the haze of smoke, Begg watched as a young girl got up from a table and made her weary way to the dance floor. Meanwhile Smith's band, an accordionist, a snare-drummer, and a violinist, struck up another dusty tune, and soon the crooks and their molls were in each others' arms, shuffling around the floor in a parody of pleasure.

In a doorway overhead a silhouette passed, then, stepping quickly down the rickety staircase crossed the room to where, in shadows, Begg waited.

From habit, Dirty Duck was incapable of anything resembling a direct route and approached Begg's table via the bar, where he bought himself a pint of beer, looking around as if for a seat. Only then did he make his way towards Begg.

All denizens of Smith's had a habit of talking softly from the corners of their mouths. The conversation between Begg and Duck took place in that style, using a whole variety of jargon and cant which, to an outsider, would have sounded like a foreign language. The exchange was brief. Money passed. And then, if anyone had been observing, Begg appeared to vanish. A moment later Duck had vanished also.

Only one party had taken an interest in the conversation. His head moved to follow what had almost certainly been Duck's route out of the Kitchen. He wore smoked glasses and gave the impression that he was blind but, as his fingers flew over the accordion's keys in a lively Empire Medley, the eyes behind the glasses were deep in thought.

Half an hour later Begg had reverted to his usual smart appearance, his favourite "Petersen" stuck comfortably in the corner of his mouth, and lay deep in his Voysey armchair poring over a large book, a glass of single malt whisky readily to hand. From time to time he would reach and consult his latest International Airways Guide. Eventually he got up and put a gramophone record on his machine. Then, as the strains of Messiaen's *La Source du Vie* began to fill the room, he returned his attention to his books and documents.

When, that evening, his confidant and sometime assistant, the cabby Tozer Vine, knocked on the door of Begg's Sporting Club Square apartments, he was shown in by Mrs Curry, Begg's housekeeper. Begg himself was fast asleep in his chair, his pipe unlit, his whisky scarcely tasted. But there was a large pad full of notes beside him now and an expression of satisfaction on his aquiline features.

Begg woke immediately, as if aware of Tozer's presence. "Ah, the trusty Tozer! Did you get my message, old friend?"

"Yes, Sir Seaton, and I did just as you asked. We might expect delivery between eight and nine tomorrow morning."

"Excellent!" Begg was alert and fresh. He had long mastered the art of catching what sleep he could where he could, making the most of it. "Now Tozer, I want you to take an envelope for me and deliver it to an address in Whitechapel which I shall give you. You must not linger there and if asked you will deny any knowledge of the one who gave you the envelope. Merely say that a customer paid you to deliver it."

"Right you are, Sir S." The cabby's massive face split in a grin.

His red cheeks positively glowed with pleasure. He loved nothing better than being party to Seaton Begg's cases.

When the amiably ugly cabby had departed on his errand, Begg frowned for a moment and glanced at his watch. Then he settled back into his chair and returned to the Land of Dreams.

~❦ CHAPTER THREE ❧~

A Fresh Twist

M onsieur Zenith arrived exactly on time. At Begg's suggestion he had come directly to Sporting Club Square.

Begg personally took charge of the albino's hat, cloak, and ebony cane, noting its peculiar silver crest. Monsieur Zenith moved with his usual alertness, all senses finely tuned, his strange eyes noting everything, yet remaining apparently languid. In Begg's sitting room he paused until the detective had indicated the easy chair opposite his own, and then he went to sit down. His manner was graceful and insouciant, yet in no way offering discourtesy to his host. When Begg spoke, the albino listened intensely and with respect, nodding from time to time and interjecting the occasional word of enquiry or embellishment. What he heard appeared to impress and delight him.

"Excellent," he murmured. "Doubly excellent! Sir Seaton, you are a gentleman after my own heart. It's a daring plan, but I think it will work."

"We shall need to rehearse all this," Begg added. "And that is when your own intimacy with the king and his family will be crucial. Are you willing to discuss such matters and empower this individual with the necessary secrets?"

"Absolutely! I must admit my mind was running along similar lines. After all, if I am careful, the information will be of no special use to anyone. But what next? What shall we do?"

Begg waved his copy of the International Airways Guide. "What we do, Monsieur, is take tomorrow's aerial packet. The journey will encompass three days, in all, because of the poor connections. That leaves us two more days before that fiend's deadline expires."

"And what am I to do in the meantime, Sir Seaton?"

"Contact the dictator's people. Tell them what we have agreed. And tell them the time and the date we shall be arriving in your capital. Do you have the necessary means, Monsieur, of achieving this within a few hours?"

"I have certain codes and access to a telegraph. If you will permit me, Sir Seaton, I shall be on my way at once. I shall report to you here by supper-time—when I hope you will join me at a pleasant restaurant not a stone's throw from your door. The Tambourine? Do you know it? They serve the most delicious goulash."

"I should be delighted, sir." Sir Seaton closed his front door on his visitor. He frowned for a moment, then smiled to himself, nodding as he returned to his Voysey chair and his fire. "Of course," he murmured. "Of course."

Reaching for his smoking materials, he chuckled to himself. "It seems this is to be an intriguing and stimulating affair, Monsieur."

Monsieur Zenith was back somewhat later than planned. He had telephoned ahead and now entered Begg's door with a murmured apology for the lateness of the hour. There was a shadow in his eyes. It might have been concern or even hopelessness. As soon as he was seated he leaned forward, lit one of his little brown cigarettes, and proceeded to explain.

"I did exactly as I told you I would do, Sir Seaton. I was lucky. Within an hour of leaving here I had telegraphed to a secret address on the Continent and had received a reply. The dictator has agreed to our proposal but—as a "sign of good faith"—he has also demanded a hundred thousand pounds in Bank of England ingots! That is impossible for me to organise. My funds are frozen; my friends could not produce the necessary cash in time! Of course, in normal circumstances, I could arrange a draft on my Paris bank. In England, at present, I have no credit to speak of. Where could I, a hapless exile, borrow such a sum in gold?"

It was almost as if Begg had anticipated the problem. After a few minutes' thought he picked up his telephone and spoke rapidly into the instrument. He listened carefully for a moment, uttered a brief word of assent and thanks, dashing a note on a pad in his elegant copperplate.

"If you take some form of identification to this address, your highness, I think you will find yourself very soon in possession of the necessary bullion. My brother Warwick will expect you. The hour is late and we must be as fresh as possible for our adventure tomorrow. When you have received the bullion it will be your responsibility to oversee its transfer to the 8.30 airship from Victoria."

The albino was clearly astonished by Seaton Begg's powers of persuasion, not to mention the value of his word of honour. "Sir Seaton, I cannot tell you the extent of my respect for your efficiency and the excellence of your connections. Needless to say my adopted country and myself shall be forever grateful to you. You are risking your reputation on behalf of a small nation of which half the world has never heard!"

"I risk nothing, sir. Because we shall succeed!" And with that Begg leapt from his chair and hastened to his bureau, there to write three notes—one to his amanuensis, Tozer Vine, another to his friend, Doctor "Taffy" Sinclair, the third to a high-ranking member of the British government. The envelopes sealed and stamped, he disappeared into his private chamber to emerge wearing his Crombie and battered trilby. "I can just catch the midnight collection. These will be in the right hands by morning!" He accompanied his guest out of the door where a comfortable electric cab waited, its engine softly running. At the wheel was the shrouded figure of Tozer Vine, his breath steaming in the cool spring air, his yellow lights cutting through a faint mist which clung to the trees of the square. Handing up one of the letters, Begg instructed his friend and chronicler to take Monsieur Zenith to the address shown on the envelope. The others he would put in the corner pillar box himself.

He watched as the cab started up and began to move off, Vine making expert play with the gear-lever. "Good luck, Monsieur. I will see you at Victoria in the morning. We shall lunch in Paris!"

But Begg had first to call upon the services of that beneficial wonder-drug Koa-Kaine which, when used in moderation, had a powerful effect upon the intellect. Only in the hands of the addict type could it become the very opposite of beneficial. Not for nothing was it known as the Devil's Snow. But Begg was a qualified doctor of medicine, specialising in the natural drugs of South and Central America, and had produced the definitive handbook upon the subject. As he carefully prepared his dosage, he attuned his powerful mind to a singular problem which, within a few hours, he hoped to solve by an effort of logic and imagination of which few were capable. These mental powers had made

Begg's mind as admired internationally as his physical skill and daring. He had two or three ancient books to hand, and a leather case containing a certain much sought-after scroll whose whereabouts were generally considered an insoluble mystery. One book bore only the picture of an ornate goblet stamped into its leather and no title as such within, merely a description of the book, which was a testimony written down by a Brother Olivier of Renschel Abbey, the long confession of a certain Count Ulrich von Bek made upon his deathbed in 1680. The others were of early and late nineteenth-century appearance, all having in common the same crest, suggesting they came from a single library. Using his expertise at speed-reading, Begg settled to absorb the texts.

By two the next morning, as the oil in his lamp began to run out and he was forced to employ the gas, Begg had his theory. His eyes were still bright with the remains of the wonder-drug, though the effects were already fading. However, it was not the Devil's Snow which fuelled his elated emotions. It was the pure delight of an exceptional creature doing what it did best. As a fine greyhound pursues the hare, so did Seaton Begg pursue the truth!

─◆ CHAPTER FOUR ◆─

Conventional Treacheries

Seaton Begg settled back in his comfortable aerated chair and relished the passing view below. His aquiline features were a silhouette against the bright sky. "Another hour and we shall be in the French capital, Monsieur," he addressed the albino who relaxed in the chair opposite. Monsieur Zenith wore a pair of plain, round smoked glasses to protect his eyes against the glaring sunlight pouring into the window. The albino had turned his head and was taking an interest in another passenger, who had boarded with them at the same time. Suddenly he seemed unusually nervous. Perhaps the burden of his responsibility, having given his own note in return for a hundred thousand pounds' worth of English gold, was weighing upon him.

Begg leaned forward to catch Monsieur Zenith's attention. "In precisely five hours, you and I shall have conferred with the king and his family. Then, in the company of a third individual, whom we shall meet at the station, we shall take the Orient Express to your country's capital. At this point we shall be met by the dictator's guards, forewarned of our company. The bullion will be transferred to a waiting van. We three will accompany it to its destination—the Kraskaya Fortress—where the exchange will be made. Your task, Monsieur, will be to get the gold out of the dictator's hands and into those of your counterrevolutionary council. Once the council is in power, you will control the treasury, so the British government is sure of her investment in your courage and integrity, Monsieur."

"I'm honoured, Sir Seaton." The albino waved a languid cigarette. Once again, he seemed to have lost all sense of urgency and took only the most casual interest in the fate of his kinswomen. Perhaps the opium was his means of "switching off" his brain, just as Begg used the mantras and prayer balls of the High Kandooni, the so-called Abominable Snowmen who inhabited the upper reaches of the Himalayas. "You can rely upon me, I think. Your task, Sir Seaton, will be to ensure the safety of the young women. That, we have agreed, is of top priority. Once I know they are on their way to freedom, I can complete my own job at the fortress. It will be some little while, I fear, before I can join you. I must stay with our third party as long as possible, or our plan will not work and his life will be forfeit."

After this perfectly coherent speech, Monsieur Zenith turned his bespectacled eyes upon the heavens and appeared to stare lazily at the elemental vision which, until a few years earlier, had been the prerogative of birds, of angels, and of the Almighty.

A little while later, Begg saw the spires and elegant towers of the City of Light glittering upon the horizon. He felt the elation of all travellers when they recall the beauty and civilised taste of Europe's most gorgeous modern capital.

"Paris next stop. Next stop Paris, sir," cried the smartly uniformed steward as he proceeded along the aisle. "Don't forget your hat, sir. Don't forget your bag. Paris, ladies and gentlemen. Next stop Paris. Remember to take your property. Paris. Paris next stop."

The sun caught the crystalline facets of the towers. As the airship manoeuvred towards the mast at Orly field, Paris appeared to burn with all the colours of the spectrum, like a single, mighty gem.

Seaton Begg glanced at his watch. "Bang on time," he said. "We shan't miss our lunch, after all."

Their business in Paris concluded, Seaton Begg and Monsieur Zenith now shared a private compartment with a third man, clad in a grey, military greatcoat and a badgeless grey, military hat, his face shaded by both lapels and peak. He rarely spoke when they were in the presence of any other person. He seemed disconsolate, ill at ease. The guard who took their tickets believed that Begg and the albino were high-ranking officials escorting a disgraced prisoner back to his country, but he had detected no sign of manacles. Doubtless the military gentleman was on his honour.

The Orient Express provided the most comfortable and delicious means of travelling to what seemed almost certain death, but Begg and Zenith were both in good spirits and, when alone with the other man, shared a private, rather black, joke or two.

As already recorded, Begg's spirits always rose when in pursuit of the truth. But Monsieur Zenith was fired by a different prospect. While he clearly cared for the liberation of his adopted country and the release of his blood-relatives, there was another matter on his mind—one he had not shared with the famous detective.

The box, carried as cargo by airship, was now at their feet. It was oblong and wrapped in scarlet velvet, bound with ropes of gold and silver. In the lid was emblazoned a single motif, the crest of a certain noble European family to which both Begg and Monsieur Zenith belonged. Their papers described an heirloom being returned to its original home. Yet it was not the bullion which interested the albino. Indeed the man in the greatcoat, who perhaps did not know what the box contained, showed more curiosity towards it than either of his companions.

The Orient Express pulled into the station at dusk when the capital was already growing silent under the vicious curfew of the new regime. The city had never recovered from the civil war which had shaken it in the early part of the century. Once she had boasted the flower of European architecture from Gothick to the Belle Epoque, but now only her ruins were picturesque and the new city was a monotony of red brick and stark concrete modelled upon the German modernist schools.

Descending to the platform, Begg, Monsieur Zenith, and their mysterious companion watched as porters loaded the box upon a sturdy hand-cart and began to push it along the pitted marble towards the exit.

As the trio gave up their tickets to the attendant, a loud cry rang out, echoed in the high ceilings of a more elegant age. A sudden silence fell upon the whole station.

Then, through the passenger arch of the main gate, there appeared a great, gleaming Rolls Royce. The open tourer of the kind once used by staff commanders in the Great War was painted a gaudy yellow and black, the colours of the fascisti warlords who had seized power from the democratically elected government. Banners fluttered all over the car. It was surrounded by an escort of motorcycle riders with the forked cross of their ruling Party on their armbands and helmets. Behind them, similarly uniformed, rode a crack cavalry regiment which had been "loaned" by a foreign power friendly to the regime and had a reputation of utter ruthlessness when "crowd discipline" was the issue. Their hardened, scarred faces glared from helmets as brightly polished as the steel tips of their lances. Before this swaggering entourage the public melted, hurrying in all directions, taking any exit rather than arouse the passing irritation of just one of those riders, who had carte blanche to perform any infamy they pleased.

The Rolls Royce drove up to within an inch of where Begg, Monsieur Zenith, and their companion waited. No one flinched.

The fierce, arrogant stare of the car's main occupant was met and returned as a fearless challenge. He was not used to such resistance and found an excuse to address one of his aides who saluted and spoke to the trio.

"We are glad you have decided to do your patriotic duty, gentlemen." Fritz von Papen, the dictator's aide, spoke with a distinct Bavarian accent. "And we are pleased to welcome you to the new, invigorated nation where we are sweeping away all the old symbols and systems and heralding in new, modern ideas which will soon make us one of the richest and most dynamic countries in Europe."

"I should hardly think you would require the services of a king, gentlemen."

The voice was amused, a little brutal, a little defiant. The speaker folded down his lapels, pushed back his cap, took a slow pull on his cigarette holder, and smiled directly at the aide. But it was the dictator who gasped with triumph.

"Good evening, your majesty," he said.

CHAPTER FIVE

Reversals and Revelations

The Martyrs' Tower was as grim as its name, a massive pile of unclad granite pierced by a few slender windows until the top, where a narrow, castellated walkway allowed prisoners a minimum of exercise. It was from here that the famous martyrs had jumped to their deaths rather than renounce their innocent and reverential belief in the Injinkskya Heresy, which had since become incorporated into the orthodoxy of the church.

Now containing Dictator Doktor Andros Papadakia, a small, stooped individual with trembling, clawlike hands who led the local Master Race with his aide, a certain Fritz von Papen, the Rolls Royce drove the three arrivals through cold, rainy streets where normal illuminations were abolished and roving search lights moved between the bleak, characterless brick blocks, where soldiers killed on sight anyone not in the uniform of the fascisti.

"You are a man of your word, I know, Sir Seaton." Dictator Papadakia combed at his straggling grey beard, casting a cunning glance at the box now carried in the tourer's boot. "And, I, of course, am the same. The little girls will be released the moment we have opened the box and noted the contents. We have our king home again, and his reinstatement will be a costly business, as you can imagine. Here we are. The young ladies have been perfectly comfortable. They are so far unharmed—though they are very pretty and one or two of them have caught the eye of my lusty uhlans. They know how to handle a woman, eh?"

Later Seaton Begg would remark that he had never in his life expected to see an albino pale, but he swore that Zenith's bone-white features drained of any remaining vestige of colour at this last remark. Yet still the nobleman controlled himself while the king stared around at his old capital, apparently with a newborn interest, as if he had failed to take in the enormity of Papadakia's implied threat.

The grim-faced praetorians dismounted and formed a foot escort. The dictator and his aide led the party through the lowering portcullis of that pitiless pile until they crossed a small bailey, cobbled and dark red with the blood of centuries, to enter the daunting hallway of the tower, its roof low and dank, as if never built for Man.

Bats and other flying creatures flapped about in the mephitic eaves while upon the slimy flagstones things hopped and skittered and crawled.

"I must admit," declared the dictator by way of apology, "that not all of our tower is as salubrious. We keep this to show our visiting foreign guests. Sadly, the rest of the place is in somewhat poorer condition." He led the way along a passage and up a circular staircase which wound forever, it seemed, above an unrailed drop whose bottom lay far below the tower's foundations. Behind them followed the guards, carrying the precious box. "They say it's haunted."

It was eminently clear that no one could escape the Martyrs' Tower by this, the only means of coming and going. It was always guarded. Every few yards they passed uniformed soldiers armed with the very latest repeating rifles from a famous Continental manufacturer. Their orders were the same as the curfew's: Unless accompanied by men in the fascisti uniform, all who moved were to be shot on sight.

The king, noting this, murmured something to Begg who did his best to reassure the man. It was clear the king was beginning to regret his decision. Perhaps he had never seen the infamous haunted tower of Mirenburg at firsthand before. After hearing him out, Begg murmured something which only the king caught. "Courage! You cannot weaken now or all is lost. A few more hours and our plan will be successful—as long as we keep our nerve."

His words appeared to strengthen the king's resolve. And now they were at the top of the tower, entering a circular room at the centre of which was a huge cage and within the cage, clad only in flimsy nightclothes, trembling miserably in the icy wind, were seven beautiful young women, like angels come to earth and caught in some supernatural fowler's net.

"You fiend!" The words burst from Monsieur Zenith's lips as his eyes fell upon that dastardly scene. His first instinct was to whip off his cloak and pass it through the bars to the women. Next, his jacket went to comfort them.

Dictator Papadakia watched in contemptuous amusement as the men lent their outer garments to the seven virgins trembling against that cold steel.

"Soon they'll be back in their own little beds, proud to have served their country as they have. They are, after all, only potential martyrs."

Zenith turned on his heel. The white of his shirt and waistcoat was now relieved only by his perfectly pressed trousers and his gleaming pumps. Although lean, he was perfectly muscled, showing that he took care of his body with a rigorous application of diet and exercise.

"You have everything you demanded of us, Monsieur Papadakia. Now I would ask of you the courtesy of a key." And he held his pale hand to his foulest enemy.

Laughing crazily, Doktor Papadakia dropped the ring into Zenith's hand. "A cheap price to pay, you must think, your highness—for your daughter's safe release!"

Only then did Begg note, by the slightest flicker of a muscle, the albino's jaw clench, and relax. Monsieur Zenith fitted another cigarette to his holder. The aide lit it for him, bringing the flame of the lighter hard against his bone-white skin. Still Monsieur Zenith did not flinch, did not for a moment betray that he felt the flame. After a while Fritz von Papen fell back like a defeated lover and with an animal snarl returned the lighter to his pocket.

Monsieur Zenith handed the key to Begg who went to unlock the cage, glancing briefly at the box which had yet to be opened. As the door swung back and before the girls could fling themselves through, Dictator Papadakia cried "Stop!" and again the world froze for a moment, save for Zenith the Albino, who continued to smoke his cigarette and watch the action as if he lazed in a box at the Opera and suffered an indifferent performance of Wagner.

"First, you will give me your key, your highness," rasped the dictator, his birdlike hands clutching towards the albino. There was a rapid movement and, as if from nowhere, the small gold key had landed in the dictator's hands. He passed it to his aide, who knelt before the box, frowning over the insignia and making as if to cross himself, until he caught the dictator's secular eye.

The key turned easily and the lid was opened with little effort to reveal ingot upon ingot of gleaming gold! English gold, from the greatest bank in the world. Dictator Papadakia's eyes glittered. He drooled with delight, considering the power such gold would bring him. He sniggered in triumph at his ability to coax so much wealth from the lair of the British lion and to show his power over what he perceived as a government enfeebled by the lies of liberalism. Papadakia's simple love of gold was as banal as the rest of his miserable impulses, his spurious dreams, and Begg could not disguise the expression of contempt which spread across his features. It was quite obvious what the dictator's ambitions were. Other little, pompous fools like Mussolini had taken control of more than one nation, so why shouldn't he? With free weapons and this gold, he looked upon his neighbours with greedy anticipation.

Begg stepped forward but was halted in his tracks by Zenith. "No, Begg. Your job is to look after the women."

Reluctantly Seaton Begg fell back, helping the young women out of the cage and across the stinking fester of the floor.

This was as far as the plan went, as far as they had agreed, but Begg had other intentions. As soon as they were past the guards and out beside a waiting Daimler bearing the official crest of the country, he spoke a few brief words to the grateful virgins and ushered them into the car. But Begg did not drive off with them. Instead, he turned and marched back into the tower, for all the world as if he had official permission!

Begg shared few of his secrets. His only real confidants were "Taffy" Sinclair and Tozer Vine, the cabdriver. He would speak of the next incidents only to Sinclair, who was on a mission of his own, and to Vine and then only after some days had passed. Often he told Sinclair he wished that he had left things as they were, escorted the women out of Mirenburg and had done with it. But his curiosity must be satisfied.

The plan he had not discussed with anyone, save the authorities in London, was now put into process. He made his way secretly back to the top of the tower where four men stood around an open box of bullion. Now none of them were in conflict, it seemed, but were sharing a comradely joke.

Begg's suspicions were confirmed. This kidnap plot was all a fiction dreamed up by the four who gloated over a hundred thousand golden pounds.

"You have done well, your highness," congratulated the dictator. He bowed, offering a sickly grin. "I mean 'Monsieur Zenith.' And you see I kept the bargain. That fool Begg has taken your daughter to safety, we have the English government's gold, and you can return to exile. Where will you go? As soon as Begg understands the truth, he will make sure it appears in the papers. Your reputation will be ruined."

"My reputation was never perfect." The albino spoke casually, taking a long pull on his holder. "And twenty-five thousand in gold will be some small compensation. I hope I can be of service to you again very soon, monsieur."

"I am sure we shall have further business in common, Monsieur Zenith. And I will be as good as my word. I will introduce you to my own 'guardian angels,' the Brotherhood of the Beast. They will be glad to adopt you into our ranks."

"Well and good, gents." The king now spoke in the louche accents of suburban Kent, "but I've done my bit I think, playing the king as long as I have. Can old Captain Quelch have his little percentage and be on his way? I am planning to catch the next train back to civilisation."

Whereupon Begg, hiding in an alcove behind a rotting hanging, saw a large packet of American dollars change hands. The "king" was none other than Quelch the famous gunrunner, more lately a successful confidence trickster operating chiefly in the European "midi," whom Begg had known to be King Jhargon's double. It was Begg, via Dirty Duck and Tozer Vine, who had located Quelch and commissioned him. But Monsieur Zenith had anticipated this part of the plan. Observing Begg in Smith's Kitchen, Zenith confirmed that Captain Quelch would be involved. Only then had he contacted Quelch and put the plan to him—to steal a hundred thousand pounds from the Bank of England. By using the reputation and honour of Seaton Begg!

Begg was unmoved. Almost all of this he had already determined. But now it was important that somehow he reach the bullion box. For there was one other item carried into the country which only Begg (and his Whitechapel carpenter) knew about.

There was nothing for it but bluff.

Coolly Begg stepped into the room confronting the four conspirators.

CHAPTER SIX

Manifestations and Mysteries

Monsieur Zenith was the first to respond to Begg's sudden reappearance. He smiled and bowed gracefully. "Well, well, Sir Seaton. You were, as always, thoroughly underestimated. But now that the truth of our little deception is out, what do you intend to do about it? I would emphasise that there is no escape from the Martyrs' Tower and you are rather considerably outnumbered. What of the girls?"

"I took the liberty of inviting my friend, Tozer Vine, to follow in a special carriage with our Daimler. He is even now carrying the beautiful hostages across the border into friendly territory."

"I am grateful to you, Sir Seaton."

"Enough of this ridiculous charade!" cried Fritz von Papen. "What can you gain from this, Begg? You are doomed! You have returned only to die!" And he reached towards his holster, unbuttoning the flap. But the dictator's eyes were narrowing and he stopped his aide.

"No! He must have some other helping him. Perhaps there are spies amongst our people—or you, so-called Zenith the Turncoat. You turned once—you can turn again, eh?"

"If you'll finish this discussion without me, gentlemen, I'll be off." With a tip of his military cap the king's double, Quelch, made his exit.

"That's improved the odds a little." Begg permitted himself a small smile. "Presumably you gentlemen have not looked closely at the bullion box just yet, or you would have noticed that those 'ingots' are a masterpiece of the forger's art. I took the precaution of doing a little background research on your histories. I was not going to guarantee a hundred thousand pounds of our sovereign wealth without so doing. What I read and what I learned elsewhere led me to believe that there are dark forces at work across Europe. You, gentlemen, are at the very heart of the evil. If you will permit me . . ." With this, Begg stooped, released a secret catch which sprang open to drop into his bands a magnificent double-barrelled hunting gun in gleaming steel, ivory, and walnut. This he levelled at the dictator's chest.

"This is a Purdy's, Herr Papadakia, and, as I'm sure you know, there is no more reliable gun made. It is loaded with a particularly large shell of peculiar manufacture. It is capable of destroying an elephant but is perhaps rather more suitable for hunting devils, if you follow me!"

Fritz von Papen fell back, ghastly pale, staring at the remaining conspirators. He understood Begg's meaning completely and only now, it seemed, realised the nature of the creatures with whom he had been dealing.

Begg crisply ordered the aide to go ". . . and take your uhlans with you when you do!"

Von Papen was quick to obey, scrambling down the steps and yelling for his men to follow. A moment later departing hooves clattered on cobbles.

An unearthly silence had fallen upon the tower. Still a small smile played about Begg's firm lips and was mirrored in Zenith's own expression. The two men knew they were equally matched and had nothing but admiration one for the other.

"Angel shot," said Dictator Papadakia with a shrug. "Is that what you think? I'm some agent of Satan?"

"I believe you to be an agent of evil, certainly," said Begg. "And I also believe Monsieur Zenith here would have nothing to do with you, save that you kidnapped his daughter. Yet you are two of a kind, are you not?"

Now Monsieur Zenith was laughing openly. "I believe only Captain Quelch will come out of this particular adventure with any profit. And I, of course, have my daughter safe. For that, Sir Seaton, I owe you much. But you are mistaken if you think the equation demands three such supernatural forces. Quelch was the second for whom your other barrel was designed. I am the first. This creature—this horrible thing—is nothing. I had meant to perform my task alone. I fear it must be witnessed by the man I admire above all others on this planet. Yes, Sir Seaton, you have the power to slay me. Only you have the knowledge and the resources to do that. It is true that one cartridge from your barrel will end my span of near immortality. So I will allow you therefore to be both witness and judge of my revenge. For revenge it will be, Sir Seaton, and a terrible one. Upon a creature who thought he could turn my family away from its work, from its massive burden of supernatural responsibility. Aha! I see that you understand, cousin. At least if I die, it will be with your respect, I think."

To this last statement Begg assented by declining his head a fraction.

Whereupon he was flung back suddenly by a blinding force which drove him against the wall and almost tore the elephant gun from his hands and, if the safety had not been on, would have caused him to blow both deadly barrels.

The dictator was scampering for the exit but was drawn back, it seemed, by a long, silvery arm which flung him into the cage so recently vacated. Doktor Papadakia cowered at the bottom like a terrified canary while Zenith the Albino strolled towards him grinning. The count's skin rippled with a thousand colours. His eyes glowed, shifting, distorted, faceted, as if they looked upon a million worlds at once. From the monster's shoulders spread two mighty wings, silver feathers clashing. At his belt was a blade, an ebony broadsword of massive proportions on which crimson runes, in some prehistoric language, writhed and murmured.

And Seaton Begg knew that he looked upon an Angel of Destruction, a creature of almost limitless power who might, centuries before, have been human, but had lived too long in the wilder reaches of the multiverse. Monsieur Zenith was a key player in the Game of Time. The scroll had revealed much to Begg. It was a tale of a family doomed forever to do the Devil's work, seek nothing less than resolution and reconciliation between God and Satan.

As Begg watched, the creature's ruby eyes flared with terrible energy. The silver teeth clashed in a silver skull. A noise came from the silver throat. It was neither human nor bestial, but the growling anger of an angel, of a jugador, a mukhamir, a seasoned player in the long Game of Time, where Law and Chaos warred across the multiverse.

The sword was lifted, almost ritualistically, howling and shrieking and singing in a key so alien, a melody so exquisite, that Begg almost allowed himself to drop the gun and cover his ears. Yet he weathered this storm of supernatural symphony and witnessed the creature that had been born His Highness Count Zoran Ulrich Rudric Renark Otto von Bek-Krasny, elected Protector of Wäldenstein, hereditary Prince of Mirenburg, Defender of the Grail, Blood-guard of the Holy Roman Emperor, King of Crete and Damascus, Order of the Moravian Hierarchy, Antagonist-in-Waiting to Pope Clement the Dane, Curator of the Ariochan Temple, Knight of Saint Odhran and Saint Mungo, President of his adopted State and master thief extraordinary, transform itself entirely into a creature of purely mythical proportions and appearance, slipping a mighty black sword into the cringing body of the dictator and drawing the filthy soul-stuff, not for itself, but to dispose of it as another might dispose of a fouled rag, flicking it into the farther ether.

The sword seemed to grumble as it feasted, as if it felt it deserved better nourishment, but it continued to drink, continued to discard, as the silver angel howled like the Wolf of All-Time and bayed out a song of revenge which was payment for the cruel horrors and infamies committed by the dictator and his minions. The sound was caught by every bell in the city until they rang in crazy unison. And still the runesword drank. And still the albino howled.

When all the filth was gone, nothing remained of the dictator Papadakia who had only lately pranced and raved and boasted and handed out casual death to all. Now he was a limp, blank thing, passive and obedient. There was a wound in him.

He was allowed to slump into a chair. His eyes were fixed on a spot above Zenith's glowing head, and when Begg followed the dictator's gaze he thought he saw, for an instant, the outline of a pulsing cup, covered in rubies and bearing a cross of silver and gold. When the vision was gone, Begg looked back. There was now no sign of a wound on Papadakia's body.

Begg could stand no more. He lowered the gun and turned to go. He did not know if Zenith were devil or angel or another kind of being altogether. He only knew that he had never wanted the privilege of such a vision and would regret it for the rest of his life. Here was a truth which even the great Seaton Begg was reluctant to face. The "gold" was worthless, a mere decoy to hide the gun. He could leave it. He wanted no more of the affair.

Then, to Begg's frank terror, the thing that was Papadakia lurched from its chair, hands grasping horribly at the air, eyes widening and rolling, its mouth the red maw of a rabid hyaena.

But it was not Begg it attacked, for suddenly the claws were turned upon its own throat. Begg watched in fascinated impotence as the dictator strangled himself relentlessly to death!

Looking up at last from the remains on the floor Begg found himself staring into the faintly amused eyes of Zenith the albino, a small brown cigarette gracing his elegant jade holder as he bowed and raised his silk hat a fraction. "I think our work is completed here, don't you, Sir Seaton? Already my government in exile returns. What you witnessed seemed the simplest way of settling the affair. To my regret your intellect is so finely tuned that you detected something of my intention. You made only one mistake, Sir Seaton. You assumed that poor wretch to be one of us. I assure you, he is no player in the Game of Time. Merely a mortal who exploits it. But he is gone now. At this moment throughout the Kingdom our people are taking over. All's well that ends well, I think. No hard feelings?"

Begg was removing the cartridges from his gun and slipping them into the pocket of his Norfolk. "I am not altogether sure of that, Monsieur. You did hope, did you not, to defraud the British government of a large sum? Your associate Quelch is already on his way to freedom with his bit of blood-money, what? I will grant that you have put an end to an injustice but I cannot approve of your methods. I discovered your family's motto, you know—Opus Sathanus —but I had not expected to see it demonstrated so dramatically."

And at that he reached out impulsively and took the albino's hand.

"We'll meet again, Monsieur Zenith, though I fear next time we shall not be on the same side."

"Well, Mr Detective, let us hope we remain friends, even as we play the parts of enemies. Farewell, Seaton Begg. I will never forget the help you gave our family."

Begg shrugged. It would be some years before he would be able fully to accept the fact that, here at the Martyrs' Tower, he had for a few seconds set eyes upon the Holy Grail. Or that the Grail had been summoned by one whom the world knew as a criminal or worse.

He put the empty gun over his shoulder and allowed a small smile to form on his manly lips.

"You forget, Monsieur," he said gently, "that it is my family also."

Epilogue

It was not until they were back in Sporting Club Square and a discreet, if only partial, report lodged with the Foreign Office, that Seaton Begg told the whole story to Tozer Vine. The loyal cabby sat in his familiar Voysey on the other side of a glowing fireplace, enjoying a brandy and soda served by his old friend and hero.

"Well, sir, for all that," mused Tozer, making a few deft notes in his personal shorthand, using the slender silver pencil and notebook presented to him by a very senior member of the Royal Family, "that there count didn't seem a bad sort of cove, did 'e, guv'nor? After all, the dictator bloke forced Count Zenith to act. 'Is plan suited 'is sense of honour but didn't endanger your life. 'E pitted 'imself against the best, didn't 'e! But 'e always made sure that nobody got 'urt—just the true villain—that Papadakia feller. What we in the trade call 'the original instigator' of the evil. I don't fink the count's a rotten 'un, guv'nor, but I fink 'e's learned to put 'isself an' his nearest an' dearest first in this crool world." He winked. "A true fallen angel, yer might say. Cynicism's 'is name, an' that's the shame of it. What a waste!"

"You'd have to admit, Tozer old man, that it's a rum sort of business all in all, what? Pretty unusual, even in our line of work?" Seaton Begg drew massive brows to the centre of that noble, intellectual forehead.

"Rummer than most, sir," agreed Tozer. And, closing his eyes, the cabby displayed his amazing literary memory by quoting from Milton—

> "Black it stood as night,
> Fierce as ten Furies, terrible as hell . . ."

Begg sat back in his chair, his whole attention upon the poem, his eyes shut, staring at impossible memories, even as he enjoyed the warmth of his familiar hearth, knowing how it was just possible that, for a few hours, he had entertained in his simple Hammersmith bachelor chambers, the Prince of the Morning personified. For the moment, an evil had been confounded and

Chaos held at bay. One day, however, he and his noble albino adversary must inevitably fight to the finish. When Tozer was done, Seaton Begg's own, deep tones filled the darkening room. Firelight brought fierce resolution to his features and flung his massive purple shadow upon the Persianate walls as he, too, quoted from the great Christian epic, *Paradise Lost* . . .

> Impendent horrors! threatening hideous fall
> One day upon our heads; while we, perhaps,
> Designing or exhorting glorious war,
> Caught in a fiery tempest, shall be hurl'd
> Each on his rock transfix'd, the sport and prey
> Of racking whirlwinds; or for ever sunk
> Under yon boiling ocean, wrapt in chains,
> There to converse with everlasting groans.

He reached for his pipe, offering Tozer his pouch of Meng & Ecker's Special "O." Soon the pleasant fumes of opium tobacco filled the study, and the two men contemplated in profound silence the import of all that had befallen Seaton Begg at the Martyrs' Tower in Mirenburg, in the land of Wäldenstein, somewhere in the multiverse, in the year of Our Lord 1937.

(With grateful acknowledgements to Anthony Skene)

⇥Crimson Eyes⇤

~❧ CHAPTER ONE ☙~

Crimes of the City

We are all familiar with the wave of murders, scandals, and suicides coin-
ciding with the collapse of BBIC and culminating on Christmas Eve
with the bizarre death of a profoundly unpopular Prime Minister.

"That poor fellow captained the most incompetent crew of self-impressed
scamps ever to tangle themselves in the rigging of the ship of state," declared
Sir Seaton Begg, heading the investigation. "But, however apt, I wouldn't
wish a fate like his on anyone." A Callahan Home Office appointee, Begg had
led the inquiry into the financial affairs of his own nephew, Barbican Begg,
whose mighty frauds had drained the country.

Barbican himself had disappeared, but the aristocrats, politicians, and
famous plutocrats left to face trial made a sensational list, especially as they
began to be killed. Barbican Begg himself had been married to the Prime Minister's sister, Wendy, who had overdosed two years earlier. A certain coolness
between the two men had not interfered with their association. The government
depended heavily on Begg's help. It had continued to endorse BBIC while the
cabinet gave authority to large-scale money laundering in the British Caribbean
territories, for Begg was underwriting some of its most lunatic flotations.

The first murders in what soon emerged as a pattern had been discovered
a year earlier, preceding Barbican Begg's exposure by months. At Marriage's
Wharf, Wapping, three armed skinheads had been killed by a large blade
leaving a single, identical wound which at first looked like the imprint of a pair
of lips. The detective in charge believed the skinheads to have been slaughtered

in self-defence. KGB, he thought. There was something subtly Slavic about the method. A former MI5 man, given to unfashionable and over subtle analysis, he could not easily explain the corpses' grotesque colour nor the hideous terror marking the dead faces, unless, he suggested, the blade had been poisoned.

The pathologist brought in was a retired Scotland Yard man whom Begg had known in his private detective days. Dr "Taffy" Sinclair's respect for Begg was returned. In the past, Dr Sinclair had discovered causes of death previously never imagined but admitted bafflement in this case. "Clearly they were all stabbed," he told his old colleague over Christmas pints of foaming Ackroyd's at The Three Revenants, "yet I couldn't swear they'd been stabbed to death." The pathologist's high, pale forehead had creased in a frown. "It's fanciful, Begg, but if you asked how they'd died I'd have to say, well, that something was sucked out of them. Not blood, especially. Not even their lives, really. Something worse. And by some filthy means, too." He shuddered.

Seaton Begg had inspected several victims. Long after the Marriage's case, a senior Lloyd's officer was discovered in a Streatham brothel. His costume had greatly excited the popular imagination but Begg had been impressed by his horrified expression, the peculiar silvery sheen of the skin, the bloodless wound like a kiss. Save for the wound's position, the Prime Minister had died in exactly the same way. "As if their souls had been drained?" Begg ordered two more pints of Vortex Water.

Sinclair was enthusiastic. "Quite. It's not the first time you and I have run up against so-called black magic, but this affair beats everything, eh? Witnesses?"

Begg had no useful witnesses. Those who had heard voices from the Prime Minister's sitting room could not tell if the other speaker was native or foreign. Someone had glimpsed what he described as a "stained-glass window" full of every imaginable colour which seemed to take the shape of a jewelled cup, its gold and silver blazing so powerfully he was almost blinded before it vanished. The piteous, blood-curdling cry awakened Downing Street at 4AM. Someone heard the front door close. Sleeping soldiers and police outside were discovered unhurt. "But I'm seeing two chaps tomorrow morning who sound better. One claims he spotted the murderer leaving BBIC on the night in question, when most of Barbican's closest associates called a crisis meeting at their HQ and were identically murdered. Noises, like music or singing, and a brilliant glow were reported, but the assassin was invisible. I gather my first witness believes he saw the Devil."

Begg added: "Only once before have I felt so thoroughly in the presence of the Supernatural. Rationally we must assume this is a clever murderer using superstition to terrify his victims in advance, enabling him to kill them without any significant resistance. That night he murdered fourteen of the City's cleverest men, including Sir John Sheppard, Lord Charles Peace, Duval of the Credite Lyonesse, Thomas King, Ricky Turpin, and all three Al Glaouis. Only a day later he killed a whole school of Wall Street sharks over here in similar haste—Bass, Floyd, Cassidy, J W Harding, the James brothers, Schultz, the Bush boys, and several others equally renowned. Not a bad score."

"You don't suggest this chap's done the world a favour?"

"Those who feed like parasites upon their fellows pretty much deserve to have the life sucked out of them, I'd say. The amounts of laundered crack money alone were obscene. This business sickens me, old man. Cabinet ministers are dying faster than they can resign. I've no love of the vigilante, but I cannot say I mourn the rascals' passing. My chief regret is that they did not die with their Swiss account numbers branded on their foreheads."

Begg's uncharacteristic pronouncements surprised Sinclair. "You seem to have more sympathy for the assassin than his prey."

"Absolutely true," Begg agreed. "Believe me, Taffy, it's my very sympathy which should soon bring me face to face with our murderer!"

~⊚ CHAPTER TWO ⊚~

An Interview with Lady Ratchet

The Prime Minister had not been the only politician to die violently on Christmas Eve. Over in Limehouse, in identical circumstances, while his wife and children were at church praying for his mediocre soul, the education minister, Oswald Quelch, was discovered at the centre of a pentacle, not part of the seasonal decorations, designed to save him from the demon he believed he had summoned.

Seaton's first witness claimed to have bumped into the murderer as he was leaving Eel House, Quelch's eighteenth-century merchant's mansion. There were only two entrances to Eel House—the first from the river, the second from a low gate into an apparently dead-end alley where Ken "Corky" Clarke, a small-time sneak-thief, had been, as he put it, "catching his breath" in the heavy fog so characteristic of London since the repeal of the Clean Air Act. Hearing a soft movement behind him, he had turned to see what he first took to be two disembodied eyes.

"Red and troubled as the flames of Hell, Sir Seaton. Coming out of that evil, muddy fog. I swear I hadn't had a drop." Corky's gin-bloated features contradicted his claim, but Begg was inclined to believe him. It was Boxing Day. They sat together in Begg's rather austere morning chamber at Sporting Club Square where pale light, filtering through old lace, gave the room a silvery, rather unreal, appearance.

Clarke had glimpsed bone-white skin "like a leper's," a dark cape revealing a scarlet lining and the hilt of a massive sword in black, glowing iron, set with a huge ruby. "I thought he must be the Devil, Sir Seaton. You would have done, too. He came at me so sudden and horrible! His eyes pulled my heart out of my chest and left me gasping, tasting that sharp, oily fog as if it was the sweetest air of Kent, and so grateful for my life! I heard his footsteps, light and bright like a woman's, tapping off up Salt Pie Passage. Oh, Lord, sir! I never want to endure that again. I thought all my sins had caught up with me. Those crimson eyes! I'm a new man now, sir, and conscience bound to answer your poster."

"Mr Clarke, you've done well and I commend you!" Seaton Begg was excited. "You bring to mind an old neighbour of mine!" Corky's description had triggered a train of thought Begg was anxious to pursue. "I note you've joined Purity Bottomley's Born Again Tolstoyans and work for the relief of the homeless. Good man!" He pressed a couple of "shields" into the fellow's palm.

"God bless you, Seaton Begg!"

"It's you, Mr Clarke, God will surely bless! Soon all Britain will have reason to thank you. Farewell, my good chap. I must shortly interview my next witness." And with a flourish Begg opened the door for the reformed crook, telling his housekeeper, Mrs Curry, to preserve his peace at all costs for the next hour. Whereupon he went immediately to his shelves, selecting a large German quarto, a jar of his favourite M & E, and a baroque meerschaum. Reading eagerly he flung himself down at his table, his pipe already forgotten. Begg was smiling thoughtfully to himself when Mrs Curry announced his next visitor.

Hamish Ogilvy worked as a porter-attendant at the New Billingsgate Fish Museum. Still in his uniform, he was a small, eager man with a soft Highland accent. On special leave, he was clearly in awe of the famous Seaton Begg as the investigator kindly coaxed his story from him.

On the night of the BBIC murders, Ogilvy, staying late in attendance on a pregnant cuttlefish, had missed the evening bus and decided to risk the walk to Liverpool Street. Ogilvy was soon lost in another fog, arriving at last in Crookburn Street at the corner of Sweetcake Court where BBIC's brutal architecture was softened by the weather. Pausing to read a sign, he heard a cab behind him. Hoping to ask his way, he saw the cab had come for a shady figure hurrying from BBIC. "I saw her face through the taxi window, Sir Seaton. She was staring back, terrified out of her skin. It was that poor, loony Mrs Ratchet, who used to be in the government. Pale as a ghost. I could almost hear her teeth chattering."

Ogilvy was also rewarded and thanked, though less enthusiastically. Reluctantly Begg decided to follow up the account. Apart from Barbican Begg, Lady Ratchet was the only surviving BBIC director. Under the impression that she was variously the English Queen, the Israeli Prime Minister, the American President, and Mary, Queen of Scots, she was at best an unreliable witness. She had moved South of the River on the assumption that her enemies could not cross running water and refused all visitors, even relatives. She went out only to "go over my books." She did not trust modern electronics so her accountants kept a large ledger which she inspected every month. She agreed to a telephone interview only after Begg threatened, under his new powers, forcible entrance of her Esher Tudor castle.

Gentle and firm as possible with the babbling old creature, Begg believed a small, cunning and perfectly coherent mind lay beneath "interference" designed to bully and exhaust opposition. Steadfastly he refused her threats, whines, pathetic lies, and claims and continued to demand an account of her whereabouts on the night of the murders. "Nonsense," she insisted, "I was never there. I was not very well that evening. A touch of Alzheimer's. My doctor will swear to it. I was at the pictures. Whoever you saw, it wasn't me. An imposter. You'd better question your chum Elizabeth. She never liked me. They were after the cup, too, you know. They said it was theirs by right. Poppycock! They knew how much it was worth. We planned to set up an office in York. But it's not safe there any more."

Begg insisted he meet her and talk "chiefly for your own protection." Eventually he persuaded her, by wonderfully veiled threats, to meet him or be arrested for murder.

"Very well, Sir Seaton." She was suddenly brisk. "I respect your family name. Be ready to receive me this evening at six o'clock in Sporting Club Square. But please be prepared also to take responsibility for your actions . . ."

"I am very grateful, Lady Ratchet. By the by, would you try to recall on your way if you ever knew a fellow by the nickname of 'Crimson Eyes'?"

A cold pause. At length Lady Ratchet replaced the receiver.

~❧ CHAPTER THREE ❧~

The Last Victim

Heavy snow was falling as the Boxing Day sun set over Sporting Club Square. Lady Ratchet, mad as she was, had never been late. Begg went to his sitting room windows and pulled back the rich, tawny Morris curtains on which the firelight made a new, dancing geometry. He peered through the blackness, through the big white flakes, through the sharply defined branches of plane trees, down into the square, towards the elaborate iron gates where "Mad Maggie" would enter.

At three minutes to six he was sure he heard a taxi setting down. Since then, save for the occasional muffled stamping of snow-laden feet, the Square had grown silent. Glancing again at his gleaming Tompion, Begg saw that it was four minutes past the hour. At that moment the soft winter air was pierced by the high-pitched shriek of a police whistle. Begg started, as if struck by a new idea, and hurried to don his overcoat. He reached the policeman outside the gates in less than a minute. "What's up, officer?"

The answer lay before them, already touched by a thickening layer of snow. Begg instantly recognised the frail, twisted little body from the shoes subtly clashing with the skirt. It was poor old "Mad Maggie." Noting the black leather trophy case in her left hand, Begg knelt beside the body, feeling uselessly for a pulse. The corpse seemed to shrivel as he watched, as if it had been animated solely by its owner's lunacy. Her face stared up at him through snow still melting on her fading paint. It was an expression of unmitigated terror. There was no sign of a wound. Maggie had died clutching at her own throat. Who had known she was on her way to see him?

Begg looked around for footprints. The snow had already obscured the trail. By the way she lay half in the gutter and half on the pavement, Lady Ratchet had met her death as she entered the square.

"By God, sir," exclaimed the policeman, "it's like she ran into Jack the Ripper and Mr Hyde at the same time. What do you think she saw, sir?"

"Oh, I'd guess something much worse than either," said Seaton Begg.

~◉ CHAPTER FOUR ◉~

Old Blood

A t one in the morning, Boxing Day over and snow continuing to fall, Begg, wrapped in a heavy Ulster and fur cap, stood in the darkness of an archway on the third floor of a Sporting Club Square mansion only five blocks from his own. Begg's stoicism was famous, but tonight he felt his age. At last he heard a soft footfall in the snow outside. A door opened almost silently. Light steps sounded on the carpeted stairway, and at last a tall figure in full evening dress appeared on the landing, stepping forward with a latchkey held out in its bone-white hand.

Than Begg revealed himself.

"And did you enjoy the Messiaen, Monsieur?"

A death's head whirled round to confront him. The eyes were covered with thick, round tinted lenses, as if sensitive to the faintest light. Gauntly handsome features showed amusement as Begg struck a match to reveal his own face.

"The Messiaen had its moments, you know," said the albino. "But the English play French music impossibly badly. Good evening, old neighbour. You see I'm back in my chambers. We last met in Mirenburg when you did me a great service."

With a movement of his head Begg let his old adversary open the door. A small oriental man appeared and took their outer garments, showing them into a sparsely furnished Japanese sitting room.

"A drink, Sir Seaton?" The albino removed his dark glasses to reveal crimson orbs whose strange light threatened to reach into Begg's very being.

"If you still keep that St Odhran Armagnac, Count Ulrich, I would love some." Begg's own eyes held steady, meeting the albino's.

"I'll join you!" To his servant: "Bring the St Odhran" and then to his friend, "Well, Sir Seaton Begg, explain this small-hours melodrama!"

"You know my interest in the histories of our family's various branches and my special fascination with our common Central European ancestors. If you would spare me a little time, I would tell you a story?"

"Late as it is, Sir Seaton, I'm always glad to listen to your yarns. A detective tale, is it?"

"Nothing less. It concerns an event frequently recorded in poetry, plays, novels, and films all across that part of Europe where Slav meets German. Perhaps you recognize this doggerel?

"A call to the Cautious, a Word to the Wise;
Tonight's the Night when Crimson Eyes,
His face bone-white and his Mouth blood-red,
Disdains the Body, but tastes the Head."

Count von Bek laughed easily. "Some Rauber und Ritter nonsense? It means nothing to me. I have never been, as you have, fascinated by the patois and folklore of the streets, Sir Seaton."

"The poem's from Mirenburg." Accepting a glass from the servant, Begg paused to enjoy its aroma. "Your family's real home for centuries. Until Wäldenstein was absorbed into Austria, then Germany and then Czechoslovakia, the Saxon von Beks played a pretty important part in local politics. The legend I know from German literature is 'Karmesinangen.' The French called him Le Loup Blanc. Your family is closely associated with that and several other enduring Middle European legends.

"A recurrence of albinism is said to manifest itself every two generations through the maternal line of Lady Rose Perrott, kinswoman to Anne Boleyn, who married Count Michael von Bek in 1560 in Mirenburg and gave birth to albino twins, Ulrich and Oona. The albino line is traced back, people believe, before Attila, before the Romans, but like the story of your family's special affinity with the Holy Grail and a black sword carved with living runes, the tale is comparatively recent. The event on which the poem is based took place in 1895 when Mirenburg was terrorised by a sequence of appalling murders. The victims were slain by a sword making a singular wound and leaving horrified corpses oddly coloured. A group of Rosicrucian exiles had obtained a jewelled cup they claimed was the Holy Grail and summoned a demon to help celebrate an unholy ritual. The 'demon,' drawn some say from Hell itself, was none other than a revived Count Ulrich von Bek, otherwise known as 'Crimson Eyes,' whose lifespan is far longer than a common mortal's, thanks to his sword.

"Not a demon at all, but an avenging angel! It is the von Beks' duty to defend the Grail at all costs. Mirenburg legends say the family has a destiny to achieve the resolution of God and Satan." Begg savoured his St Odhran.

"Old folk tales, Sir Seaton. How people love to chill their blood! So much more mysterious and romantic than the prosaic truth! Regrettably, we have little time to chat further. I'm off on my travels tomorrow."

"I would imagine your business here is over," agreed Begg. "There's talk Barbican fled to the Caymans."

"By coincidence, exactly where I'm bound, Sir Seaton." The albino drew a case from his jacket and offered Begg a thin, brown cigarette, taking one for himself when the investigator refused. "I'm growing too soft for these London winters."

"The tale continues," Begg went on equably. "It seems a City and Wall Street consortium came by an old von Bek family heirloom mislaid in 1943 when the Nazis arrested the count in Mirenburg. A Polish officer sold a cup which, it was said, could heal or even raise the recently dead! The potential profit from such a thing was enormous. But it would only display its powers in the presence of Barbican Begg, its steward, who tried to sell his interests to shore up BBIC. Well, as you know, members began to die pretty regularly, first in ones and twos, then by the boardroom-full. Every man who helped set up the vast BBIC fraud was being wiped out. In 1895 the Mirenburg press noted that Crimson Eyes never killed a woman, a child, or an innocent. Crimson Eyes could not kill old Lady Ratchet. He let her run away and eventually cross the river into Esher. Her poor, baffled brain was addled once and for all. She locked herself up.

"Ironically, she had nothing to fear from Crimson Eyes. Neither she nor I knew that the von Beks had kept their Sporting Club Square flat. She ran into you while she was leaving her taxi and you were trying to catch it, because you were late for a supper concert at the Wigmore Hall. You did not even recognise her! But she knew you. She saw your eyes. She thought she had met her nemesis and she died of shock. Or, you might say, she died of guilt . . ."

Trained to hide his feelings, Count von Bek could not suppress a slight, sardonic smile. With a sigh, he sat back in his chair, his moody red eyes staring thoughtfully into the amber of the glass. "So it's done at last. Apart from your nephew, of course, who seems to have taken the cup with him. I had not realised he was still in England until last week."

"Hiding at Lady Ratchet's. She'd grown to resent him. He believed she'd betray him. If he has the cup, you, presumably, have the sword?"

"A grotesque old family relic, really. Would you like to see it?" The albino's voice had taken on a peculiar edge.

"That would be a privilege." Begg's own voice was steady as steel. Rising, von Bek swiftly crossed the room to open a door in the wall. From within came a distant murmuring like swarming bees. Von Bek stooped into the space and withdrew an ornate broadsword, scabbarded in heavily worked leather. A huge sphere in the hilt glowed red as the slender albino came to stand before Begg with the long scabbard stretched upon both white palms. "There's our famous Mittelmarch blade, cousin. A rather rococo piece of smithery, you'll recall."

"Perhaps you could slip it from the scabbard?" Begg suggested evenly.

"Of course." Frowning, von Bek changed his grip and drew out a few inches of the blade. His arm shook violently. Now the sound became an angry alien muttering. Seaton realised he looked upon a living thing. He sensed something horribly organic about the black metal within which red words swarmed, words in an alphabet Begg had seen only once before on three broken obsidian tablets buried in a tomb below a temple in Angkor Wat. Those runes bore no resemblance to anything else on Earth, and Begg could not free his eyes from them. He was in their power. Inch by inch the blade slipped from its scabbard, taking control of the creature who held it.

Then with an enormous effort of will, Begg broke from his trance to shout: "No! For the love of God, von Bek! Master your sword, man!"

He stepped back, watching as the albino, his red eyes blazing in their deep sockets, battled with the blade until at last he had resheathed it and fell exhausted back into his chair. The sword continued to mutter and shriek in thwarted lust.

"It would have taken your soul," said vok Bek coolly, "and fed me my share."

"I remembered that," said Begg. "I know the secret of your longevity. We have the murder weapon, eh? The chief motive was retribution. And we know the method. Barbican and company needed your experience when the Grail stopped 'working.' You were invited to London and came ashore at Marriage's Wharf. As you realised what BBIC were up to, you took it upon yourself to 'balance the books.' I can't say I approve."

"You have evidence for any of this?" Von Bek lit another drugged cigarette.

"The blade doubtless matches the wounds, but I'm not sure we want to release it into the world, do we? You are right, Count. I am unable to arrest you, but it has given me some satisfaction to solve this case and confront, as I had hoped, such an unusual killer. At a stroke or two you have considerably improved the probity of politics and business in this country. Yet still I dis-approve of such actions." He would not shake the pale hand when it was offered.

With a regretful shrug, Count Ulrich turned away. "Differing times and cultures refuse us a friendship. Can I offer you some more of the St Odhran?"

But Begg, oddly depressed, made his excuses and left.

Returning home through the old year's snows, he reflected that, while one act of barbarism did not justify another, he could not in his heart say that this had been an unrewarding Christmas. He looked forward to returning to the warmth of his own fireside, to opening the black trophy case Lady Ratchet had brought him, to stare with quiet ecstasy into that blazing mir-acle of confirmation, that great vessel of faith and conscience: the Grail, of which he was now the only steward.

⇥ The Ghost Warriors ⇤

～⊛ CHAPTER ONE ⊛～

El Lobo Blanco

Shorty, Pinto Pete, The Breed Papoose, and some of the other hands were up on the West Range pretending to mend fences and find strays but were actually, as their boss was aware, searching out shade and sweet water because the heat was so hard and dry it felt like a sack of old cement on your sweat-soaked back. The real reason Tex, head wrangler and owner of the outfit, had sent them up there was to keep some kind of look out, which was just as well because Shorty squints up from where he's standing neck high in a pool of mud and shades his eyes and says to his dozing compadres "Ain't that Swedish Charlie makin' dust yonder?"

Shorty was the binoculars of the Circle Squared Ranch on account of his extreme long-sightedness, so it was a while before his identification was confirmed. It was indeed, the rest agreed, Swedish Charlie, sometimes known as "Sarajevo," who was riding in as if he'd eaten ten bowls of chilli and was about to soil his breeches. He was standing in his stirrups when he reached them and brought his pony to a spectacular "Mexican skid" so that he was on the ground before his mare knew she had stopped galloping.

He was all dust. His eyes shone out of the dirt like frightened diamonds, and it only took him two words to explain his condition.

"*El Lobo*," he said, and pointed behind him. He went off to relieve himself against a yucca while Shorty and the others saddled up and checked their Winchesters.

"Damn," said Shorty, cinching himself into his gear and wishing he'd paid more attention to his weapons when he should have. "I thought that sucker was supposed to be six feet under!" He took his Peacemaker from its battered holster and tried to spin the chamber. "Oh, god-damn!" From one chamber he dug out a disgusting mixture of oil and hair, but the gun was no better for his attention. He put it away, relying as usual on his rifle.

"I've been sayin' about that pistol," said Grumpy with deep satisfaction, swinging up alongside him.

"You've been sayin' 'I told you so' all your life, Grumpy," says the Breed Papoose, squinting his handsome eyes to show he spoke in fun. "I'm lookin' forward to the day I take an arrow or a bullet an' find your ugly mug leanin' over me to tell me how I should've seen it comin'." And he patted his own holster. "An' when it happens, Grumpy, don't say I didn't warn you . . ."

Emphatically the Papoose turned down the brim of his wide Mexican sombrero and kicked his pony forward, whistling *The Streets of Laredo* in that ostentatious, elaborate way of his.

Over his shoulder Charlie told them that at least one war party of Kiowa Apache, employing their usual clever strategies, were maybe twenty miles off but moving in fast. He had seen two other distant war-bands and heard of more—though they could be reports of the same parties. If the Apache's leader wasn't the real *El Lobo Blanco* he had certainly convinced the Indians that he was.

One thing was certain—they were coming together and their War Chief bore the Black Lance, the lost totem, their legendary symbol of redemption and revenge. Following this potent weapon, which was also their *ginam*, nothing less than an Apache army was on its way. News was that they'd already taken and gutted the Pecos Express and destroyed tramlines as far as De Quincey, making it impossible for the army to bring up troops quickly.

Charlie said that the general wisdom was that the White Dog Society was on the warpath because *El Lobo Blanco* had returned from the dead and was leading them. He had been the most feared Apache on the border—cunning, clever, and supernaturally lucky, and he had nearly destroyed the Circle Squared once before. Leaving Grumpy, Windy O'Day, and Swedish Charlie to follow as rearguard, the other cowboys took off like bullets for the relative security of the Brady Ranch.

The big sprawling fortified house and its various outbuildings were arranged around a good, deep well. The ranch was capable of withstanding for months anything but overwhelming numbers. Its situation, on a lush plain, gave it every advantage, and it could not be taken by surprise. Tex Brady's father had built the place in the years when Indian raids were common and there was no cavalry station nearby to make a savage think twice. Here, single-handedly, he had defended his cabin while his wife gave birth to his son and half the Apache nation seemed to descend on them as if some instinct told the Coaxinca, the Merengo, the Kakatanawa, and the Chirichaua that a great warrior was being born to the whites—a warrior who, if he survived, would become their noblest and most admired adversary! They seemed determined that he should not survive.

But survive he did—and grew to young manhood at Dulwich College in England—until recalled hastily to Texas with the news that his father was murdered and the Circle Squared Ranch possessed by Mr Paul Minct, the notorious land-grabber. That tale of vengeance, redemption, and love has been told already.

Now the boys skidded into the compound and dismounted in a storm of dust, their chaps flapping about their legs as they ran towards the big house just as Jenny Brady, Tex's beautiful and very recent bride, and Don Lorenzo, his grey-haired old mentor, came out onto the porch. Shorty wasted no time conveying to his mistress and her friend what Swedish Charlie had conveyed to him.

Jenny and Don Lorenzo immediately sprang into action. Barricades were raised, rifle-slits were tested, ammunition was brought out, and two Gatling guns were mounted on their swivels, covering the greater part of the surrounding range while a rider was sent to Los Pinos to warn the citizens and bring the boss back.

Tex was helping out at the circuit court where his friend, the "Prairie Green Incorruptible," Judge Abraham Peakiss, was dispensing that evenhanded law which had made him the most respected authority from Galveston to Port Sabatini. When Shorty found Tex he was about to enjoy an evening drink in the Gin-U-Wine Oyster Bar just down the street from the old French courthouse. The judge was with him and so was one of the plaintiffs the judge had just fined, shaking him by the hand, buying everybody a drink, and thanking the old man for his verdict.

Swiftly the foreman blurted out the news. Nobody asked him to repeat himself. Judge Peakiss hurried off to send some telegrams. Captain Gideon went to order an express rider to Austin requesting urgent reinforcements. Mayor Borden called a general town meeting. Lizzy La Paine demanded someone's protection, preferably Tex's. Sheriff Omar Hunt was at the Mac-Gregor farm delivering the usual writ. The plaintiff goggled, turned pale, and seemed to be looking around for something to kill himself with. *El Lobo* had that kind of credibility.

Tex Brady ran to his hotel, grabbed up his simple kit, and followed Shorty to the ostlers, where his greathearted stallion Geoffrey was already saddled and waiting. As always, he was eager to be off. His ancestors had borne the chivalry of Arabia and galloped with the British at Alhambra, Bengazi, and Wadi-al-Djinn. Toledo steel was in his bones. Marekshi powder was in his blood.

Soon the two cowboys were riding hell for leather across the open prairie. The only difference was that now Tex Brady wore the famous blue and red costume with the black mask and white sombrero of his *alter ego*—the legendary Masked Buckaroo! His reason for donning the costume was his reputation amongst all Indians as an honest broker. That might be the edge which saved their lives. Everyone respected the Masked Buckaroo.

They used neither quirts nor spurs, simply calm, encouraging words, to maintain that wild pace. There was not a motor—steam or electric—to match them in their own element where man and mount became the same creature, thinking and acting as one. Tex's father had always maintained that justice and kindness made simple economic sense. "You get more out of an animal and more out of an Indian if you treat 'em with respect."

A stern disciplinarian and a great patriarch, that old Cattle Baron thought cruelty made no sense at all. He had coexisted with the Indians by acknowledging their ancient rights and customs, for which they were perfectly prepared to allow him some modern rights and customs. He knew that a balance of power existed and that if he was ever at a disadvantage, depending upon their prevailing mood and practical needs, they would finish him and everyone else on his ranch. They assumed the same of him without understanding that he believed alternatives to be available. He had no romantic notions about the kind of people they were. They saw their funda-

mental survival to be dependent upon their military ascendancy, their reputation as vicious conquerors. They had been practising tribal genocide as a
way of life since time began.

Like the Indians, he was acting from what he took for profound moral
imperatives. He did not know how much invisible power he derived, in
Indian eyes, from those people in Washington he so despised. For the times,
however, his views were enlightened. Behind his back, because they dare say
nothing to his terrible, battle-scarred face, the other ranchers and towners
called Meredith Brady an Indian-lover.

The mystical Secret Circle of the Kiowa Apache known as the White
Dog Society had tested his sentiments. As he said, "It was one of those cults
which catches on and spreads from tribe to tribe faster than slurry through a
swimming-hole. A desperate substitute for real power, maybe, but it causes
a lot of trouble while it's running."

The chief shaman of the White Dogs was a Kiowa Apache troublemaker
called Ulrucha-na-o, which means "Pale Wolf" in his dialect. They believed
that, as a presentiment of his coming death, a warrior saw a pale wolf following him. However, if the wolf ran ahead of him, that meant his life ran
on also, so long as he followed the wolf.

Pale Wolf's charismatic personality as much as his religious proseletising
drew in bored young braves with no future and a history of defeat who
believed it might be possible to drive back the whites with magic and drugs
as well as courage. When Ulrucha gave the word and lifted up the Black
Lance they were ready to take the war-path confident in the understanding
that they were protected by powerful magic and that their weapons were
equally charmed. This made them even braver and their attacks all the fiercer.
And it carried the luck of the devil. For eight months they did seem to lead
charmed lives, running roughshod over Texas in one last, cruel, spiritually
enhancing bloodletting. This seems common to the generality of religions,
whose adherents justify the most elaborate horrors and torments in the pro-
motion and establishment of their faith.

No one called Colonel Meredith Brady an Indian-lover after he had led the
war against Ulrucha and his White Dog Ghost Soldiers. The final battle between
him and the fighting shaman was a proud legend amongst both peoples. Suffice

to say, Ulrucha's scalp was brought back to his enemy's lodge. How Brady's son made reconciliation with the Kakatanawa Apache and became their blood-brother is another story. After it was over Tex had thought there could never be war between Apache and Texican again. Yet here was the worst news possible!

Hours later, after some tense moments and faster than seemed physically possible, the two men reached the compound of the Circle Squared and threw themselves off their exhausted ponies, calling for hot water and fresh ammunition. After a few moments they noted the eery silence of the ranch. Though it was evening, no lamps had been lit. From somewhere came the noises of chickens and hogs, the whicker of a horse, the sound of a hammer rising and falling, but no human voices greeted them. Shorty silently pointed out the still, dark shape on the porch. The body of a black Labrador retriever. It had been shot through the eye with a white-fletched Kiowa Apache arrow.

"You ever seen that dog before, Shorty?" murmurs Tex, putting fingers to the creature's throat.

"Nope," says Shorty. "Looks like a man's good hound dog, though."

A sharp sound from somewhere inside.

Tex Brady grew instantly alert, his hands falling onto the pearl handles of his twin revolvers.

"There's something funny going on here, Shorty," he gritted. "And I have to admit I don't like the smell of it . . ."

⤙ CHAPTER TWO ⤚

The Scent of the Wolf

As the two men listened, the slow, regular hammering continued to come from the bunk house. Their guns in their fists, the young cowboys warily approached the big building, kicking open the doors and ducking quickly into the shadows.

In the middle of the common room, tied to chairs which had in turn been placed on the old oaken table at the centre, were Grumpy, Pinto Pete, Windy O'Day, Swedish Charlie, and The Breed Papoose. They were wearing nothing but their pink union suits, boots, and hats. They were gagged. Some of the other boys were equally discommoded, lying in corners of the room. The Breed Papoose had made the noise rapping on the table with his fancy silver boot heels.

"Somehow," said The Masked Buckaroo as his Bowie knife expertly sliced through rope and cloth, "this has none of the earmarks of an Apache raid."

"What about the arrow?" Shorty said. "That looks and smells right."

But Tex said nothing, merely frowning as he thought the problem over. He would make no judgements until he had heard the boys out.

Windy O'Day, Tex's oldest sidekick and confidant, told what had happened. Not four hours after the hands had ridden in to the Circle Squared the entire ranch house and its outbuildings had been surrounded by shadowy Apache riders who arrived with the dusk.

"It was right spooky," said the fungus-faced oldster, rubbing at his wrists and ankles and glancing around at his companions for confirmation of his view, "like they was dead. Not a sound out of any of 'em, and all kinda glowin' with that faint, silvery light."

"Natural phosphorescent paint found in the Guadalupe Mountains of New Mexico can give that effect. It is a favorite warpaint of the Kakatanawa Apache and is said to scare the bejeezus out of their enemies." The Masked Buckaroo helped Windy outside to his usual rocking chair.

"Well, boss, I guess it scared the wixwax out of us, too," said Windy philosophically, "because we was impressed. Especially when they didn't attack. They seemed to be darin' us to shoot at 'em. This stand-off went on for a couple of hours and then they kinda faded back into the darkness. We didn't feel too easy about this and were waiting for their next trick when this mist came up all of a sudden, and we heard this single voice calling against a wild wind. My blood ran colder than a Wyomin' weasel . . ."

"He's right, boss," confirmed the usually sceptical Pinto Pete. "It did things to yore insides, that singin'."

"Couldn't have been worse than Windy's yodelling." Shorty winked at his old friend.

"Come to think of it, it *did* sound a little bit familiar!" The Breed Papoose joined in the fun.

"Well," said Windy, "I don't know about the rest of you boys, but I was barely in control of my bowels *or* my bladder."

Suddenly sober, the experienced old hands nodded their agreement. The scene, the noise, the fog had all combined to terrify them and somehow blind them to the fact that the Indians were sneaking into the compound, weaving in with the mist, getting through the doors, and taking over the entire ranch without a single blow falling or a shot fired. When the boys got a hold of themselves again, they were tied up and sitting on the table. Miss Jenny and Don Lorenzo were in the hands of the Apache. And no time seemed to have passed between the events. They did not feel like they had slept or been drugged.

"It was more like a dream," said Grumpy, after some thought. "Like magic might be . . ."

"Yet it didn't seem bad or crazy, did it?" said Pinto Pete. "We weren't threatened . . ."

"They took Jenny and Don Lorenzo," said the young vigilante very quietly, his steel-blue eyes glittering behind his mask. "I would call that an act of aggression, I think."

"They didn't seem scared, either," offered Windy. "And I can always tell, boss, when Miss Jenny's scared."

This set the Masked Buckaroo to thinking for a moment. Then he was forced to put intellectual speculation behind him and turn to more pressing action. The Indians had been gone only three or four hours and had left a substantial trail, heading southwest towards the US border. The Buckaroo had no trouble following. Not for nothing was he respected by the Kakatanawa as "Pa-ne-e-ha-ska-na-o-nee-pa-no-sta" or *Sniffing Dog*.

"They have made no attempt to hide their trail. This in itself is significant," said the Buckaroo, reining in on a bluff as the vast, bloody sunset turned them all into black silhouettes and the yellow sky darkened against the blue of the night to reveal a silver wash of stars. He pushed back his sombrero and brushed dust from his face. "They mean for us to follow them."

As soon as his loyal riders were gathered around him, the Masked Buckaroo explained his strategy. They would camp here for the night, but the two men with the freshest mounts would ride out before dawn racing for Port Sabatini via San Antonio with all the information Colonel R. G. "Thunderclap" Meadley could be given. Once they had delivered their messages to Colonel Meadley in San Antonio they would then ride to see Captain Blackgallon Jones, the Welsh Engineer, and hand over the remaining documents.

"The army has some of the best modern inventions at its disposal," the Buckaroo assured his audience. "The wild Indian of today has little chance against such resources. Now we shall see how Texas's investment in modern transport and communications pays off.

"But meanwhile," he reminded his listeners, his voice growing deeper and sterner and his fists hardening around Geoffrey's reins, "my wife and oldest friend are prisoners of these mysterious 'Ghost Warriors,' and my guess is they're luring us into a trap."

"But why?" The Breed Papoose had already dismounted and was lifting the saddle off his tired bronc. "They could've taken us all at the ranch. They only had to wait for you, Buckaroo."

"That's what's puzzlin' me," admitted the young vigilante, "and that ain't the only thing. There's a whole lot to this affair which stinks higher than a Pecos fish pond in summertime. No Apache I ever came across behaved like these hombres. Sarajevo, did you ever get to see any of the atrocities you heard they'd committed?"

Sarajevo removed his battered sombrero and scratched his head. "I can't say I did, boss."

"And did you ever meet a man who had seen anything at first hand?"

Sarajevo frowned and thought back carefully. After a while he shook his head. "Nope."

"What are you drivin' at boss?" the Papoose wanted to know.

But the young rancher was not yet ready to speak. While the others made camp, he took his portable writing kit from his saddlebags and penned messages to the necessary personnel. This done, he sealed each envelope, then stretched out with his head on his saddle to sleep.

The Buckaroo was up before his companions, waking them to the smell of fresh coffee on a boisterous fire. Windy unlimbered his pans and provisions and began preparing the hearty breakfast all the boys looked forward to when on the trail. Then messengers were despatched, full of ham, eggs, beans, and java, riding like the wind, and the Buckaroo issued instructions to his remaining men.

Soon the little party on the bluff was reduced by a further two. As the sun rose into a blue, misty sky and moonhawks sailed far overhead, the Masked Buckaroo and his loyal companion Windy O'Day continued on the trail the Apache had left for them. Tex knew he was taking a chance, but he was a natural born gambler. He was staking not only his own life and that of his companion—he was staking the liberty and well-being of his wife and mentor.

Soon the two partners were the only moving objects to be seen for scores of miles in that bleak landscape on which the sun fell with savage intensity, casting the long shadows of cactus and jedediah tree across the stirring dirt. Yet the Apache trail was impossible to lose.

"They've driven a highway for us," said Windy, still puzzled. He was used to having a harder time than this tracking Apache. "Is this a band sent to draw us off while something bigger happens somewhere else?"

"I've allowed for the possibility, Windy," the Buckaroo reassured the old-timer. "As I've suggested, modern communications coupled with the most up-to-date transport systems should solve that particular problem. But the mystery remains—where are they leading us and for what purpose?"

"Maybe just one of their devilish tricks," suggested Windy. "Who can figure what goes on in the head of an Apache?"

"I can usually make a pretty good guess," Tex answered modestly. He had, after all, lived the life of an Apache brave and gone through the harshest trials of manhood to the approval of his bloodbrothers. In other words, Tex *could* think like an Indian. This affair, however, baffled him.

An hour later they arrived at the Telegraph Station to find it a gutted, smouldering shell. The wires had been cut and used to bind the operator and his wife. The couple had been laid across the nearby tram-tracks which had been dynamited and were unuseable from this point on. Their personal property had been removed from the station and piled nearby on the line, as if the thief had ridden off in haste.

As the Buckaroo swung out of his saddle and stopped to cut the man and woman free he looked meaningly at Windy. "Ever hear of the Apache doing this?" he asked.

Windy scratched at his tangled beard and frowned hugely. "Can't say I ever did, boss."

The telegraph operator was, as so many in his profession, a mute, but his pretty and agreeable young wife spoke enough for both of them. Not that she had any clear idea what had happened to her. The Indians had turned up out of nowhere and surrounded the station. "They just sat there on their ponies staring in at us." They had the look of ghosts, she said, but she guessed they were wearing some kind of warpaint. Their leader carried a massive black-bladed war-lance and had, she would swear, the eyes of the devil—"Red and glaring like the fires of hell!" She blushed and apologised for her language.

"Ma'am," said the Buckaroo quietly, "there are some experiences which call for strong language. I suspect this is one of them. What happened next?"

She was not sure. She spoke of a silvery mist growing so thick that it entered the cabin. In some way she could not quite remember the Apache had entered the station. The chief had spoken a few words, but she had not understood them. The sound was awful and made something inside her head hurt.

She had been lying on the tracks, watching the fire, before she realised what had happened to them. She was unable to remember earlier events. It was, she said, as if certain things had simply not happened.

"As if Time itself had been cut up at random and then put back together again with pieces missing?" suggested the Masked Buckaroo.

"Exactly," she gasped. "How did you know?"

But the young Texan did not reply. His mind was elsewhere. He was trying to recall a book he had read long ago while at school in England. The book had been in Old German and had been given to him to study. He had become fascinated by its arguments and its odd narrative; and something about this business reminded him of that book, but he could not think what.

Remembering his manners, the Buckaroo touched his gloved hand to his hat. "Just a hunch, really," he answered. "Well, ma'am, we're expecting a track-mendin' team along soon. I don't expect you'll be bothered by the Apache again. Are you willin' to wait here until the army arrives?"

"Since your trail clearly leads after the Indians," she said, "I think I would prefer to await the army." She went to help her balding, red-faced little husband to his feet. She dusted at him vaguely with a cloth. Beaming, he accepted this attention as a show of affection.

"Excellent!" exclaimed the young Texan, taking out his writing set. "I will leave a message with you. It can be despatched as soon as Colonel Meadley's 'Flyin' Tracklayers' arrive and fix everything up."

Clearly delighted that the famously romantic old soldier was on his way, the woman accepted the envelope the Buckaroo handed her.

A moment later Tex was mounted again. Geoffrey's forelegs stamped against the air. He was impatient to be off.

"Good luck, Buckaroo!" The woman waved with the envelope as Tex and Windy disappeared rapidly in a dust cloud of their own making.

~@ CHAPTER THREE @~

The English Detective

Hours later after following a waddy for a few miles, they found themselves in semi-desert with nothing but the jaspers, joshuas, jedediahs, jeremiahs, mesquite, and tumbleweed for company. In the far distance was a scattering of bluffs while even further away they made out the faint, blue outline of a mountain range. They reined in to take stock of the trail. It looked as if the Indians were heading for the mountains. They determined to press on while there was still daylight left.

Windy O'Day was uncertain, however. "What if these redskins are leading us off so they can do something really bad?" the greybeard proposed.

"I have sent the appropriate messages, Windy." The Buckaroo brandished a grey glove he had discovered on the trail. "This means they're leading us to Jenny," he said. "And, old pard, that's all I reckon I care about just now . . ."

Windy could not disagree with him.

He was about to reply when a voice sounded behind them, startling them both.

Tex whirled in his saddle, his fingers falling to the handles of his revolvers. Then he relaxed, laughing.

"There's only one hombre could sneak up on The Masked Buckaroo like that," he said with admiring respect as he stuck out his hand and addressed the newcomer. "And that's Sir Seaton Begg! Good evening, my old friend. What brings you to this part of the prairie?"

It was indeed the famous English detective, who had last worked with The Masked Buckaroo on the exhilarating *Case of the Glass Armadillo* when the two lawmen had joined forces to solve a particularly sticky mystery and rounded up some pretty ornery hombres in the process.

Sir Seaton was dressed for the bush with a wide-brimmed hat, hunting whites, and a voluminous dust-coat. His horse was a sturdy black Arab. In her long holsters were two rifles—a Winchester and a Purdy's. The rest of the detective's simple kit was rolled behind the saddle. He himself was a man in middle years, lean and fit and with an alertness of bearing which might have belonged to a much younger individual. His aquiline features emphasised the eagle sharpness of his grey-blue eyes, displaying a superb intelligence, one that for many years had been used to singular effect against the criminal fraternity.

"I picked you up a couple of hours ago," the detective told his friend. "And because I couldn't initially be sure it was you, I took my time revealing myself. Besides, I rather enjoyed the fun of wondering when you'd spot me."

"I couldn't want a better companion in this escapade," declared the young Buckaroo. "But what are you doing here, Sir Seaton, if I might ask?"

"I would guess it is what you are doing," the detective replied. "I am on the trail of a first-class troublemaker."

"Would he be known by any chance in these parts as Pale Wolf?" asked the Buckaroo.

"That is not the name by which he is most familiar to me," declared the detective, "but I am aware of it. What is your business with him?"

Laconically the Masked Buckaroo recounted the events of the last couple of days.

As they continued to ride, Sir Seaton took out his big onyx pipe and packed it full of his favourite ope. Soon the surrounding air was filled with the wonderful smell of aromatic M&E.

"It certainly doesn't sound like Apaches," opined Windy, after the Buckaroo had finished his tale.

"Well, I think you'll find Apaches are involved," Sir Seaton gestured with the pipe, "and perhaps more than you have bargained for. You are right, however, in suggesting that these are not Apache tactics. They are, in fact, the tactics of the man I seek."

"And who is that?" Tex squinted his eyes against the darkling sky. He could no longer see the range, but the buttes stood black and tall with the sun behind them.

"I am not sure he has a name you would recognise, Tex," said Sir Seaton, "save one, of course. His Kakatanawa Apache name."

"Lib-nu-pa-na-da?"

"He is called that in many languages. I mean the name he has adopted."

"Ulrucha?"

"Just so. For it is not his true name. He adopted it from the first Ulrucha—the man your father fought so long ago. That man was killed in a famous duel."

"I know the story," said the Buckaroo, "and I've seen the evidence for it. Ulrucha's long, white scalp hung in my father's smoking shed for a number of years. Until I gave it back to the Apache."

"You gave it back? Aha!"

As it grew too dark to ride the three riders headed for a sheltered gulch, making camp some distance from the water and preparing the surrounding ground against the mob of varmints which would be attracted to them in the night. Windy O'Day had soon cooked up a tasty meal, and they ate in silence for a while, looking up at the bright stars and listening to the distant song of the coyotes.

"There's nothing like a night spent under the stars in the American wilderness," said Sir Seaton offering his pouch of M&E to his friends.

They agreed enthusiastically as they packed their pipes.

Soon all three men were smoking thoughtfully, their eyes on imagined scenes, as they considered their situation.

After some time Windy spoke. "I reckon they ain't hostiles at all," he said. "Not in the regular sense, anyway."

"Your instincts are perfect as always, Windy," said Sir Seaton. "How do you explain their apparent ability to make themselves invisible?"

"Indians believe they're invisible. Sometimes that's enough, they're so tricky at not being seen, anyway." But even Windy realised his explanation did not fit the stories they had heard, let alone his own experience. "I just can't see how they slipped past us. Hardly a man in the bunkhouse ain't an experienced Injun fighter, and Don Lorenzo knows more about Apache than Geronimo. Yet we wasn't drugged. Unless there was somethin' in that smoke. How could so many get past us?"

"It might not have been many. One, with the appropriate skills, would be sufficient. It's an old trick," Sir Seaton spoke abstractedly, his mind elsewhere. "Almost a favourite, I'd say."

"You mean you know how it was done, Sir Seaton?" Tex wanted to know.

"I believe I do, Tex. Indeed it is his timeless method. That isn't the mystery. What interests me is how he was able to employ it here."

"Were we drugged, Sir Seaton?" asked Windy, his whiskers bristling.

"Not exactly, Windy. We are confronting forces which don't need to slip anyone a mickey finn in order to do their work. You may think me mad or worse, gentlemen, but I believe we are dealing with nothing less than the supernatural!"

"You mean we really are fightin' ghosts!" Windy's eyebrows leapt to join his unruly mop of grey hair.

"After a fashion." Sir Seaton fell again into a thoughtful silence, unable or unwilling to answer Windy's many questions.

Tex, too, said nothing but stared into the heart of the fire. It was clear to Windy that his mind was not on supernatural speculation but on the fate of his beautiful young wife, Jenny. It was the Buckaroo's way to make little of his personal fears, but there was no doubt he was in an agony of anxiety.

A little later when the moon came out and turned the whole prairie into a silver fantasy, Sir Seaton got up. They saw him sit down on a rock to inflate an Association soccer ball. When they finally put their heads to their saddles, Sir Seaton was still out there amongst the cactus and the jerrymanda punting the ball expertly through the assymetric goalposts formed by a bent yucca, muttering to himself, making complicated, almost mystical passes with the ball, and puffing periodically on his vast pipe.

They were up again before dawn and on the trail with Tex leading the way. He was even more anxious than before to catch up with the men who had captured his wife. For the first time since he had set out in pursuit he began to wonder if he would ever see her again.

Sir Seaton apologised if he had disturbed them with his activities. "I have a rule about exercise," he said. "Especially when I need to think something over. And, of course, usually I have a rod with me. But here—" With a helpless gesture he indicated the dusty, waterless plain.

The mountains were now clearly distinguishable. Glowing like copper in the sunlight, the ancient, eroded peaks were the most southeasterly tip of the Nova Guadalupes, close to where they joined the Guadalupes proper.

As they rode Sir Seaton explained what had brought him to this bleak plain.

Called upon to investigate the third theft of the Fellini Chalice, otherwise known as the Garth Cup, this time from the rooms of his own brother-in-law, the detective had uncovered an extraordinary story which had already brought him face to face with the League of the Cobbler's Last, the Gateshead Leopard Men, and the lost tin miners of Cornwall, and had him crawling through an endless succession of tunnels, storm drains, deep galleries, shafts, and corridors in pursuit of his quarry. "For most of my recent experiences, I must say, have taken place underground! A week ago you would have found me sailing the five great subterranean canals which meet at the Quai des Hivers in Paris. I found it rather a relief to take the express zeppelin to Austin and then ride alone under these wide skies."

"What led you to Texas?" asked the Masked Buckaroo leaning to rebuckle a strap.

"That's a very long story indeed," Sir Seaton told him. "As I said, I am on the trail of the one who has been called Pale Wolf by the Apache. I believe he has gained possession of the Garth Cup and means to use it in a ceremony intended to increase the power of Chaos in our world!"

"Are we talkin' Loo-cif-her, here," Windy wanted to know.

"If you like," said the English detective.

The old-timer shuddered. "I can take pretty near anything the Apache think up," he said, "but when it comes to devils an' ghosts, sir, I am not your man. I guess my brain don't believe in such things, but my feet never seem to listen to my brain."

Sir Seaton clapped a friendly hand upon Windy's shoulder. "Don't worry, Mr O'Day. You shan't be called upon to deal with the supernatural. That's my business, I'm afraid."

"I ain't sure I'm much better at handling that stuff than Windy," said the Buckaroo doubtfully. "I must admit in my wildest dreams I didn't really believe old Ulrucha was a ghost!"

"He is not a ghost," Sir Seaton declared quietly. "I assure you, Tex, he is something far more powerful and terrible than that."

With a grim, distant expression, he urged his horse into a gallop and for a while raced ahead of his companions, lost in the contemplation of his own appalling knowledge.

~● CHAPTER FOUR ●~

The Will of the Wolf

The three adventurers dismounted at the mouth of a towering canyon and looked in awe at the strange red limestone formations all around them. The Apache trail led relentlessly to this spot and into the depths of the canyon. What Tex and his friends had to work out now was what kind of trap it was . . .

Although Tex's every instinct was to ride like fury into the canyon and with both guns blazing rescue his wife, he knew that he must continue to use his brains and self-control if he was going to get Jenny free.

Suddenly there came the thin whine of an aero-engine. Glancing upward they saw the dark blue and gold hull of a Texan flying battlecruiser easing herself over a mountain peak and hovering above them.

Tex needed to see no more! While Sir Seaton took out his pocket holo-
graph and exchanged messages with the ship, he removed his Winchester
from its scabbard and checked the rifle's action.

"Are we ready, Tex?" Windy wanted to know. He squared his shoulders, ready
to face the Devil himself if necessary but not looking forward to the prospect.

"We sure are, Windy," declared the young cowboy. "But you ain't comin'
with us, pard. I need you here to signal."

After a quick word of explanation, the Masked Buckaroo shook hands
with the old-timer, grinned his famous go-to-hell grin, loosened his twin
guns in their holsters, and galloped to ride side by side with Sir Seaton Begg
into the shadows of the vast canyon.

The silence was profound. All the men heard was the creak of their own
harness, the sound of hoofs thudding rhythmically into the soft sand of the
canyon bottom. Very evidently many horses had recently come this way.

"I would guess there's maybe fifty warriors," Tex suggested, when Sir Seaton
questioned him. "And then there's captives, maybe loot. The waggons aren't too
heavily loaded, and the horses pulling them are fresh enough. If I was readin'
these signs as I usually would, I'd say it was a whole tribe, or at least a big village, on the move. Has he got his women and children with him, do you think?"

"Not his," said Sir Seaton.

Tex shuddered.

The canyon grew steeper, taller, and darker, and still the two men rode
steadily on until at last they came to a place where the high limestone walls
widened into a rough circle and light from above poured down to give the
effect of a single beam focussed on the center of the clearing.

The shadows were full of restless shapes. Tex could smell them all around
him, but he did not reveal this. He looked steadily ahead into the pool of
light where three figures now moved, as if they had been waiting for him.

The first was his beloved wife, Jenny, clearly unhurt and not especially
frightened. The second was his wise old friend, Don Lorenzo, his sombrero
brim turned down against the blazing sunshine. And the third was a thin,
muscular figure in an Apache breechclout and bolero jacket, far taller than
the average Indian, whose skin had a strange silvery tinge so that Tex's first

thought was "the man's a leper!" From a long, tapering, handsome skull stared two dark, crimson eyes which seemed to burn with fire so ancient it had petrified. And slung over his back was a monstrous war-lance, bigger than any normal Kiowa weapon, its wide blade of black iron burned with a pattern of writhing ruby red hieroglyphs in a language neither man recognised, perhaps some ancient semitic alphabet. The man stared at them with a haughty, almost bored expression. It was as if his chief attention were elsewhere, as if those strange eyes stared into another world entirely.

Tex was immediately struck by the air of melancholy which exuded from the warrior. He had the manner of someone who had lived for ten thousand years or more and had seen nothing to confirm any faith he might ever had had in the world's improvement.

Sir Seaton Begg rested in his saddle, his arms folded over his pommel, his reins loose in his hands. "Good afternoon, your highness," he said sardonically.

The Apache leader turned his head to regard Begg, and his eyes seemed to narrow in a smile. "So you have found me, Sir Seaton. I had not expected to meet again so soon."

"Always a pleasure." Begg took his pipe and baccy from his coat and offered the pouch to Pale Wolf who shook his head, declining gracefully. As the detective filled his bowl and lit the mixture, puffing luxuriously, Tex could contain himself no longer.

"I need to know, sir," he said to the War Chief, "if my wife and friend are your prisoner."

"No longer," said the Apache chief. "They are free from this moment. They have served their turn."

"And what turn was that, sir?" demanded Jenny sharply, moving rapidly to her husband's side. Tex dismounted to embrace her. Thankfully he shook hands with Don Lorenzo. "You were never clear on the issue," Jenny continued, "even the other evening, at dinner."

Pale Wolf smiled wistfully at this. "I apologise," he said. "My problem is not that I lie, but that the truth is unacceptable to most people. Sometimes it is impossible to disguise or even modify. Everything, or almost everything, can be summed up in a brief equation: $Z = z^2 + c \ldots$"

He spoke a melodic, vibrant, faintly accented English which made it immediately clear how he could lead so many young warriors by the power of his words alone. The great black war-lance was in his hands and the red engravings seemed to come alive within the metal, reflecting his blazing, ruby eyes, giving his face the sheen of a silver mask.

"Let us finish this," he said.

And then he smiled.

~✿ CHAPTER FIVE ✿~

Apache Dreams

As the strange albino lifted the war-lance to strike, the Masked Buckaroo pushed Jenny behind him and lifted one gloved hand.

From somewhere high above came the familiar notes of a Texan Cavalry cornet calling a complicated "Alert." The sound seemed to go on forever, and the young vigilante looked in astonishment as the silver-faced warrior threw back his long head, the white hair cascading and curling about his shoulders, to howl in sudden, impossible unison with the bugle's call.

The black blade itself now began to vibrate and moan, making that hideous nauseating crooning many had reported. Yet gradually the pitch changed until it, too, sang in unison with the other voices.

Had Pale Wolf planned everything for this moment?

From out of the shadows came a small, crooked individual, carrying a great jewelled chalice which, once the light from above touched it, also began to vibrate in harmony with the bugle, the sword, and the man.

From somewhere above a voice was calling—perhaps a warning—but those in the canyon did not hear. Their attention was on the scene taking place under that concentrated beam of sunlight where a bizarre silver-skinned warrior in the full war-gear of a Kakatanawa Apache raised his voice in unnatural, inhuman music, performing a ritual which none doubted to be of the darkest, most powerful magic. As the echo of the bugle began to fade, the albino brought the great, black blade down into the rock at his feet, his voice rising in hideous crescendo. The chalice held by the dwarf seemed to swell and shatter, and the blade bit down into the ground, splitting it wide, revealing a great opening in the darkness, a natural stairway leading into the unknown.

Out of this sudden fissure came a deep, suffering groan, as if Mother Earth herself stirred in her sleep, dreaming of all the evil her children had done. And none there dared imagine what kind of creature bore such pain or uttered such sounds.

Sir Seaton Begg took the initiative. He stepped to the opening and stared down into it frowning.

Behind him Pale Wolf smiled. "So you have lost none of your courage, old enemy."

"Should I be afraid?" Sir Seaton looked up and met the Apache leader's strange eyes directly.

Pale Wolf shrugged. "I suppose not."

"I must credit you with excellent strategy," Begg said. "You have completely outmaneuvered us in the best traditions of Apache generals! You guessed how young Tex here would act and think. You put yourself in his shoes, imagining how he would cover all possible eventualities, leaving as little as possible to chance because his wife's very soul could be at stake. You knew he would find a way to get the army here, and that's exactly what he did . . ."

Pale Wolf reached into his breechclout and removed a compact silver case. From this he took a small, brown cigarette and placed it between his lips. He lit it with a match and drew deeply of the dark smoke. He appeared to have nothing to do in the world but listen in a relaxed, easy posture, as Sir Seaton Begg continued:

"You didn't want Jenny Brady or Don Lorenzo or even Tex himself. You were using Tex's brains to make sure the army would be here at a certain moment. And you didn't really want the army. You wanted the army trumpeteer, that wonderful cornet which, of all the armies in the world, only the Texas Cavalry boasts. You did not really want the trumpeteer. You wanted his cornet. Or rather, you wanted a particular sequence of notes on that cornet, which occurs in the formal 'Alert' blown by Texas's bravest. And it had to sound at a particular moment, when the light fell in a certain way and when man, chalice, and blade could give voice together, casting the great spell which would open the doorway you needed into Moo-Uria, the Realm Below."

At this the albino's eyes narrowed. His handsome features seem to display a strange, bitter amusement. His long-fingered hands, the colour of bone, played with the ornate red shaft of the lance. "I believe I have underestimated you, however, Seaton Begg. For I did not anticipate your presence here. Neither did I prepare for it. Neither was I aware of your knowledge."

"Acquired in the course of a long investigation," murmured the detective. "I have been seeking you and the chalice for some while. Since you stole it from Sir John Soanes' Museum in London three years ago. The Museum of which my brother-in-law is director."

The albino seemed surprised and made as if to deny the charge, then shrugged and pulled deeply on his aromatic cigarette.

"Well, Sir Seaton, you could easily have thwarted me, it seems. Yet you did not. Why so?"

Begg pursed his lips and frowned, as if he had not considered the question before. At length he said: "Curiosity, I suppose. Which is, after all, my abiding and defining vice."

"Then I am obliged to you," said the albino, swinging the now dormant blade onto his back and signalling to the people in the shadows.

As they emerged, Tex saw that they were emaciated creatures, pale from every deprivation. Tex thought one thing when he saw them: "Reservation Indian." Their undernourished bodies spoke of terrible hardship. Only their eyes were vital and, as they began to ride and walk slowly down the causeway into the earth, they bore themselves with a strange, new self-respect. Men, women, and children, waggons and horses, moved slowly down into the darkness, their voices ringing with wonder and fresh confidence so that those above ground almost felt envious of them and what they were seeing.

"You mean, Pale Wolf, that you made such an elaborate plan simply in order to save those poor creatures?" gasped Jenny.

"I am not so altruistic, Mrs Brady," said the albino with an ironic glint in his strange, red eyes. "But I guessed my self-interest would combine with theirs to our mutual benefit and so it proved."

"Where are they going?" Don Lorenzo asked.

"Home," said the albino tossing the remains of his cigarette into the shadows. "Home to the land of lost nations, of recollected pride and purpose. Home to the Reforgotten. Home to the Realm Below." His eyes met those of his old adversary. "Would you deny them that peace of mind, Seaton Begg? That pride?"

The English detective took an interest in his pipe. "My question has always been, your highness, whether you would deny me my peace of mind in achieving yours. It is the great fundamental debate. How do we achieve satisfactory compromise?"

"They intend you no harm," insisted the albino. "And as for myself, I believe you know how deeply uninterested I am in your kind and its ambitions. As long as I am left alone."

"Left alone to murder and steal, sir." Sir Seaton Begg reminded the strange creature. "Why, you have killed half the British parliament! Lady Ratchet herself dropped dead merely at the sight of you! While this made you something of a popular hero, you are still guilty. I made the mistake of loaning my special charge to the museum from which you stole it, threatening my brother-in-law, the curator, with shameful ruin! You have stolen that great national treasure and apparently destroyed it. You have put everyone, moreover, to a considerable outlay of time, concern, and money which could have been better spent elsewhere. Sir, the rogue wolf is left alone only when he hunts in his own territory. I cannot believe you to be unaware of the fallacious nature of your arguments. You have not left us alone, sir."

At which a deep sigh escaped the albino's lips and he glared around him impatiently. "Am I to be forever plagued by dullards and fools splitting hairs in abstract arguments? I am tired of the abstract, gentlemen. How I long for the concrete!"

"I can offer you as much concrete, sir, as you please," said Sir Seaton Begg. "Her Majesty's prisons consist of little else."

The albino turned brooding eyes upward, studying the tiny figures who now rimmed the canyon. He spoke dreamily. "Did you bring the entire Texas army here, Mr Brady? I am flattered. Please give Captain Gideon my compliments, and tell him I shall have to meet him another time."

With that he had mounted his pony and, without looking back, urged it at a rapid trot down into the fissure.

A few moments later they heard his laughter issue from the echoing depths. The caverns enlarged and expanded it, giving it a rich, eternal bitterness so that it seemed Satan himself addressed them in tones full of tormented melancholy and longing.

"Farewell, old friend! We shall meet soon enough, no doubt, in the Realm Below."

And he was gone.

A moment later a thin voice from the heights called down: "Could someone let us know what's happening?"

Tex recognised the voice of his friend Captain James "Bible" Gideon.

"All's well down here, Captain Gideon," he shouted back, and the echo continued "giddy-on, giddy-on, giddy-on . . ." until it was spent.

Sir Seaton Begg continued to stare thoughtfully down into the fissure.

"Are you planning to follow them, Sir Seaton?" asked the young vigilante, half joking.

"Not immediately," replied the detective, "though it is my duty. I know my limitations. I lack certain fundamental equipment. I have no instinct for the underworld." He took a long pull on his pipe. "Yet that creature, that demon, as some believe him to be, can negotiate the most alien landscapes without any hesitation. You heard that equation he offered. Almost a mantra. He has that ability to sense routes and avenues which you and I could never find, even with maps. He is not the only one of his family to have that talent, of course. But it is why he can so easily pass between one realm and another. Few possess such skills."

"But what *is* he?" Jenny Brady wanted to know.

"They are sometimes called 'eternals,'" the detective replied slowly, "and they are able to walk the roads between the worlds. The entire multiverse is theirs, yet some of them are still prisoners, still victims of their own stories."

"I am really not quite following this, Sir Seaton," said Jenny.

The detective gestured with his reins. "That is why, dear Mrs Brady, I make so few attempts to offer explanations. I assure you it is nothing to do with your intelligence, which is extraordinarily high. But there are some things about our realities that only a certain number of people seem to be able to comprehend. And there is no persuading them. They simply cannot see what I see or indeed what that poor white-faced creature who has just left us can see."

"I do not believe I would want to see what he sees," said Don Lorenzo, lightening the atmosphere a little. "Especially at this moment."

"Oh, my dear sir," said Seaton Begg feelingly, "you do not know the beauty he experiences as he wanders the impossible caverns of the Grey Fees where the organic and supernatural infrastructure of the planet intertwine. He will see jewelled halls so high and vast that twenty great cities stand in them, each upon a peak, high above mercury rivers and bronze mists of the valleys which draw their light from phosphorescent rain dripping steadily from the distant roofs, making fresh formations everywhere, through which move the native folk of the Grey Fees, the *Offmoo*, so tall and thin and silent, drifting like phantoms through whispering rock forests and jangling crystal gardens, practising their rituals and legalities with obsessive, mindless insistence. And you have not heard the great natural organs playing when all the cities make music at the same time, and dying travellers come from thousands of miles to spend their last ecstatic hours borne upon so many wonderfully weaving melodies. No music is more sophisticated or more moving."

"Then should we not follow him this minute?" said Don Lorenzo a little drily. "Who could resist such a paradise?"

But Seaton Begg shook his head refusing levity. "It remains, for all that," he said, "an *alien* paradise. It is an alternative. The Realm Below is a compendium of lost dreams. All the defeated people arrive there, vowing return, revenge, and those other satisfactions with which we seem to perpetuate our miseries. But when they have been there for some time they become infected with a peculiar sadness. It is Pierrot's world, after all, without sunlight. That melancholy is characteristic of almost every denizen of the Realm Below. They live, they flourish, they have pride, and their achievements are spectacular.

"The great American civilisations are there, as well as the African, the Indian, even the Etruscan. For the Realm Below is where the Reforgotten know triumph, where the disenfranchised and the marginilised find renewed power, where noble memory is made concrete. Where justice exists. Yet all but the *Offmoo* know that they are not native to the Realm, that they are for-ever exiled."

Riding back up the canyon now they could hear military voices raised in command, the busy clatter of equipment.

"Do none of them ever yearn to return?" Jenny asked the detective.

"Some dream of it. Some even make plans for conquest of the Realm Above. But that pervasive melancholy usually informs their final decisions. It is hard to make war while enjoying such emotions. They compensate for their lack of martial vigor by aspiring to a high standard of civilisation."

When they had reached the canyon's mouth again, the first person they saw was Windy O'Day, his whiskers bristling with anxiety. He sat his horse expectantly, counting the riders as they emerged and brightening as soon as he saw their faces. Behind him it was possible to see the practical magic Tex had worked, enabling Captain Gideon to get to the canyon hours ahead of the Apaches and position his men.

Nothing would have been possible, of course, without Colonel Meadley's famous "Flying Tracklayers" who had constructed a temporary bed across the prairie enabling Captain Blackgallon Jones to bring up his mighty double-decker war-trams loaded with men and ordnance. These so-called gun-tubs with their electric gatlings could be of spectacular effect in plains conditions and had been employed to full effect at the Battle of El Paso against what Texas still insisted on calling The Californian Threat.

Express trams had transported the cavalry, and now Captain Gideon's battle-hardened squadrons lined every vantage point of the surrounding country! This vast display of military coordination brought a small smile to Sir Seaton's lips as he looked around him. He was too well-bred to observe what his companions also understood: that it had taken a great deal of organ-isation and a great many men to ensure that a certain cornet note sounded at a certain moment in the wilds of the New Guadalupe mountains!

Two master strategists had, for a short time, joined in a game whose rules were known only to one of them. Pale Wolf had used the Masked Buckaroo's famous strategic skills for his own purposes.

"I first smelled a rat," declared the Buckaroo, "when I felt for that dog's pulse.

That animal had died of natural causes. The arrow had been shot into it much later. Did you notice that no one was killed in those 'raids.' Nobody was even seriously hurt." The Buckaroo could only admire the way in which he had been tricked.

He was not sure, however, how he was going to explain it all to Captain Gideon and his men.

As if he had had the same thought, Sir Seaton Begg leaned across in his saddle and murmured: "Remember what Pale Wolf said about not lying— that people usually refused the truth?"

The young vigilante nodded.

"Well," continued Sir Seaton, "I think we had best not explain all the details of how your dear ones were restored to you and what happened to Ulrucha and his miserable band."

Tex was inclined to agree with him.

"But first," he said, "you must tell me something about that queer fellow, Pale Wolf. He's clearly not an Indian. He's definitely a white man. But he didn't look much like an average white, either. What is he, some kind of cross?"

"He is at once the last and the first of his race," said Seaton Begg. "I should perhaps explain that he is a relative of mine. We have ancestors in common. The family is from Germany. They are the von Beks of Bek in Saxony. The family is better known, however, in neighbouring Wäldenstein. Most of its sons spent more time abroad in Mirenburg, the capital of Wäldenstein, with whom they are identified. They intermarried with the local aristocracy and share an intimate history with the place. The man you met is Ulrich, Prince of Mirenburg, who carries the ancient curse of the Bek blood . . ."

"Curse? More melodrama?" said Tex, almost wearily, but the Englishman ignored him.

"Every few generations they give birth to an albino. Every few centuries they give birth to identical albino twins. And about every five hundred years they give birth to albino twins who are a girl and a boy. When that occurs there is a certain stir created in the occult world. A proliferation of magical swords is one phenomenon associated with such a birth."

"What are they?" asked Don Lorenzo in some distaste. "Vampires? Were-wolves? What?"

"Some of them, as I said, are called 'eternals.' They live according to dif-

ferent rules and conditions, but few have sinister ambitions where we are concerned. Indeed they are often fairly benign, even altruistic. No others possess
the warlock's powers you saw demonstrated just now. But 'Monsieur Zenith,'
as that individual sometimes styles himself, is a master of magic, though his
familiars are not always available to him here. His mind holds ancient secrets.
His regular companions are the restlessly damned, the dispossessed, the
abnormal. He consorts with criminals in the lowest dens of vice. And he plays
the violin like an angel. No, Don Lorenzo, this is not an ordinary monster.
Neither, in the usual sense, is he damned. I expect to meet him again. And
when I do, I hope I shall have the luck to best him. Even extraordinary mon-
sters, my dear sir, have no place in decent society."

"Which is why they deserve the freedom of the wild underworld at least,"
said the Masked Buckaroo with some feeling. He had been thinking over those
events. "I propose we should leave them alone. Why pursue them, Sir Seaton?"

The detective sighed. "'Monsieur Zenith'—or Pale Wolf as you know
him—is a criminal. It is my duty to bring him to justice. And that means I
must follow him wherever he hides."

The Englishman rode over to have a word with Captain Gideon. The
officer issued instructions and soon several saddlebags were handed to Sir
Seaton. He rode back, lifting his hat to Jenny. "Goodbye, Mrs Brady. A
pleasure to meet you." He shook hands with the others who were rather surprised. They had not expected the detective to leave them so soon.

None asked him where he was going. Then he turned his horse about and
began to ride into the shadows of the canyon on his way to the Realm Below.

They watched until he disappeared. "A man after my own heart, that
Englishman," said young Tex. "I almost wish I was going with him."

"Where he goes, he goes alone, I think," said Don Lorenzo, frowning. He
murmured some sort of prayer under his breath and crossed himself. "Today
is Ash Wednesday." This last remark was made to no one in particular.

"Well, I seem to be the only person looking forward to getting home,"
said Jenny with a grin. "After this strange experience I'll never be bored with
the ordinary routines of the Circle Squared."

By now they had ridden up to where the tram-tracks began. Captain
Gideon stepped forward saluting.

The Masked Buckaroo thanked him for responding so rapidly and efficiently to his messages.

"I'm glad we could be of help," Gideon insisted warmly.

"You will never appreciate the full extent of your help, captain," said young Tex dismounting. As they climbed the steps of the heavy war-tram and took their places on the mahogany bench seats, the young buckaroo put a manly arm about his wife's shoulders. Soon the vehicle was in motion, racing back across the plains as a second machine collected track behind it, a demonstration of the skill and ingenuity of "Thunderclap" Meadley's famous "Flying Tracklayers," who had done so much for Texas's military reputation. Within a few hours they would be back at the Circle Squared.

Yet for all Jenny's talk of a return to normality, the young avenger knew that life would never be quite the same again. No matter how much he blocked it from his conscious mind, he would continue to dream of that subterranean world Sir Seaton called The Grey Fees. He would long to experience its alien wonders. And one day he knew his curiosity would get the better of him. He would give in to his impulse, saddle his horse, and retrace the trail to the Realm Below.

Something in him yearned for that day to come, but he was not to know how soon his desire would be fulfilled!

For that is another story.

The Girl Who Killed Sylvia Blade

CHAPTER ONE

Dangerous Curves

She came through the door with a gun in her hand and tears in her eyes. I didn't know what I was going to get first—the gun or the tears. Thought of either depressed me.

I said: "Hello, there . . ."

She was five feet tall in a green paisley trouser suit, with long blonde hair and a pastel pink skin. Her eyes were big and blue. She reminded me of Alice in Wonderland after a particularly hairy ordeal with the Queen of Hearts.

She didn't say anything. But she lowered the gun and began to cry.

I sighed and moved in, easing the little .38 from her soft hand. The tips of my fingers on her arm, I guided her across the carpet to the big guest chair. She sat down with a bump. I went to the bar and poured her a large gin. I put it in the hand that had held the gun. It seemed a fair trade. She drank the gin, downing half of it in one swallow, and when she looked up at me she wasn't crying any more.

"You're Beck?" she said. "The reporter on the *Trib*?" She had a whispering New England accent that did something to me. I nodded.

"I'm Belinda Fayre."

"Uh-huh," I said. "I saw you at The Black Room two nights ago. I like the way you frug. What's your problem? Why come in without knocking? Why the gun?"

"I just killed someone." She said it flatly, with a hint of surprise in those wide, blue eyes. "At The Black Room. I shot her."

I picked up the gun and sniffed it. "Someone certainly fired this recently. Shot who?"

"Sylvia."

"Wow," I said. "Sylvia Blade." Sylvia Blade was a top star at the discotheque—The Black Room—where, to powerful beat music, Belinda frugged twice nightly in a golden cage above the dance floor. Sylvia's act was the most popular. It involved a long bull whip and a male partner. I'd only heard about it. That stuff isn't for me.

"I didn't mean to," she said.

"They never do. You want help?"

"Yes." The word was the sound of a summer breeze through a Maine meadow. She looked at the rug. "I'm sorry—"

"Lady," I said, "so am I. You're not the first to ask me for help. You killed a woman. You think I can get you off a rap like that? I work with the law, not against it."

"But, I didn't mean to kill her. She attacked me. She—she was vile, Mr Beck. The gun was hers—she kept it in her dressing room. She—"

"Why did she attack you?"

Belinda wasn't listening to me. She just kept talking, getting it out fast. She had been dating a youngster who attended the disco. Dating customers was against the rules. Sylvia had found out and threatened to tell the management unless—.

"Unless I agreed to meet some friends she had—and—do things—with them—let them do things to me . . ."

I didn't ask what kind of things. I didn't really want to know. This was 1964 after all, and adults were adults. But this had nothing to do with consent. Sylvia had tried to blackmail Belinda into joining some kind of orgy, and Belinda had refused point blank. From what Belinda could gather, Sylvia had already made a guarantee to the people she knew that she would get Belinda for them—they'd seen her at the disco—and when Belinda had said no, Sylvia got mad and tried to force her out of the place and into a car. Belinda ran back to the dressing room. Sylvia produced a gun. There'd been a struggle. Belinda had gotten hold of the gun and shot Sylvia. It was manslaughter, maybe even self-defence. I told her she had little to worry about if the cops believed her story. She didn't seem impressed.

"It's just my word," she said. "Nobody saw anything."

"I believe you," I told her. "Why shouldn't the cops?"

"Even if they did, what about the jury?"

She had a point. I frowned.

"What if we could find some member of this group Sylvia mentioned?" I suggested. "Someone who might testify that Sylvia had been commissioned to get you for them? That would convince the cops. And maybe the jury."

Her lovely face brightened and then sank again. She shrugged. "Nobody would come forward. Who'd want to give that kind of evidence, admitting they were a member of a vice circle?"

She was right. I went to the closet and got my hat and coat.

"Where are you going?" She grew alarmed again. The tears threatened.

"To see what I can dig up," I told her. "If we can't persuade a volunteer, I might be able to get something on these orgy organizers. Force 'em to come forward. Stay here. If the cops ask me where you are, I'll have to tell 'em, but don't worry."

I put a Lucky between my lips as I left, paused outside the door and lit the cigarette. I was thinking what a fool I was. I'd gotten in trouble again, playing knight errant for some dame who was probably making a sucker out of me. But I'd believed her. I wanted to help her. Maybe in the back of my mind I thought that if I did her a favour she might do me one. I'd fallen for that Alice in Wonderland innocence.

I went out to the rainy, neon lit sidewalk and hailed a cab. I gave the address of The Black Room. The driver told me it was closed. I told him I knew that. It was ten after one in the morning and I was beginning to feel sour.

~ CHAPTER TWO ~

Beautiful Corpse

The Black Room was at basement and street level of a Southside block in a district that had been seedy but was becoming fashionable. Rain silvered the night in long streaks. The sidewalk was a strip of black ebony gleaming under the lamps. No cops to be seen. The body hadn't been found yet. It was Wednesday. I knew the discos generally closed early on Wednesdays. There was no one in sight, just a few cars cruising by, their tires hissing on the wet asphalt. I paid off the cab and went round to the back door marked STAFF. It was wide open, swinging in the wind. I walked through and found the dressing room. The lights were still on. I saw the body. Sylvia was dead all right, lying in a litter of clothes and makeup in the tiny dressing room. The big, black whip she used in her act lay near her, its thong curled around her upper calf.

She was tall, well built, with lovely legs and firm flesh. She wasn't particularly young. Her long red hair was spread behind her head, and her eyes were closed, her full mouth slightly open, as if to receive a lover's kiss. The only kiss she'd be getting now was from the skinny guy with the sickle who came to collect her wicked little soul.

Her arms were flung out at her sides and her legs were spread apart. She hadn't been wearing any underwear, and the flimsy white dress had risen to her thighs, revealing her black garter belt. It wasn't sexy, any of it. It made me want to weep.

There was something dark and corrupt about her appearance, even in death. Just looking at her, without knowing her act, or knowing what she'd wanted from Belinda, you sensed she was a woman who revelled in perverse sexuality.

I didn't touch her. I started to search the room, hoping I could turn up some clue to the identity of Sylvia's "friends."

I found her purse and opened it. It contained the usual stuff—and one unusual item. I frowned, looking at the bronze badge and wondering how it came into the picture. It showed the Roman fasces—the bundle of sticks tied together that symbolised order and justice. The last people to use a badge like that had been Mussolini's Fascists! I thought of Mussolini. I thought of Italy. I thought of the Mafia. I thought of my old enemy Big Tuna Bastori, Capo of The Organisation, the local Mafia in these parts. I thought I was going crazy. Didn't the Mafia hate Musso as a more successful rival? Still holding the badge, certain that it was the clue I'd been looking for, I went to the phone and dialled the number of the Homicide Department.

I told them to put me through to Lieutenant Sinclair.

Ike Sinclair wasn't there. They asked me if I wanted to talk to anyone else. I said it could wait. I dialled Ike's home number and held on. I didn't have to hold on for more than a few rings. Ike's voice answered, alert as usual. He could come out of sleep in seconds. I told him the good news. He cursed me and said he'd drive round. I said I'd be there.

As I turned, still fingering the little badge and wondering about it, hoping Ike could tell me something, the door opened and something glossy walked in.

The guy was in white tie and tails. His brilliantined hair outshone his patent leather shoes. Six feet two with a cleft chin, he had the good looks of a college football player. But looks were deceptive. He must have been forty. The mouth had odd lines on it. The eyes were very hard. I knew the face. We'd printed it in the *Trib*'s gossip page before. It was Rudy Klosterheim of the Klosterheim millions. A big man in Lake City. A powerful man who backed politicians and racketeers and other deserving causes.

"Give me that badge," he said.

"No," I said.

"Don't be foolish," he said.

"Who's foolish?" I said.

He chewed his lip. "I'll buy it."

"How much?"

"Five grand."

I whistled. "So it's worth five grand."

"Only to me. Know who I am?"

"I do."

"Don't cross me, chum," he said.

"You know Sylvia's dead?" I asked politely, nodding towards the less-than-decorous corpse.

He didn't turn his head, but he took a gun from the pocket of his top-coat and he pointed it contemplatively at my stomach.

"So you knew," I opined. "And you came back for this? The old Fascist badge? What is it? The badge of the club you belong to? The one Sylvia tried to get Belinda to join?"

"Oh, I'll enjoy killing you." That was hard to say between clenched teeth.

"Go ahead," I said. "Wish I could enjoy the sight of the cops arriving just as you do it."

"You called the police?" His voice became nervous. "The local precinct?" He sounded as if he could handle the local precinct.

"Ike Sinclair of Homicide," I told him.

He put the gun away. "You a cop?"

"I'm Beck of the *Trib*. I'm worse than a cop. I'm a fearless reporter. Tell me about your group, Mr Klosterheim. Can anyone join? Or is it exclusive? We'd like to do a story on it."

"Write a word and I'll make sure you never write another," he said.

"I was hoping for a more original quote."

There was the sound of a siren and tires squealing.

He left the dressing room in a hurry.

He must have managed to avoid Ike Sinclair and his boys, because when they came in they didn't say anything about him. I decided I wouldn't say anything either. I put the little badge in my pocket. I felt Mr Klosterheim was the lead I needed.

Behind his glasses Ike Sinclair had that bitter look every cop wears when wakened in the middle of the night to come look at a corpse. He took off his hat and ran his hand over his high, balding head.

"How'd you find the body?" he asked, bending over Sylvia's cold, curved cadaver.

"Her killer told me where to look," I said.

Ike straightened up. "No games, Hank. The full story. Fast."

I thought he might even hit me if I didn't tell him. I told him. When he'd listened he pursed his lips and looked around the room, finally fixing his eyes back on the corpse.

"You say you believe her?"

"I believe her," I said. "And I want to find some witness who'll verify her story."

"You're crazy," he said. "Who'd—?"

"I'm going to find someone," I broke in.

"In how many weeks?" Ike's mouth wore a sardonic tilt.

"Tonight," I told him.

He shrugged. "You try. We'll pick up the girl. She's at your apartment now?"

"That's where she is."

"We'll go together," Sinclair said.

CHAPTER THREE

Sinister Street

When we got there the apartment was bare and Ike offered me a long, hard stare.

I shrugged. "Sorry."

"Know where she'll be?"

"Her address will be at the discotheque, I guess." I said.

He walked out of the apartment without a word. I had the feeling he didn't like me too much that night.

I gave him a couple of minutes while I hunted up a few things I might need for the excursion I planned, then I followed him out.

There were no cabs around. I began to walk. I was thinking of paying a call on Mr Rudy Klosterheim. As I turned the corner of the block, I heard footsteps behind me. I swivelled round. Three men stopped and looked at me. There wasn't much doubt that they'd been waiting for me. I was pretty sure of another thing—they wanted to do me serious damage.

Two were small, ratty-faced men with the look of cheap hoods. The other man was bigger, with the look of a cheap hood who was making money. He was the tough one. He was the one who snarled at me. I made out the words.

"Give us the badge you found at The Black Room."

"Mr Klosterheim ask you to ask me?" I said politely.

"Just hand over the badge, baby," said the big one.

"What if I don't?"

"We'll hurt you," said one of the rat-faces.

"You don't look so tough," I remarked.

They came at me then. I didn't bother too much with the little ones, but I kicked the big one's shin as he reached for me. It gave me time to slam the two little rats' heads together. I left them reeling about and got a good judo grip on big boy and let him push himself over my shoulder. He landed on the sidewalk with a solid sound. He stayed there. One of the rat-faces had drawn a knife. I chopped down on his wrist and he let go of the knife. I clipped him a short one on the jaw and he crumpled. I swung on the last member of the rough-up party and my fist dented his chin, too. They lay there in a heap. I walked away from there. I stopped at the nearest phone, called the cops to pick up the three, and called the local cab stand.

As the cab took me uptown, I saw the police wagon arrive.

I'd decided that I now had a personal score to settle with Mr Klosterheim. I was going to get him to be the witness Belinda needed. I was definitely going to get him.

⟩⟩ CHAPTER FOUR ⟨⟨

Too Late for Tears

The Klosterheim house was big, ostentatious, and glossy, like its owner. It had a wall around it, and gates. The gates were closed. I told the cab to wait. I climbed over the gates and moved around the house.

There was light coming from the french doors at the back of the house.

I slunk towards the light and peeked in through a chink in the drapes.

Belinda hadn't gone home. She hadn't done anything of her own free will. I cursed myself for opening my mouth to Klosterheim too much. He must have realised who I was, found my address, sent his men around to pick up Belinda.

She was wearing the same pale green paisley trouser suit which she wore for her dancing act and which she'd worn to my apartment. She was sitting in a high-winged chair with Klosterheim standing over her holding his gun. There was a little bruise on the right side of her mouth. She looked very scared indeed. She looked like she needed protection. I felt protective. I drew my S&W and poised myself to kick in the windows, hoping I could do it with one kick. Just as I was ready, I saw a movement through the chink and had another look.

Klosterheim was pushing Belinda towards the door. Since they were leaving the room I decided I could be more subtle. I had the compact cracksman's tool kit that Hymie Janson had given me taped to my inner thigh. I could try a key on the door.

As I was going through the somewhat complicated routine of getting at the tool kit, I heard the front door slam.

Klosterheim must be taking the girl away somewhere.

I ran round the house in time to see him forcing Belinda into a big sky blue and white restored Duesenberg, as ostentatious as everything else Klosterheim owned.

Frustrated I crept towards the fence and huddled in the shrubbery as Klosterheim drove the car up to the gate. Keeping Belinda covered with his gun, he opened it to let the car through.

As soon as the car was gone, I signalled for my cab. It came smoothing up and I jumped in. I told him to follow the Duesenberg.

We headed back downtown and were soon Southside again. The Duesenberg entered a narrow alley and doused its lights. I had a word with the cabby, paid him off, and moved cautiously down the sidewalk until I reached the entrance to the alley. Peeking around the corner I saw Klosterheim shove Belinda out of the car and through a doorway. A dead neon sign could be seen. It said PORTIA'S DISCOTHEQUE—MEMBERS ONLY. Lake City was full of discotheques. The boom had started a year ago. Maybe I'd found the head-quarters of the vice group Belinda had mentioned. If so, I had a scoop for the paper, the evidence I would need to support Belinda's story, and possibly the prospect of being found next morning floating face down in Lake Kakatanawa.

It was still raining as I walked down the alley towards the club.

It wasn't raining bricks, though.

It was a brick that fell on my head.

Or something like a brick.

A gun butt or a blackjack, I figured later.

Whatever it was, it put me straight to sleep. The world slid sideways, and I slid downwards. Just then, I didn't much care what was happening.

✤ CHAPTER FIVE ✤

Caged

When I woke up, the world was still swaying. I opened my eyes and turned my head as it began to throb, throb, throb. It wasn't only my head, either. There was music—wild, Tamla Motown music turned to maximum volume. I saw bars, bright light above me from a central hanging chandelier, a gold speckled wall beyond it. It looked like a discotheque in its decor. Then I realised where I was.

I was in one of the cages suspended over the floor where the girls danced. It was hanging from a couple of heavy, central cables from the ceiling.

I heaved myself to my feet using the bars for support. The cage was swaying. Its anchoring cables had been removed.

I looked down at the floor.

I closed my eyes.

When I opened them again I saw what I'd seen before. This time I looked longer.

Klosterheim wasn't wearing his monkey suit any more. He was clad in a pair of black tights and jackboots. Nothing else. The girl who knelt before him, a big, heavy blonde in an attitude of supplication, was stark naked. Her head was thrown back and there was a yearning expression on her face.

In one hand Klosterheim held a long, slender rod. He reached out with it and stroked it over the girl's face, breasts and stomach, caressingly. Her mouth opened and closed pleadingly. Her breasts, heaved up and down. I felt sick.

Then, as I turned away, I saw something that made me feel even worse.

It was Belinda, also completely naked. She was spread-eagled, hanging from golden chains suspended, like the cage, from the roof. There were chains pulling her legs apart and anchored to the floor. Her stomach was about level with Klosterheim's head.

There were other people in the room. A dozen men and women. I recognised faces. All top society people.

I knew I'd found the vice group, but there wasn't much I could do about it.

Klosterheim looked up then, and a thin smile crossed his face.

"Hello, Mr Beck. Welcome to Portia's Discotheque. The floor show is about to begin. I thought you'd like to see it. You've got a great view."

I didn't say anything. I didn't let him see any expression. I just stared at him hard. He shrugged, raised his rod, and brought it down with a great thwack across the kneeling girl's back. She moaned and fell on her face to the floor in front of him. He started to whip her in time to the roaring music. I retched.

Below, the others were also beginning to leap around in time to the music, flailing at one another in an ecstasy of sadomasochistic glee.

Klosterheim stopped long enough to point his slender rod at Belinda and shout to me.

"You see, she finally let herself be persuaded to join us. She's going to die, Mr Beck. Can you guess how?"

Belinda moaned and writhed in the chains. My heart was full of pity for her, and my mind was clouded with hatred for Klosterheim. The man was insane.

I grasped the slim metal bars. They weren't that thick, but they were too thick to bend with my bare hands. And they were too narrow to let me squeeze through.

I had to do something.

I looked around. I saw the chandelier that gave light to the hall. I saw the sprinkler system above me on the ceiling. On the wall nearest me I saw the pipes that fed the system. At one point they curved in a U on their way down the wall. There seemed to be a gap between them and the wall.

A desperate idea began to form in my sickened mind.

Klosterheim leapt forward and brought the rod down across the front of Belinda's thighs. She shrieked in agony. I couldn't take it. I had to try and go through with the plan, no matter how desperate it was.

I began to swing the cage from side to side as the music pounded on and the sick wretches below continued to perform their disgusting ritual.

Faster and faster I swung the cage, hoping that Klosterheim and his friends were too absorbed in their perverted activities to notice what I was doing.

Then I did it. The cage swung out and struck the chandelier with a great splintering of glass and sparks. The lights went out.

Still the music pounded, but below they had fallen silent.

There was still a little dim light from the single skylight window high above. It was all I needed to swing the cage in the opposite direction and claw out to catch the water pipe at the U-bend. My muscles strained. My whole body shook with agony as I managed to wedge one of the bars behind the pipe. Then I put my back to the cage and used my feet as a lever, trying to bend the bar outwards.

The pipe creaked. Inch by inch, the bar began to bend.

When it happened, it happened suddenly.

The bar bent outwards and the water pipe came with it. Water began to gush from it on to the floor. That gave me another idea.

The cage was swinging free now. The bar bent enough to let me through. As it swung towards the light cable, I grabbed it as I passed and swung the cage harder until I was close to the gushing water.

Down below people were shouting. Then I heard a gun bang.

"Stop it, Beck, whatever you're doing!" It was Klosterheim's voice. "I'll shoot you Beck!"

I grabbed the twisted pipe. Water poured out of it in a steady stream to the floor. Carefully I touched the naked light cable to it.

I felt good then. I heard them screaming. What I had done was use the water to conduct the electricity to the floor, and I was giving the people below a heavy shock. It wasn't enough to do them serious injury, but it was enough to give them something to think about. It stopped Klosterheim's shots.

Then what I knew would happen did happen. The electricity fused.

While they were still in confusion, I squeezed through the bars, hung for a moment, and then dropped to the water-sodden floor. Every light in the building was probably out of commission now.

I saw Klosterheim loom out of the gloom as I ran towards Belinda.

His face was a mask of hatred as he pointed the gun at me. I didn't stop to think. I just leapt at him. We both fell to the floor. He was still holding the gun.

We rolled about on the floor, grappling, as I tried to get the gun from his hand.

I felt someone else grab me. It made me even more desperate. I managed to free myself from Klosterheim and clipped him a short, hard punch on the jaw. It made him groggy. I got hold of the gun.

I stood up.

Now that my eyes were used to the gloom, I could see all the people standing around me, tensed. Some of their faces were full of fear. They guessed how the cookie was crumbling.

I relaxed and grinned. I motioned with the gun.

"Bunch up," I said, "so you're all together." Klosterheim was now on his feet. I shoved him towards the rest of the perverted crew.

Nearby Belinda was sobbing quietly. I waved the gun again and pointed at one of the naked women in the crowd, the wife of a well-known local politician. "Get her down," I said.

As the woman helped Belinda to the ground, I decided there was one more thing I wanted to do.

I'd left a message with the cab driver to fetch Ike Sinclair and his men. They should be arriving soon.

I wanted to wrap up the job neatly. I thought I knew how to do it.

~◉ CHAPTER SIX ◉~

Desire

When Sinclair arrived, I'd managed to get the emergency power working. He looked surprised when he saw what I'd prepared for him.

While waiting for him to arrive, I'd made the whole sick gang get into one of the cages. Then I'd winched it up above the floor. They were all in there. The expressions on their faces ranged from stark fear at the knowledge that their careers and reputations were finished, to Klosterheim's utter hatred.

Belinda was beside me, wearing her trouser suit again. I had my arm around her. In my other hand I held the gun I'd taken from Klosterheim.

Ike couldn't keep his cool.

"For chrissakes, Hank, what is this?"

"All the evidence you need," I said. "There's the members of the vice group that tried to get Belinda. There's half a dozen major raps you can hand 'em. I don't think Belinda will have any trouble getting acquitted."

Ike recovered.

"Why send for the Homicide Department," he said sourly. "This is a Vice Squad job, you know."

I grinned at him. He grinned back.

Belinda hugged me tightly.

She was grateful.

Very grateful.

She showed me just how grateful she was for several nights that followed.

Oh, and of course, I had one of the hottest scoops for the paper the world-weary Lake City had ever known.

It got me a raise even though the story didn't appear under my byline.

But mainly it got me the gratitude of Belinda Fayre.

I wasn't complaining.

The Case of the Nazi Canary

-ᴥᴥ CHAPTER ONE ᴥᴥ-

Message from Munich

It was, or would be, the misty autumn of 1931. A suite of comfortable bachelor apartments in the highest tower of London's exclusive Sporting Club Square. Sir Seaton Begg, former MI5 special operator, now metatemporal investigator, reached across the fire grate, singeing the sleeve of his smoking jacket. His aquiline, unconventionally handsome features were caught by the firelight. "What d'you make of this, Taffy?"

I. J. "Taffy" Sinclair, Begg's best and oldest friend and leading Home Office pathologist, accepted the rectangle of yellow paper. The balding giant had the mild but sturdy rectitude of an East End bishop. Balancing a cup of Darjeeling in one hand, he sank back into the depths of his armchair to read. Moments later, with an impatient expression, he set the telegram aside.

"The National Socialists?" Taffy frowned. "Sort of German Mussolini-ites? Aren't they even worse than the Commies for going around beating up honest citizens? And, of course, there's that lunatic anti-Jewish muck."

Begg smiled a familiar, almost sly, smile. "I gather they will restore 'German pride' and so forth, meaning, no doubt, the military. A very attractive message to the heavy industrialists, naturally, who find more profit in swords than ploughshares." He lifted delicate bone china to his full, masculine lips. "The armourers and their jackals."

Like Sinclair, Begg supported world disarmament under the League of Nations and was disappointed when Woodrow Wilson had been forced to placate the parochial exigencies of his Congress by quitting the League.

Begg continued with some emphasis. "Look here, Taffy, read that thing again and let me know any other names you recognise, apart from their Little Corporal destined to become their German Napoleon."

"You mean that awful oik who looks like Charlie Chaplin? Musso's effeminate pal Mr Hitler? The Nazi general secretary or whatever he styles himself. Nothing new is it?"

"I'd agree he seems to be preaching a familiar line of *l'intoxication special*. The bankers are offered financial stability, the people are offered full employment and security. Everything they fear will be extinquished."

"Of course, you can't keep the illusion alive forever. Sooner or later you need a good war to take people's minds off your failed promises." Sinclair reached a taper into the fire and relit his pipe. "These chaps have been getting more dangerous since the successes of Primo De Rivera and Mussolini, of course." He puffed heroically on his briar. "Nothing spreads faster than a bad idea."

"I agree, old man," Begg glanced into the fire, his aquiline features in silhouette. For an instant his eyes burned an angry red. "But desperation is a poor bedfellow for democracy, as we've found already. Come on, Taffy. Be a pal and glance at that wire again."

Reluctantly, Sinclair adjusted his spectacles. "Well, Hess is a pretty common German name. Could this be your acquaintance the Baron von Hess, kinsman to your cousin, Count von Bek?"

"Von Bek?" Begg laughed at this mention of his old sparring partner, known to the British public as Monsieur Zenith, the Albino, Count of Crime. "I doubt if my cousin would deign to involve himself in this. It's not what you call an epicurian crime, eh? Anything else?"

"Well, the thing's from Briennerstrasse. Seems to be genuine. That's a pretty posh avenue in the salubrious bit of Munich. Papal Nuncio's there and all that. So these chaps seem to have some powerful backers, as you say. Naturally, Begg, you wouldn't consider working for such people!"

"Well, I agree it might be a bit unsavoury to take their money, but I'm curious. Fascinating, eh, the dreams of power of failed shopkeepers and frustrated shipping clerks?"

"That's downright perverse, Begg!" exclaimed the sensitive Celt. "Keep 'em away with a ten-foot pole, I say."

"Currently President Stalin's favourite foreign policy strategy, the ten-foot Pole." Sir Seaton referred to Lenin's successor, who lead the Bolshevik Party in the Duma and was spouting nationalistic rubbish every day, winning votes from Monsieur Trotski, the liberal internationalist. "Poland as a buffer zone in case civil war breaks out in Germany. That could be the touch paper for another world conflict."

"Germany's safe enough," Taffy insisted. "She has the best and most just political constitution in the world. Certainly better than ours. Even sturdier than the American."

"A people who have never been really happy with their constitution's restrictions. A good-sized chunk of the American press and public rather likes Signor Musso and his disciples. I suspect Germany would have to declare war on the United States before the House stopped favouring stability over freedom. So we can't rely on Roosevelt, any more than Stalin, to stop a civil war if one started. Some of his admirers already call Roosevelt the American Mussolini. They say he wants to set up an enlightened fascist state in the United States and destroy the British Empire."

"All of which," Sinclair offered a dry smile, "is scarcely on the cards, what?" Like so many old Harrovians, but unlike his former schoolfellow Begg, Sinclair had a comfortable, phlegmatic belief in the good sense of the commons and their strong survival instinct both as social democrats and as self-interested individuals with jobs and businesses to ensure. He shook his head, waving the telegram dismissively.

Begg took back the German wire and read it aloud, translating swiftly. *My dear Sir Seaton: Here in Germany we have long admired the exploits of your famous English detectives. We are sufficiently impressed with your national virtues as a detecting folk to enquire if you, paramount in your specialised profession, would care to come at once to Munich where you will have the satisfaction of rescuing a reputation, bringing the guilty to justice, and also knowing you have saved a noble and betrayed nation. The reputation is that of our country's most able philosopher-general. I refer, of course, to our Guide Herr Adolf Hitler, author of* Mein Kampf *and bearer of the Iron Cross, who has been devastated by the murder of his ward, Fraulein Angela Raubal, and whose reputation could be ruined by the scandal. With a view to seeing the triumph of justice, could we, the National Socialist Party, enjoin you to lose no*

speed in taking the earliest Zeppelin from Manchester to Munich? While BOAC pro-
vide an excellent run from Croydon and appears quicker, there is a long delay making
stops at Berlin and Frankfurt. Therefore we recommend you take the modern German
vessel which leaves Manchester Moss Side field at 5 PM and arrives at 10 AM the next
morning. An excellent train from Kings Cross at 2 PM connects with the airship, The
Spirit of Nuremburg. *Please excuse the brevity of this telegram. My inner voices tell*
me you are destined to save not merely Germany but the entire Western world from an
appalling catastrophe and become the best-loved Englishman our country has ever
known. On the presumption that you will accept our case, as you accept your historic
destiny, I have sent, via courier, all necessary first-class travel documents for yourself
and an assistant, together with papers enabling you to bring any personal transport
you favour. We are, you see, familiar with your foibles. I will personally be at Munich
International Aerodrome to meet the ZZ 700. I look forward to the honour of shaking
your hand. Writing in all admiration and expectation that your famous sense of fair
play will move your conscience, I am, Yours Most Sincerely, Rudolf Hess, Deputy
Leader, The NSDAP, Briennerstrasse, Munich, Bavaria, Germany.

"Rum style, eh?"

"About as laconic as his countryman Nietschze," reflected Sinclair with a snort. "No doubt the poor blighter's trench crazy. Harmless enough, I'm sure, but still barking barmy. I mean to say, old sport, you *are* the multiverse's leading metatemporal snooper, and this case is merely a particularly grubby murder of a girl, who was probably no better than she ought to be, by a seedy *petit bourgeois* who sets himself up as the saviour of the world. He'll likely find his true destiny, if not on the gallows, among the sandwich board men of Hyde Park Corner, warning against the dangers of red meat and Asian invasion. A distinct case of an undersatisfied libido and an overstimulated ego, what?"

"Quite so, old man. I know your penchant for Viennese trick cyclists. But surely you wouldn't wish to see the wrong cove found guilty of such an unpleasant crime?"

"There no chance he's guilty, I suppose?" Sinclair instantly regretted his words. "No, no. Of course we must assume his innocence. But there are many more deserving cases around the world, I'm sure."

"Few of them cases allowing me to take the very latest in aerial luxury liners and even put yourself and 'Dolly' on the payroll without question."

"It's no good, Begg, the idea's unpalatable to me . . ."

With an athlete's impatient speed, Begg crossed to his vast, untidy bureau, and tugged something out of a pigeonhole. "Besides, our tickets arrived not ten minutes before you turned up for tea." He grinned and held out imploring arms. "Oh, say you'll do it, old man. I promise you, if nothing else, the adventure will be an education."

Taffy began to grumble, but by midnight he was on his feet phoning down for his Daimler. He would meet Begg, he promised, at Kings Cross, where they would travel to Manchester that afternoon on the high-speed M&E Flyer so as to be safely aboard the Zep by 4:30.

Begg was delighted. He trusted and needed his old comrade's judgement and cool head. Their personalities were complementary, like a couple of very different fives players. This time Begg felt he had involved himself in a job which would have him holding his nose for longer than he cared.

As for the Presbyterian Taffy, he would still be debating the morality of accepting the tickets when they met the next day and began the journey to Munich.

⤳❧ CHAPTER TWO ❧⤶

ℋomicide or 𝒮uicide?

𝒮ir Seaton and Taffy had fought the "picklefork brigade" for too long to hate them. They understood that your average Fritz wasn't so very different from your average Tommy and that it took self-interested and foolish politicians to make men kill one another. Yet for all his certainty that the War to End War had done its work, Begg knew that vigilance was forever the price of freedom. Few threats to our hard-won rights came from the expected sources. The unexpected angle of attack was generally successful. Authority is by nature conservative and therefore never truly prepared for surprises. It was Seaton Begg's job *always* to be prepared for the unexpected. That was why the Admirality, the War Office, the Home Office, and the Foreign Office continued to pay him substantial retainers. It was also why they encouraged him to take the occasional foreign case, for he was equally admired by the Quai D'Orsay and Aleksanderplatz.

The service aboard the *Spirit of Nuremburg* was impeccable. This made Taffy a little nervous. "Sort of military feel about it, if you know what I mean. Sometimes I think I prefer the old, sloppy cockneys we get on the Croydon-Paris run."

Begg was amused by this. "Sit back and enjoy it, old man." He had asked for that morning's newspapers. Their front pages were full of the bomb attempt on the half-finished Miami-Havana raillink. Begg, however, was scanning the interior pages with great concentration, especially, for some reason, the entertainment columns.

To Taffy's discomfort, not all the papers were of the better type. Some of the sensational French and Italian sheets mingled with more respectable journals.

"There's some fascinating reading about Herr Hitler's relationship with Fraulein Raubal? Does her name mean anything to you, Taffy?"

"Her nickname, 'Geli,' is, like Raubal, fairly common, I believe, certainly in Southern Germany and Austria. Who is she, do you know?"

"Herr Hitler's mistress, my dear chap." Begg smiled self-indulgently at his own relish for scandal. "They are also close relatives."

Disturbed, Sinclair shook his head. "I don't follow the Continental gossip columns."

"You should, old boy." The lean detective settled himself in his chair, an empty pipe clenched between his teeth. "You'd learn a lot more from them than from any piece of biased front-page news. I've been reading 'em religiously since Germany started to wobble again, and Italy began her various disastrous 'wars' on marshlands, drink, crime, poverty, and other social ills. Bad precedent, rhetoric like that. Also France is a great source of pillow talk, eh?" He waved at the untidy stacks of *Munchner Neuesten Nachrichter*, *Il Popolo d'Italia*, *Actuelle*, *La Vie*, *Moi Aussi*, *Der Spiegel*, *Svenske Dagbladet*, *Berliner Poste*, *Der Gerade Weg*, *Volkischer Beobachter*, and *Münchner Illustrierte Presse*, which shared not always agreeable space with *Le Figaro*, *Les Temps*, *Al Misr*, *The Times of India*, *The Cape Times*, *El Pais*, *Il Giornale d'Italia*, and the Berlin-published

Munda Veritas. Few were open at the early pages. "Do you know the name, for instance, of Mussolini's powerful art advisor and long-term mistress?"

"Naturally not, it's none of my business."

"Do you know which 'pretty boy' Hollywood actor, the greatest of Mussolini's American supporter's, the Duce's film-actress mistress is secretly 'dating'?"

"Of course not!" Taffy was almost insulted by these questions.

"Mussolini's art advisor is Signora Margarita Sarfati. Jewish, as it happens. Signor Mussolini has no defeated nation to console. For him, certain socialists and other rivals are enemies enough. To answer my second query, William Randolph Hearst's mistress is Marion Davis. She is having an affair with Max Peters, the Jewish cowboy 'star.' Peters is a friend and admirer of Mussolini. William Randolph helps support Mussolini by paying him for articles, which Hearst publishes in his newspapers. The day could dawn when *Il Duce* will seem almost moderate in his power addiction! As you can imagine, Hearst's rivals are glad of any news likely to embarrass him.

"What's more, the Raubal murder case has proven meat and drink for the German left-wing press. They are thirsty for any sign of Mr Hitler's downfall, it seems. But the public still expects evidence if its going to change its loyalties now!"

Taffy, deprived of his *Times*, contented himself with the *Munchner Post*'s crossword puzzle, which he found surprisingly straightforward.

The wind and rain thudded hard against the huge airship's canopy as she swayed at anchor between forward and stern masts. In spite of the stirring waltz tunes coming over the tannoy, there was still an air of adventure about boarding an airship, especially in bad weather when you realised how much you were at the mercy of elemental nature. Outside the windows, Moss Side Field was obscured by mist, and even Manchester's famous chimneys were hardly visible, wrapped, as they were, in cloaks of their own making. Begg had been pleased to see the smoke. "Those chimneys are alive, Taffy," he had said upon boarding. "And a live chimney means a living wage for those poor devils in the factory towns."

Since Begg needed to make notes, they had ordered cabin service. At seven PM sharp, as the lights of London faded on their starboard bow and they saw below the faint white flecks of waves, there came a discreet knock on their door. At Begg's command, a short, jolly, red-faced waiter entered their little sitting room. They had already decided on their menu, and the efficient waiter soon converted a writing table to a dining table and laid it with a bright, white cloth. He then proceeded to bring the first courses which, while of the heavy German type, were eaten by the pair with considerable relish. A good white wine helped the meal down.

The signs of dining magically removed, Taffy took up a light novel and read for an hour while Begg continued to make notes and refer to the newspapers. Eventually the pathologist could stay awake no longer and with a yawning "Good night, old man," decided to turn in. He occupied the sleeping cubicle to the left of the main room. He knew from experience not to compete with Seaton Begg, who needed at most five hours sleep in twenty-four.

Indeed, when Sinclair rose to use the well-designed hidden amenities, it seemed Begg had done no more than get into his pyjamas, retaining his place and posture from the previous night.

Only the scenery below had changed. They had crossed the North Sea and were now making their way above the neat fields of the German low-lands. In another two hours they would berth in Munich, the *Spirit*'s home port. Meanwhile there was a full English breakfast to consume and wash down with what, even Sinclair admitted, was a passable cup of Assam.

Munich Aerodrome had the very latest in winching masts. Disembarking from the fully grounded Zeppelin, Begg and Sinclair descended the ship's staircase. They were greeted at the bottom by a tall, rather cadaverous individual in a poorly fitting Norfolk jacket of chocolate brown, two swastika armbands in the German colours of black, red, and white, rather baggy riding breeches, and highly polished polo boots. He offered them a "Quo Vadis" Roman salute, made famous in the popular film drama, then immediately began to pump Begg's hand.

"This is such an honour, Sir Seaton. I have read about you so much. I myself have a natural affinity with the British atristocracy. I so admire your Prince of Wales. The best of English and German blood breed fine specimens of humanity, eh? Might I know your eating habits?"

Begg, as Sinclair could tell, was a little taken aback by Herr Hess's intensity. "Eating habits?"

"I had heard a little rumour that you were a vegan." Hess was almost coy in this suggestion, giving Begg no option but to pull his leg.

"Vegan? No, sir, I am a typical London mongrel, a bit of everything, a unique and sturdy breed. Anglo-Saxon brawn and Jewish brains, Irish sentimentality and French phlegm."

Hess snorted and arranged his odd mouth into a smile as if he tried to enjoy a joke he didn't understand. "You are not carnivores, I hope, ha, ha."

"I'm afraid we are, dear boy. Roast Beef of Old England and all that. The Steak and Kidney Pie of Sidcup. Or, in a pinch, the Bangers of Old Bavaria." It was dawning on the Englishmen that Rudolph Hess, given his preferences, would wear a very hairy Bernard Shaw tweed suit, rope sandles, a bushy set of chin foliage, and spend his weekends, rain or shine, at a nudist camp. The Nazi Party, or at least its leadership, began to seem both more and less sinister.

"I ask because of lunch," Hess confided.

Begg gave every appearance of insouciance as he replied. "Anywhere that serves those delicious local white sausages and a pint or two of your marvellous beer will be fine with us, old chap."

Hess frowned. "Both Alf—" he coughed, anxious to let the investigators know he was on such intimate terms with Hitler—"I mean Herr Hitler and myself are both convinced vegans. We are firmly against the cruel treatment of animals and understand the dangers to health involved in eating their slaughtered meat." He shuddered. Clearly he was making more than one point. "Adolf Hitler is a man of considerable feeling. He would not harm a fly, let alone another human being. I hope you don't judge us all by Berlin decadence or aggression, which is largely a foreign and alien invention anyway."

As they talked, they strolled through the passenger foyer of the great modern aerodrome. Over a dozen pairs of steel masts held ships, or awaited vessels from all over Southern and Eastern Europe. The 'drome was one of Munich's very latest monuments to municipal pride.

The weather was much improved and a warm, golden sun was reflected in the silvery hulls of the airships. Through massing white clouds, rays of sunlight struck the distant outlines of Munich herself, her twisted gables and glittering spires. As they reached the exit, Begg was delighted to see "Dolly" waiting for them at the kerbside.

"Dolly" was, of course, Begg's massive Deusenburg tourer, custom-made by the great American motor company whose reputation in their homeland was as considerable as Rolls Royce, Ferrari, Citroen, or Mercedes elsewhere. "Dolly" possessed the latest type of batteries tuned to take the great automobile up to seventy-five miles an hour if necessary.

Sinclair slipped discreetly into the shadows of the back seats, leaving Hess to sit next to Begg as the detective engaged the engine and gears. With a mighty purring of the modern electric engine, they were soon on their way to Munich, following Hess's precise directions. In what seemed a quixotic request, Begg asked Hess to give him a quick tour of the city and take them to the Nazi HQ, the Brown House, before lunch. Knowing the ways of English detectives to be mysterious and circuitous, Hess did not hesitate in obeying.

Sinclair had visited the city several times and had an affection for it, but Begg knew Berlin much better. He remarked on Munich's pleasant architecture, the broad tree-lined avenues and parks, her well-appointed public galleries and museums.

Hess had lived here for much of his life. He pointed out the various sights. Munich was a busy provincial metropolis with an excellent public transport system, chiefly trams and metro. As her many churches indicated, she was predominantly Catholic by religion. The old Bavarian capital had the baroque quaintness usually associated with the German regions, tributes to the taste and vision of her princes and governors.

"Dolly" was soon through the old quarter of the city, making a circuit of the huge, covered market, then driving along another avenue sparsely occupied by large mansions and official buildings, some flying the flags of other nations. Here Hess gave the order to stop. They had arrived at their first destination, the "Brown House," HQ of the National Socialist Party. The salubrious surroundings made one think twice about the party's lack of respectability. The huge silk Nazi "hooked cross" banners were very striking as they stirred in the faint, westerly breeze.

Once at the Brown House Hess's status was confirmed. Smartly uniformed SA men in their odd ski cap headgear and brown uniforms sprang to open the doors of the car, and the three occupants were greeted with a barrage of "Heil Hitlers" and lifted arms as they entered the busy vestibule decorated in the very latest "Bauhaus" or Viennese *avante garde* styles. Bustling as it was, the place had a mournful, depressed quality, as if everyone in it grieved for their leader's loss and feared for his safety. All knew, as they were quick to inform Hess, that Hitler was the victim of an enemy's plot.

Now Hess became a different man. He took on the authority and manner of a high-ranking officer as he led the two Englishmen through the simple, quasi-rustic foyer and up the low, wide staircase.

"This is the Führer's own office." Hess guided them into a large, triangular room dominated by a portrait of Hitler himself, his hands in Napoleonic pose, his stern, cool eyes fixed on the problems of the Nation and those who would threaten Germany's security again. Outside at the back there was a large amount of building work going on. "We are making a barracks for the SA boys," explained Hess. "This place, of course, is a natural target for Sozie attack." Sozie was the slang for Socialist, just as Nazi was slang for National Socialist. The street clashes between the various groups had become notorious throughout Germany where uniformed militia, the so-called Free Corps, swaggered about, doing as they pleased. Recently Hitler's ablest general, Captain Ernst Röhm, had organised them all under the same banner as the SA or "Stormtroops" and brought a certain rough discipline to the hooligans. This gave Röhm command of a powerful militia, probably superior to the regular army.

"I'd be obliged, Herr Hess," said Begg, "if you wouldn't mind telling us again exactly what you know about the circumstances surrounding the discovery of poor Fraulein Raubal's body. I know you were the first party member on the scene."

"Naturally the Winters called me first," agreed Hess. His black, bushy eyebrows twitched with a life of their own. He pulled at his earlobes and, grinding his teeth, stared into a middle-distance where he seemed to be looking at a cinema screen presenting the events he described.

"Geli is Alf's ward, you know. His niece. His half sister's child. When he moved into his new apartment in Prinzregensburgstrasse he needed someone to look after the place, so he invited his sister to come and be his housekeeper. He

insisted she bring her daughter Geli, too. He was, I will admit, a little infatuated, but more in the way a childless man might yearn for a daughter. He doted
on the girl. He bought her whatever she wanted. He paid for drama lessons.
Singing lessons. Dancing lessons. He took her with him everywhere he went."

"Even to political meetings?" asked Begg, making a note.

"Even to those. His career had begun to prosper. The SA were glad to see
him with a girl from time to time. He paid for the singing lessons, because
she had a talent for operetta, which Adolf loves. Of course there were more
puritanical party comrades, such as Heinrich Himmler, who disapproved of
this relationship. Himmler felt it detracted from Hitler's seriousness and
made him vulnerable to the anti-Nazi press. There were vile rumours, of
course, but those are always attached to successful politicans.

"Geli caused the odd scene in public, and Alf seemed unable to control
her. Alf knew how Himmler felt, but he ignored him. Geli fired his political
engine, he told Himmler. Without Geli he could not give the speeches which
swayed the crowds."

But not only Himmler noticed how much less the rich ladies would give
to party funds when they saw their beloved Herr Hitler, who on other occasions had laid his head in their laps, with his niece. They influenced their
husbands. And the industrialists Adolf wanted to win over were not too sure
about a man who took his niece everywhere he went.

"I know there were strong arguments in this very room. Once Adolf
became so incensed by what he said was interference in his private life that
he fell to the floor and began to tear at the carpet with his teeth. He can be
very wearing sometimes. That is why few of us ever wish to upset him . . ."

"The carpet?" declared Sinclair. "With his teeth?"

"I wasn't there on that occasion, but Röhm, Strasser, and Doctor Göbbels
were, as I recall."

"You have told us about Captain Röhm, but have not explained about
Herr Strasser and Doctor Göbbels."

"Personally, I prefer Röhm, for all his predelictions. He is at least an honest
soldier and as loyal to Hitler as I am. Gregor Strasser is the leader of our party
in the Reichstag. He's a bit of a left-winger. A very distinguished man, but
rather at odds with Adolf over the direction of the party. Strasser is more

socialist than nationalist. Doctor Göbbels is the intellectual of the party. A frail little man with a club foot. He represents what I call 'the Berlin faction'—those who have more recently attached themselves to our party's destiny."

"And would any of these think the death of Geli Raubal would benefit Herr Hitler and the party?" Through the window Begg inspected the construction in what had once been a rather pretty garden.

"Oh, all of them would probably say something like it." Hess nodded absently, looking about the room, its sparse furniture, rather as if he saw it for the first time. "But saying and doing are very different things. I can't see Röhm, who thought Geli a bit of a doxy, Strasser, who was the last one to want scandal, or Göbbels, who is our chief propagandist, threatening either Hitler's career or the party's prospects by killing Geli. And Captain Göring has no interest in such things. Göbbels might have made her an offer she couldn't refuse. Röhm might have frightened her away. Strasser would have told her to keep her nose clean and not embarrass the Führer."

"And this Herr Himmler?"

"He's a cold fish. Head of Hitler's personal body guard. He did hate the relationship. But he, too, knows that the party is on the very brink of sweeping the country. As far as I'm aware he is in Berlin. Why would he jeopardise his own career? You see, there are no real suspects within the party. Our self-interest would not be served by scandal."

"True," agreed Begg. "So you believe there was no political motive for her death. And what about a personal one?"

"You will have to ask others about that." Hess was suddenly very subdued.

Under Begg's clever prompting, Hess revealed all he knew of the Geli Raubal murder case.

Hitler was becoming increasingly jealous of Geli, who grew steadily bored with his prolonged absences from the flat. His political career took him further and further from Munich for longer periods. She, being a young, spirited woman, wanted more gaiety in her life and eventually asked her Uncle Alf if he would pay for her to go to Vienna where she had friends and where she could get far better voice lessons than in Munich.

Hitler had objected to this. He had not wanted her to go to Vienna. He had not wanted her to leave their flat. He was becoming even more suspicious of her. He threatened and wheedled, and it seemed she calmed down. Then on the morning he was due to leave for an important speaking tour, there was another row. "It was to involve some crucial secret meetings, for there are those in our party who do not believe Alf should be courting the rich at all. Yet without them, we are nothing." Hess paused, his voice taking on an increasingly retrospective tone.

"That same morning, Geli had found one of her pet canaries dead on the floor of its cage and became hysterical. She threatened Hitler. She said that if he did not let her go to Vienna she would kill herself. Then she threatened to spill the beans about 'everything.'"

"Everything?" Begg lifted an eyebrow.

Hess did not know what "everything" was, he said. But Sinclair recognised Begg's sudden alertness.

"Well, Hitler's car was to call for him early that morning after breakfast. He could not cancel his engagements. But Geli demanded that he either stay with her or let her go to Vienna. Again Hitler refused. Even as he got into the car, Geli appeared on the balcony above. "So you won't let me go to Vienna?" she had shouted.

"Hitler's reply had been a terse 'No.'" Then the automobile had driven away."

Hours later Hitler was meeting his new backers. He stayed overnight at the Deutscherhof in Nuremburg. There were many witnesses. Meanwhile, in the morning, Annie Winter, the housekeeper, arrived at Prinzregensburgstrasse to begin work at 8:30. The flat was silent. Frau Winter knocked several times, without getting a response. Eventually she sent for her butler husband to force it. They found Geli.

"She appeared to have killed herself. Beside her lay the dead canary spattered with her blood. She was shot in the heart." Hitler's Walther 9.5 mm automatic pistol lay near her hand. She had been dead for some hours. Hess had been called. Eventually he called the police. "You have to be certain who you call, Sir Seaton. The Munich police have a decided anti-Nazi bias and would love to use something like this against the Führer." The police had soon decided Fraulein Raubal could not easily have shot herself at that angle and that she had probably been murdered. Nobody believed it was suicide.

"And it could not have been Alf, Sir Seaton! Alf was miles away in Nurem-burg when the crime occurred. You can see how easy it will be, perhaps, to prove he paid someone to kill her. But he loved Geli, Sir Seaton. He lived for her. He is too gentle. Too idealistic. I fear that if the case isn't cleared up rap-idly by one such as yourself, it will mean the end of Alf's career and, because he is our most important spokesman, the dissolution of the Nazi Party. Please stop this from happening, Sir Seaton. Please say you will help us!"

Begg's features were hidden from Hess and the astonished Sinclair as he spoke reassuringly. "Of course I will, Mr Hess. It's not the sort of problem one solves every day. And we do love a challenge—don't we, Taffy?"

The pathologist was taken aback. "If you say so, old boy."

Sometimes even Taffy Sinclair found his friend's game very hard to follow.

↝⊕ CHAPTER THREE ⊕↜

Leading the Master Race

Begg's first stop after lunch was to the murder scene itself. Prinzregens-burgstrasse was the smart area where "Führer" Hitler now lived. On the way Hess explained how the Winters had called him and he in turn had tried to telephone Hitler in Nuremburg. But Hitler had already left Nurem-burg and was travelling to his next appointment. Apparently he was singing snatches of song, entertaining the other occupants of the car with jokes, impressions of people they had just met. "Many people, Sir Seaton, have no idea what a marvellous entertainer Alf is. He used to keep us in fits of laughter on those long tours. He could impersonate anyone. Pompous innkeepers, party officials, intense old maids, famous politicians! He could have gone on stage as a comedian had he not been chosen to lead his people."

Hess recollected the question. "Well, the hotel sent a boy after Herr Hitler's car, and when he got the message Alf almost collapsed. Everyone says it was completely unexpected. Indeed the first words from his lips, I understand, were 'Who has done this?' He had the car turned, his appointments cancelled, telephoned me the first chance he got, and came back at once to Munich. It was my suggestion I next call the Munich Police Head Quarters and he assented. And then I sent you a telegram. My staff arranged your tickets and so on."

"The police weren't suspicious concerning the time you waited before telephoning them?"

"I explained that I myself had been in a state of some shock after seeing poor Geli's body." He paused and then looked with a strange, new innocence into Begg's face. "I know I am a suspect, Sir Seaton, but I seek peace and security and pride from the Nazi Party, not violence. This is what most of us in Germany want. The thought of killing a mouse makes me sick. The thought of killing some poor, foolish creature who had been flattered and cajoled into waters well above her natural depth, that is abominable. You must not judge us all by those who 'goosestep' through the main streets of our towns with banners and bludgeons. Yet remember those poor lads were boys when they went to war, and what they saw in the trenches and learned to do in the trenches never left them, especially when they found they had no jobs . . ."

Rudolf Hess continued this apologia all the way to the flat in Prinzregensburgstrasse, an imposing modern classical building built on the corner of a broad, quiet avenue. Hitler's flat was on the second floor. It was light, airy, and luxurious in a subdued, up-to-date way. Doors led in several directions from the main vestibule suggesting servants' quarters and guest apartments. Certainly there was every way in which Hitler, his half sister and niece could live together in such a flat very respectably indeed.

Minutes later the investigator was interviewing Herr and Frau Winter themselves. The couple had found Geli on her own carpet, only partially dressed, as if she had been disturbed at her toilet.

The Winters were clearly shaken by what had happened. At that moment Frau Winter resembled a bewildered mole, in her grey cardigan, grey blouse, skirt, and stockings. This was not, Begg guessed, natural to her. Usually she probably wore a fairly cheerful expression. Herr Winter's features were habitually surly, yet his voice was agreeable enough. Neither man nor woman was of very high intelligence. They both confirmed under Begg's questioning that Hitler and his niece had quarrelled increasingly as his political career made demands on his time. But the party needed Hitler.

"Even I have fallen under his oratorical spell," said Winter seriously. "It is almost impossible to escape his charm when he wants something from you. Crowds love him. Without him the party would be lost. But as a result, he spent even less time with Geli. You couldn't really blame her. She grew restless, he grew jealous."

"He had plenty to be jealous about, too," Frau Winter interjected with an angry twitter. "She was not a good girl, Sir Seaton."

Herr Winter reluctantly conceded. "I think she had a fair amount of company when Herr Hitler was gone. In particular that tall, blond SS man who wanted her to run off to Vienna with him . . . Himmler's chap."

"You saw them?" Begg demanded.

"Just as we saw the whips and the blood after one of Herr Hitler's 'sessions,'" she said primly.

"Whips?" asked a startled Begg. "Blood?"

Herr Winter interrupted hastily, too late to silence his wife. "It was Herr Hitler's way of relaxing. He carries heavy responsibilities. It is often the way with important men, not so? We are people of the world here. We all know what goes on in Berlin."

Having verified with the Winters the events of the recent past, Sir Seaton Begg thanked them gravely and made to leave. Taffy Sinclair in particular seemed glad of some fresh air.

Back in the Duesenberg, Begg asked a further carefully considered question of Hess. "Tell me, old boy, did Herr Hitler ever have his niece watched? And was he ever blackmailed?"

"Aha! I knew I had approached the right detective. You realised. Unfortunately since the blackmail he's grown suspicious of everyone. Yes, he did have a couple of SA men in plainclothes keeping an eye on her, but they were incompetent. Himmler wanted to use SS people. He thinks they're more efficient. So yes, he watched her, but you can't really blame him for that."

"Blackmail?" said Sinclair from the shadows in the back, unable to contain himself. "Your leader was being blackmailed?"

"A couple of years ago. That's not what the blackmailer called it, of course, Herr Sinclair. But Putzi, Hitler's foreign press secretary, handled the details of that. Putzi's half-American, a great source of vitality, you know. We all love him. Only his jokes and piano-playing can cheer Alf up when he's really depressed . . ."

Begg had begun to realise Hess had to be kept on course or would wander off down all kinds of twists and turns in the story. He slowed the car behind a stopping tram, then indicated that he was going to pass. Slowly he increased pressure on the accelerator. "Putzi?"

"A nickname, naturally. Putzi Hanfstaengl was at Harvard. He's an art expert. Has a gallery in Munich. His firm publishes the official engraved por-traits of Hitler, Strasser, Röhm, Göring, myself, and the other eminent Nazis. Anyway, Putzi took the money to the blackmailer. We weren't rich in those days. It was hard to scrape together. He got the material back. Probably nothing especially bad. But, of course, Alf became much less trusting after that."

"Does Herr Hanfstaengl usually enjoy a drink at the Hotel Bavaria?"

Hess's enormous eyebrows almost met his hairline. "Mein Gott, Sir Seaton! You are indeed the genius they say you are. That is remarkable deduc-tion. Putzi's natural American vitality has been drained, it seems, by recent events. He has never really been at ease since we began to gain real power. A little bit of a playboy, I suppose, but a good fellow and a loyal friend."

After that Begg asked no more questions. He darted Sinclair a vindi-cated glance, for he had got that information from one of his much-loved "gossip columns." He told Hess he would like to drive around and think the case through for a while. Hess showed some impatience, but his admiration for the English detective soon reminded him of his manners. Heels were clicked as Hess was dropped off at the Brown House. Then Begg had touched the featherlight wheel of the superb roadster and turned her back towards central Munich.

CHAPTER FOUR

Fear and Trembling

As usual Sinclair was amazed at Begg's extraordinary retentive memory which had drawn itself a precise map of the town and was able to thread "Dolly's" massive bonnet through the winding streets of old Munich as if the driver had lived there all his life.

Soon they were leaving the Duesenberg in the safekeeping of the Hotel Bavaria's garage and strolling into the plush and brass of the old-fashioned main bar. Clearly the Bavaria was more popular with those who preferred to be in bed with a good book by eight PM. The bar was large but sparsely occupied, save for one middle-aged couple dancing to the strains of Franz Lehar played by an ancient orchestral ensemble on the distant dais. At a shadowed table two smart young men at second glance turned out to be smart young women. Against the walls leaned a couple of sleepy-eyed old waiters and at the bar sat two young couples from the local "cocktail set" who had lost their way to the latest jazz party. Slumped alone as far away from the couples as possible, wearing a great, bulky English tweed overcoat, sat a giant of a man nursing a drink which seemed tiny in his monstrous hands.

With his huge pale head and irregular features, an expression of solemn gloom on his long face, the lone drinker looked almost comical. He glanced up in some curiosity as they entered. Begg wasted no time in introducing himself and his colleague. "You are Herr Hitler's foreign press secretary, I understand. Too often in Berlin, these days, I suppose. We've been hired to prove your boss's innocence."

Herr "Putzi" Hanfstaengl did not seem greatly surprised that Begg knew his name. He lifted his hand in a salute before returning it to the glass. "You guys from *The Times*, are you?" He spoke in English with an educated American accent. He was clearly drunk. "I told your colleagues—when *The Times* turns up, that'll be a sign this is actually an international story." He let out an enormous sigh and drew himself to his full six and a half feet.

"You've been trying to keep all this speculation out of the papers, I suppose."

"What do you think, sport?" Hanfstaengl tossed back his drink and snapped his fingers for a refill. "It's not doing anyone much good, least of all Alf himself. He's gone under the bed, as we say, and won't come out. And I'm talking too much. Have a schnapps!" Again he snapped for the waiter who disappeared through a door and a little later appeared behind the bar to serve them. Begg and Sinclair modified their orders to beers, but Hanfstaengl hardly noticed.

"We're not from the newspapers," Begg told him before the drinks arrived. "We're private detectives employed by Herr Hess. Anything you tell us we will use in the processes of justice."

The lumbering half-American seemed relieved to hear this. He loosened his big coat and made himself more comfortable. As he listened to the tunes of Strauss and Lehar, he relaxed. "This isn't for publication. I have your word on it?"

"Our word as English gentlemen," said Begg.

For a while "Putzi" chatted about the old days of the Nazi party when there were only a few of them, when Hitler had been released from prison a hero, the author of *Mein Kampf*, which was published in Munich by Max Amman. "We have a concession on pictures of the Nazi heirarchy and Amman publishes what they write. It's pretty much our only business. This scandal could wreck us." Since the party's success in elections, sales had climbed. *Mein Kampf* (*My Struggle*) was now a best seller, and it was money from royalties, Hanfstaengl insisted, not from secret financiers, which was paying for the Mercedes and the place in Prinzregensburgstrasse. He seemed to be answering questions neither Begg nor Sinclair had asked. And when Sir Seaton threw the big query at him, he was rather surprised, glad that he did not have to hide something from the detective. It was dawning on him at last who Begg and Sinclair were.

"You really are the ace sleuths they say you are," he said. "I know those Sexton Blake things are heavily sensationalised, but it's surprising how like him you are. Do you remember *The Affair of the Jade Skull?*" Blake was, of course, the name said to disguise the identity of Sir Seaton Begg in a long series of stories written for *The Union Jack*, *The Sexton Blake Library*, and other popular British publications known as tuppenny skinnies and fourpenny fats.

"I'm surprised they're read at all beyond the London gutters," said Begg, who made a point of never reading the "bloods." "Speaking of which—what about that material itself. I've seen some of it of course. The stuff Hitler was being blackmailed with? Weren't you the middleman on that?"

Only Taffy Sinclair knew that his friend had just told a small, deliberate lie.

"What earthly need is there for you to know more? If you've seen how dreadful that stuff is—?" Hanfstaengl's brow cleared. "Oh, I get it. You have to eliminate suspects. You're looking for an alibi." He sipped his drink. "Well, I, too, dealt through a middleman. An SA sergeant who had got himself mixed up in something he didn't like. Called himself Braun, I think. Nobody ever proved it, but he pretty much confirmed who the blackmailer was and nobody was surprised. It was that crazy old Heironymite. Stempfle. I'm not sure how a member of an order of hermits, like Father Stempfle, can spend quite so much time drinking in the seedier Munich beer halls, but there you are. He has a certain following, of course. Writer and editor, I think. He worked for Amman once."

"The publisher?"

"Do you know him? Funny chap. Never really took to him. He's putting Hitler up at the moment. My view is that Amman could be cheating Hitler of his royalties. Could Geli have found something out, do you think?"

"You mean she knew too much?"

"Well," said Hanfstaengl, glancing up at the big clock over the bar, "she wasn't exactly an innocent, was she? Those letters! Foul. But his pictures were worse. It was my own fault. I was curious. I wish I'd never looked." He let out a great sigh. "Party funds paid the blackmailer, you know. The stuff was impossibly disgusting. I said I'd burn it—but he—Alf—wanted it back."

The orchestra had begun to play a polka. The couple on the dance floor were having difficulty keeping time. Begg studied the musicians for any sign of cynicism but found none.

Hanfstaengl's tongue, never very tight at the best of times, was becoming looser by the moment. "After that things were never the same. Hitler changed. Everything turned a little sour. You want to ask crazy old Stempfle about it. I'm still convinced only he could have had the inside knowledge . . ."

"But where could I find the hermit?"

"Well, there's a chance he'll be at home in his cottage. It's out in the Munich woods here." He jabbed his hand towards the door. "Couple of miles or so. Do you have a map?"

Sinclair produced one and Hanfstaengl plotted their course for them. "Be a bit careful, though, sport. There are lots of homeless people in the woods these days. They could spell danger for a stranger. Even some of our locals have been waylaid and robbed."

Begg shook hands with Hanfstaengl and said that he was much obliged. "One last question, Herr Hanfstaengl." He hesitated.

"Fire away," said "Putzi."

"Who do you think killed Geli Raubal?"

Hanfstaengl looked down.

"You have an idea, I know," said Begg.

Hanfstaengl turned back, offering Begg a cigarette from his case, which Begg refused. "Killed that poor little neurotic girl? Almost anyone *but* Hitler."

"But you have an idea."

Hanfstaengl drained his glass. "Well, she was seeing this SS guy . . ."

"Name?"

"Never heard one, but I think they planned to go to Vienna together. Hitler knew all about it, of course. Or at least he guessed what he didn't know."

"And had her killed?"

Hanfstaengl snorted sardonically. "Oh, no. He doesn't have the guts." His face had turned a terrible greenish white.

"Who does—?" Begg asked, but Hanfstaengl was already heading from the room, begging his pardon, acting like a man whose food had disagreed with him.

"Poor fellow," murmured Begg, "I don't think he has a taste either for the poison or the antidote . . ."

CHAPTER FIVE

The Politics of Exclusion

An hour or so later Taffy Sinclair was shining the hand torch down onto their map, trying to work out what Hanfstaengl had shown them. All around them in the woods were the camps of people who had been ruined by Germany's recent economic troubles. While Munich herself seemed wealthy enough, the homeless had been pushed to the outlying suburbs and wood-lands to fend for themselves as best they could. The detectives saw fires burning and shadows flitting around them, but the forest people were too wary to reveal themselves and would not respond when Begg or Sinclair called out to them.

"I suppose it's fair enough that a follower of Saint Jerome the Hermit makes himself hard to find," declared Sinclair, "but I think this place was less populated and with fewer caves when—aha!" His torchlight had fallen on the pencilled mark. "Just up this road and stop. Should be a cottage here."

The car's brilliant headlamps made day of night, picking up the building ahead as if lit for the cinema with great, elongated black shadows spreading away through the moonlit forest. An ancient, thatched, much buttressed cot-tage was revealed. The place had two main chimneys, three downstair's win-dows and three up, including the dormer, which had its own chimney. The whole place leaned and inclined in a dozen different directions so that even the straw resembled a series of dirty, ill-fitting wigs.

"This has got to be it." Sir Seaton climbed from the car and walked across the weed-grown path to the old door of Gothick oak and black iron, ham-mering on it heavily and calling out in his most authoritative tone: "Open up! Metatemporal detectives! Come along, Father Stempfle, sir! Let us in."

A grinding of locks and rattling chains confirmed Sir Seaton's inspired guess. A face which looked as if it had been folded, stretched, and refolded many times regarded them in the light of the lamp it held over the chink in the door, still latched by a massive row of steel links.

"Open up, sir."

Seeing their faces seemed to weaken the old man's resolve, for another bolt turned and the door creaked slowly open.

Begg followed Stempfle into the hermit's horrible candlelit den which stank of mould, old food, woodsmoke, and dust. Everywhere were piles of books, manuscripts, scrolls. There was no doubt the man was a scholar, but whether he followed God or the Devil was hard to determine. In a small grate a sparse, damp fire admitted a little heat.

"You're a close friend of Adolf Hitler, I gather, Father?" Begg hardly gave the unshaven old man in the filthy cassock a chance to catch his breath.

Father Stempfle stuttered. "I wouldn't say that. I have very little to do with him these days."

"You helped him write his book—*Mein Kampf*, is it?"

Now Begg's long hours of reading and study were coming to his aid as usual. Sinclair remembered how impressed he so often was with his friend's ability to put together a jigsaw with pieces from so many apparently disparate sources.

Father Stempfle began to turn scarlet. He fumed. In his mephitic cassock and sandals, he stamped about his paper-strewn study until it seemed the unevenly stacked piles of books would fall and bury them all alive. "*Helped* him, my good sir? *Helped* that illiterate little trench terrier, that scum of Vienna's perverts' quarter? *Helped* him? I wrote *most* of it. The manuscript was unreadable until his publisher asked me to work on it. Ask Max Amman. He'll confirm everything. He and Hitler fell out over it. Or perhaps he has now been persuaded to lie by Röhm and his apes. My arguments are the purest and the best. You can tell them because I offer a much more sophisticated analysis of the Jewish problem. Hitler's contribution was a whine of self-pity. For years Amman didn't publicise the book widely enough. Now, of course, it's selling very well. And do I get a pfennig in royalties?" The squalid old monk shuffled to a stop, his face breaking into something which might have been a grin. "Of course, it'll sell even better once they know about the murder . . ."

Begg had no stomach for this. He drew a large handkerchief from his pocket and blew his nose. "You think Hitler killed her?"

"Nobody seems to think he's up to it," murmured Sinclair. "Not a strong man, physically at least. A pacifist, we were learning today . . ."

Stempfle crushed old parchment in his hands as he moved towards the fire. Something had made him feel the cold. "He says he hates violence. But you should see how cruelly he treats that dog of his. Wulf? He calls it such a name so that he can demonstrate his own masculinity the better. I think he is capable of any violence."

Sinclair stepped forward. "What about those pictures—those letters—the blackmail attempt?"

"Oh, he's calling it blackmail now, is he? I simply wanted fair reimbursement for the work I'd done . . ." Stempfle glowered into the fire which seemed to flicker in sympathy.

"If you still have some of that stuff, I could see that it got into the appropriate hands. Would it not strengthen the case against Hitler?"

Stempfle snorted. The sound was almost gleeful. "It would top and tail him nicely, true . . ."

"That material is here?"

Stempfle grew cunning. "The originals are elsewhere, in safe keeping. Still, I don't mind showing you the copies."

"I am prepared to pay one hundred pounds for the privilege," declared Sir Seaton.

At this the old man moved with slightly greater alacrity, ascending a ladder, moving a picture, rattling a combination, then going through the whole process backwards again. When he came down, he had an envelope in his hands. Begg paid him in the four crisp twenty-five-pound notes he held ready, and Sinclair accepted the envelope, casually drawing out the first photograph and then blanching at what he saw. He returned the photograph to the envelope and covered his mouth. "Great Jehovah, Begg! I had no idea! Why would any woman involve herself in this? Or any man demand it?" Now he knew why Angela Raubal could not help being a disturbed young woman and why Hanfstaengl had left the bar so swiftly.

Stempfle's crooked body shook with glee. "Not how Adolf might wish to be remembered, eh? They would make excellent illustrations for certain works of the Marquis de Sade, no? I think I've been very modest in my request for my share of the royalties. Since I suspect you are already representing him, you can tell him that the originals of these are much more expensive!"

"I've yet to become a blackmailer's runner, Father Stempfle," Begg protested mildly. "Goodnight to you."

He ducked beneath the warped lintel and began to make for his car, Sinclair slightly ahead of him. At that moment Sinclair shouted "Hey!" and headed for the Duesenberg. Then he was grappling with a couple of shadows, two of the forest people who had been trying to break into the car. Sir Seaton weighed in instantly, and now the heavy, desperate, fighting shadows came from everywhere. It seemed they were bound to go down beneath the sheer weight of the wretches. Then, from the darkness came the distinctive sound of a Mauser shot being fired. Had the bullet passed them, unnoticed, in the darkness? Had it been meant for them at all? Begg wondered if some kind of unacknowledged civil war might already be taking place in those woods. The next time he heard the shot, the thunk of a bullet in wood came dangerously close to Begg's head. Drawing his own Webley he turned to seek out the rifleman and saw instead the forest people fleeing back into their shadows. Within seconds the danger was over. The scene was quiet and peaceful again.

With a sardonic bow, Begg replaced his pistol and opened Sinclair's door for him. "Someone trying to shut us up, do you think, Taffy?"

"I'd call that a warning," the pathologist agreed.

Within the wholesome comfort of the great automobile, Sinclair held the packet of photographs, continuing to vent his disgust. "How could he make her—? I mean—?"

"Not a position any sane creature would volunteer for," Begg agreed. He began to reverse the car back down the short drive. "I think it's time we paid a call on the local copshop, don't you?"

⟿ CHAPTER SIX ⟾

The Federal Agent

As it happened there was no need to visit the police station. Arriving back at their hotel's foyer and collecting their keys, they were immediately confronted by an extraordinarily beautiful young woman who rose from a couch and came towards them smiling. Her full red lips and dark red hair worn in a fashionable wave were complemented by her green evening dress as she stretched a gloved hand towards Sir Seaton.

He bent to kiss it. Of course they had immediately recognised the woman. Once a ruthless adventuress whose love affair with Begg had resulted in her decision to make herself his ally, she was now a freelance. Unlike him, she accepted retainers from any government that valued her skill.

From her reticule the woman took a small book on which was fastened a metal badge. After they had glanced at it, she returned it swiftly to its place.

"My dear Countess von Bek," exclaimed Sir Seaton, "I had no idea you were in Munich. Are you staying here?"

"Nearby, Sir Seaton. I wondered if you had seen my cousin lately?" This was prearranged code. Countess Rose von Bek wanted to speak urgently and privately. Begg immediately led them into the deserted sitting room, ordered some tea, and closed the doors.

Once they were settled and the tea served, Sir Seaton relaxed. "So, my dear Rose, we appear to be working on the same case? Can you say who your client is?"

The adventuress responded with her usual charm. "I have made no more a secret of it than have you, Seaton. The German Federal Government Special Political Service. They sent me down from Berlin to give support to the local cops—the ones who don't actually believe Herr Hitler to be the next world saviour and that Jews are damned to hell for not accepting the messiah. So far I've met a good number of decent cops and some very clever newspapermen."

"So we find ourselves on different sides in this case. I take it, therefore, you know who killed Geli Raubal?"

She took an ironic sip from her Dresden cup. "We've been working on the broader political associations."

"But surely everything we need to know hinges on the circumstances and solution of this case?" Taffy Sinclair chipped in.

"No doubt, Mr Sinclair. But the government's priorities aren't always our own." She spoke softly, anxious not to offend him. "I agree it is possible to argue that Fraulein Raubal's death is emblematic, if not symptomatic, of her times, but at the moment we're worrying that the National Socialists have a sizeable representation in parliament. And a large amount of armed support. We are thinking 'civil war' here. *Cherchez la femme* is not a game we often play in my section."

Taffy mumbled some polite apology and said he thought it was time he turned in, but Begg insisted he stay. "I think I'm going to need your help tonight, old man."

"Tonight?"

"Afraid so."

Sinclair rather reluctantly poured himself a fresh cup of Earl Grey.

"Was the corpse still in the apartment when you arrived on the scene?" Begg asked his old paramour.

"Hinkel of the *Taggeblat* called us. He's our best man down here. So I caught the express from Berlin and was here in time to have a look at the body."

"You're certain she was murdered?"

Rose was certain. "Someone's made a clumsy attempt to make it look as if she'd shot herself through the heart. Hitler's gun—easy accessibility. Dead canary nearby—she'd been carrying it around all day—no doubt adding to the impression that she was suicidal. But the angle of entry was wrong. Someone shot her, Seaton, while she was lying on the rug—probably during an amorous moment. Half undressed. Evidently an intimate. And Hitler was certainly an intimate . . .

"You've seen these pictures?" He handed her the envelope.

"No wonder the poor girl was confused." Even the Countess winced at what she saw. "They might have tried to *push* her towards suicide, but she wouldn't fall. Eventually someone shot her at close range, then put the gun in her hand so it seemed suicide. Only there were too many clues to the contrary."

"Any chance of taking a look at the corpse?" Taffy's dry, decisive tone was unexpected.

"Engaging your gears at last, are we, Taffy?" said Begg jumping to his feet. "Come on, Countess. Get us to the morgue, post haste!"

Responding with almost gleeful alacrity, Countess von Bek allowed Sinclair to open the door for her. "Dolly" was still outside, so within moments the investigators were on their way to the Munich police headquarters.

The Countess had already established her authority there. She led the way directly through the building to a door marked *Inspector Hoffmann*. The round, red-faced inspector assured them that he knew them all by reputation and had the greatest respect for their skills. He was grateful, he said, for their cooperation.

"However," said the bluff Bavarian when they were all seated, "I ought to tell you that I'm convinced Hitler killed her during quite a nasty fight. Fortunately for your client, Sir Seaton, he has the best possible alibi—with dozens of witnesses to show he could not possibly have committed the murder. Hess? What do you think? Was it Hess who contacted you, Sir Seaton?"

They all agreed Hess was an unlikely suspect. Indeed, very few of the party heirarchy had motives. Others had perfect alibis. Vaguely mysterious figures had been reported as coming and going, but Geli, of course, had not advertised them. "Coffee?" Hoffmann touched an electric bell.

After coffee, Hoffman led them down to the morgue, a clean, tiled, up-to-date department with refrigerated cabinets, dissecting tables, and the latest in analytical instruments. Taffy was visibly impressed, unable to hold back his praise for the splendid facilities. "I can't tell you how old-fashioned Scotland Yard looks in comparison. You can't beat the Germans at this sort of thing."

Herr Hoffman was visibly flattered.

"Practical science and sublime art," murmured Taffy.

Inspector Hoffmann rather proudly crossed the mortuary. "Wait until you see this, my friend." He went to a bank of switches, each with a number. He flipped a toggle and then, magically, one of the drawers began to open!

"The wonders of 'electronics'!" cried Begg enthusiastically. Then he moved quickly towards the projecting steel box where he knew he would find the mortal remains of Hitler's mistress.

Begg's expression changed to one of deep pity as he studied the contents. Even Sinclair stood back, paying some sort of respect to the corpse. Begg touched the skin, inspected the wound, and then, frowning, bent as if to kiss the frozen lips.

A shocked word froze on Sinclair's tongue as Begg straightened up, his nose wrinkling almost in disgust. "See what you think, Taffy."

After Sinclair had inspected the corpse Hoffmann turned the switch to send the temporary coffin back into its gleaming, stainless steel housing. "I know we're on opposite sides in this, Sir Seaton, but I think the obvious suspect is the masochist. Herr Hitler. Mysterious lovers? How could we find them? The Winters noted only one lover but hinted at many others. They would not be on our side in court. I suppose I shouldn't be saying this. But I know your analytical powers, Sir Seaton. And your thirst for justice."

"And you know something of the science of psychiatry?"

"Of course, I first studied in Vienna. To me this Hitler matter seems a classic case of the father figure and the bored young protégée. The father becomes obsessively possessive. The more he grows like that, the more she seeks to break free in the only way she knows—affairs of the heart. One after another. The father, unable to watch her hourly, pretends it isn't happening. The daughter grows bolder. No one can ignore what is going on. Her *affaires* become common gossip. Eventually his ego can be suppressed no longer . . . you saw the marks on her face and shoulders?"

"Indeed I did," said Begg.

"He had beaten the poor little thing black and blue!" Sinclair barely controlled his anger. "They were fighting, as you say, and brought Hitler's gun into play. Next thing 'Bang' and the girl's dead on the carpet."

"Lovers quarrel?" queried Rosie von Bek. "Maybe. But I prefer to believe the girl knows too much about our suspect's sex life as well as political plans. Election coming up. She tries blackmail. Second time it's happened. Could she have been behind the first attempt? He snaps." She spread her hands, palms out. "Open and shut." She made fists. "This isn't the first time Herr Adolf Hitler has been involved in some Sadistic business or other, I take it."

Hoffmann nodded emphatically. "But, if it could be proven, Hitler's enemies would be dancing in the streets. His chances of wheedling any more concessions from Hindenburg would disappear at once. Hindenburg already considers him a parvenu. So he has to go to great lengths to build an alibi."

Begg became uncomfortable at this. "You clearly hate Hitler," he suggested. "Yet you seem to be a conservative yourself . . ."

"I hate Bolshevism," Hoffmann searched through a gleaming filing cabinet for the documents he needed. "But I am also a Catholic, and all the Nazis' antireligious talk, especially against the Jews, who are amongst the most law-abiding people in the nation, is too much for me to stomach. I know Hitler did this murder, but that alibi . . ."

"No way he could have come back, committed the crime, then returned to Nuremburg?" asked Sinclair.

"Too many people know him in Nuremburg. He is very popular there. They would have noticed something. Of course, he could have used another car altogether, and a disguise. I think you'll agree the bruises might have been delivered earlier than the gun shot?"

All three nodded.

"So," continued Hoffmann. "She knew too much. There was a fight. The gun. A shot. I don't say it was premeditated. Then he gets into the car and heads for Nuremburg, guessing nobody would want to disturb her until the next morning. He locked her door with his own key. No doubt he had had it made long before."

Begg smiled almost apologetically, adding: "And then she appears on the balcony. No doubt she has at last got Hitler's message. Stemming the blood from her wounded heart she calls: 'So you won't let me go to Vienna?'"

"Pretty clear, I'd say." The Countess recognised Begg's rather inappropriate black humour. "I think Hitler beat her up. Then one of his henchmen went back and shot her. Maybe some kind of 'Murder in the Cathedral' situation? I gather that's how Mussolini learned he was responsible for his first murder. Overzealous followers. So who shot her? Röhm? He's ruthless enough, and he doesn't much like women. Himmler? A cold fish, but too far away at the time. Same with Göring or Goebbels, if we assume they didn't come to Munich incognito."

"I think our people would have known about it," said Rosie.

"Ours, too, most likely," confirmed Hoffmann, rubbing at his red jowls. "They have orders to keep track of who goes in and out of the Brown House."

"So we have a dozen suspects and nothing which leads to any of them." Sinclair lifted his eyebrows. "But two of you at least are convinced Hitler did it. What about you, Begg? What do you think?"

"I'm beginning to get an idea who killed Geli Raubal, and I think I can guess why. But there is another element here." Begg frowned deeply. "I think in the morning we'll set off for Berchtesgaden for Herr Amman's little hideaway. You, presumably, have already interviewed Hitler, Inspector Hoffmann?"

"As soon as he arrived back from Nuremburg, of course. He seemed in a state of shock, but, as stated, his alibi was airtight. Of course, you will wish to prove he didn't do it, Sir Seaton, and I admit the cards are stacked in your favour?"

"Not exactly, old boy. But I agree with you that as things stand, any case against Herr Hitler couldn't be proven in a court of law."

With a courteous good night to the policeman, Begg escorted his two friends outside. In the street his car was being guarded by a uniformed constable who saluted as soon as he recognised Countess von Bek and opened the doors for them.

It was only a short drive to the hotel, and most of it was spent in silence as the three investigators thought over what they had learned.

"I suppose there's no chance of me coming down with you?" asked the countess. "Since Herr Hitler isn't my client."

"Exactly," murmured Begg, concentrating on the unfamiliar streets. "And I think even you'd agree, Rose, that client confidentiality, at least at this stage, is sacrosanct."

While Begg waited with the engine running, Sinclair saw the beautiful adventuress through the doors of her hotel. As they drove off, Sinclair said: "She wants our Mr Hitler hanged, no doubt about it. She's afraid you'll get him off the hook. Are you sure he didn't do it?"

"I merely noted," said the detective with what seemed inappropriate cheerfulness, "that there was no evidence directly linking Hitler with the murder of his niece. Nothing to convince a jury. Don't worry, Taffy. One way or another justice will out. I have a feeling we will meet at least one more old acquaintance before this business is over."

Interview with a Saviour

Hess took the Duesenberg's back seat. "I think they are also trying to assassinate me," he said. "Someone shot at the Brown House while I was in there this morning. It could even have come from the Papal embassy. A high-powered rifle, no doubt, with a telescopic sight." They had been driving for some hours, making for the lodge at Berchtesgaden where Adolf Hitler retreated, apparently in deep mourning for the loss of his niece. The surrounding scenery was both dramatic and beautiful with high hills and pinewoods giving the air a rich, invigorating quality.

"We must be careful not to lead such an assassin to the Führer. Any attempted violence would be disastrous. He is very sensitive. His mind is of a higher order than most. He always comes here when things go wrong. Here he collects himself and makes something of his experience." The hero worship in Hess's tone was tangible and had become extremely familiar to the two Englishmen.

Sinclair's expression, could Hess have seen it, would have revealed that he had already had far too much of this sort of talk. But Begg remained apparently affable. "Bit like Mr Gandhi, I suppose," he suggested.

"Perhaps." Hess seemed uncomfortable with the comparison.

"So we think someone with a Mauser is taking potshots at the party chiefs, do we?"

"We have powerful enemies," mumbled Hess. Then he fell silent for a litle while.

They turned another corner of the winding road. Ahead was a pleasant, rustic hunting chalet of the kind many Germans built for their summer season. As they drove up, a tall, thickset, grim-faced man, with a head so thoroughly bald it might have been shaven, hurried from the door to greet them. They were, of course, already expected.

"Ah," declared Sir Seaton Begg, climbing from his car, "I take it I have the pleasure of addressing Reichstag Leader Strasser?" He put out his hand, and it was firmly shaken.

Gregor Strasser's face was clouded, but he knew his manners. He spoke in a soft, well-educated voice. "We are so glad you have come to help us, Sir Seaton, though I am not sure Herr Hitler is in any real condition to speak to you." He was almost disapproving. "Hitler has gone into one of his hysterical states again. Always been one to hide under the blankets during a crisis. Hasn't been out of bed since he got here. Won't talk to me. Will hardly talk to Röhm."

"Captain Röhm is here also." Begg was clearly pleased. "Excellent. You, I presume, don't believe that Herr Hitler's guilty?"

"I speak, of course, from loyalty as well as conviction. But Herr Hitler loved his niece. He was, of course, very possessive. Even when my brother Otto expressed willingness to take her to a dance, Hitler furiously forbade it. I felt sorry for her. A bit of a bird in a gilded cage, you know. But while Hitler might speak rather fiercely in public, he rarely exposed Geli to that side of himself. It was Himmler who hated her. Even Alf knew that! But I really think she must have killed herself."

"The police evidence suggests she was murdered, as you probably know." Now all three men had paused on the verandah outside the front door.

"Surely you don't believe—?" The big politician purpled.

Begg put a reassuring hand on Strasser's arm. "Fear not, old sport. I think we are going to be able to tell you something about the real killer soon. But I really must speak to your Führer, you know."

The house was decorated like a typical hunting lodge, though without the usual trophies of animal heads and skins. Hitler hated such signs of violence against animals, and his host pandered to him. Otherwise, with its coatracks of antlers and its heavy rugs and old, comfortable furniture, it felt familiar and secure. Off the main reception room a broad staircase rose up into the darkness of a landing where, no doubt, the bedrooms were. A big fire burned in the grate. The surround was carved with bears, stags, and other game. Leaning against it was a short, stocky individual with a hideous scar marring half his rather pudgy face. He was dressed in what, apart from its brown colour, resembled the regular uniform of a Wehrmacht officer, with

Nazi emblems on collar, cuffs, and sleeves. Knocking back a ballon of brandy, he came forward, greeting them in a surprisingly hearty rich Bavarian accent. In private, none of these men used the Hitler salute. "Grüss Gott, Sir Seaton. Just as we're at the point of real power someone's trying to sabotage the party's chances. What can you do for us?"

"A miracle would help," said Strasser, pouring schnapps for the two men.

Captain Röhm helped himself to another large cognac.

Only Hess did not join them in a drink. He almost immediately made an excuse and disappeared upstairs, presumably to report to his old friend and leader.

Röhm was the worst for drink. He leaned easily, excessively relaxed as the habitual drunkard usually is. In spite of his hideous appearance and his tightly buttoned and belted uniform, there was an almost sensitive set to his features, a haunted look to his eyes which suggested he knew and rather approved of the arguments against almost every statement he made. His rough charm, his loyalty, his bluntness allowed him to thrive. Not long after he had returned from Bolivia, affectionate Spartan letters from Röhm to a young cadet had been published in the yellow press. Yet somehow Röhm had survived the scandal and even today made no secret of his Greek tendencies.

"Herr Hitler has taken his niece's suicide to heart," began Begg and was immediately interrupted by a gusty, brandy-laden laugh at once sardonic and angry.

"*Suicide!* Absolutely, my dear Sir Seaton! *Suicide!* Certainly! And I'm the bloody Virgin of Lourdes." Still chuckling, the Brownshirt leader, considered by many to be the most powerful man in Germany, turned to throw his cigar butt into the flames.

"Perhaps if we had a word with Herr Hitler himself?"

Again the Herculean snort. "Good luck, my friend. He's a wreck. Maybe you can get more sense out of him than we can. He's a classic Austrian. All mouth and trousers and useless in a crisis. Feckless as they come. Yet he's my leader, and I live with it. I am an infantile man, at heart, and a wicked one. I offer my loyalty to whichever general best serves my interest. I have too many weaknesses to be more than an ordinary soldier taking orders."

"You've known him a long time?" Begg asked quietly.

"I threw in with Alf, as we knew him in the trenches, soon after the Stab in the Back of the Armistice. Just as we were on the verge of winning, victory was stolen from us by Jews and Socialists at home. I didn't need to explain anything to Alf. We had a lot in common. He was a great infiltrator. Used to get in with the commies, find out what they were up to, then report back to me. They say he won the Iron Cross for bravery, as a runner in the trenches, but that's not his talent. My guess is that he was terrified the whole time. No choice. Run the lines or be shot as a coward. He's always managed to slip away from the violence. Bad precedent, of course, in a soldier. Learns the wrong lessons." Röhm shrugged. "I doubt if he ever had to shoot anyone personally in his life. Good luck to you, my dear sir."

Strasser was sober and collected. He put down his glass half finished. "Let me see if the Führer is ready."

As he walked up the staircase, Sinclair murmured to Begg. "Classic case of manic depression, eh?"

From the landing above, Rudolph Hess peered down. "I have very good hearing, Mr Sinclair. We reject the debased jargon of the Jew Freud. We have perfectly good German words and good German precedents to describe our leader's state of spirit. Goethe, himself, I believe coined several . . ."

"Our Anglo-Saxon phrase would be 'barkingbarmy,' Herr Hess." Sinclair craned to look at their customer. "Would that be better?"

Clearly not understanding, Hess adopted a haughty manner. "Perhaps," he said. "Herr Strasser. Would you like to bring them now?"

With a somewhat theatrical movement of his hand, Gregor Strasser motioned for the two Englishmen to follow him up the stairs.

Hitler's room was at the far end of the landing. There was only faint flickering candlelight issuing from it. When at Hess's knock they entered, they found a dark, ill-smelling room in which guttered a few church candles of yellow wax placed here and there on dressing table and nightstands. The Englishmen were immediately reminded of Father Stempfle's den. The mirror of the dressing table reflected a man's naked legs, scrawny feet. The knees were bare. The man had hastily pulled on a raincoat in lieu of a dressing gown.

Adolf Hitler sat at the end of his bed. Clearly he had just allowed himself to be coaxed out of bed. He sat hunched with his hands folded in front of him and did not look up as Begg and Sinclair were introduced. Then a thin, whine, like a distant turbine, started in the man's throat. "No, no, no. I can't. I can't. I can't."

Strasser stepped forward. "Just a few minutes, Alf. They want to find out who killed Geli. This means you'll be able to punish the culprit and put an end to suspicion within the party. It will save your career."

"What do I care for my career now that my angel is dead?" The soft, Austrian accent was unexpected.

When the man looked up, a ghastly intelligence in his unslept eyes, even Begg was shocked. Hitler had the familiar red blotches on his cheek bones, the drawn lines of anxiety, a face so mad and yet so utterly without redeeming character that one might have been looking at a damned soul in Limbo. It was all the two men could do not to turn away in disgust.

Now Hitler began to mumble in a monotone. "She loved life. She loved her Uncle Alf. We had so much in common. She would never have killed herself. Somebody shot her!"

"It is a possibility we're looking into, Herr Hitler. Do you have any suspicions?"

"Naturally, I am convinced who killed her, but how can we hope to bring them to justice. They are masters of this kind of conspiracy. Oh, Geli, Geli, my perfect angel." He began to weep then, with tears streaming from those mad eyes. He spoke with sudden clarity and force. "They'll get me next, you know. They killed her with my gun. To make it seem as if I had done it. And where are they now, these traitors and saboteurs? Returned to Berlin and Moscow. You'll never catch them. They come and go like poisoned gas. They couldn't kill me, so they killed poor Geli. You waste your time, Englishman. I am already doomed. I carry too great a burden on my shoulders. I am a lone voice against Chaos and Bolshevik Jewry."

"Quite a responsibility!" agreed Sir Seaton, backing towards the door. "We'll take up no more of your time, Herr Hitler."

As they walked down the stairs, strange, mewling noises continued to come from Hitler's room. Hess had remained with his master. Strasser shook his head, speaking softly. "You wouldn't believe it, gentlemen. Hitler's a different creature on a public platform."

They had returned to the fireplace where Röhm still lounged, and he agreed vigorously. "It's as if the crowd feeds him energy. He stands there sometimes for minutes before he speaks, drawing it in. He's a kind of vampire, I suppose." The SA leader drained his glass and sighed.

Strasser interrupted. "He's our best bet for Chancellor. We all know that. He has something the crowd responds to. But once we are in power, we'll find him a more suitable position—head of propaganda, perhaps." He started as, softly, upstairs, a door closed.

Strasser dropped his voice still lower. "In a few days Hitler has an appointment with Chancellor Hindenburg. It looks as if, so long as we keep our noses clean, old Hindenburg will name Alf as his successor. But if Alf remains like—like what you saw upstairs—he won't make any other impression than the obvious one. So you don't have much time, I'm afraid, Sir Seaton."

"I'll do my best, Captain Röhm. And, of course, I'll be grateful for any help." Sir Seaton reached to shake hands, but Röhm was taking his cap and greatcoat down from the antlered peg.

"Give me a lift back to Munich. I might have a lead for you," he said.

Sinclair was astonished at how rapidly Röhm had sobered.

Hess decided that he should remain at his leader's side, and Strasser had also decided to spend the night, so Röhm joined Sir Seaton in the front while Taffy again found himself in the profoundly comfortable leather of the back. Against his will, he began to doze and did not hear the whole exchange between Röhm and Begg.

"She had only one lover, you know that?" announced Röhm, "He might have been assigned to guard her. My chaps were keeping a watch. She had a lot of guards, but this one was special. I think she was infatuated with Captain Zeiss. A tall SS captain, by all accounts. Blond. Always wore dark glasses. He's disappeared out of the picture since the shooting. They say Zeiss was Himmler's spy, but he didn't seem to be following anyone's orders much. Himmler hated old Geli, you know. I had a soft spot for her. Bit of a whore, like myself. Maybe she died because she knew too much. Maybe that's what'll happen to me, too." Again that monstrous, grunting laugh, far too big for the size of the soft, battle-scarred face.

Captain Röhm was staying at the Brown House that night. His own flat, he reported with a laugh, was full. It was dusk as they dropped him off. "Where to, now, Seaton? Bed?" Sinclair asked hopefully.

"I'm afraid not, Taffy. There's just time to catch the last few musical numbers and get a decent glass of Russian tea at the Carlton Tea Rooms! You remember I was studying the entertainment pages on the way over. This will help take the taste of that schnapps out of your mouth, eh?"

CHAPTER EIGHT

The Violinist of the Café Orchestra

As Taffy Sinclair enjoyed the strange mixture of black Russian tea and a plate of small *weisswurst*, he relaxed to the strains of Ketalby's *In a Persian Market* played by the band of tuxedo-clad musicians on the stand. It was their last performance of the evening. All the players were seated save for their leader, a tall man with close-cropped hair and wearing impeccable white tie and tails. He stood in the shadows of the curtain and played the violin with extraordinary beauty and skill. When Begg tipped the waiter heavily and put a folded note on the plate, Sinclair thought his friend was asking for one of his favourite sentimental tunes, such as *The Gypsy* or *The Merry Widow Waltz*, but neither of these was played before the musicians brought their performance to an end.

Sinclair was surprised when the tall violinist, having replaced his instrument in its case, strolled over to their table. Then, when the albino removed his dark glasses, Sinclair realised with a shock that he sat across the table from Sir Seaton Begg's cousin and archenemy, the notorious Monsieur Zenith, wanted for countless daring crimes throughout the Empire.

The red-eyed albino had a charming, crooked smile. "So, gentlemen, you have discovered how I earn my living, these days . . ."

Begg grinned almost boyishly at this. "Good evening, cousin. Perhaps I am too familiar with your aliases. I looked in the entertainment pages on the way over. The Zodiac Tea Orchestra rather betrayed you? But I hear you work for Heinrich Himmler now . . ."

For a split second Zenith's expression changed to one of anger. Then again he was all urbane affability. "Is Himmler claiming that? Scum like him can't employ me, Sir Seaton?" He sat back in his chair, lighting a pungent, black cigarette. "However, you might find that Himmler and the others have all been playing my game . . ." He chuckled with deep pleasure.

Sinclair, who had been up for too long and drunk too much schnapps, lost his usual discretion then. He leaned across the table. "Look here, Count von Bek, did you kill Geli Raubal? You seem to be the only one who had the opportunity, if not the motive! You are the mysterious SS man, eh? And have you been loosing off a Mauser at people by any chance?"

"Captain Zeiss," said Begg.

Zenith drew a deep, ennui-ridden sigh. Ignoring Sinclair, he addressed Begg directly, reaching across the table and handing him a pasteboard card. "I think you deserve the coup, my friend. You have solved the case, I know. I was at this address until yesterday. You might find it interesting. Even useful." He turned, bowing, to Sinclair. "We all work in the ways which best suit our temperaments, I think, Mr Sinclair? Who is to say whether, in our good or our evil intentions, we unknowingly serve the causes of law or chaos?"

With that the albino turned on his heel, picked up his violin case, and disappeared into the night.

Sinclair was all for pursuing him, but Begg restrained his friend. He continued to sip his tea, studying the card. "We don't need to follow him, Taffy. He has left us his most recent address."

Begg frowned down at the card in his hand. "Do you feel like making a visit to the Hotel Rembrandt? It's just around the corner. We can walk."

"This is unbelievable!" Taffy Sinclair was staring aghast at a handful of papers and photographs. He had just opened the writing bureau in Room 25. Zenith's room at the Hotel Rembrandt looked as if it had been hastily vacated. Sir Seaton was inspecting the wardrobe. There on hangers was an SS captain's uniform. The metatemporal detective displayed it to his friend. "Look at this, Taffy. Bloodstains. They fit perfectly with the suspected shooting." He reached into the back of the closet and emerged with a black Mauser rifle. "And here's our red herring!"

"Letters from Himmler to Captain Zeiss, ordering him to seduce that poor girl, compromise her, then kill her, so that Himmler could continue his blackmailing of Hitler through a third party." Sinclair inspected a piece of stationery. There's a note here that even suggests Himmler was responsible for the initial blackmail a couple of years ago! The most damning evidence! So your cousin, von Bek, is a common murderer, after all! And in Captain Himmler's employ?"

"It certainly appears so." Begg looked around for a bag of some kind. "Come on, Taffy. We'd better take these togs to Hitler."

"Surely we should get them to Inspector Hoffmann as soon as possible! Zenith must be captured!"

"I remind you again, Taffy, that Herr Hitler is our paying client and it is our duty to show him the evidence before it is presented to the police."

"But Great Jehovah, Begg, this overrides any client loyalty!"

"I'm afraid not, Taffy. Come on. I remember the way to Berchtesgaden. You'd better ride out there with me, old man, whatever your scruples. I need a witness and someone at my shoulder if the client decides to kill the messenger."

Only this persuaded the pathologist to accompany his friend, but he did so in brooding silence. Begg seemed completely insouciant, whistling fragments from musical comedies as the great car bore them relentlessly up towards Hitler's retreat.

Only because Rudolph Hess was convinced they had good news for Hitler were the Englishmen allowed into the fusty stench of the Nazi leader's lair. Again he greeted them in nothing but his mackintosh, his eyes as mad as ever. He moved between gross self-pity and rage against his niece's killers, sometimes in seconds. But when he at last looked at the evidence Begg and Sinclair had brought with them, he was stunned into a cold, sudden pseudo-sanity.

"Himmler! He always hated her. He has grown closer and closer to me, building up the SS on my behalf, he says. They warned me he had Jewish blood, but I laughed at them. And all the time he plotted against me in this subtle way, getting at me through Geli, using one of his own men to—ugh!" He stood up suddenly, bowing with both hands at his sides, and brought his bare heels together. "I am most grateful to you gentlemen. You have done everything Hess promised. Naturally you will receive your fee. Herr Hess will take you to the Brown House at once."

Even Hess seemed surprised by this sudden *volte face*.

"No need, old boy." Sir Seaton Begg lifted his hat. "Have this one on me. I am happy to serve the cause of justice."

Though dressed only in a mackintosh, Hitler visibly grew an inch or two. "You have served not only my interests and those of my great party, Sir Seaton. You have served the interests of the entire free world. Hess. We shall need the Mercedes. There is something I must take care of at once. Thank you again." He lifted his arm in his familiar salute.

"Only too happy to oblige, old chap." And with that Begg steered an open-mouthed Sinclair into the fir rich air of the sub-Alpine forests.

"Take a good gulp, Taffy," he murmured.

"Are you out of your mind, Begg. That chap's about as unbalanced as it's possible to be without falling off the planet. You've no idea what notions you've given him."

"Oh, I think the ones he was meant to be given, Taffy. Perhaps you already suspect the truth? In this case we served a client other than we thought!"

By now "Dolly's" headlights were piercing the dark shadows of the German night. Taffy, still deprived of his usual amount of sleep, began to doze in the seat beside his friend. He was awakened to realise that Begg was driving far slower than usual and that the headlamps of another car were coming from behind. He watched in some astonishment, as if dreaming. The great Mercedes swept past them, overtaking at almost one hundred miles an hour. Sinclair made out Herr Hitler in the back seat. Hess was with him. Strasser appeared to be driving. Before he began to fall back to sleep, he remembered noticing that Hitler appeared to be wearing a suit and a tie. He asked Begg where the Nazi leader was going at this time of night.

"Berlin, I'd guess." Sir Seaton kept "Dolly" at a steady pace.

"We're going to Berlin?"

"Good Lord no, old boy. Our work's done here. We're going home. If I put on a little speed at the crossroads, we should be just in time to catch the dawn Zeppelin for Manchester."

Without Sinclair's knowledge, Begg had already stowed the luggage. There had been no hotel bill to settle. By dawn they reached the great Munich Aerodrome and were soon installed in a comfortable suite. Through the portholes came floods of intermittent sunshine caused by the movement of the ship in her cables. A radio bulletin playing on the State Radio took on a rather excited air, and as soon as he had disrobed, washed, and settled in his seat, Begg turned the volume up.

He listened in some amusement, but Sinclair was aghast at the news. He even failed to notice the almost effortless lifting of the huge liner as she uncoupled from her masts and began her journey to Moss Side aeropark.

Effectively there had been a complete disintegration of the Nazis. Already the Reichstag party seemed divided into opposing camps headed by Strasser and Göring. Nazi officials were issuing contradictory statements since the arrest earlier that morning of Adolf Hitler, self-confessed murderer of the man he termed the "Jew Fifth Columnist Himmler," hitherto his trusted aide and an ex-chickenfarmer. Hitler understood that he could no longer hope to be Vice Chancellor, but now it scarcely mattered, since he had in his own words "torn out the heart of the hydra sucking the life from Germany, keeping the nation safe against injustice and horror for a thousand years!"

"You effectively put the gun into Hitler's hand and killed Himmler!" cried Sinclair. "Really, Begg, sometimes . . ."

"I told you, Taffy, that I did what I was supposed to do. Zenith knew only too well that there are few better and more trustworthy messengers than you and me. So he sent us to Hitler with the evidence he had carefully manufactured over months. Those papers were enough to convince almost anyone and in a bad light they were even harder to detect. But they were forgeries, old man. Planted for someone to find. When Zenith knew we were on to him, he simply made us his 'runners.' Pretty audacious, eh."

"But Zenith killed that poor creature, Fraulein Raubal," insisted Taffy.

"Not at all, Taffy, though you could argue Hitler effectively drove her to her death. She killed herself, as everyone insisted. She tested the poison first. You smelled that distinctive odour as readily as I did."

"Cyanide!"

"Exactly. The smell of cyanide, if taken by mouth, lingers on the lips long after the taker has gone to the hereafter. That dead canary the young lady carried around all day? She had already tried the stuff on the bird and saw that it worked. She took a pretty heavy dosage, I'd say. The police remained deceived by the gunshot. The way she lay on the floor made it seem to others that she had died in the throes of passion. But I believe she died in the throes of death."

"But she was shot, Begg. Shot by Zenith!"

"True."

"So Zenith is the real murderer . . ."

"No."

There was a knock at their door and Begg called "Come in!" A busboy with a salver presented him with a card which he glanced at, smiled, and tucked into his upper waistcoat pocket. He offered the boy a silver coin. "Ask Countess von Bek to join us at her pleasure." He beamed across at a bewildered Taffy.

"No?"

"No. Zenith was, of course, Fraulein Raubal's lover. He played the violin by night and courted her by day. By whatever clever devices, he had provided himself with the assignment of keeping guard on her, knowing that he planned to seduce her. But I think he also planned to save her. He took some conventional 'glamour' pictures of her. He made those Himmler forgeries we showed Hitler. I don't think he had any plan to kill the girl. But he did want her to run away with him. So he suggested they go to Vienna together. He told her to demand of Hitler that she be allowed to stay with her relatives and study singing there. It was a plan she had already toyed with. So she did as she was told. But Hitler, as we know, had reached the end of his tolerance." Begg rose to his feet to open their door, bowing Countess Rose into their rather cramped quarters. Offering her his chair, he brought her rapidly up to date and then, leaning beside the porthole, continued.

"Someone, probably an SA spy, had reported the 'secret lover,' even if they had not been able to say who it was. So Hitler refused. Under no circumstances could she go to Vienna. She again threatened suicide. He did not believe her. Neither, I suspect, would 'Captain Zeiss' have believed her. But when he let himself into the apartment late that night, he found poor Geli

Raubal on the floor, having tasted the torments of cynanide. She had left a note, no doubt. This went against his plans, but he had to go through with the rest of it. He pocketed the note. He found Hitler's gun, shot the already dead Geli through the heart in a way deliberately to draw suspicion on someone, placed the gun in her hand with equally deliberate clumsiness, then left the police and investigators, like ourselves, to conclude that the young woman had been murdered, either by Hitler or one of his lieutenants."

The Countess Rose sat back in her seat, her eyes gleaming with admiration. "So Hoffmann and myself were completely fooled. Only the fact that Hitler had an ironclad alibi stopped us from arresting him."

"Zenith already had his original plan, which he modified. He knew that Hitler could not be 'framed.' So he planned to let his men discover the clothing and documents at the Hotel Rembrandt. Since I caught up with him so much sooner than he expected, he merely decided to use me as his messenger! He was always a clever customer. Even those pictures, released to the press, would be enough to threaten the fortunes of Hitler and his party. But Zenith wanted to be dead certain. That was why he had forged some Himmler documents to make sure all in the party were suspect. He hoped they would find their way to Hitler. I made sure that they did. The consequences then followed like clockwork. Leading to a satisfactory resolution, I think you'll agree, Taffy. Sometimes it is just about possible for two wrongs to make a right."

Rose von Bek clapped her hands together as another knock came at the door. "Ah. That will be our breakfast champagne!"

But Sinclair's Presbyterian soul was not yet ready to accept the full burden of these unwelcome demonstrations. He rose gracefully, so that Begg might have his chair.

"If you'll forgive me, I'll take a stroll up to the dining hall and avail myself of the full English breakfast. I think an occasion like this calls for some honest fried bread, fried tomatoes, mushrooms, and black pudding. Traditional fortification."

"Very well, old boy. To each his own poison. I trust you'll rejoin us as soon as you can." Begg lifted a victorious glass.

Declaring that he would probably take a turn or two about the observation deck before he rejoined them, Sinclair stepped into the corridor and closed the door on his colleagues.

Once in the corridor the pathologist stared thoughtfully at the tranquil, dreaming German fields and villages passing below. A man trained to follow the law and to play the game by the conventional rules, Sinclair reflected that this was not the first time that his association with his friend Seaton Begg troubled him.

He shook his head, the delicious scents of frying bacon drawing his attention back to breakfast. He put the problem behind him. For all his moral dilemma, Taffy Sinclair was forced to admit that once again, by the most unconventional, even cynical methods, by the most circuitous path, justice had been done.

❧ Sir Milk-and-Blood ❦

What's the time?" he says. "Pad—what's the time? My watch has stopped."

"Four-thirty," says Patrick. "Shouldn't he have turned up by now?"

"He's always on time. He'll be here. God knows I'll be glad to get the release." Reaching for his cup. "It's bothering me, Pad. I can't get rid of the guilt."

"There are no 'innocent victims' in a war," says Patrick. "Not in this war, anyway. Just remember how many of our children died to make them rich."

"Pad, I can't keep doing this. I really can't. It's getting to me. I didn't join to kill kids. I don't want to do it any more." As he looked at his companion's frowning face he knew he was saying too much. Even if you thought it, you never said it.

"Well, it's not likely either of us will have to do it any more," says Patrick, ignoring this breach of etiquette. "In a little while we'll have our new passports and be out of here. Anywhere we like, so long as it's not Ireland or the UK. We can go to America. You've got relatives there, haven't you?"

"They read the papers," he says. But, anyway, he thinks, he won't be free there. He's ashamed to see his family. He already knows what they think of him. There isn't a news channel in the world that hasn't shown the pictures of the ruptured tram, the children's bodies thrown everywhere, the weeping mothers. And his and Patrick's unshaven faces staring crazily out at them, their eyes reflecting the harsh flash of the camera. "By God, Pad, don't you wish you'd never got into this?"

"I don't think like that," says Patrick. "Since I was thirteen all I've ever done is this. I mean what else is there? What would you be doing now if you hadn't joined the movement?"

"I was going to be a schoolteacher, God help me, before I got into politics." He lights a Gitane and goes to stare through the streaked grey window at the rain falling into the filthy water of the canal basin far below, where all six of the city's great underground waterways emerged into daylight and met at the infamous Quai D'Hiver. "I thought I could do more good in the movement."

As soon as he and Patrick were identified as the surviving bombers and their photographs had been published, they left London and travelled all the way to Paris from the Hook of Holland on a barge. It had taken a couple of weeks, but after a fortnight the authorities assumed they were far away from Europe. As it promised, the movement looked after them. Now their orders are to stay put until their "release" comes. They have been told who to expect. When he arrived, there would be no mistaking him.

"I just wish it hadn't happened," he says.

"Jesus, don't you think I wish that, too! But it wasn't your fault. It wasn't my fault. And your bloody brother died a hero's death. It's him you should be grieving for. You think too bloody much. You have to put it behind you. Now, stop moaning on, will you? Honestly, it's really not cool to start up like this." Patrick seemed to regret the harshness of his tone. "You know that as well as I do."

He knows he's condemned to silence for the rest of his life. Once you join the movement, you never retire. You're "released from active service" and that means the movement looks after you until it needs you again. He has never before longed with such passion to be free of it all.

"Well, look at it this way, we got a bit of collateral. That thing will make it easier for us, eh?" Patrick goes to the table and hefts the heavy newspaper parcel.

They had just left the tram at Waterloo Bridge when the bomb went off. Tony was going on a stop or two, would leave his bag under his seat and then get the train at Charing Cross. They had both been thrown flat by the blast, and as they got to their feet, trying to catch their breath, it was as if they had had a vision. The glass of the silversmith's was blown out and all the stuff in the window had been flung everywhere, apart from the one heavy object that had been central to the display and hadn't shifted or been damaged. An instinct developed from a lifetime of looting moved Patrick to grab the thing and then run for it. When they met up later, they discovered that Tony, sitting downstairs at the front of the tram, still had the bomb on his lap when it went off.

"Have another bloody drink, man." Patrick pours whisky into two glasses. "Go on."

"It doesn't work for me."

"God, you're a bloody morbid bugger! You're bound and determined, aren't you?" Patrick drains his own glass and takes the other. "It's a waste of time, this brooding on what can't be changed. Put it behind you, mate." He moves about the little room with impatient, aimless steps, as if his body tries to escape even as his brain tells him he has to stay. "You know as well as me that in a war there are no innocents. We all regret the civilian casualties, but there it is. I don't have to remind you of this. You taught me. Was it our fault that the bomb went off too soon? If your stupid brother had set the bloody timer right none of us would be in this jam now!"

"Well, he's dead. And so are ten other people, mostly kids. Going home from the pictures on a Saturday night, looking forward to their tea."

"Oh, man will you stop it! You're making it worse for yourself. Nobody was supposed to be hurt. The bomb should have gone off when the tram was in its shed. You know that. The sheds were supposed to be empty. The orders were clear. No casualties. Just do maximum damage to the turning plates. Our job's to disrupt travel and communications, not kill kids."

"But we did kill kids. And I can't get them out of my head. I can't stand the thought of another day of this! Oh, Jesus God, I want to be free of it, once and for all." Again he saw the disturbed disapproval on Patrick's face and fell silent.

"Well, you will be, any minute now." Patrick shows great self-restraint. "Who is this bloke? You know him, don't you?"

"He's a German, I think. I've been in the same company as him once or twice." He tried to keep his tone normal or at least controlled. "I always thought there was something odd about him. You can't tell how old he is. But he must be older than he looks. Mick says he was the youngest colonel in the SS." He sits back down in his chair, feeling a little better for talking. It takes his mind of the bombed tram.

"After the war he went to South America and he was in Spain for a while and North Africa. He's been running guns for as long as I've been in the movement. And he's helped us with other stuff, of course. He was our main contact with Libya until that went sour. You could call him a soldier-of-fortune, a mercenary—I think he's nothing but a renegade. He has no loyalties at all. No cause, no religion, and, as far as I can tell, no damned conscience."

"He sounds a superior sort of chap," says Patrick, emphasising his consonants the way they do in Kerry to announce sarcasm.

"Oh, he is, sure." He sighs. "No, I'm not kidding. There's something about him. When I was a kid, we used to have this story. It's one of those old Irish things that seem to be just local." He puts out the Gitane and lights another. The room is misty with his smoke. "My granny used to tell it as 'Sir Milk-and-Blood' in English. She didn't speak much Gaelic, but I thought the name had to come from old Irish and I looked it up. I found something that sounded right in Cornish—*Malan-Bloyth*."

"You said he was German."

"My granny's story had him finding the Holy Grail. He came from Brasil, which was probably the Scilly Islands. But *Malan-Bloyth* wasn't a knight-errant on a quest for the Holy Grail, as he was in the *Sir Milk-and-Blood* version. His name means, as close as I can give it in English, *The Demon Wolf . . .*"

"For the love of God, what a bunch of crap," says Patrick, sitting down with a sigh on the corner of the iron bed. He looks about, as if for escape. "Holy Jesus, I could do with a cup of decent tea. Why the hell are you telling me a kid's story?"

"To pass the time. To take our minds off things. I was talking about this bloke."

"The German bloke?"

"My point is: he reminded me of the hero in my granny's story. Red eyes and very white skin. That was why he was called Sir Milk-and-Blood. That's who this German fellow was like. He was a supernatural creature, a son of a Sidhe man and a human woman. In granny's version of the story, he looked for the Holy Grail. In the other version, he sought the Magic Cauldron of Finn MacCool. You know . . ."

"I don't bloody know. I was never that interested."

"It's the sort of thing a patriot ought to know." He manages a smirk to show he speaks in fun, but Patrick chooses to bridle anyway.

"Maybe. And maybe a patriot wouldn't keep going on about some poor bloody civilian stiffs he couldn't even know were on the damned tram." Patrick finished his whisky and took a Gauloise out of his pack. "So this is the bloke we're waiting for. What is he? A bloody werewolf?"

"Some believe that he was."

"I'm not talking about the fairy story. I'm talking about the real bloody bloke. What's he got? Leprosy?"

"Maybe. I first met him in the Med off the coast of Morocco. He was with Captain Quelch, another damned renegade, on that boat that almost got blown out of the water off Cuba the other day—the *Hope Dempsey*. We were dealing with some kind of volatile cargo. Nobody ever told me what it was, but I could guess, of course. My job was to check the boxes and pay over the money. I was always a better quartermaster than I was a field soldier . . ."

"Tell me about it," says Patrick, glaring disgustedly into the rain. He hears a movement on the uncarpeted stairs and rises from the bed.

The two men wait, but it's a false alarm.

"Well, he's a cold fish, by the sound of it," says Patrick. "What else do you know about him?"

"Not much. He's some sort of German prince, but everyone calls him 'Monsieur Zenith.' He spent a lot of time in the Far Atlas, speaks their languages, does business with the Berbers. They say he has one of those big villas in Las Cascadas. But Donald Quinn told me he lives in Egypt most of the time."

"Why is he interested in that?" With his unlit cigarette Patrick indicates the newspaper parcel.

"It's his price. The movement arranged it."

"Well, let's hope he brings cash," says Patrick scratching at his bottom and sighing. "I don't know about you, but I could do with some sunshine. Another few days and I'll be on a beach in Florida soaking up the rays."

"What happened isn't that important to you, is it, Pad? You've already put it behind you."

"No point in doing anything else," says Patrick. "An incident in the ongoing struggle. Better to forget it. You can't make it not have happened.

A bad dream. Leave it behind, mate, or it'll fester forever. Or go and see a bloody priest and get it off your bloody chest. Jesus Holy Christ! You're no bloody fun any more. I'll be damned glad to see the back of you!" And he begins that agitated pacing again, so that neither of them hears the soft knock. A second knock and Patrick is rushing for the door, dragging it wide.

"I told you he'd be on time."

And there he is. He would be a little less terrifying if he wasn't smiling.

"Well, thank God, at bloody last!" says Patrick, studying the tall stranger with nervous resolve.

Although it is only late afternoon, Monsieur Zenith wears perfect evening dress. Thrown back over one shoulder is an old-fashioned scarlet-lined opera cape and on his head is a silk hat. His eyes are hidden by a pair of round, smoked glasses which further emphasises the pallor of his skin. He has a long head with delicate bones and his ears seem to taper. He has an almost feminine mouth, sensitive and firm. In one white-gloved, slender hand is an ebony cane trimmed with silver. In the other he carries what appears to be a long electric guitar case which he now stoops to rest on the floor.

"Good evening, gentlemen." He speaks in a soft accent that is difficult to identify. "Such confidence is flattering. I believe you have something to show me?"

Patrick backs into the room as Monsieur Zenith carries in his burden, puts it down again, takes off his hat, closes the door carefully behind him, and nods a greeting. Slipping a slender silver case from his inner pocket, he removes a small, brown cigarette and lights it. He comes immediately to the point. "I have your release, gentlemen. But first I must be sure that you are who you say you are and that your circumstances are as they have been described to me."

"What do we have to bloody prove?" says Patrick. "That we blew up a Number 37 tram in the Strand? The movement knows who we are. They sent you, didn't they?"

"Not exactly. I volunteered to come. I had heard about that—" he gestures with his cane at the parcel on the table. "And when I learned what I was to receive for my services, I put two and two together. So that was your bomb on the Number 37?"

"It was," says Patrick dropping his cigarette to the boards of the floor and crushing it out.

His companion is silent. Monsieur Zenith removes his smoked glasses and lifts a pale, enquiring brow.

Patrick now takes note of the albino's ruby eyes which burn with suppressed pain and melancholy irony. Caught for a moment in their timeless depths, Patrick feels suddenly lost, as if his entire universe has fallen away from him and he is absolutely alone. Gasping, he turns and almost runs towards the table, tearing at the newspaper. "You'd better have a look at this cup . . ."

"No," says Monsieur Zenith. "I don't want to see it. Not quite yet. I know what it is, believe me. I'll wait. Until you're gone."

"So you trust us?" says Patrick. He looks expectantly towards the guitar case. He is very anxious to leave. His companion, however, sits quietly in his chair. His nod to his old acquaintance has a reconciled, submissive air. He makes no effort to prepare himself for departure.

"To be who you say you are? Of course I do! Who else would claim such a crime?"

"Jesus God Almighty," says Patrick. "Crime is it? I can't stand another damned moralist. I'd be prepared to bet you've just as much blood on your hands as we have."

"Oh," says Monsieur Zenith lifting the case onto the table. "Infinitely more, no doubt."

This confession of complicity, as he sees it, relaxes Patrick a little. He gestures to the bottle and glasses. "A drink, pal?"

The albino moves his head a fraction. No. His strange, almost angelic face turns to the window and notes that it is overlooked by nothing.

"You brought cash I see," says Patrick. "And travellers checks, like we asked, I hope?" He hesitates as the albino rapidly snaps open the case's catches and begins to lift the lid. There's a walkman or something in there, playing what sounds at first like modern North African music. The noise deepens until it vibrates all the glass in the room and makes Patrick feel faintly ill. Some sort of alarm, perhaps.

Then the case is fully open. It is lined in red velvet. The whole of its length and much of its breadth is taken up by an enormous broadsword. The thing is so impossibly ancient its iron has turned jet black. And along the length of the blade run a series of disturbing red runes which, even as he watches, seem to move and reshape themselves constantly, in unison with the strange, deep howling which springs from the trembling metal. In the hilt what looks like an enormous ruby pulses in harmony with the sword's unnerving voice.

"What the hell is that?" Patrick valiantly demands, trying to guess where the money's hidden.

The albino seems amused. For a moment, he has a panting, wolfish air to him as he reaches both hands towards the case.

Somehow the black sword, almost as tall as he is, settles into the German's grasp, its voice changing to one of profound satisfaction as it unites with its master. It shudders as if with eager anticipation. Now, with a new calmness, Monsieur Zenith turns towards the seated man, and there is still an element of compassion in his flaming red eyes.

The whole world fills with the sword's rising song. The runes race and whirl, forming and reforming to create whole new languages of power as they writhe up and down its black length. The universe trembles. The room fills with darkness. That same darkness floods out of the window and silences the Quai des Hivers.

As Patrick begins to vomit uncontrollably, the albino smiles.

"It is your release," he says.

The Mystery of the Texas Twister

The Invasion of Begg Mansions

All the gold and glorious scarlet of the shaded stage erupted around her as Miss Una Persson strutted out of the wings, the audience at once in her outstretched, imploring hands. *"Won't you please take pity on a girl who's lost her pretty, her pretty little tit-for-tat?"* she sang, lifting sweet eyes of winking innocence to the boys in the boxes, the gallery mashers, and the lads in the stalls, while the band struck up in concert with her swirling skirts and even the curtains joined in her sensual waving red, white, and blue, the costume she had made her own.

In the audience the multiverse's leading metatemporal investigator shared a chorus with his fellows while his old friend Taffy clapped in unison, his enthusiasm less vocal but if anything more ecstatic. *"Then the old gent from the city sat on my little pretty, sat on my pretty little tit-for-tat!"* Cocking her hat over that uncreased forehead, a bare shoulder lifted in a coquette's shrug, marching to the rhythms of the waves she had set in motion, even pausing to watch a hat or two lift into the air, saluting it as it fell back into the crowd. *"And now he's stuck another feather in my darling little titfer, my pretty little darling little cap."* Even the electric limelights danced to her stride.

"And who'd have guessed," said Sir Seaton Begg later, "that she was once considered the most dangerous woman in London. The rival, at least, of Rose von Bek."

Tipping the driver generously, he and his friend, Doctor "Taffy" Sinclair, the Home Office pathologist, descended from the electric hansom. There was still a light on in the hallway of the Sporting Club Square penthouse, which served Begg as both home and consulting rooms and even contained a suite of apartments for Sinclair whenever he chose to remain in Town. Sinclair's own house lay in rural Hackney, not far from the infamous marshes. Begg's housekeeper, Mrs Curry, by now almost certainly in bed, had left them a cold collation for their supper. The evening was the first of a weekend they were determined to enjoy as a holiday.

The following Saturday morning the two men rose late and met for breakfast in Begg's pleasant dining room which looked out onto the elegant square with its wonderful collection of mansion blocks in every architectural style from Gothic to Art Nouveau arranged around the park and tennis courts. The morning was disturbed only by the occasional passing car, its engine buzzing faintly as it glided along the perfect smoothness of the tarmacadam. Dr Sinclair, who remembered without nostalgia the old days of horses, commented as usual on the cleanliness and relative silence of modern transportation as he helped himself to kidneys and bacon and brought his plate back to the table. Begg's grunt of acknowledgement was all Sinclair expected. He took a newspaper from the pile beside Begg's chair and began to read. As usual Begg was buried in the back pages where he insisted all the real news was to be found. Mrs Christie's *The Mousetrap* had just entered its fortieth year on the London stage. British goods were back in fashion in the Antipodean Republic (popularly known as Anzacia). Relatives were concerned about the recent disappearance of the Brazilian wizard Luis O'Bean from his seaside holiday home in Mexico, the furthest northern province of the Brazilian Empire. The photoplay actress Miss Vivienne Leigh was about to divorce her fifth husband, Mr Simon Russell Beale. Mr Ian McKellen, currently Iago in the Stratford Royal Shakespeare production, was being cited as the co-respondent by Sir Dirk Bogarde, currently Othello. The female guilty party was Dame Fenella Fielding, who played Desdemona. It had become impossible to buy a seat for the production. Crowds remained outside the theatre every night. Returns were changing hands at fifty guineas. A new airship, the *Queen of Newcastle*, had just been christened by Princess Anne in the

New Tyneside yards. Her steam turbines were the very latest in modern technology. To a barely hearing Sinclair, Begg noted that the Francophone Confederation was anticipating record harvests in Central Africa. Sinclair scarcely responded. "Your fascination with the minutia of world events baffles me. I'll tell you frankly, Begg, I'm not sure it is especially wholesome." Laughing softly at his friend's concern, Begg suggested that they get some fresh air.

Returning to Begg's sitting room from a stroll around Sporting Club Square, the two friends took to their armchairs on either side of the fireplace. Awakened almost immediately from a pleasant doze by the sound of the doorbell ringing somewhere in the depths of the house, Begg grunted. "Mrs Curry's popped out. Would you mind, old boy?" Doctor Sinclair agreed reluctantly and rubbed his eyes. He was looking forward to the lunch Mrs Curry had promised them by way of celebrating his fortieth birthday. Coincidentally it was also the anniversary of his first meeting with Begg, many time zones away when serving on the Northwest Frontier under the redoubtable General Oswald Bastable. Bastable had long since disappeared into the limbo of alternative branes sometimes called "the Grey Fees," but since that affair, commonly known as "The Adventure of the Afghan Astrologer," the two men worked almost exclusively for the British government. Of late, released to act in the private sector on the understanding that no case would be against British interests, they had recently taken on increasing numbers of different assignments.

To be disturbed at this hour of a Saturday morning was, under any circumstances, pretty unusual. Begg's brow lightened as he heard Mrs Curry return and speak to their visitor.

"Bit odd," agreed Begg in answer to Sinclair's raised eyebrows. "Still, we can safely leave it to Mrs Curry's discretion as to whether the caller has important business or not."

He cocked his head to listen to the sound of a loud American accent raised in desperation on the stairs below. "No, no, ma'am. I will not be sent away. My business with Sir Seaton is highly urgent. There is no time to lose! My life is in danger! That damned turncoat albino intends to assassinate me, I'll swear!"

Again Mrs Curry's firm tones attempted to calm their agitated visitor.

"His accent," mused Begg, "is that of East Texas if I'm not mistaken, modi-fied by exposure to French, Spanish, and Washington English. What do you say, Taffy? Is this some sort of charade? Shall we have him up?"

Sinclair frowned, a little annoyed at the disturbance to a day he had already decided was to be their own. But he too knew why his friend was intrigued, and it was not simply by the accent. Indeed, his own curiosity was also whetted. Nodding, he reached for his briar, stuffing it with ill-smelling M&E. "I thought I heard him mention the albino also."

Moments later a small, pugnacious middle-aged man in a well-cut suit with an evil looking tie and matching handerchief burst into the room removing his massive sombrero to reveal a balding head. His ruddy features spoke of a dangerously high blood pressure, and to Sinclair's trained eye it seemed he must collapse on the carpet at any moment. Even before he spoke the visitor popped a couple of tablets into his mouth and was served with a glass of water by the disapproving Mrs Curry, a lifelong Christian Scientist. The formalities over, the man introduced himself as Mr Dick Shiner, a leading member of the Texan Senate and vice president of Texas Power Inter-national. He came straight to the point.

"Tell me, Sir Seaton. Have you ever heard of a crimson-eyed albino who goes by the name of 'Count Zenith'?"

Begg settled back in his chair. "I understood from the newspapers that he was acting as an advisor to your company's president, popularly known as George 'The King' Washington Putz. Your people gave him immunity, since which time he's done very well. With your help, I understand. Has there been trouble?"

Mr Shiner's expression indicated that there had been more than a little trouble. "This Zenith guy was supposed to be on our side. He'd been working for the Wahabi Confederation. They have some idea of developing a kind of chemical-fired engine. The fast-heating chemicals produce steam quicker and less clumsily than the conventional steam engines used on airships. Moreover, they are supposed to be far lighter motors." Dick Shiner scratched his bald head and grimaced. "I'm no Faraday, Sir Seaton, I'll admit to you, so I don't understand the precise details, but, as a scientist, Count Zenith was per-suaded to work for the Republic of Texas, specifically for our company, which as you may know acts as Regent Corporation on behalf of the ruling Senate. We are developing this new engine and its secret fuel. We had no idea, of course, that Zenith had a criminal record."

"I am all too familiar with Count Zenith's activities, Mr Shiner. I follow them with keen interest. Although I am more familiar with him and his deeds than most, I understand he is known to most of the world's police forces. Not Texas's, it appears. I should imagine your somewhat tolerant treatment of an ex–international crook has made him the envy of his kind. As I understand it, Texas needs to develop a practical heavier than air flying machine. It is crucial, therefore, that you find a way of manufacturing an engine for your existing 'autogyro' capable of delivering power far in excess of its weight. The new chemical engine would make your machine airworthy. I gather the French abandoned the invention several years ago after extensive tests. Yet you and your colleagues continue to see it as the future of modern flight, what?"

"Sir Seaton, you're as smart as they say you are." Dick Shiner accepted a chair, mopped his brow, and placed his glass on the table. "I take it you're privy to British intelligence sources and that's how you know. Yes, Zenith claimed to have the plans for a chemical engine which would easily develop enough power to lift our rotary plane. The 'Texas Twister,' as we call it, would be able to fly fifty miles or more without refuelling! We were dubious at first, but the crook convinced us. I take it you know something about this man, Sir Seaton."

"He and I are acquainted. You could call us old duelling partners."

"I follow your meaning, Sir Seaton. He came to us on excellent authority. Now I wish we had thought to ask you before we hired him. Mr Putz's brother swore that he was a good egg."

"That would be the chap currently doing five years in the Florida hulks for vote tampering, as I recall?" Sir Seaton could not suppress a small smile. "Otherwise known to the Washington constabulary as Gentleman Jed."

Dick Shiner cleared his throat. "We place great value on personal relations in our country, Sir Seaton, as well as on personal liberty. But occasionally the system, I'll grant you, lets us down. The Texan Republic is run by a Senate of good men and true, appointed for their intelligence, integrity, and character. Whatever you say about it, there are fewer mistakes made than you find in most of your much vaunted democracies, even your own democratic monarchy. It is well known, for instance, how corrupt the Democratic Republic of California has become. Those guys take the cake. Funding terrorism is the least of their crimes. Hell, the whole so-called Texas Libertarian Front is bankrolled by California. Who else could it be?"

Taffy Sinclair, who had strong political views, cleared his throat. At once Sir Seaton answered swiftly. "Just so, Mr Shiner. I assume, therefore, that there is no truth to the rumours that your Senate planned to offer a crown to the head of Texas Power? Your own president?"

"Perhaps in the event of social instability, Sir Seaton. Which, of course, could easily arise if California declared war on Texas. Only Navajonia stands between us and conflict at the moment. Them and the pope. If this Count Zenith has sold our gyroplane to the Californians, then we will have little choice but to demand it back. And, if it is not forthcoming, we will be forced to annex Navajonia for aiding our enemies. We should be forced to march on Sacramento."

"You can afford to do that?"

Mr Shiner thrust out his chins. "We will not be alone, Sir Seaton. We will have allies."

Seaton Begg had no wish to involve himself in the notoriously unstable politics of North America, with its constant belligerence and changing alliances between red men and black, white men and red, French and Spanish, Spanish and Navajo, English and American. The thought of capturing his old antagonist Count Zenith tempted him. Dr Sinclair, on the other hand, was dubious, as was evident from his expression. America was too volatile and intemperate a continent for his taste.

"I have it on good authority," continued Dick Shiner, "that, once he has our Twister working, Count Zenith will lead the Californians against our capital of Waterloo. The Californians are greedy for any chance to attack. We have evidence that the Democratic Republic has stores of poison gas they intend to use against us. This could easily be spread from fast flying machines. Within a few days the whole of Texas could be dying of some deadly disease. That, sir, is why you must lend us your powerful intelligence."

"How can you be so certain that the Californians mean to attack?" Taffy Sinclair wished to know.

"We have discovered a document detailing such plans." Dick Shiner was grave. "Before he left their employ Wolfy Paulowitz stole it for us from their own council chamber! A memo from Governor Arnold Zinoviev to his most trusted associates. The poison gas attack will coincide with aerial bombardments by great flying ironclads. The Bank of Texas, the Haliburton building, our electrical grids, and other key targets will be subject to cowardly bombing raids from thousands of feet up. Our citizens will have no means of fighting back."

"If you are so certain that there is to be war between your nation and California, Mr Shiner, what point is there in your engaging us? Are you merely hoping to use us to legitimise your plans?"

Shiner bridled at this. "We will do anything to avert war, Sir Seaton. We Texans are a peace-loving people who abjure conflict in all its forms. The Lord knows that we have experienced enough of it in our own backyard. From wild Apache to the so-called Texas Republican Movement. We are currently having to take unusual steps. Terrorists in our own nation hate our way of life and are jealous of all we have. You've heard of the 'Masked Buckaroo'? I thought so. We are constantly threatened from within by that mysterious bandit and his 'libertarians.' That is precisely why we must track down Zenith as quickly as possible. Only when the 'Texas Twister' and its secret engine is in their hands will the Californians dare attack. Until then we are probably safe. The Californians, of course, deny they are sheltering Zenith. If you could prove otherwise or, indeed, capture Zenith, it would give us the breathing space we need. You could avert serious conflict."

Still uncertain Begg frowned. "I'm not sure our time lines are sufficiently close for a safe crossing, Mr Shiner . . ."

"The year is the same as your own," insisted the vice president. "At most there is the difference of a week between zones." As he began to offer more detailed information there came a further disturbance from below. With a murmured apology Begg left his consulting room and crossed to the top of the stairs. In the hallway stood a uniformed policeman explaining himself to Mrs Curry.

"'E come in 'ere Missus, I'll swear to it. Smooth lookin' character in a posh suit a bit too good fer 'im if yer take my meaning. I knew 'im straight away. We've a poster up at the station. Yank crook by the name of Wolfy 'the Gent' Paulowitz. The Yard wants 'im picked up on sight. Escaped from a posh loony bin. Armed an' dangerous. Delusions of grandeur. I've sent for the CID."

"An 'ow could this Yankee spiv get past my door without me a-noticin' of it?" Mrs Curry wished to know, folding her arms firmly on her chest and continuing to block the officer's entrance.

Before the constable could finish another sentence the sharp report of a pistol came from behind him, and Begg rushed back to find his friend staring open-mouthed at the scene. On the floor slumped Dick Shiner, apparently dead, while standing over him, gun in hand, stood the man the policeman had just described as Wolfy Paulowitz.

"So die all traitors!" cried Paulowitz, lifting his pistol above his head. "So die all terrorists and those who deny our Texan freedoms!

"Hang on a second, old boy," said Begg engagingly. "While I'm inclined to join in any such celebration, I'm not entirely sure of the issues here."

The assassin drew back his lips in a sneer. "If you don't know who is against you, you don't deserve to know. Do not steer me adrift of the path of righteousness, or I shall be fored to punish you also!"

"You seem to have put your finger spot on the problem, old chap." Chatting amiably, Sir Seaton moved casually closer to the American assassin. "Now, how many enemies would you say you currently have—?" In one split second Begg had pounced and put "the Gent" down with a perfectly aimed right to the jaw, his weapon firing harmlessly into the air.

"Good heavens, Begg!" gasped the mild-mannered pathologist. "He was a determined fellow! It all happened far too quickly for me. One moment you had left the room, the next our friend came from behind the curtain—" Sinclair indicated the open window, "and shot Mr Shiner point blank without hesitation! I must say he seemed frightfully confident. A mad glint in his eye and all that!"

Begg picked up the Smith and Wesson and trained it on the awakening gunman. "Better get the cuffs on this customer, officer. I recognised him as you did. Mr Paulowitz isn't your common sort of criminal. He doesn't even recognise himself as a criminal. He belongs to a terrorist outfit known to the police as 'the Family of Fear,' though they usually term themselves something grander. Their ambition is to take over entire nations via their governments. Recently Wolfy Paulowitz has been concentrating on Whitehall. Rumour has it he had already corrupted more than one high-ranking Member of Parliament, who, I'm glad to say, has since resigned."

"That's wot I was tryin' ter tell yer, missus," the policeman exclaimed. "'E came up the back wall from the alley. I'd read the reports in last week's *Gazette*. Wolfie is famous as a backdoor man, so we've 'eard. Fastest climber in the game. But a lousy shot by all accounts. 'Course I didn't know 'e 'ad a Film Fun on 'im or I'd 'ave blown me whistle."

Now that a glaring "Gent" had the gyves on him, Begg handed his pistol to the officer. "Better take the 'Film Fun' as evidence," he said. "Aha! There you are, Coutts."

The infamous battered bowler hat of Chief Inspector Coutts, Scotland Yard's finest man, floated through the door. Beneath it the stern bulldog features regarded the room. "Good work, Davey," Coutts told the policeman. "There's a car downstairs. Ensure this customer hops in it. They'll take you to Marylebone Central to make a formal charge. I'll be along first chance I get. Tell the ambulance chaps to come up as soon as they arrive."

Dr Sinclair was examining Shiner's body. He drew in a surprised breath as he found the man's pulse. "Not a mark on him. The bullet—? Aha!" Tearing open the Texan's shirt, Sinclair revealed a heavy "bulletproof vest" of the kind favoured by certain police forces and armies on the other side of the Atlantic. "He's merely winded. Fainted, I shouldn't be surprised. Unless he's had some sort of stroke."

But Shiner was already groaning as he came round. He sat up and was helped into a chair by Sinclair. He took a large elaborately embroidered handkerchief from his top pocket and mopped the sweat pouring from his grey forehead.

"Phew, a lucky escape. I guess. You see the kind of desperate men we're dealing with, Sir Seaton. Paulowitz knows me well. Clearly he's working for the Texan insurgents. For some time the Masked Buckaroo's 'freedom fighters' have been a thorn in our side. I'm well defended on my home ground, going nowhere without my own detachment of Rangers, so no doubt

Wolfowitz thought he'd have a better chance here. You people hardly know the meaning of homeland vigilance."

"Desperation certainly seems evident, Mr Shiner," Inspector Coutts agreed dryly. "You had a fortunate escape, it seems. Few of us have the foresight to go about the West End wearing armour."

"These days that's second nature for us." Shiner accepted the brandy Sinclair poured him. "Fellows like Wolfy are a little quick on the trigger and self-righteous enough to justify any violence."

"You know the chap, then?" Sinclair asked in some surprise.

"He's a former business partner turned gangster. A special kind of gangster. You know about 'The Family'?"

"The Family of Fear?" repeated Coutts with a knowing tilt to his lips. Begg's brief glance in his direction suggested the metatemporal detective would rather his Scotland Yard colleague had not shown familiarity in the matter. "I was just mentioning them, sir." For all their friendly rivalry, Coutts was generally pleased to be associated with Begg's cases. "Sir Seaton encountered them in that odd affair in Washington we both investigated." Obviously the policeman showered his whole store of information upon the Texan. "Most are born-again Marxists of the worst sort, sworn to bring down the governments of the world by any means available, including assassination!" Coutt's snorted his disapproval. "They dignify their motives with all kinds of high falutin' words, but they're still common criminals in my view."

"Exactly, Mr Coutts," Shiner seemed relieved he did not have to explain too much. "Former fundamentalist Christians and right-wingers who have secretly come together to institute a programme of 'reform' from top to bottom. Popularly known as the American Taliban, they've infiltrated every level of society, recruiting the likes of Paulowitz with promises of amnesty and political office. To them any method is acceptable if it brings about the end they seek. And I am one of their chief targets for, in fact, I was briefly with them. Their actions, however, are repugnant to my moral principles, to my free Texan blood, to my respect for Law and my commitment to Jesus Christ, whom I accept as my personal saviour."

"Just so, just so." Begg helped his visitor to stand. "Inspector Coutts here will need you at the Yard to make a statement. Meanwhile—"

"You'll take the case, Sir Seaton?"

"It certainly intrigues me," declared the famous detective.

"No doubt we shall meet again soon. If not in London then in Waterloo. Good afternoon, Mr Shiner. I offer you congratulations on your happy escape."

With that the metatemporal detective ushered Inspector Coutts and Shiner from the room. He turned to observe with some amusement the expression on his old friend's face.

"Good heavens, Begg!" exclaimed Sinclair. "Surely you're not going to accept the case? This is merely a blood feud between different clans of American zealots. Such feuds are scarcely uncommon on that conflict-torn subcontinent. The place teems with secret societies and armed militia. The north is made up of warring industrial states. The Family of Fear is typical of its many quasi-criminal political groups. Evangelicalism is virtually the only industry most of those impoverished and unstable nations know. The internal feuds between members of the Ku Klux Klan are good news only for the gun makers. The rate of lethal shootings remains the highest in the world! All the various factions believe their viewpoint to be the only valid one, blessed by God or Karl Marx, and they back their arguments with lead and cold steel. Everyone knows they could have the second-greatest economy in the world. Yet they fritter away their wealth on constant internecine rivalries and conflicts in which one biblical sect spends its entire time seeking to impose its own interpretation on the others. So much for there being only one true God!"

"Quite, Taffy. I could not have put it better."

"So why on earth—?"

"One name," Begg said. "That's all it took to intrigue me. Zenith's never up to something small, even if it isn't what Mr Born-Again Shiner suspects. And you know how I yearn to finish our game. So far I have beaten him and averted the worst of his plans. But I have yet to put the steel bracelets over those elegant wrists. This time I think I have the chance. We can catch tomorrow's express and be in Waterloo, Texas, in under four days!"

With an air of resigned martyrdom, Dr Sinclair rang the bell to order his celebratory lunch.

CHAPTER TWO

Waterloo, Texas

Her great engines snorting and throbbing, the *Duchess of York* descended majestically, a mass of scarlet in the deep golden blue sky. She turned her blazing nose towards the glinting silver masts of Waterloo. The sprawling aerodrome awaited her below. Long, slender tethering poles swung to lock the great ship into place.

Seaton Begg turned from his stateroom's observation window. "There she is, Taffy. Waterloo, the Texan capital since Sam Houston's day. Not a bad city all in all. Built by idealists. Not maintained by idealists, I fear." Wide expanses of green park, rivers, and lakes. Large public buildings mostly in a low, classical style. As his friend moved to look down, Sir Seaton Begg finished their earlier conversation. "You know as well as I that Count Zenith is an expert falsifier, a creature able to reproduce almost any appearance and most emotions. Some of Europe's oldest blood flows in his veins. A devastating seducer, he can draw the full range of emotions from those he fascinates. Many, to their later regret, have fallen in love with him."

Through his dining room Sir Seaton Begg led the way back to their sitting room, a somewhat troubled Dr Taffy Sinclair striding beside him. "But charm hardly describes Zenith's astonishing powers of persuasion. He is, of course, quite without conscience, though he has a code of honour of his own from which he never swerves. If he has an Achilles' heel, that is it. You remember how he tricked us time and again during those early days when we were together on the Northwest Frontier, how he united the Pathan tribes against the forces of Law?

"Yet Count Zenith almost never works for another. That is why I find it hard to believe most of Mr Shiner's story. Those Texan senators want us here for secret reasons, perhaps as part of an elaborate alibi designed to obscure one country's invasion of another! That's why I'm so curious to discover their real game. Our own interests are involved here, too. Zenith's contempt for most human creatures is never disguised. He would have no time at all for such narrow puritanism as Paulowitz's and his kind. Zenith holds his own life as cheaply as he holds those of others. His behaviour is never for our approval but only his own. He is a self-serving monster, as you say, dear Taffy. But not a common one. He is as addicted to risk as others are to whisky."

"He has to be admired," reflected his friend. "There are few who can get the better of you, Begg!" Taffy Sinclair's face clouded with embarrassment. "Forgive me, that was ill-mannered."

"Not at all, Taffy." Begg readied his bags for the porters. "Count Zenith has bested us a number of times. More than once he has spared my life when he could have killed me. As I have always spared his. Unlike our American cousins, I do not regard the duel or the bloodfeud as anything but a very primitive form of justice, long since obsolete and setting a very bad example to the community at large. If I cannot bring the likes of Zenith before the courts, then I shall have failed the Law I serve, as if I had committed a crime myself. And Zenith would have won!"

"Noble adversaries," murmured the pathologist, not without irony.

Seaton Begg accepted the comment. "Perhaps. But we must never forget that Zenith has taken many lives in the course of his escapades. Most of those lives have belonged to poor examples of the human race, but we must treat him as any other killer. He cannot be allowed to go unpunished. I say, what's this?"

Begg leaned forward to inspect the seat before him. Gingerly he picked up a slip of paper with a few words written on it. "Well, perhaps Count Zenith has a rival in this particular game!" He handed the note to his friend.

Frowning, Taffy Sinclair read the words printed there. *"Whose is the hand which moves 'The King'? Beware the mysterious 'Doctor Spin.'"* We have been gone from the cabin only a few minutes, Begg. Who could have placed this here?"

"No doubt we shall find out in time." The note of the great steam turbines was changing now as the ship backed air before she descended the last few hundred feet to her mooring masts.

"Doctor Spin. Isn't he the chap we chased across Red India?"

"Yes, indeed. The trail took us all the way to the People's Republic of Bengalistan where we lost him. An area long coveted by the Anglo-Texan power cartels for its constantly flooding territories. They planned to dam those great rivers and sell the electricity around the globe. But even King George Washington Putz, Managing Director of TPI and head of the Texas Senate, has been unable to come up with either the finances or an excuse for invading the country."

"He's called Doctor Spin by the few who know of his existence. Some say the name's a shortening of Spinoza or Spinetti and that he's a Red Hand don who quarreled with his fellows. Some believe the name refers to his ability to create a web of conspiracy wherever he goes. I happen to know he is not Italian. However, he is rumoured to be associated with Wolfy Paulowitz, the failed assassin of Dick Shiner. So connections are already being offered to me . . ."

"But what have Doctor Spin and Wolfy to do with Count Zenith, Begg?"

With a shudder the *Duchess of York* connected to her great grappling cones. White-uniformed stewards ran along the companionways. "All first-class passengers please assemble on the disembarkation deck." Dogs barked as they were reunited with their owners. Children cried with excitement. Outside a brilliant sun reflected off the aluminium domes of the airship sheds and tiny figures darted about seeing to the mooring.

"That's what I don't know, Taffy." Begg gave up his suitcases to the porter and left the suite. "Zenith holds the Family of Fear in deep contempt. It is unlikely they are allies. If in fact they are working together, we're looking at a pretty ambitious crime." He hesitated, then joined the lines of slowly moving humanity in the common passageway.

They proceeded forward with a small party of Saudi Arabians, mostly women in heavy burkas, their dark eyes full of excitement as they looked out at the surprisingly green woods and fields of the Texan Hill Country with its great chain of lakes and rivers. The bearded Wahabim men were stern and dignified behind their smoked glasses, murmuring amongst themselves and studiously ignoring all other passengers. From an item in the *Waterloo Chronicle* Begg knew that they were here to discuss the building of hydroelectric systems for their own domestic uses. Even though Arabia was a fairly impoverished region, Texas Power courted her these days. The raising of cattle was still the nation's main income so the Texas government had long experience of making the most of what water existed in otherwise arid land. Knowing they could only extend their wealth by extending their farming capacity, the

Saudis were willing to spend whatever gold they had on improvements. There had even been some talk of installing a national tramway service, similar to the one that now laid a lattice of steel and copper across the modern Texan plains.

The walkway to the waiting customs and immigration buildings was gently sprung and gave Sinclair a certain lightness of step. He was whistling under his breath as he opened his cases for the hard-eyed officers.

At last they had disembarked. Begg went to supervise the unloading of his pride and joy, the sleek all-weather electric brougham made by the great Duesenberg racing company especially for his needs and affectionately nicknamed "Dolly." She had been charging while in the air and was ready to go.

Guided by the great marble dome of the Capitol, they were soon purring on their way up the only paved road into Waterloo. Here at the impressive Graeco-Roman edifice of the Driskill Hotel, they had arranged to meet Dick Shiner. As Mr Shiner had already told Begg, democracy, such as was enjoyed in England, was not regarded as a sensible system for governing Texas. It was an idea which further divided them from their Californian rivals on the other side of the predominantly barren deserts of Dinéland or Navajonia, itself ruled by a council elected, according to the custom of the Diné people, by native men and women, by ranchers, distillers, and owners of entertainment establishments. California, however, remained a populist democracy, subject to demagoguery and shifts of fashion, regarded as hopelessly unstable compared to Texas and her powerful neighbor the Southern Confederation, whom cotton had made rich.

In no time at all the metatemporal detectives located the Driskill Hotel, a local landmark patronised chiefly by wealthy cattlemen. A negro boy jumped on the running board and directed them into the cool lobby, receiving a coin for his services. Here their bags were taken up and their brougham garaged. Adjoining suites had been engaged for them by Dick Shiner's people. After showering away the sticky Texan heat, they met for a cocktail in Begg's suite, then sought out the Long Bar, already generously patronised by men with expensive Stetsons they never removed and ladies in white buckskins and turquoise whose stacked hair resembled grain silos in miniature. Like most wealthy kulaks, they seemed amiable, self-satisfied, and not much interested in two strangers. It took a moment for the Englishmen to recognise Dick Shiner, who also wore a large white hat. He was deep in conversation with another Texan but looked up, saw his guests, clapped his companion on the back, and advanced towards Begg and Sinclair, hand extended.

"So glad you made it, gentlemen." Shiner's face was ruddy and beaming but his small eyes had a somewhat haunted look, as if he still anticipated assassination from the "Family of Fear." He glanced around the big, dark bar. Begg noticed a number of hard-faced men who were evidently bodyguards of some kind. These were no doubt the "Rangers" Shiner had mentioned in London. "You'll presumably want to rest after your journey and begin work tomorrow. Since we spoke I have strong evidence that Monsieur Zenith is operating in California, no doubt with the connivance of their government, somewhere close to the border with Navajonia. I have to admire your courage in taking this case. There is murder in the air, gentlemen!"

"Then the sooner we meet your President Putz the better," suggested Sinclair briskly.

A distant explosion suddenly shook the room. Though a few laughed, most ignored it. Another went off, closer this time. Sir Seaton smiled. "More terrorists, no doubt."

"No doubt." Shiner's face clouded. "The president and key members of the Senate have had to go into hiding. The terrorist risk to them is too great, so the Rangers advised them to leave the capital for the time being. They are in a secret location. The affairs of the nation are still firmly and safely in their hands."

"Indeed." Begg sipped his malt whisky. "So where would you suggest we begin tomorrow, Mr Shiner?"

"Zenith's trail is still warm. Naturally it would be considered an act of aggression if we officially entered California. But you, gentlemen, can follow him easily. As Englishmen you require no special passports to travel through Navajonia or California. I have an idea where Zenith might have landed the gyroplane he stole. It will be well guarded. Your task will be to capture Zenith and force him to fly the plane back to Texas. To her owners."

Dr Sinclair's expression of shock was clearly evident. Before he could speak, however, Begg silenced him with a touch.

"Mr Putz is at his ranch, perhaps? The old Engelbrecht farm in Crawford, if I'm not mistaken." Begg stared keenly at Shiner, watching his reaction.

"I regret in these troubled times I'm not at liberty to say, Sir Seaton. A question of homeland security."

"Quite." Begg finished his whisky. "Well, back to the quarry. We know that Zenith is an expert aeronaut. Do you think he had help stealing your plane?"

"Possibly." Shiner showed little interest in these somewhat crucial questions. "But he had already demonstrated his new engine to us, so we must assume he acted alone, fitting it to the gyroplane without our knowledge."

Begg was about to ask another question when he noticed a newcomer enter the bar. With a motion of her head, she acknowledged the many lifted hats and deep bows of the gentlemen greeting her. A stunningly beautiful woman, she dressed in the very latest fashion, her vivid scarlet gown blazing like a firebrand in the shadowy room. Never had a woman looked more elegant or self-assured. His eyes meeting hers in a secret exchange, Begg's frown cleared as if he at last understood something which had been puzzling him. Apparently she did not see Shiner and his guests and was soon absorbed in a flirtatious exchange with two cattlemen. Sinclair, too, noticed her, but Shiner had his back to the door. Neither Englishman remarked on her presence.

"And now," Shiner put in quickly, "how about some barbecue? Beef is our national dish, just as it is in England. Texans know how to roast meat, Sir Seaton! Only we prepare it with a little more fire and sweetness."

"And you also serve it with your wonderful maize," Begg responded. "They say Texas corn is the finest in the world."

They moved towards the restaurant, followed by at least half a dozen plainclothes Rangers. Almost at once the train of the newly arrived lady joined in behind them. Though she was surrounded by behatted suitors, it became impossible to pretend they were unacquainted. "Good evening, Mrs von Bek." With a bow Begg introduced all parties. Shiner already knew her, he said. With a half-growl he moved towards his table and sat down immediately. She in turn graciously shook Begg's and Sinclair's hands before strolling away to a distant table. It was not until the meal was in progress that Shiner produced a map marking the fastest road to California across what he called "Indian territory." Zenith might have taken over the old experimental aerodrome of Los Alamos near the Navajo border with Eastern California. "If so, Sir Seaton, you could use your famous resourcefulness to capture Zenith and force him to fly the gyrocopter back to Waterloo. We are prepared to pay a high price in Texan silver for the return of that machine. If you can't persuade him to return it peacefully, I authorize you to take whatever means necessary to achieve our desired objective. We're aware of your reputation, sir. You will not fail us. You know when to stick to the law's letter and when there is a greater justice to be served. And, of course, there will be a similar sum in Texas silver for Zenith's head . . ."

"Most generous, Mr Shiner," murmured the investigator. "It seems a simple enough case. Almost too simple. It's hard to understand why your president could not have put this plan into operation with his own people."

"Because he understands all about British discretion. Moreover, he cannot be seen to be doing these things himself. Our intelligence must seem to come from an individual, preferably *not* a Texan. It's the realities of modern politics, sir. Any other action would lead to too many awkward questions. And as I've said, our people would not be welcome over the border. We know you Brits to be subtle fellows, better at this sort of deception."

A quiet smile passed across Begg's lips as he exchanged a sardonic glance with his friend. "You flatter us, Mr Shiner."

"When will you set off after our friend?" Shiner wanted to know.

"Tomorrow morning would seem a sensible time."

"Very well. To save battery power you can take your brougham on the tram with you and transfer at the Navajonian border." Shiner got up, shaking hands. "I wish you good night and good luck, gentlemen."

"All seems distinctly fishy to me, Begg," said Taffy Sinclair when they were back in their suite. "It would not be the first time someone has tried to use us as what these chaps call 'the fall guy.' Are you really going to let him manipulate us like this? There seems to be at least one twist to which Shiner hasn't referred . . ."

"You mean the arrival of Mrs von Bek? Quite. I doubt she has been commissioned to perform the same peculiar task as ourselves. But I would bet my soul on her business being connected with ours. She almost certainly came over on the *Duchess of York*, probably disguised. It strikes me, Taffy, that the Wahabim sheikhs might have had one more wife than they realised, if they had stopped to count. She's playing her own game, and it would not be fair to spoil it, at least until we know whose side she's on. It's quite possible we are not actually on opposite sides . . ."

"Could she be in league with the mysterious Doctor Spin?"

"Oh, I suspect there could very well be a connection." Begg did not seem greatly upset by the prospect. "Perhaps we'll meet later."

"Are we really going to leave for California in the morning?"

"You know me too well, Taffy, to ask that question. Of course we're not. Shiner was too eager for us to follow his plan. There's already too much that doesn't quite add up, and the presence of Mrs von Bek further complicates the case. Before we do anything at all we're going to pay a visit to the Engelbrecht farm. I need to get some idea what 'King' George Putz and his people are really up to. Why doesn't Mr Shiner want us to meet his president? Happily he's provided us with a fine map, and it will be possible to go a good distance before stopping to recharge Dolly's battery. Meanwhile I must return to the public parts of the hotel. I have some unfinished business there. My advice to you, old boy, is to get a spot of sleep while you can."

And with that the metatemporal detective moved softly from the room and was gone. For a moment Dr Sinclair thought of asking a question; then his head sank into his pillow and he gratefully gave himself up to Morpheus.

In the bar Begg knew where the only single woman would be found. Mrs von Bek was, as he had predicted, sitting near the automatic piano listening to the electric music rolling from its jet and brass amplifiers. The singer was a grinning fellow wearing a fortune in gold dentistry. Nobody appeared to appreciate it as he exercised his mouth. Mrs von Bek was so still she resembled a beautiful statue. Her smile was spontaneous enough, however, when Sir Seaton courteously asked if he could join her at her table.

He wasted little time with further politeness. "I would guess it is not a coincidence that we both came over on the same ship?"

Her smile broadened. "So you guessed, cousin. What surprises me is that you should be lending your talents to such men as Shiner and his boss. These people are worse than common bandits."

"Well, most dynasties start as bandits, my dear. But I take your point. I have to make up my own mind about all this, and then I shall decide what I must do. You, I gather, are working for some foreign government not entirely friendly to Texas?"

"Quite so. How did you guess?" She arranged a stray lock of gleaming auburn hair.

"Mr Shiner wasn't exactly pleased to see you." They ordered drinks from the waiter and for a while sat listening to the music. "You're up to something significant, I take it?"

"If you like. I didn't entirely expect you to stay the night. I thought you'd be out on the prairie chasing wicked outlaws."

"The night's young." Their drinks arrived.

"Well, welcome to Waterloo." She raised her glass in a toast.

He smiled and lifted his own glass. "Thanks. Would you be here on an engineering matter also?"

"You could call it that."

She was not going to tell him anything substantial. He had expected nothing less. Instead, he enjoyed his drink, chatted casually with her for a while, and then bid her good night, satisfied that his instinctive judgements were, as Coutts would say, definitely on the money.

Back in his own apartment, Begg made some notes in the small book he carried, using his own special code to record his ideas. Then he closed the book, put it back in his pocket, and crossed to Sinclair's suite, gently shaking his friend awake.

So used was he to being wakened by his friend that Sinclair came alert in seconds. "What's the game, old boy?"

"We're paying a visit to the headquarters of the president of TPI. I need to know just a little more about our employers . . ."

Sinclair pulled on his trousers. "I should have thought it was jolly obvious what those chaps were—jumped up crooks, justifying their actions with mock politics and self-serving zealotry."

"Indeed they are, Taffy. But I suspect they are rather dangerous at the moment. If they start some kind of war down here, it could spread across the American Midwest, even involve the Yankee republics and the Confederation. Given that half those states are within the European sphere of influence, the way France owns most of Kansas and Wisconsin, such a war could easily draw in the entire civilised world. Years of peace in Europe would come to an end. You know the consequences. You've visited those hells which are the alternatives to what we and our kind hope to sustain. Do we want a world war here?"

"I take your point entirely, old boy." Sinclair's face was grave as he quickly buttoned his waistcoat.

"We can make it there and back in a few hours, Taffy, if we leave now." Seaton Begg busied himself with a small bag. He removed a case in which lay a pair of handsome Webley revolvers, handing one to his friend. "Better take this. We are going into territory where they shoot first and ask questions afterwards." He laughed. "A bit of a *Chums* jape, eh, old man!"

Within a quarter of an hour the Driskill's well-trained mechanics had eased Dolly from her stall in the hotel's underground garage. Then the two men were speeding out of Waterloo as a huge Texas moon shone down upon the hills and rivers around them. They followed the tramlines in the road, two silver streamers meeting in infinity, driving between huge live oaks and pecans until slowly but surely the trees became more stunted and the hills higher. The electric lights of Waterloo dropped behind them and vanished. Above them was the wide, velvet Texas sky, the vivid stars scattered across it. The silence of their drive was broken only by the occasional howl of a coyote or the hoot of a giant owl.

Waterloo was not a large city, and Texas was still chiefly cattle country, so it was not long before the road took the two detectives across wide prairie grazing lands on their way to the Sporting Dwarf Ranch, as Putz had renamed his farm, at a distance beyond the limit of the car's power. Only once did they come to a recharging station, Shorty's Power Stop, and, after a short wait in which they were able to refresh themselves with strong black coffee, were again on their way, knowing now that they had enough electricity to reach the ranch and return to Shorty's for a recharge.

Soon they came to a sign informing them they were now at the entrance to the old Engelbrecht place. PRIVATE PROPERTY. NO TRESPASSING. INTRUDERS WILL BE SHOT. The signs were everywhere.

"The more people put up such signs, the more they have to hide," murmured Begg. "Clearly the Texas Republic is not a believer in transparent government!" Disguising their brougham with branches in a nearby copse they proceeded on foot.

The long driveway ended at a set of gates guarded by uniformed men with carbines crooked in their arms. Texas Rangers.

Begg and Sinclair slipped into the shadows, listening to the chirping of cicadas, the occasional bark of a dog, the croaking of distant frogs. Begg had come well prepared. It took him no time to cut through the fence with the clippers he drew from his overcoat pocket while the only dog which bounded towards them was swiftly silenced with a single shot from his veterinarian's gun. The large mastiff would sleep peacefully for some hours.

The well-lit ranch house blossomed with the loud talk of men in convivial intercourse. Every so often a wave of laughter burst from the rooms in response to the comments of one drawling voice: "We must strike first before they hit us. But we need at least the silent acquiescence of the Europeans." Begg did not pause to listen. His prime interest was in the black outline of a large shed behind the house. It seemed too big for workers' quarters or stables.

"I had a feeling we might find something like this," he murmured as, cautiously, they approached. The building, black against the full moon, was also guarded, but Begg silently led his friend to the rear, shining the thin beam of a bullseye lantern on a set of large windows most of which were locked. One, however, was open, and through it the pair slipped noiselessly.

They entered a massive shed. Sinclair thought it must be several storeys high. Like Begg, he recognised it immediately. Though disguised on the outside as a barn, it was actually a gigantic airship hangar, and it did not take a moment to discover that it contained a huge flying leviathan. But, when Begg shone his flashlight's slender beam over the bulk of the ship above them, it became immediately obvious that this ship was only partially finished. Her control gondola, moreover, was queerly shaped, supporting engines very different in appearance from conventional steam turbines. Sir Seaton frowned as his beam picked out the insignia already painted on the great hull.

"Good lord," whispered Sinclair. "Have they stolen her? Red, white, and green. Those aren't the Texan colours. That bear is the emblem of the Californian Republic! Tell me, please, Begg. *Is* she stolen?"

Begg did not answer. His attention was now on the floor below divided into work cubicles. Here stood the conventional engines removed from the ship overhead so that she might be fitted with the new ones. But it was not the discarded engines which interested the detective. His flashlight beam fell on a pool of liquid. Blood? He crouched to inspect it, then straightened again, frowning.

Staring around him at the bizarre scene, Sinclair lifted his hand involuntarily to protect his nose, remarking on the acrid smell. Begg noticed it too. In one of the working cubicles he again squatted to look at something his beam had captured. It was a yellow-back novel with a typically vulgar cover. Leaning to pick it up he laid one hand on the floor and withdrew it quickly with an expression of disgust. Finding a rag, he wiped off whatever was on his hand and slipped the book into his pocket. Their beams continued to search until Begg exclaimed softly, spotting smashed remnants of some kind of electrical device, including a long strip of oddly shaped metal. This, too, went into his pocket, together with a small, beaded bag lying close beside it.

Suddenly alert, the detective straighted up. He had heard a noise from outside. "We'd better get clear, Taffy."

Quickly the two men crept to the window through which they had come. Within moments they were back in the open air, listening to the voices of guards as they talked amongst themselves. Thinking he had spotted something suspicious, one of the men was being reassured. Meanwhile Seaton Begg and Taffy Sinclair stole through the shadows, towards the long ranch house ahead. The men's voices from within had grown louder with drink. The detectives could hear their conversation clearly now.

"This way we clean up, gentlemen! The invasion of California will provide the distraction we need. Meanwhile we build a fleet to make us invincible. Since we'll be key suppliers of the fuel, no nation on earth will dare to resist us!"

"I would surely love to put a face on that speaker," murmured Begg. "It sounds like 'King' George Putz himself to me!" He was being drawn closer and closer to the ranch house as his curiosity got the better of his common sense. Sinclair, knowing his friend well, made some attempt to stop him.

This time their luck no longer held. All at once the area was flooded with powerful electric lights! They had set off a motion-controlled security device. The main door of the house was flung open, and Begg's suspicions were confirmed. Into the now illuminated porch stepped none other than "King" George Washington Putz, president of TPI, Texan oil, leader of the Senate, the most powerful man in Texas. He threw up a protective hand, staring out into the yard as Begg and Sinclair sought the shadows of the perimeter. "Who the hell's out there?" Now at least Begg was assured of the identity of the speaker!

Sinclair gasped in astonishment, his sense of decency outraged. Had he really been listening to the president of an international business enterprise?

The King's heavy, simian features clouded with confusion and anger. He waved a massive sixgun in his fist. "I'm gonna warn yuh! We shoot first and ask questions second in this neck o' the woods!" His high voice was at odds with his belligerent words.

Sinclair saw that they were slowly being surrounded by Rangers. He reached into his pocket and felt the grip of his Webley. Should he draw it? But Begg had guessed his dilemma, and a hand on his shoulder stopped any further movement. Disguising his voice Begg called from the blackness. "My apologies, sir. Our vehicle broke down some hours ago and we approached your ranch in the hope of getting help."

"This is private property," retaliated "King." "The only help you'll get from us is a butt full of buckshot. Can't you fellows read?" His scowling, heavy brow was furrowed with mystified hostility. "You don't even sound like Texans to me. What are you? Some kinda Californian snoopers?"

"No, sir, we have been commissioned . . ." Begg was about to try telling the "King" at least a version of the truth when from behind the ranch house came a confused shout and the sound of pistol shots.

Then out of the broken silence of the range came a thrilling whistle, a shriek, a howl, and all attention was on the darkness. Suddenly, disguised in various ways so that their features could not be seen, came an army of riders, cowboys and soldiers and Apaches, as disciplined a mixed light cavalry as

Begg had seen. From a moment's glimpse in the beam from the ranch, Begg was sure he recognised at least one of them.

All attention was on this new event. The detectives took the opportunity to seek the scant cover of the ranch's split-rail fence.

"Who are they?" whispered Sinclair.

Begg put his finger to his lips until they had found their way back to the paved road.

"Texas Volunteers, some call them. Terrorists according to Shiner's friends. Soldiers in the Army of the Republic of Texas." Panting, he paused, turned, and, in the wandering beam of a searchlight, clearly saw a figure on a white palomino, his white stetson firmly on his blue-masked face, his white bucksins trimmed with scarlet. "Aha! And here's an old acquaintance of mine! The Masked Buckaroo!" He raised his hand to wave even as Sinclair tried to suppress his gesture.

Hearing boots on the gravel, they turned again. They had not expected the roads to be guarded. But, even as the Rangers called for them to put up their hands, there came a further distraction.

At the Northern end of the ranch house stood a corral, but no animals were held there. Lights began to play over a shape which crouched like a giant insect on the ground. Begg and Sinclair made out the shadows of a score or so of men, all armed and milling in confusion. Again they were able to avoid capture as "King" George and his Rangers ran towards the corral yelling orders, firing their weapons seemingly at random until the sounds were suddenly drowned by a whining roar, a mighty, rising scream as if the insect creature on the ground was finally fighting back, hissing like a monstrous snake while emitting great clouds of steam that whirled into the appearance of a writhing tornado. Then came the animal roar of a powerful engine as the creature in the corral rose rapidly into the air and hovered, silhouetted for a moment against the moon. A bizarre flying machine, like a winged mantis, elongated and with two sets of short stubby wings stacked one above the other with a kind of umbrella device spinning rapidly above them. Meanwhile front and rear propellers began to turn as well. A wild, fierce wind blew, threatening to flatten the onlookers with its remarkable strength, and they were forced into a crouch, their coats flapping like sails.

"Zenith!" hissed Sinclair.

The angry men on the ground were now all firing upwards as the riders disappeared into the night and that bizarre, howling shadow rose against the moon, tilted slightly to the west, and moved rapidly away. An authorative shout silenced gunfire. To their relief Begg and Sinclair were forgotten.

"Now that turncoat Zenith's stolen *all* our aces!" they heard someone growl.

"He can hold us up to pay anything he asks, and he knows it. We've got to start working fast before he makes any more alliances with our neighbours."

"It's part of his weird personal code to offer us first refusal on our own secrets," said another. "He hates trading. If the price is right, he'll agree and that will be that."

"Call that guy what you like," said another, "he's got Texan nerve."

The King's reply was a grumbling mutter which could not be made out.

"While our luck lasts, I think we'd better make ourselves scarce, Taffy," whispered Begg. "I had not planned on there being a second autogyro. We're probably in rather more danger than I anticipated. While the King and his court are distracted, I'd suggest we make a run back to the wire!"

Sinclair was hard behind Begg as they dashed through the compound, almost tripping over the sleeping dog, and found the break they had made in the wire.

Suddenly there was a shout from behind them. A shot sounded. A bullet struck a fence post just as they began to climb through. Another shot. This time Sinclair winced, feeling the breeze of a shell passing his face. Now a virtual barrage of pistol fire whistled around them before at last they reached the copse where they had hidden the brougham and jumped in. Begg disengaged the brake and reversed into the driveway, turning the car as a dozen men rushed after them, some of them jumping to grab for the steering wheel. Sinclair struck out with the trained fist of a boxer catching one man on the side of the head, while another was kicked clear as he mounted the running board. More guns barked.

Then the car gathered speed, purring up to full momentum, diving into the darkness. The shots and the shouts receded as Dolly's superb electric motor took her up to almost a hundred miles an hour.

"Lost 'em!" declared Taffy, rubbing his knuckles.

"Not quite, old boy," Seaton Begg leaned forward over the wheel. "They have cars, too. Though Dolly has the edge on them, I'm sure. We still have to make it to the recharging station!"

"Do you think they saw the car clearly?"

"I doubt it. But they could have colleagues ahead—and they do have telephones. We'll put Dolly's top up to disguise her profile a bit. And we should put our hats on, too. That way no one will be certain it was us at the ranch."

"Was that really the Texan president we heard making those terrible plans?" Sinclair was still a little dazed. "I can hardly believe it!"

"*Calling* yourselves president or the Senate and *behaving* as such bodies are supposed to behave, are two different things down here, Taffy. People are still in the habit of honouring the name. They seem to have forgotten that titles go with the function. 'King' George and his boys are clearly in the process of dismantling any form of honest, representative government and replacing it with what is little more than gangsterdom with respectable names! I must admit this is rather what I suspected. Which was why I was attracted to the case. I want Zenith. But if we can alert the Texan people to the way in which they are being betrayed by their own leaders, so much the better!"

Begg's face was set in grim determination. It did not relax even when the lights were far behind them and the detectives switched on their own lamps. They passed one or two vehicles on the road, including several horsedrawn buggies. Begg slowed the mighty Duesenberg, anxious not to drain her batteries. To a contemplative Taffy it seemed no time had passed before they drew into the electricity station to hand the car over for Shorty himself to begin the recharging. They took their places at the same table, ordering coffee and sandwiches. Outside, whistling the latest cowboy hit off the marconi, the dwarfish Shorty McAllister, sole proprietor of the station, began the process of "juicing" Dolly up.

Under the bright lights of the café, Begg noticed how filthy his right hand was. It was stained almost black by whatever viscous stuff had been on the floor of the airship hangar. Not blood, but some sort of lubricant. Excusing himself, he went to the station facility and began scrubbing hard at the stuff, failing, after many minutes, to get his hand completely clean.

While at the basin he also took a surreptitious look at the piece of metal and the paperback book he had found in the great shed. He would give both more attention later, but already his brain was active, already putting together all his recent discoveries.

He was in no doubt at all that Shiner and his cronies intended to use two respectable Englishmen as cover for their nefarious plans. Begg was furious that his honour should be tainted in this way, and he meant to teach Shiner and the Senate a lesson.

Back at the table Sinclair was eating his sandwich. "So what do you think, Begg? At least we can be pretty sure that our friend Zenith's not in league with President Putz and his 'Family.' Any idea what happened back there?"

"None at all, old boy, apart from the obvious. I suspect we witnessed a very brazen sort of theft—and perhaps not just of a second gyroplane. Clearly the 'King' and his men weren't expecting someone to fly away with their Mark Two machine! Our presence inadvertently helped distract the guards while the thief made good his escape. I fear they won't think much of us for our part in the business, inadvertent as it was."

Doctor Sinclair snapped his fingers. "Aha! So there are *two* of the things. Another important point Mr Shiner 'forgot' to inform us about! No doubt we saw Zenith returning to steal the one he'd left behind!"

"It certainly looks that way, Taffy. But I don't think it's wise to confide in Mr Shiner any further, do you?"

"Are we going home to London?"

"Certainly not. Mr Shiner and his boss need to be taught a lesson. You don't drag the honour of old England through the mud for your own debased purposes and expect to get away with it! I intend to unravel this mystery and, when possible, teach a self-appointed Senate of a faux Republic the consequences of its actions!"

So engrossed was Begg in his plans and thoughts that it was almost too late before he looked up and found himself staring into the startled eyes of Mr McAllister. Shorty's gagged head was framed by half a dozen chromed six-guns held in the hands of stetson-wearing masked men all sporting some kind of homemade star on their clothing, the badge of the Republic of Texas.

In silent eloquence the men herded their three captives back into the darkness behind the diner. For some while they walked in silence. The Texan terrorists exchanged a few inaudible words.

After a fair distance they stopped. "Far enough, boys," announced one of the outlaws. "I guess we'd better do ol' Shorty here first. As he kindly explained to us, he was only working for the money 'King' George offered. But this other couple seem to be turncoats and spies of the worst order. We have special ways of dealing with them!"

In spite of their protests Begg and Sinclair were forced to watch as Shorty was relieved of his boots and jeans and told the way to the nearest town. A few pistol shots sent him, lively in his pink underwear, on his odyssey. Begg and Sinclair had no idea what was to be their fate, if that was the outlaws' idea of mercy.

At last they reached the foothills of a long line of eroded red mountains as the moon rose to illuminate the scene. Here the outlaws were joined by more of their number, this time mounted and bringing spare horses with them. With hands tied in front of them, Begg and Sinclair were each put on a horse.

The outlaws rode at a clip in silence for several hours before they eventually eased back and guided their ponies into a box canyon. Here they came to a stop. A match was struck and a brand lit. The leading horseman rode up to join them. He was a grizzled, amiable-looking oldster in a worn pair of blue denim overalls, a shock of grey bushy beard beneath permanently astonished blue eyes.

"Good evening, Mr Windy!" With difficulty Sir Seaton Begg attempted to raise his hat. "You look younger every year that passes!"

"I'll be goldurned," chuckled the ancient cowpuncher. "I know that voice an' I know that face—if I aint—tarnation!—it's Seaton Begg. My old pard as I love an' spit."

The firelight displayed the cheerful bewhiskered features of Windy O'Day, the Masked Buckaroo's well-known sidekick.

At that moment Tex Brady, the Buckaroo himself, rode up grinning, his mask pushed back. "Don't worry, Sir Seaton. I don't suspect you of any villainy whatsoever, though we're mighty curious to know why you're tanglin' with that varmint Georgie and his friends. There's not a true Texan amongst that bunch of sidewinders and coyotes. On the other hand, we know that you are as straight an hombre as every rode down the trail. You're a friend of true libertarians everywhere. You two are very welcome, gents.

"We had heard that Mr Shorty had instructions to alert King Georgie if any car came through these parts. So we thought we'd make things a little harder for Georgie's gang. And, we hope, a little easier for you."

"I appreciate your help more than I can say, sir." Sir Seaton had nothing but admiration for the young Texan, whom he saw as the best type of American, brave, rugged, and honest, with a love of liberty in his blood. "And you know you have my full support in your attempt to free your country of its self-elected tyrants."

The cowboy outlaws led Begg and Sinclair to the road where their car awaited them, fully charged and inspected and ready to go. "Georgie and his boys will be even more likely to suspect you now," warned young Tex Brady. "You are in greater danger than ever, gentlemen."

"Oh, I think we're safe enough," Begg reassured him. For a moment he exchanged a few quiet words with young Tex. This was the first time Taffy Sinclair had met the famous Masked Buckaroo, although he knew the story of how young Tex's father had been a friend of Sir Sinclair's and how the two had formed a bond. The first Buckaroo had brought justice and law to the wild Texas plains, then had donned the famous uniform in order to fight as a vigilante against big land corporations. His son had followed in his footsteps, as events demanded. Their famous red, white, and blue uniform had struck fear in the hearts of violent men, whether native or settlers. There were few who loved liberty more and understood its price better.

Sir Seaton engaged the motor and with a comradely wave to the mixed squadron of cowboys and Apaches, he and Sinclair made the rest of their journey in record time, had the car garaged and were in their room by three AM precisely. Begg showed no sign of tiredness. Instead, he placed the beaded bag and the strip of metal he had found on the table. "Are you too sleepy to take a look at these tonight, old man?"

"Not a bit, Begg." On a case, Sinclair showed some of his friend's own tirelessness. "What else did you find?"

"This book."

Sinclair picked it up. "Why, it's in Spanish! *Os Mundos Dividos*? Pretty garish cover. Some sort of science thriller." He looked at the other objects Begg had placed there. "A queer looking strip of metal. And a small red, white, and blue beaded bag. Looks like it was made by the local aboriginals."

"It's Navajo, Taffy, or Diné, as they prefer to be known. It links Zenith in some way with the Diné people. I'd call it a fetish bag of some sort. Its owner would be glad to get it back. What do you make of the metal strip?"

The pathologist's eye was as keen as his friend's. "Hmmm. This is odd. Two things like—what?—poppers, a seamstress might call them. The sort of thing you find on clothes instead of buttons, only larger. And these marks. A plus sign and a minus sign. Why, it reminds me of what they clip on to car batteries when recharging 'em!"

"Exactly."

"I understood this new engine to be of a chemical nature. Yet this suggests they were experimenting with conventional electrical motors. Or are they steam-generated like the big airship engines?"

Sir Seaton glanced down at his hand. It was still dirty. "Evidently they have modified those steam engines. If rapidly heated chemicals are the secret, this could be the chemical in question, Taffy. A very thoroughly refined oil, such as that used for clocks or guns."

"Well, I'm no scientific genius, I'm afraid, Begg, and I hadn't realised Zenith was either." Sinclair stretched and yawned. "And where do you believe Zenith is conducting his experiments? Did he take that gyrocopter back to California? Surely—?"

"I know what you're thinking. The range would be too great for him to get all the way to California. The plane would have had to stop more than once. Unless, of course, the engine was already delivering the kind of power Zenith promised! I don't think, incidentally, that Zenith is the inventor of any of this. In the past he's paid people to invent things for him, or stolen formulae, or otherwise acquired some invention, like the tanks he intended to use in the big jewellery theft he planned and which we foiled. So I'm sure he did steal this idea, probably from the Wahabim. But what puzzles me is why the Arabs have not pursued him with greater vigour. Could they, like the French, have abandoned their experiments and actually lost interest in what Zenith tries to do with their leftovers?"

"Very likely, old boy. Makes sense." Stifling another yawn, Sinclair nodded. "I wonder where the mysterious Doctor Spin fits into all this?"

"I suspect he doesn't, Taffy. I can guess who hoped to divert us with that note."

"And who would that be? Someone I know?"

Sir Seaton smiled. "Sleep on it, old man. There are a couple of things we need to do as early as possible. Check the guest records, for one thing. They should confirm my suspicion!"

He did not elaborate, and Doctor Sinclair was far too sleepy to question him further.

~✺ CHAPTER THREE ✺~

The Third Factor

Next morning both men breakfasted earlier than usual. As he laid down his marmalade knife, Begg asked Sinclair to give the apartments one last look round and follow him to the ground floor in a few moments. "I know how Doctor Spin likes to operate, and this doesn't feel like him. I just need to confirm for myself that he has not stayed in or visited this hotel at all. There's at least one very clever mind at work here, Taffy. My current need is to eliminate which of those suspected minds it is. Then we shall have the beginnings of the solution to our puzzle. Now for a word with the reception clerk, since they often know far more than they realise. A routine check of the hotel register should tell us if a particular, favoured pseudonym has made its appearance. It's surprising how easy and dull much detective work can be!"

Taffy Sinclair was in fact further surprised when, choosing the stairs rather than the elevator, he emerged into a secluded area of the hotel to find his friend taking coffee with Mrs von Bek.

Somewhat embarrassed, Doctor Sinclair made to leave, but Sir Seaton rose, beaming. "I bumped into Mrs von Bek in the lobby, and she asked me to join her for coffee. We were just saying goodbye. Won't you join us, Taffy?"

"Very kind of you. Better not. Thanks all the same. Everything else checked out, old boy, did it?" asked Sinclair. "I've seen to the bags and so forth and the car . . ." His voice petered out. He did not know how much to reveal in Mrs von Bek's presence.

"Aha! The car. Did they pack it before bringing it round?"

"I believe they did."

"It seems we are to say farewell again, Sir Seaton." Mrs von Bek rose elegantly from her place and offered the detective her hand. "I should have liked to have spoken with you a little longer. But meanwhile I wish you a pleasant journey."

"As always, Mrs von Bek, I am in your debt." Sir Seaton bent to kiss her beautiful fingers. "I will remember what you have told me. We are dealing with ruthless individuals, it seems."

"More ruthless than most in this degenerate age, Sir Seaton."

On their way out of the hotel, they paused only briefly in the lobby so that Sir Seaton might scribble a quick note to Shiner who had paid for their room in advance. Their business done, the two men left the lobby and were about to enter the massive tourer when Begg paused at Dolly's side and looked down between the two front seats. From the leather, he picked up the small object wedged there.

"Hello!"

Holding the thing delicately in his still partly blackened hand he sniffed. "That's interesting. It hardly seems to have been casually dropped. What would you say it was, Taffy?"

Sinclair took it and put it to his nose. "By heaven, Begg! It's an ebony cigarette holder containing the remains of an opium cigarette. Hardly a mystery as to who was here, eh? There's only one man I know of who smokes cigarettes like that. Monsieur Zenith. That crook genius is everywhere! How on earth—?"

Smiling cheerfully Begg dropped the holder and its drugged cigarette into his pocket, pushed his hat up from his forehead, and mounted the Duesenberg. "I wouldn't be at all surprised if Dolly didn't contain one or two other mementoes indicating that Zenith has been enjoying her company!" Before he started the motor he leaned back and surveyed their luggage, testing the steadiness of the stack, pulling at the securing straps. He sniffed again, tugged a dressing case from the pile and pressed it to his ear, then put it firmly back into place.

"You don't think he's stolen anything, do you, Begg? Or sabotaged the car in some way?"

"I don't think Zenith has committed *any* crime against us, Taffy." Begg started the car and let the powerful purring motor pull forward.

Distant hills, gentle fields with grazing cattle, rural ponds with ducks and geese, all these fled by as they headed westward out of town. This part of Texas was atypical of the rest of the nation. Its landscapes resembled those of Gainsborough rather than Corville. There were no romantic Turkish-Texan cattle herders and their camels festooned with weapons and savage dandyism. Here were groves of gentle oaks and loblolly pines in pastures tended by men in wide sombreros and blue overalls where lowing cattle were taken in and out for milking. Something of an English idyll even at night, and by day it tugged at any European's heart. It seemed to be Eden rediscovered after so many disappointments. Yet here, too, were serpents.

It would be another two hours before they needed to make a recharging stop.

"I had absolutely no idea that this part of the world was so attractive," said Sinclair. "It's like Oxfordshire. I'm surprised so few people have settled here."

"A great many people by Texas standards, old boy. But there will doubt-less be more if the nation ever gets a chance to exploit her true potential. I can see a splendid future ahead, especially if she were to accept French investment."

"Can you see the present establishment moving this country forward, Begg? I can't."

Begg made no reply. On that note they continued out of Gainsborough country into semi-scrubland where longhorn cattle looked up with sleepy eyes to watch their car go by. At this junction Begg turned Dolly off the road and stopped the car.

"What is it, Begg?"

Not answering, Sir Seaton unstrapped the bags, sniffing each one and lis-tening to them as he stacked them beside the car. Then suddenly he seized the small dressing case and flung it over the fence into a nearby stock tank. There came a tremendous explosion. Muddy water gouted up, spattering them and the car, leaving Dr Sinclair decidedly pale. In the distance a herd of longhorns stampeded away throwing up clouds of dust.

"Good heavens, Begg! How on earth did you guess the case was booby-trapped? Zenith?"

"Perhaps, Taffy. But I noticed the lock of that particular valise had been tampered with and had an idea our lives were in danger. No doubt it was a bomb timed to explode when we crossed the border from Texas, either into Dinéland or California. That, I'm afraid, I couldn't risk investigating. Not only did I hear the ticking of a clock which should not be in the case, but I smelled cordite. One of the parties we encountered last night wants us off the job!"

"What a cowardly thing to do. I did not think the Albino would sink to such methods. *Cherchez la femme?*"

"I know you always look for the woman in the case, Taffy, but here I am not so sure. Certainly clues were planted to make it look like Zenith's work. No doubt there are others, apart from the opium cigarette. But the distant assassination of an old enemy like myself? I think not. I suspect a cruder hand altogether. Zenith would be a useful name to attach to our murder, of course. It would strengthen the Family's cause. Oh, do not believe we are free of him. Zenith might still stalk us, but he has a better sense of melodrama! I doubt if he fears us just yet."

"He has proven himself highly successful so far!"

"It appears so. Come on, old man. Give me a hand reloading this luggage. The greater the speed we can make today, the better."

Already a curious rancher was riding over the prairie towards them, anxious to discover the source of the explosion. Unwilling to be involved in lengthy explanations, Begg cupped his hands to his mouth and shouted an apology and a reassurance. They were not harmed, and he hoped no damage was done.

Some fifty miles further down the road they watched a big vehicle transporter pulling into a tram station. Begg was tired of driving but did not want to stop to recharge. After a simple negotiation with the ticket master, they drove Dolly onto one of the vacant flat cars and were soon enjoying the interior comfort of the very latest in luxury trams. Moving smoothly towards the border, the powering car's equipment automatically "juiced" the great Duesenberg. By this means the metatemporal detectives were able to catch up on their sleep. Overhead power cables sparking and spitting, the scarlet and brass Keswick-built J-Class tram bore them steadily westwards on gleaming rails while the sun rose above, beating down on the tawny ochre and golden scrub of the semi-desert. They lunched from an excellent, if limited, menu and by afternoon caught their first glimpse of Narbona framed against a pale blue sky. They were about to cross the border into the Constitutional Monarchy of the Diné People, known in Texas as Navajonia. The CMDP's wealth, courtesy, and pacifism were watchwords throughout the civilised world.

Gradually the streams of traffic increased as the roads widened becoming broad bypasses or feeder roads into parts of the city herself. She was a model of modern architecture. Begg admired the logic and common sense which had been put into her design. "I hope other cities take note," he said to Sinclair. "Europe still has much to learn from Navajonia. But will she learn, old boy? The question sometimes seems moot. Only in a few places like Narbona does reason seem to have taken precedence over mindless greed. Once it was impossible to build too quickly, so that structure and infrastructure grew together. Now so many of these places remind me of imitation buildings. Stage sets. Shapes erected by cargo cultists to attract good fortune. In Narbona everything works. Function comes first. But in Waterloo, for instance, I noticed that form preceded function. Many of the things they have built do not and could not actually work. Did you notice how poor the plumbing was? They are there for show. As if that is enough."

"And do you draw any conclusions from this, Begg?"

Begg was laughing at himself. "Only that illusion is more important than actuality these days. I suspect you and I knew that already, Taffy."

Still smiling he joined the flow of the traffic.

Narbona was a bustling metropolis, her tall white buildings predominantly in the Pueblo style. A network of tramways and overhead lines crisscrossed clean, busy streets crowded with every type of electric carriage. Wealth poured into the city from many sources, not least Dinéland's silver mines and her stock exchange. She was known as the Queen of the West, the commercial and cultural apex of the region. In Las Vegas, capital of Dinéland, her hereditary princess and her parliament, based on the British model of constitutional monarchy, administered a programme of social services and educational systems which were a model for the world. Her buildings, constructed primarily in artificial adobe and aluminium, were not especially distinguished, though here and there a magnificent piece of modern Pueblo architecture rose up. In Narbona all the Diné's business was done, attracting every kind of trade and trader, not all of them beyond reproach, but subject to the strict laws and high taxes of the Diné nation. In "Navajonia," as opposed to her neighbour, Texas, people were content to pay their taxes because they received excellent value in exchange, including a small but thoroughly modern constabulary.

Crossing the border from one country into another, Begg and Sinclair were glad of their fluent Spanish while Begg was also able to hold a passable conversation in Diné. Their British passports were handled with respect and duly stamped, but not a single word of English was spoken. It was well known that the Diné were sensitive concerning their neighbours' ignorance of their own language. While they knew they could never get a Texan to learn Diné, they at least had the satisfaction of making him learn some Spanish.

Suddenly all the road signs were in Spanish or Diné with only a few offering English. The Diné people spoke and published in their own language, but the *lingua franca* they had adopted was the legacy of old Spanish missionaries. Smartly uniformed and friendly customs people saluted the detectives. Within moments they were driving through the barriers and into the streets of Narbona, seeking signs to the highway Begg had chosen.

"Not California, then?" said Sinclair.

"As you guessed, Taffy. I think we'll have the most luck if we head in the general direction of Las Vegas. And then I trust you'll keep your eyes peeled for what we were talking about before we left the hotel! You know the sort of installation we're looking for. The kind put up by gas prospectors."

"I think I've seen those structures before, as we were driving through Texas. But why would the Navajo build them, too?"

"For one reason, Taffy. So that they can experiment with the same type of engines. But it is not the Navajo who are worrying me! As you shall soon discover, I hope!"

Suddenly, without explanation, Sir Seaton Begg swung Dolly off the main highway and up a small side street.

"So it's not Las Vegas, after all . . ."

Sir Seaton smiled apologetically. "No, we're still on the right road, but I had an exchange of telegrams while at the Driskill and am hoping my codes were understood. We're looking for a modest, suburban house." Slowly the car eased her way through the leafy roads. "Aha. Number Seventy-two Cypress. Here we are. I'm so sorry I couldn't risk revealing this information to you, old man, but I know you'll understand."

Dr Sinclair did not care for the kind of surprises Begg seemed to love, but he tightened his lips and said nothing as they disembarked from the car and walked up the drive of the small, neat house. The door was opened before they could ring the bell. They were ushered into the gloom of a place clearly not lived in and rarely visited. In one of the big easy chairs sat a middle-aged woman whom Sinclair instantly recognised. He gasped with surprise and scarcely knew how to comport himself. Recognising his distress, she smiled and stretched a hand towards him. "How nice to meet you, Doctor Sinclair. We have heard so much about you and your clever companion."

And with that Taffy Sinclair was allowed to kiss the hand of the Princess of Navajonia, the most powerful individual in the land. He scarcely heard as his old friend quickly discussed the situation with the princess and her advisors.

"It is quite possible, Sir Seaton, that Count Zenith is using a secret base somewhere in our country. Our foreign minister has a map of places of the kind you are interested in. They were spotted by our airships but proved generally pretty inaccessible from the road." A young man, wearing traditional tribal clothes, stepped forward and offered Sir Seaton a folded sheet of paper. With a short bow, he retired.

"But we have no arrangement with Count Zenith, Sir Seaton," the princess continued. "It would be against all we stand for to allow a common criminal like that to work for us."

"Only the true shall build what is true."

Her round, kindly face suddenly beamed. "Oh, you know us well, I think, Sir Seaton. We are pleased with our institutions. They work for us. We have no wish to impose them on anyone else. All we wish to do is live at peace with our neighbours, trade with them, and otherwise interact with them on a friendly basis. It is not a question of gaining an upper hand but of us all improving our fortunes together. This does not impress King George or Dicky Shiner as a good idea. They want to be seen to be 'winning,' and sooner or later that kind of thinking gets you in exactly the opposite place you want to be. Eventually they will be seen to be 'losing,' at least in their own eyes. Sadly, Sir Seaton, they represent a very variable and uncertain element in the politics of this region. While we would never consider attacking Texas and have an army which exists only to defend us, we are sometimes tempted to wonder what would become of her if she had a better and more democratic government!"

"Naturally you can only pray for that day," said Sir Seaton gravely.

"Naturally," said the princess. "And our sympathies are, after all, our sympathies. I hope you will be staying for dinner, gentlemen. We have other guests I'm sure you would like to meet. Mr and Mrs Brady I think you already know. Also Mr O'Day. But there are more . . ."

"Not the Brazilian, I take it?"

"Unfortunately not. I gather the problem is in hand."

"The most competent hands I can think of," said Begg with a bow and a smile. "I fear time is too pressing, your majesty, much as we are honoured by the invitation."

The princess made her gracious farewells. "I wish you the very best of luck, gentlemen," she said. "You are true Englishmen, and you are about to do a very brave thing."

"Brave?" enquired Taffy Sinclair when they were in the car together and back on the road. "What did her majesty mean by that, old man?"

"Oh, you know these foreigners. Always exaggerating." And that was the only answer to his question Doctor Taffy Sinclair ever received. He was, however, becoming aware of a pattern of foreign politics as his friend pieced his own puzzle together. He was about to speak when Begg smiled again. "You are quite right, old man. We have stepped into the story, as it were, after it has begun. There's a complicated bit of international politics going on at the moment, and I have to admit to you now that I have known about the problem for some time, as has our own government. At the present moment a number of factors are coming together. If we can act in a timely manner and in a certain way, we have some chance not only of keeping this world stable in every sense of the word, but of adding to that stability."

"That's all I need to know, old boy," replied a satisfied Taffy Sinclair. There were good reasons why this man of iron integrity and modest demeanour was the trusted companion of the multiverse's greatest metatemporal detective.

The day remained magnificent as the great web of tramlines gave way to a few single tracks. The eroded mountains and hills of the semi-desert rose around them. Sage brush and saguaro cacti became common and the landscape was coloured by great blossoming jeremiahs and yucca. Sinclair was content to admire it until, suddenly, he became alert, lifting his powerful binoculars to his eyes. "Over there, Begg! I think I see exactly what we're after. What extraordinary luck! If it is luck, of course." He smiled. "Your instincts remain as keen as ever."

"I assumed we would have to be on a route between major cities, old boy. And one must be on the watch for specific features, as you were. We know the whys and wherefores of the situation. We also know that certain supplies have to be brought in, even if the main ingredient is on the doorstep, as it were. Let's have a look." And Sir Seaton Begg stopped the Duesenberg, accepting the glasses from his friend. "Aha! This could be it. And look—narrow-gauge temporary tramlines leading directly into the area. They must have been specially laid. Now all we have to hope for is a road!"

They drove on until they came to a small dirt track winding up through low hills. A barrier stretched across the path and a sign in Diné and Spanish forbid entrance.

"Which means," said Begg, smiling, "we should proceed on foot. Here we go, Taffy. Do you still have your Webley?"

"I certainly do, Begg. Am I going to need it?"

"Not against the law-abiding Diné, I'm sure. But if that gas prospector's rig and site refinery you spotted is anything to go by, we might have found our man Zenith. If not, we must keep looking. Yet every instinct in me tells me—"

Leading the way Begg began to climb over the barrier and then froze suddenly as a familiar voice spoke from the nearby rocks. "You disappoint me, Sir Seaton. I understood you to be fluent in Spanish. Yet you don't seem to be able to read a simple sign."

Holding a pistol which she trained firmly on the two men, out stepped the stunning woman they had both seen at the Driskill Hotel the previous evening. She gave no indication that she and Begg were intimates. She was dressed in a lightweight travelling coat of cream linen. The wide brimmed sombrero covered part of her face but did not hide her green, mocking eyes.

With a bow Sir Seaton Begg lifted his hands. "I am at your mercy, Mrs von Bek. It is a pleasure to meet you again so soon. I was misled. I understood you to be about to enjoy dinner with a very distinguished group of Texan libertarians. Are we coming or, as it were, going? You are an elusive person, Mrs von Bek." His smile denied any accusation.

Stepping from cover, Mrs von Bek made a movement of her left hand. Half a dozen well-armed Diné police officers joined her, surrounding the two men and regarding them with expressionless faces. They wore the traditional dress of the Diné constabulary, including headbands, shirts, breechclouts, leggings, and soft boots. "I don't understand you, Sir Seaton. If I am not mistaken, you are the one who allies himself with political cynics, the enemies of all decent civilised people. At the Driskill it simply would not have occurred to me that you were really in league with such people. Has Texan silver the power to compromise you, these days?"

"You, of course, initially suspected my affiliations, I know, Mrs von Bek, and wished to keep me out of the game for as long as possible. Why else would you have attempted to divert us with that red herring concerning Doctor Spin? It was you who wrote that note." His face creased in amusement. "I am not your enemy. You will recall I am something of a friend . . ."

She smiled in open admiration of his powers of deduction. "But that still doesn't help me understand why you are working for some of the most corrupt interests in the modern world."

"You refer, I suppose, to Mr Shiner, President Putz, and the rest of those Texans who make up the local chapter of the infamous Family of Fear? Yes, it appears that I am working for them. They are indeed the ones who plan to plunge this region into war for what they believe to be their own profit and power."

Taffy Sinclair did his best to hide his astonishment. "Do you mean to say we have been so thoroughly duped by those people, Begg?"

"Not only that, Taffy, but my guess is they are the ones who tried to murder us and put the blame on Zenith. That bomb should have gone off about now, when we were well into Navajonia and neither Shiner nor his associates would be held responsible for our deaths. The opium cigarette would have pointed the finger squarely at Zenith!"

Sir Seaton Begg turned to his captor with another slight bow. "I suspect you are working for the Brazilian government, Mrs von Bek, and that your quest is pretty much the same as ours."

Mrs von Bek drew back her linen coat and holstered her pistol, but the Diné soldiers did not lower their carbines. "Shiner tried to kill you, did he? Why is that?"

"We were no longer serving the purpose for which he had brought us to Texas. We had discovered some of the truth about his employer. We knew he was lying to us. They had not anticipated this, and their instinctive reaction was to eliminate us!" Swiftly Sir Seaton outlined what he and Sinclair had been told and what they had learned since arriving in Texas. "So I assumed the business in London was a charade to whet my appetite for the case, to involve me on a number of levels. To associate me and the Texans in the mind, for instance, of Inspector Coutts. Merely for insurance purposes, I suspect. My reputation would ensure that the world perceived their motives as honest. I am still not entirely sure of their plans. I knew at once, however, that they were plotting something pretty nefarious when I saw the Californian colours painted on the side of the giant airship they have out at the Engelbrecht farm. Do you know anything about that, Mrs von Bek?"

"I have some idea, Sir Seaton." She gave a signal and her warriors uncocked their carbines. "I believe you and I have information to share which will prove of mutual benefit. I suspect we have a common enemy. I was a little optimistic about that dinner engagement. That common enemy is—"

"The man I am here to find. In order to come face to face with him I originally took this case. Monsieur Zenith, the Albino."

"Precisely." She glanced at the gates and the trail beyond. "We had better return to the road where we're less likely to be spotted." Once back on the public road, they arranged themselves around Begg's car while Sinclair took out their vacuum flask and a small hamper to share with the newcomers.

"So you have already deduced that Zenith was using a refined oil-fired motor?" she said, spreading her skirts to sit down. "I didn't suspect the Family's airship was flying Californian colours, however. How did you work out where Zenith's headquarters were?"

"I didn't," Begg answered. "I merely knew that he was using highly refined oil as the 'chemical' fuel Shiner had mentioned. What's more, Texas is well known to have large deposits of that generally useless fluid, as does the Wahab, and it seemed to me that Zenith had persuaded the Family of Fear, which effectively rules Texas now, of a use for the stuff. I think he heats it somehow and produces concentrated steam. However, that isn't why you're here is it? If you're working for the Brazilians, then you're after O'Bean."

"The Texan branch of the Family kidnapped him some weeks ago. I was commissioned to track him down after the Brazilian agents had failed."

"Last night," said Begg, "Zenith made a daring raid on their secret base where I guessed they had been holding O'Bean. I came across a paperback book. *Os Mundos Dividos*. Not in Spanish, Taffy, but in Portugese—the language of Brazil. Just before we arrived, Zenith freed O'Bean and then escaped with him in the other stolen gyroplane. Our poor engineering wizard probably had no choice in the matter—"

Mrs von Bek smiled admiringly at the metatemporal detective. Some said she was his only true rival in deductive powers. ". . . and Zenith has almost certainly brought him here. Anywhere further away would have meant a stop to refuel and, of course . . ."

". . . he can't refuel an experimental flying machine at your ordinary recharging station!" Taffy shook his head in wonderment. "Great Abraham, Begg! Your brain never fails to astonish me. Yours, too, Mrs von B. That's why you had a rough idea of where he would be! And that oil rig out there, together with a refining plant, is where he's holding both O'Bean and his stolen machines! This means that Zenith is as good as in our hands."

Both Mrs von Bek and Sir Seaton Begg laughed at this.

"Not quite, Taffy, old boy. It seems we've found his lair. But it wouldn't be the first time we've been this close to him and he's still managed to get away. Don't forget he now has *two* 'Texas Twisters' up there somewhere. Do you have a plan, Mrs von Bek?"

"I had started to work one out when you turned up. I would suggest you drive on in your car until you come to a bridge over a creek about half a mile up the road. You can easily hide the machine there. We will meet you, and I'll let you know my ideas."

"Splendid!" His eyes gleaming as they always did when the chase began to heat, Begg leapt into the Duesenberg. Soon he and Sinclair were on their way.

The pathologist had lost his usual reserve, and he looked almost as excited as his friend. "It seems, old man, that a long chapter in the annals of crime is about to come to a close. This will be an historic day!"

"One way or another, Taffy," remarked Begg, clapping his free hand on his friend's shoulder. "One way or another!"

━◉ CHAPTER FOUR ◈━

A Distinguished Guest

Little more than an hour later Sir Seaton Begg and his friend were lying on their stomachs carefully examining the collection of ramshackle huts and sheds surrounding the oil rig. The place was guarded by a high fence. To the casual eye it resembled a mining facility, of which there were dozens in the region. Through the binoculars, however, they could see that armed men patrolled the place at all times. Taffy was at last certain they were on the right trail.

"More than a simple prairie gas prospector, I'd say, wouldn't you, Begg?"

"I suspect you're right, Taffy, old boy."

A little more scouting and the detectives found that the stolen gyro-planes were disguised under large pole barns. At first there was no sign, however, of O'Bean or of the notorious albino crook.

Begg and Sinclair settled down patiently to wait.

Then, not long after tea time, Begg heard a voice he recognised. It was quiet, it was authoritative, it held a perpetual hint of irony and insouciance, and although the accent was that of a good English public school, there was a slight foreign cast to it.

Begg and Sinclair were alert at once.

A tall figure appeared at the door of one of the huts. He was clearly preparing to turn a key in a padlock and was addressing his unseen prisoner. The fact that he was powerfully built, extraordinarily elegant, and clad in full, perfect evening dress, was not the most striking thing about the man. For this was very obviously Zenith himself. He was an albino with bone-white skin, milk white hair, and blazing ruby eyes. Under his arm he carried an ebony cane. In his hand was his ebony cigarette holder.

"My dear sir, I am not going to kill you, have no fear of that. I can think of few circumstances where that would fit in either with my ambitions or indeed with that silly set of rules I give myself to live by. But I do intend to keep you here for as long as need be, while your wife and children and all your many friends are driven to distraction by your disappearance. You are a man of imagination, sir, as I am. I am not sure, however, what other qualities we share. Perhaps patience is one of them. Application, certainly. But I suspect you, Senhor O'Bean, are a little more sentimental than myself. I will bid you goodnight now. And once again apologise for any discomfort you are experiencing. We are a rough and ready lot, those of us who spend most of their lives out here in the wild."

This last was spoken on so many levels of implication that a man of imagination might well consider not only the anxieties of his loved ones but the steely cruelty which informed his captor's character. The two detectives exchanged glances. There was no bargaining once Zenith the Albino had announced the bidding closed.

Knowing how useless his life would be in Zenith's power, no matter how long he lived or how much he resisted his emotional attachments, O'Bean might actually consider giving up his secret. It was all Zenith asked of him, after all. Or so it seemed. Then, of course, thought Begg as he digested the scene before him, there will be the problem of keeping the secret one's own. A living O'Bean would always threaten that secret's security.

Begg murmured that he had no doubts that the same thoughts occurred to the Brazilian engineer. "It's a tricky one, Taffy," he whispered. "Can the Albino be trusted to keep his bargain? On the one hand, there's his famous 'honour code,' to which he sticks rigidly at all times. If he gives his word, then it is minted in gold. Yet how he phrases his word might bear close examination." On the other hand, there was the cold logic of the situation and the millions at stake. A living O'Bean was a very distinct liability to Monsieur Zenith. Perhaps the unfolding situation would reveal a development no one had yet considered. Begg's glasses followed Zenith's impeccably clad figure as it crossed from the prison quarters to a large shack which, on inspection, was far less decrepit than it had initially looked. For a few minutes there was only the silence of the high desert.

From Zenith's quarters soon issued the unworldly strains of a violin. Even Begg was astonished. Then he smiled broadly, remembering his old opponent's only apparent passion—his passion for music. The strains were assured and subtle, from an instrument of extraordinary age and workmanship. At first Begg tried to identify the piece. Clearly, he thought, some modern master. But then he realised that the composer was Zenith himself. Gradually it moved from classical to romantic to contemporary structure, a perfectly integrated piece which led the listener slowly into the nuances of the music. Moreover it was somehow in perfect resonance with the landscape itself, as if the coyotes and armadillos and hunting birds all paused to listen. Against his better instincts, Begg moved in to hear the music better. Taffy tried to restrain him but failed. Soon Begg was almost fifty yards closer to the compound, and it was still clear daylight.

Astonished by the exquisite beauty and assurance of the music, Begg was for once caught unawares as from the corner of his eye he spotted a moving shadow. A mountain lion?

No. A burly man in a check shirt and a greasy black stetson who held a big forty-five in his hands and with a gap-toothed grin gestured for Begg to raise his hands.

Begg smiled, as if beaten, and gestured with the binoculars. "What do you want me to do with these?"

For a second the man's eyes were off Begg and on the glasses. Begg used that time well. The binoculars came up and forward, flung directly at the guard's face, while Begg threw himself to one side, rolling as he did so until he reached a dry river bed below the man's line of sight.

Silent as the cat he at first thought he had encountered, Sir Seaton Begg crept forward and to one side, circling the guard until he was behind the man, whose stunned eyes still searched the ground in front of him.

Then, as luck would have it, a swooping hawk dipped behind the guard's shoulder, and he turned just as Begg was raising himself up to make the short spring towards him.

"You'd better stop playing games with me, hombre, or I'm going to start pulling this trigger. I'm a pretty expert shot with this here pistol, and believe me there's real lead in these chambers."

"I assure you, old lad, that I am only playing the most serious of games. I have been shot at and someone has attempted to blow me up. I have suffered inclement weather and I will admit ultimately rather undistracting scenery. Forgive me for any natural ill temper which might have tempted me to use the glasses—"

A crude oath silenced Begg. But it also, apparently, made him vanish.

With another curse the guard began to stumble forward again. A faint shout came from the compound. The words could not be understood. The music stopped suddenly. Silence resumed. Begg knew he had no more time. In an instant he ran around the guard once more, so that he was again at his back. Then he dashed forward, catching hold of the hand which held the gun and wresting it from the astonished man's grip. Next he moved into a ju-jitsu stance and flung the big man down to the earth so hard that he was winded. Begg picked up the guard's forty-five.

Taffy Sinclair ran up to stand beside him, looking down in horror at the big guard. With a gesture, Begg silenced him.

"Okay," Begg said in the best version he could muster of a language the man would understand, "I'll level with you. I'm an agent working for the International Crime Control Bureau. We at the ICCB know exactly what your boss is up to and it's getting too bad for us to turn a blind eye. Tonight's the big raid. We've got a net fine enough to catch every one of you. Zenith can promise you the earth, but, when it's time to set off those bombs, he won't be worrying much if they blow you to smithereens. You know what he's like. They could go up at any moment. He wouldn't much care if they killed him, too, so he certainly wouldn't care if they destroyed you. The planes are only there so he can make his getaway along with partners you don't even know about. So here's the deal, my good man—start heading for Silver City now and no longer be part of Zenith's gang, or stay here and blow the whistle on me. Then take the consequences when the rest of my boys get here. What do you say? I'm giving you a break. Zenith wouldn't give you a break like that, would he?"

"Yeah, okay. This job's gotten outta hand anyway." The man rose under Begg's vigilant eye. "He never promised us a share of the loot, which I guess is worth millions, if not billions. And we haven't been paid for a while either. So I guess I know what's best for me, mister."

"You'll be thanking us, mark my words, when you read in your Narbona newspaper what has happened here tonight."

As he watched the guard heading as rapidly back towards Narbona as he could go, Begg sighed and returned his attention to the compound. It seemed that Zenith demanded total silence from his men when he was playing his violin. But the work was entering its last movement. It was time to fall back and discuss their plans.

Already the scarlet sun was sinking beyond the hills, sending deep, black shadows across the desert. In less than an hour it would be dark. Then the detectives planned to make their move, confident that Mrs von Bek was ready to fulfill her part of the plan.

"Are you sure you want to go through with this, Taffy, old man? After all, it could prove the most dangerous element of our operation."

"It's the best thing I could be doing," the pathologist told him. "You and Mrs von Bek have other work which I could not perform."

Sir Seaton Begg patted his friend on the shoulder, an expression of profound respect and consideration on his face. "Good man."

Eventually the sun dropped below the horizon and the temperature became distinctly cooler. Gradually the noises of the night replaced the silence of the day. At last the two men rose from their hiding place and crept carefully forward. Soon they lay behind clumps of prairie grass near the very gates of the installation.

One more clap on his friend's shoulder and Begg slid back again into the shadows while Sinclair suddenly set up a great bawling and yelling as he stumbled out of his hiding place towards the gates of Zenith's compound. "I say, let me in! Let me in! You've got to help me. There's dozens of wild savages out here. They're after my gold, I know it."

One of the guards came forward with a snarl, clearly believing Sinclair to be mad. "Off with you, you crazy old loon." He spoke with a Spanish accent and was clearly of native origin. "There's no savages out there. There's nothing but a few coyotes and some rattlesnakes and scorpions. And the rabid bat that bit you!"

"No, no, I mean it. I've been mining under licence up in the hills." Sinclair's own accent was a strange mixture of English and Texan. "I was on my way to town to bank my gold when my mule train was attacked by bandits. It's the Masked Buckaroo's boys, I'll swear. Anyway, they thought the gold was on the mules, but I'd already buried a lot of it. The rest is on me. You've got to help me. There must be fifty or sixty of them."

"There could be something in it, Rick. We was wonderin' why Jimmy hadn't come in from patrol yet."

Jimmy was no doubt the guard Begg had encouraged to return to Narbona.

Sinclair kept up his play-acting. "Yes, yes, it's true, gentlemen. I am in serious danger. You could be, also. Do you have a colleague, perhaps? I think I stumbled over his body."

Now all the guards were gathered around the gate. While their attention was distracted, Seaton Begg used his pocket wire cutters to make a hole in the fence large enough for him to slip through, carefully arranging the wire so it appeared nothing was disturbed.

"There's no gold mine around here," said one of the guards. "You're crazy. Get away with you or we'll be the hombres who shoot you! This is private property and our boss *really* don't like being disturbed."

"Please help me. I must have almost a million dollars worth of dust on me and buried less than a mile from here. They've already killed that big man in the check shirt. If you leave me out here, I'm lost! Help me, please gentlemen."

"What's the trouble, Estes?" A drawling, cultured voice spoke, quite unlike those of the guards. Light spilled out from one of the buildings, silhouetting a man who stepped into the compound. In spite of his surroundings, he still wore perfect evening dress and was smoking another thin, brown cigarette in an ebony holder.

As Zenith approached the gates he looked even more eccentric than he had at a distance, with bone-white skin and elegantly groomed white hair the colour of fresh milk. His eyes, as hard, as bright, and as red as rubies, focussed on Taffy Sinclair. "What further carrion disturbs my exile in this loathsome wilderness?"

"I beg your pardon, sir." Taffy Sinclair took a step forward. "I see you are a gentleman. I ask you as one to another, could you please spare me a little shelter for tonight. I am willing to pay handsomely."

For all his elegance and breeding, Zenith the Albino was evidently still a thief at heart. His manner changed at once and became suave. "Do forgive my guards, sir, but we have our own security problems, as you can imagine. We, too, are in a branch of the mining business."

From out of the darkness of the desert came a sudden bang, the sound of a rifle. Everything went silent. At Zenith's command, the compound's powerful searchlights turned into the darkness.

"There, you see!" Sinclair's amateur dramatics were thoroughly convincing. He rolled his eyes like a madman. "They are after my gold, I swear. You must help me."

The albino smiled quietly to himself. Perhaps he suspected a plot, but it was not like him to be put off by a little risk. He gestured languidly. "Let him in, Estes, but be careful. And keep those guns trained on the gates. One slip and I will have you all slaughtered like the sheep you are." With a bow the albino greeted Sinclair. "One moment while my man deals with the locks. My circumstances are sadly reduced, I fear, but you are welcome to what little I have. You must tell me about this gold mine. I thought gold had been largely abandoned for silver in these parts . . ."

"Only I bothered to search out the original seams," Sinclair told him. "They are often what led to the silver and were abandoned when silver was found to be more abundant. That's why I bought up deeds to abandoned mines, you see, sir . . ."

From the darkness, Sir Seaton Begg grinned admiringly at his friend's dramatic and creative talent.

The opportunity to help himself to a million in gold from a mad miner was not going to be wasted, even by Monsieur Zenith.

The gates were opened and Sinclair, still giving the impression of a man out of his mind with terror, stepped through. He knew he was risking death, that Zenith killed without question, but meanwhile he had given his friend the time he needed to sneak into the deep shadows of the compound and begin his task of locating the Brazilian wizard, O'Bean.

Now he must hope that Mrs von Bek and her men fulfilled their part of the plan.

With Zenith and his men distracted, Seaton Begg found the hut he was looking for. The windows were barred, and there was the lock on the outside he had already noted.

Begg had come properly prepared for this task. Using his powerful cutters again, he severed the hasp and the door swung open. Carefully he entered. His slender torchlight quested about the place. A table, a chair, a mechanical calculator. Some notebooks. A pile of lurid yellowbacks. Then, on the bed, he saw a sleeping figure. It was exactly the man he had expected.

Pulling the door shut behind him, Begg touched the sleeper lightly on his shoulder. The handsome, middle-aged man groaned and stirred. In spite of the tousled hair, the stubble on his jaw, the red-rimmed eyes, Begg knew at once that he had found his quarry. This was Honorary Deputy Luis O'Bean, the Brazilian Wizard, who had helped turn his nation into one of the most modern in the world, who had developed the long-distance airships which all countries now used, as well as the electrical engines which powered most of the world's tramways and road-transport, and had always refused to let his talents be put to warlike uses. It was rumoured that he could build a world-destroying bomb but had had the knowledge erased from his cortex by a surgical means of his own devising. Once his inventions were developed, they were free to the whole world. O'Bean believed that no nation should have an advantage over another, and that wherever possible such inequalities should be addressed. He had done much to ensure the peace of the world in recent years.[1]

---

1. Further accounts of O'Bean and his inventions are to be found in the Bastable sequence of memoirs most recently published as *A Nomad of the Time Streams* and in the Jerry Cornelius stories including *The Condition of Muzak*, which appears in the tetralogy, *The Cornelius Quartet*.

Speaking in Portugese, Begg said softly: "Your Excellency! Deputy O'Bean, I am here to rescue you."

O'Bean opened his eyes. There was cynicism in them. "That's what your colleague told me yesterday. And now here I am in a worse prison than the last one. I don't care what fresh hell you have proscribed for me, I tell you again, I refuse to give up the secrets of my engine. I will go to the grave before one part of that secret is passed on to you. I know exactly why you want it. Why would you trade the peace of mind of my children for such a secret when that same secret is likely to destroy them as it destroys children like them all over the world? Do you think, if I have the imagination to consider my wife and children, I cannot imagine the grief of another wife, other children, another man like me? Whatever you do will not make me forget that."

"I assure you, sir, I have no intention of stealing your secret or using it for military purposes. I have always supported and admired your moral position. My name is Seaton Begg. I am a metatemporal investigator. I deduced you had been taken prisoner by the Texans and that Zenith the Albino had kidnapped you. I am here to get you to safety if I can. But we must be quick and we must be quiet."

Slowly O'Bean swung out of his bunk rubbing his eyes. He dressed rapidly and soon stood beside Begg. "That monster has the devil's patience. He was going to begin a subtle torture tomorrow by sending my family pictures of me as I am now. He wants to sell the plans for my new electrical batteries as well as the stolen aeroplanes. Together they will command any price. The price of a nation if necessary. But what nation would pay so much? I will not permit it. I delayed those Texans as long as I could while I actually dismantled and made unuseable the experimental engine they had come by. They were furious, of course, and I think some of King George's men wanted to kill me. But they were trying to persuade me to build another engine when Zenith arrived.

"Zenith pretended to be my friend and said that he wanted to help me get back to Brazil. Ultimately he stole not only the second autogyro but, as it happened, the only man in the world who knew how to build an effective engine to power it. I thought he was taking me to Brazil, of course.

You can imagine how I felt when I found myself here and in a worse situation than before."

"Just as I suspected, sir. You'll be pleased to know they could not reconstruct the engine you destroyed. I came across its remains. We were a little too late ourselves in coming to your rescue. I had deduced where you were being held. But Zenith works with incredible speed. I am always surprised by the Albino's powers of persuasion."

"I understood that Zenith and I were both prisoners of the Texans. I thought he had escaped before I did. You know he was working on an engine of his own?"

"An idea he had stolen from his Arab paymasters, yes. What is it, some kind of oil-fired steam-engine?"

"It's an infernally filthy thing he calls an internal combustion machine. It works by releasing energy through a series of rapid explosions which drive the pistons."

"Aha! And oil ignites readily, so is a perfect fuel?"

"Exactly, sir. If sufficiently refined. But he knows it to be a faulty concept. There are all kinds of reasons why it is not likely to work. So instead, to power the 'gyrocopter,' he decided he needed my battery. I have developed a way of storing enormous amounts of electricity, enabling anything using my super-battery to travel almost limitless distances. The Texans discovered that I was working on this in Brazil—and the rest you know."

Begg guessed instantly what such a battery could mean politically. The man who possessed its secret could be master of the world. Now at last the full extent of Zenith's plan was clear to him.

"Well, we'd better get you out of here and back to Brazil as soon as we can . . ."

He turned at a sound from outside.

Suddenly the door was flung open and Taffy Sinclair stood there. His face was covered in blood. His clothes were torn. He had put up a long fight. Behind him, pressing an automatic into Taffy's ribs, stood Zenith the Albino. With his free hand he lifted a slender opium cigarette to his grimly smiling lips.

"Good evening, Sir Seaton. It seems I am making quite a collection for myself. Some of the finest minds in the world gather in my little experimental laboratory. Did you think I wouldn't recognise your friend, Doctor Sinclair?"

Sinclair suddenly threw up his elbow, catching Zenith off guard, and Sir Seaton Begg leapt for the man, his fists flashing. There was a crack as his knuckles met his old opponent's jaw, and with a grunt Zenith staggered backwards, the automatic spinning from his hand. Like lightning Begg dived for it. The gun was almost in his grasp when a foot stamped cruelly on his reaching fingers and a rifle butt swiped across his skull. At the same time Taffy Sinclair's arms were pinioned behind him by a grinning crook as Zenith's guards took control. Even O'Bean fought on until he, too, was stunned by a rifle blow. Seaton Begg tried to pick himself up from the filthy floor of the hut, but vivid flashes of lightning appeared before his eyes, the room began to spin, and he sank down into unconsciousness.

The last thing he heard before he collapsed was the soft, mocking laughter of Count Zenith. "I have you at last, Sir Seaton. It is clear I must take my leave of this place. It means I'll have to dispose of my distinguished guest a little earlier and a little cheaper than I had planned. But before I do, I'll devise a perfect end for you and your meddling friend. Something suitably symbolic, you can be assured!"

⤳ CHAPTER FIVE ↢

An Old-Fashioned Death

"It is bound to amuse you, gentlemen, to know that the manner of your deaths will help me destroy all signs of this establishment's function." Adjusting his silk hat on his head, Count Zenith slipped his ebony cane under his arm and pulled on his white gloves. His ruby eyes glittered with amusement. "You were always a catalyst, Begg. And your last function will be perfectly in character!"

Sir Seaton Begg and Taffy Sinclair, tightly bound from head to foot by sturdy hemp ropes, hung suspended from the hook of a crane. The machine's arm jutted directly out within the pyramidal skeleton structure of the "rig" used to drill down to the oil pool feeding the evil-smelling viscous liquid into pipes. Initially used to carry oil to the refining plant but now disconnected, they leaked into the ground. Zenith's two captives hung directly over the deep shaft. At the bottom, oil glinted like a dark rainbow.

Smiling with some regret, Zenith tipped his hat to his old adversary. "You were a worthy opponent, Seaton Begg. I cared to pit my wits against no one else. All the rest are cattle. Their lives are as useful or as meaningless as circumstance demands. But only in my dreams could I hope to outwit you. Is it not a commentary on the nature of life? Your cleverness has defeated me a dozen times, yet one small error of judgement, and you find yourself helplessly in my power! You know I would prefer to spare your life. Sadly, that cannot be. You have interfered with my plans for the last time and must pay forfeit, just as I would expect to pay if our positions were reversed. In honour of our old-fashioned rivalry, I have devised a suitably old-fashioned death for you, worthy of my mediaeval ancestors. As you are turned into a human torch, you will ignite the oil well which will send this whole affair to perdition! All evidence will be destroyed along with you and your companion."

"If I do not bring you to justice, Zenith, someone will!" Begg replied grimly. Few men could have retained their self-control under these circumstances. He and Sinclair now gyrated slowly over the oil pit.

"What? Your colleague with the gun?" Monsieur Zenith chuckled with cruel insouciance. "He has already been dealt with. His distraction worked only briefly. Clearly your actions became poorly considered once you had tracked me down. Your deductions were, of course, completely accurate. I stole the secrets of the Wahabim's oil-fired engine and sold them to the Texan chapter of the Family of Fear, knowing O'Bean had developed an altogether better and more valuable idea. It does not rely at all on the filthy liquid your body will soon ignite into a suitable inferno! My interest was chiefly in the design of the autogyros. And, of course, the great engineer."

"So you had already planned to kidnap O'Bean and drag his secrets from him!"

"Naturally. But 'King' George, Shiner, and the rest of the Texan Family of Fear anticipated me. They captured him before I had the opportunity. It meant I was forced to modify my plans slightly. I befriended him, then escaped to my base here, stealing the experimental oil-burning engine autogyro. It was the machine I wanted, not the engine. O'Bean would be induced, soon enough, to help me install his engine. Knowing you and I were old enemies and of all the men in the world you would be most likely to find me, Shiner visited you in England. No doubt he used my name to whet your appetite for the chase! But you made a rare blunder—and here you are! The Family's plans were thwarted when I returned and made off with O'Bean and the other machine!" Zenith permitted himself a rare chuckle. "I left them only with that elephantine airship and its impossibly inefficient oil and steam engine. No doubt they still intend to bomb their own capital with poisoned gas, giving them an excuse to go to war with California, whose gold they sorely need. Have you discovered that plan yet, my old friend?"

Begg's aquiline features writhed in disgust. "A filthy plan. Even you would be incapable of such a thing. Before long the Diné, too, will be plunged into conflict . . ."

"You are right. For all that I loathe the human race, I would not myself wish to create such suffering. Still, needs must when the devil drives. What they do is up to them. Thanks to you I must now cut my losses. In a short while I'll have sold O'Bean back to the Texans and returned to Europe. They will either kill him in order to produce their oil-fired engine or torture his secret from him! The situation here will become a further source of profit for unscrupulous men like myself. But you'll witness nothing of that. You will have suffered the fate of one of your English battered cod! The Texan Family shall rendezvous here in under half an hour."

"So the Texas chapter of the Family is on its way?" Surreptitiously Begg tested his bonds.

"I telegraphed them. They'll come under cover of darkness. As a sign of my good faith they will see me burn my oil well—and our mutual enemies. You and Doctor Sinclair will be the fuse lit to begin the conflagration. Now, if you'll excuse me, I have some minor matters to oversee before our friends arrive."

And with that the albino turned on his heel, disappearing into the night.

"The man's a fiend, Begg!" Taffy twisted in his bonds. "What human creature would consign us to such a fearful fate?"

"Some doubt he is truly human, old man. It seems Mrs von Bek has failed us. And we can expect no other salvation. Neither Zenith nor President Putz can afford to have us as witnesses. We have only our own wits now, Taffy. We must try to coordinate our movements and get this thing to swing off-center. Do you see that strut? It has a raw edge. If one of us can get his hands to it and rub the rope apart we might have the slenderest of chances!"

Together the two Englishmen began to swing back and forth, increasing their momentum, until Begg was at last able to catch his feet in the strut, pulling them towards it and twisting so that Sinclair could rub his bound hands on the rough edge, sawing desperately. Overhead in the star-splashed blackness of the night they heard the increasing roar of an airship's turbines. Carrying the Family of Fear, the Texan craft was coming in low to keep her rendezvous with Zenith.

Begg was aware that at any moment one of Zenith's men would arrive to thwart them. But it seemed all the crooks were fascinated by the looming bulk of the steamer of the skies as she at last became visible. Vapour boiling around her hull, her questing searchlights picked out the sheds of Zenith's refining plan and the two grounded autogyros some distance away.

Soon the great steamer hung directly overhead, shutting off her engines and throwing down her mooring lines to be caught by Zenith's straining men. Then the Albino himself appeared, pushing the stumbling O'Bean forward into the pool of light, forcing the Brazilian's head up so that President Putz and his Texans could recognise him through the glasses they would now have trained on the camp.

Desperately Taffy Sinclair's hands continued to move up and down. Bit by bit, the strands of rope parted. Yet time was against the detectives as a silence descended, broken only by Zenith's soft chuckle as he called up to the ship. "Will you show me the money, gentlemen?"

Begg recognised "King" George Putz's fox bark issuing orders, but it was Dick Shiner's amplified voice, distorted by his bull horn, which bellowed down. "We aren't going to let you trick us again, Zenith. We're going to lower a man in our observation gondola. O'Bean gets in the gondola, then our man hands over the silver. Okay?"

Zenith shrugged. "As long as I receive the agreed price, Mr Shiner."

"Don't worry, Zenith. But first we want to see you have Begg and his friend. We can't afford any witnesses to this affair."

At this request Zenith took a flashlight from the hands of one of his men and turned it dramatically onto Seaton Begg and Taffy Sinclair, who were suddenly swinging back and forth again. "The moment I have that money in my hands, I assure you, Mr Shiner, those two interfering gentlemen become *pommes frites*, the fuse which will send the whole place up. Then we all part company and go about our own business."

There came a harsh laugh from above. "We love rare beef, but we take our limeys crisp in Texas, eh? So much for the reputation of those high and mighty British detectives! I always held they were overrated. They fell for my story hook, line, and sinker!"

The flashlight went out. Soon there came the whine of an electric winch. A small open gondola detached itself from the bottom of the ship and began slowly to descend.

Grinning evilly in the firelight, one of the crooks touched a match to a brand which flared into violent life. He muttered a cruel oath in Spanish and advanced with sadistic pleasure upon the apparently helpless Englishmen.

Taffy grunted. The crooks thought it was an expression of fear, but he had sawn through his ropes at last. Already he was removing the remains of his bonds and secretly untying his friend.

"Come on, old man!" hissed Begg. "We're cutting it a bit fine, eh?"

At a given signal, they jumped for the struts of the rig and hung there for a moment. Then, as the baffled crook swung the brand this way and that, seeking them out, they began to descend. They were stiff from the ropes and could be recaptured at any moment, leaving Zenith and the Family of Fear to go free, taking the kidnapped Brazilian inventor with them!

The crook yelled for help and drew his pistol.

Another leap on legs which threatened to give way under them, and the sleuths had reached the wall of the nearest shed just as the gondola reached the ground. They sought the temporary safety of the shadows.

Unable to hear for the whirr of the cable, Zenith and his men approached the gondola with O'Bean. A bag had been passed to Zenith and he inspected it, nodding. O'Bean was then forced into the gondola's passenger seat and a signal was given to reverse the winch.

It was only then that the smiling Zenith turned and saw what had happened. He laughed, almost admiringly, and snatched the brand from his man's hand. His crimson eyes glared into the darkness. "You fool! You've let them escape!"

He flung the flaming brand into the well and for a moment it merely guttered, threatening to go out. Then a great bolt of fire sprang into the air.

By its light the two detectives, still stiff from their bondage, became instantly visible. Their eyes darted this way and that, but there was nowhere to hide.

Casually, Zenith picked up the bag of silver. Overhead the gondola was already halfway back to the ship. Almost with regret Zenith pointed his walking stick at the detectives. His voice betrayed a certain melancholy. "Shoot them."

Utterly exposed, Begg and Sinclair searched the ground for some sort of cover or weapon. Then bravely they faced their enemies, preparing to die like gentlemen. Zenith understood this. Understanding this, Zenith tipped his hat towards the Englishmen, then turned and ran into the darkness.

Begg drew on his remaining strength, knotting his fists. "Charge 'em when I give the word. They won't be expecting it."

"Goodbye, old man." Sinclair spoke through gritted teeth. "It's been a pleasure to serve with you!"

Begg's reply was drowned by a great whining sound from out of the night. Steam hissed and rotors clashed. A bellowing wind blew the fire from the oil rig. Zenith's men yelped, flinging their arms against the flames and scattering in every direction.

Begg stared up in disbelief.

One of the gyrocopters rose into the air. She hovered on her wide wings, her overhead screws whirling. Then she banked towards the airship.

Begg and Sinclair were transfixed in astonishment as the flying machine drew alongside the gondola, threatening to crash into it. A dark figure rose from the gondola's passenger seat, leapt the distance between the two vehicles, and clung on to the side before clambering into the autogyro's spare cockpit. Seconds later the whining, rattling machine banked and flew into the night.

Suddenly there was silence. The flames from the rig seemed dormant for a moment. Then with an almost human roar, they leapt skywards with apalling ferocity as Begg and Sinclair dashed for the other side of the shed, seeking shelter from the engulfing flames and barrage of bullets. Begg saw a figure emerge from the firelight. "Quickly, Taffy! We can still catch him." He pointed.

Zenith, bag of bullion in hand, was racing for the compound, clearly planning to use the second autogyro to make his escape.

The two detectives were significantly shortening the distance. They were almost upon him when he turned, a savage white wolf, teeth drawn back in a snarl. Suddenly steel flashed in his right hand. His ebony stick had hidden a sword!

"The tables are turned again, gentlemen!" He seemed to be enjoying the irony of the situation. One swift movement of his arm and Sinclair gasped, clutching his shoulder. Zenith had struck like a snake and was already running towards the grounded autogyro now visible in the flames.

Begg paused. "Are you all right, old man?"

"A flesh wound, Begg. Get the Albino!"

By this time Zenith had drawn his pistol and snapped off a quick shot at the detective. Begg flung himself to one side. When he found his feet, he saw that Zenith had reached the gyroplane, pulled down his flying goggles, and leapt into the cockpit, switching on the engine. With a hideous noise, the forward propeller and the overhead rotor began to turn. Once, the albino looked back, his eyes hidden by the goggles, then gave his full attention to the controls.

Begg made one desperate leap for the cockpit but his still numb fingers failed to grip. The little ship rose thundering and rattling into the air, its wings wobbling dangerously as the experimental engine bore it skyward pouring black fumes and flames as it went.

Meanwhile Dick Shiner's voice came over the amplifier, yelling curses at the man in the gondola and at Zenith. Clearly Shiner believed himself betrayed by the albino.

Soon the autogyro was framed against the airship which still flew its false California colours. The massive aerial steamer began to turn about as if to follow the escaping autogyro. An aerial recoiless gun made a familiar dull thumping sound, its large spent shells rattling to the ground around them as Seaton Begg returned to his friend's side, his hands expertly inspecting the wound. "You've been lucky, old man."

"Did Zenith have a coconspirator?" Sinclair wanted to know. Before Begg could reply, two of Zenith's men came running towards them. Begg picked up the swordstick preparing to defend himself, but the men swerved and continued past them. They were in a blind panic as clearly the rig was about to blow.

"Come along, old boy. We'd better make ourselves scarce, too!"

Supporting his wounded friend, Sir Seaton Begg kept low, staggering towards the now open gate. Once through it, they stumbled over uneven ground for long minutes before pausing at last to look back.

The giant airship had engaged her turbines. The steam combustion hybrids emitted enormous clouds of black smoke and orange sparks.

"A scene from hell, indeed!" murmured the detective. Dawn was just beginning to turn the horizon pink and grey. The autogyro was still visible, turning eratically, as if on her own stationary screw. The machine was in trouble.

The airship drew closer. Zenith could be seen struggling with his controls. Suddenly a machine gun began to rattle. Zenith had got his armament working and was firing on his pursuers.

The action of the gun sent the little machine into another whirling spin. Desperately the albino tried to recover. Suddenly the ship shot upwards, high above the pursuing aerial leviathan. The flying machine's screws then stopped turning altogether. The detectives had the impression of someone trying to leap from the gyroplane as it came screaming down directly into the airship's gasbag. The oil well below erupted with an enormous explosion, and a moment later the flying machine struck the hull of the giant ship. Then came another vast noise. A mighty wind howled and buffeted them. The shockwave knocked Begg and Sinclair flat.

When they rose again, covered in bits of debris, they saw the carcass of the ship burning brightly on the remains of the refinery. The autogyro had crashed into the monstrous gasbag and brought both machines down to their ruin. It was unlikely that anyone had survived either on the ground or in the two aircraft. "It appears Zenith spoke a little too soon," breathed Sinclair, his eyes reflecting the shrieking intensity of flame. "We were not, after all, the piece de resistance of his display. Instead it's the Family of Fear who have provided us with a Family-sized Texan barbecue."

Sir Seaton Begg wasted no sympathy on the Family of Fear. "King" George and the others had got their just desserts. He even smiled in response to Taffy's grim joke. "Sweet and spicey, no doubt," he said.

The next morning they waited beside their car, attended by Rose von Bek's Diné policemen, one of whom was a medical officer qualified to patch up Doctor Sinclair's shoulder. The metatemporal detectives watched as two riders galloped towards them over the scrub. When they were close enough it was possible to make out their identities as Rose von Bek and the Brazilian wizard, O'Bean, Sinclair, who had not been party to the plan concocted by Begg and his female opposite number, began to grin broadly in understanding.

"So she did save us, after all, eh? It was touch and go, and you took some pretty close risks, but you did it! Mrs von Bek, of course, was the pilot of the first autogyro that rescued O'Bean! What a magnificent lady she is, Begg. I think we owe her our lives!"

"Well," said Sir Seaton Begg, advancing towards the newcomers, "at very least we owe her an excellent dinner. What would you say to some jugged hare at Rules's?"

Epilogue

One evening a few weeks after the Texan affair, Sir Seaton Begg and Taffy Sinclair took two ladies to dinner. They had met them backstage at the Empire Music Hall, Leicester Square, and now sat in the mirrored red plush luxury of Mr Rules's restaurant in Maiden Lane. This had been the scene of many a grand resolution to a case and was where Rose von Bek in particular loved to celebrate. Across the white linen and gleaming silverware Mrs von Bek and her old friend Mrs Una Persson smiled upon the two delighted men.

Mrs Persson looked from beneath her dark, swinging "pageboy" hair as she picked up a menu. "Yes," she said, answering Dr Sinclair's compliment. "I think we had a jolly house tonight. But tell me more, Doctor Sinclair. What's to become of poor Texas with her entire government gone? Corrupt as it was, it was surely better than anarchy!"

"There is nothing to be concerned about, Mrs Persson," Dr Sinclair reassured her. "A team of international advisers is at this moment helping Texas rediscover her original source of wealth, which is cattle and agriculture. A provisional government has been convened by Mr and Mrs Brady, provisional joint presidents of the new republic. She's to hold democratic general elections by the end of the year . . ."

". . . while the accumulated wealth of the former governors is to be donated to social programmes to fund the hospitals and schools so badly needed there," chimed in Mrs von Bek. "I must admit when I loosened the bolts of the rotors on the other gyroplane, I only hoped to stop it taking off. I certainly did not envision accidentally putting an end both to Monsieur Zenith and to the entire corrupt republican Senate of Texas! A whole branch of the notorious Family of Fear gone! Gradually the fight is being won."

"And thanks to you, my dear Rose," Sir Seaton reached a fond hand across the table, "they suffered the fate they intended to mete out to us and thousands of their fellow innocent Texans. What's more, Senhor O'Bean is back in Rio de Janeiro with his family, developing the concentrated electrical battery. Within a year it will be available to anyone who wishes to use it. It will benefit the world enormously and put an end to any temptation to develop Zenith's disgustingly filthy 'combustion engine.' Can you imagine!"

Mrs Persson had once known Zenith well. Indeed when Sir Seaton Begg had first met her she had been in league with the infamous albino. "But what of our friend Monsieur Z?" she murmured as the little café orchestra struck up a discreet waltz. "Are you certain he died in the crash?"

"We must hope so, dear Mrs P." With exaggerated delicacy, Taffy Sinclair offered his escorte his manly reassurance. Ever since their meeting he had borne the air of a creature permitted a glimpse of heaven. When she smiled at him so delightfully he felt he would swoon on the spot with pleasure. "We must certainly hope so."

For a fraction of a moment a shadow passed across Mrs Persson's exquisite forehead. Then, before anyone but the metatemporal detective had noticed, she was gay again. "What larks, eh, gentlemen!"

Sir Seaton Begg permitted himself a glance which met the ironic eye of Mrs von Bek.

The waiter arrived. He regretted that the hare was not in season until tomorrow. He recommended the young deer but they all ordered sole. Then the orchestra played *Belle nuit, O nuit d'amour* from "The Tales of Hoffmann," and they raised their glasses in a toast to the power of civilisation, the triumph of Order and Chaos in balance, and the pleasure of sublimely perfect company.

⇥London Flesh⇤

aniel Defoe was the first to write about "London Flesh," the legendary meat of the hern supposed to "confer Magical Powers upon those who Partook of it." Defoe, in fact, invested money in its unsuccessful commercial production. Perhaps that was why he wrote his famous pamphlet which, while pretending scepticism, actually gave the impression that the meat, sold mostly in the form of a paste, had supernatural properties.

De Quincey, Lamb, Dickens, and Grossmith all claimed to have sampled London Flesh, usually in pies, sausages, or patés, but only Lamb was convinced that he had briefly become invisible and known the power of flight (over Chelsea Gardens). The Flesh was rumoured, of course, to be human, and Dickens raised the name of Sweeney Todd in *Household Words*, but Doctor "Dog" Donovan of Guy's was convinced that the meat was "undoubtedly that of the female hern." That said, the rumour persisted.

The hern was never abundant. The last pair in the London area was seen in Kew in 1950. Legend had it they were raised in captivity in Hackney Marshes up until the Second World War. Patrick Hamilton and Gerald Kersh both claimed to have been taken to a hern farm (Kersh was blindfolded) and seen dozens of the creatures penned in cages hidden behind trees and bushes, where they were offered hern paté on cream crackers. "London Flesh," reports Hamilton, "as sweet and smooth as your mother's cheeks."

"There's a book in heaven," said Coleridge, who was convinced that the Flesh was human, "in which is recorded the names of all who dishonour the Dead. Graveyard Desecrations and any form of Cannibalism, including the eating of London Flesh."

London believes it remembers the horrible story of the cannibal tramwaymen of Hampstead Heath and how they devoured on Christmas Day the passengers and crew of the Number 64 tram which mysteriously returned empty to the Tudor Hamlets terminal. This is the true story of that event.

No complete list of passengers has ever been made, but we do know that a party of some dozen revellers left The Red Mill public house on Tufnell Hill and made their way to the tram stop to board the 64. Witnesses saw and heard them, commenting on their cheerful drunkenness and the somewhat lewd behaviour of the young women who, removing hats and veils, bared their entire heads at passersby. We also know that the vicar of St Alban's, Brookgate, was last seen boarding at The Tessy O'Shea stop, because his brother walked him there. A young mother with three rather boisterous children also boarded, though it was possible they disembarked before the 64 began its crossing of the Heath. The night was foggy. The gas was out across a fairly wide area, due to air in the pipes at Highgate, the GLC said. Indeed the Gas Light and Coke Co were held partially responsible for police officers not at once investigating after the tram failed to reach Tudor Hamlets. The gas being restored, the tram mysteriously returned to its own terminus. All that was found aboard was a leverman's uniform cap and two ladies' hats, which told their own grim story.

At that time there was no fashion for elaborate headgear or, indeed, the casual doffing of it as there is today. At least two young women had been aboard, yet at first the police tried to treat the case as one of simple abandonment. They thought the overhead power rail had come adrift from its connector and passengers had decided to walk home. But neither the leverman nor the conductor reported for duty. The Home Office decided to investigate the mystery and send Sir Seaton Begg and his friend Dr "Taffy" Sinclair relatively late on Boxing Day. Unhappy at being called away from their festivities, the two men came together at Tudor Hamlets, in the office of Mr Thorn, the regional manager of the Universal Transport Company.

Thorn was a red-faced, anxious man whose perspiration made dark stains on his scarlet, gold, and white uniform. He was somewhat in awe of Begg and Sinclair, their reputations being familiar to all who followed the news.

"It will be my head on the block, gentlemen," he reminded them, "if the UTC determine negligence here. Of course, we are used to tram robbers on the Heath, but in all my years we have only known one killing and that was when a barker went off by accident. It has always been prudent of levermen to obey a command when they receive one, especially since we are insured for material loss but not for the death of our employees. Guild tramwaymen never do more than wound. Those flintlock pistols they affect allow for little else. It is to everyone's advantage that their guild, formed in 1759, laid down strict regulations as to weaponry, masks, mounts, uniforms, and so on. Do you have any suspicions, gentlemen?"

Removing his wide-brimmed slouch hat Sir Seaton Begg brushed at the brim with his sleeve. "It's rare for a tramwayman to disobey his own strict codes. They would sooner lose the goodwill of Londoners and therefore their guarantees of secrecy and shelter. Nor is it like them to abduct women and children. Either this was a gang feigning to be real tramway thieves or we are dealing with rogues who hold their guild honour at nought."

"It would be yet another sign of the times," murmured the tall Welshman, the detective's lifelong friend and amanuensis. "When tramwaymen go against their traditions, then the next thing we'll see will be the looting of graves."

"Quite so," said Begg, taking out an enormous briar, filling it with black shag, and lighting it from a vesta he struck against the bricks of the terminus. Soon heavy black smoke filled the hall as, puffing contemplatively, he paced back and forth across the stone flags.

"Remarkable," offered Sinclair, "that no passengers were reported missing."

"And only the leverman's wife called in to say he had not come home." Begg paused frowning. "The conductor lived alone?"

"A widower," said Mr Thorn. "His mother is in Deal with relatives."

"Young women? A mother with children?" Sir Seatton drew thoughtfully on his briar. "Could they all have disembarked before the Terminus?"

"It's not unheard of, sir."

"But unlikely, I'm sure you'll agree. I think it's probably time we took a tram back to The Red Mill. Can you spare us a leverman, Mr Thorn?"

"We're still on a skeleton schedule for the holidays, but in these circumstances . . ." Guild rules usually demanded that every tram carry both a driver and a conductor. "I can't see anyone objecting here if only the leverman takes out the Special. I'll give the appropriate instructions. We should have her connected in fifteen minutes."

~◉ CHAPTER TWO ◉~

Grey clouds regathered over the Heath as the Special began her long climb up Tufnell Hill. The Red Mill's tethered sails strained against air, bending foliage across the horizon like mourners in procession.

Snow had melted into the grass, and mud puddles reflected the sky. Crows called with mysterious urgency, and there was a strong, fecund smell. Dr Sinclair remarked on the unseasonable warmth. Only a few roofs and the steeple of St Valentine's, Hampstead Vale, could be seen below until the Mill was reached. There they looked on to Tudor Hamlets and the suburbs beyond Highgate, red roofs, green cedars and pines, the bones of elms supporting untidy nests, all gauzed in smoke from the chimneys.

Disembarking, Begg strolled up the path, through the ornamental metal gates, and began to ascend worn granite steps to the Red Mill. Sinclair, examining the soft ground, bent to frown over something. "Hello! That's odd for this time of the year!" He straightened, now giving his attention to something on the other side of the path. "I wonder why—?"

A bass voice greeted them from the door of the hostelry attached to the Mill. "I'm sorry, gents, but we're closed until New Year's Eve." Sinclair looked up to see the large red-bearded publican standing there.

"Except for guests who ride hunters, it seems." Dr Sinclair smiled and pointed to the evidence. "One doesn't have to be a High Mobsman to know that tramway thieves always convene here for the holidays."

Sir Seaton shared his friend's humour. "Don't worry, Mr O'Dowd," he told the publican, "we're neither peelers nor wildsmen and have no direct busness to discuss with your guests. Would I be wrong if I understood Captain Anchovy to be stabling his horse here for the Season?"

A cheerful, handsome face appeared behind O'Dowd's broad shoulder as, with his famous dashing grace, a man in the white wig and elaborate long waistcoat of a guild member stepped forward, lowering and uncocking a huge horse pistol, the traditional tool of his trade.

"Festive greetings to ye, Sir Seaton. I trust you and your companion will take a glass with us?" He smiled as he shook hands with the detectives. Together they entered the heat of a public bar filled with Tobeymen of every rank. Any suspicion of the newcomers was swiftly dispelled, and within moments the two investigators were imbibing goblets of mulled wine while Captain Anchovy and his men volunteered their aid in solving the mystery. Their own honour, they said, was at stake.

Tom Anchovy in particular was inflamed with disgust. "My dear Sir Seaton, that 64 was indeed our intended prize as she came up Tufnell Hill. But it was Boxing Day, and we had no intention of stealing anything but the hearts of the ladies aboard. All were brought here. Three children were given presents, and old men of pleasant humour were presented with a glass of wine. Only a few refused our hospitality—the mother of the children, a good-hearted reverend gentleman whose abstinence we respected—and that sour fellow who had refused to quit the Inn on our arrival and refused to share his vittles with us. On any other occasion we might have taken him for ransom."

"And he was—?" Sir Seaton lifted the beaker to his lips.

"Henry Marriage, sir. A humourless walking cadaver if ever I met one. Yet even he was permitted to retain his valuables. I don't mind tellin' ye, Sir Seaton, that had it not been Christmas, I would have had his last stitch *and* kept him for ransom!"

"Is that Marriage of Marriage's Opiates by the river?" asked Dr Sinclair, placing his finished beaker on the bar and nodding with approval as O'Dowd refilled it. "The millionaire who lives in a house on his own wharf?"

"The same, Dr Sinclair. Do ye know him?"

"Only by reputation," replied the doctor. A solitary individual, they say. A dabbler in the alchemist's art. He's published an interesting book or two. No charlatan, but no great scientist, either. Many of his findings and experiments have been discredited. He's considered a mere amateur by the medical and scientific guilds."

"I understand nothing of such things, sir. But I'll swear to this—when that tram left last evening he was safe and sound, as was every living soul aboard. Though he chose to go with them, all but Henry Marriage were as cheerful as when they had embarked. If that 64 was taken, then it would have been on the high stretch of track below the ruined village."

"Why so?" Begg enquired.

"Because we watched her lights until they were out of sight, and young Jaimie Gordon here was on his way to join us, taking the low road up the Vale. He'd have spotted anything untoward."

Sir Seaton was already slamming down his glass and cramming his hat onto his handsome, aquiline head. "Then I can guess where the tram was stopped. Come on, Taffy, let's board our Special. I'm much obliged to you, Captain Anchovy."

"Delighted to have helped, sir."

After a further quick word with the tramwayman, the two metatemporal investigators were again on their way.

⟶⟨ᗩ CHAPTER THREE ᗧ⟶

A Bleriot "Bat," no doubt taking the day's mail to France, flew high over-head as the 64 rattled to a stop below the ruins of Hampstead Model Village which lay on the brow of the hill above the tramline whose branches had once serviced the inhabitants of Lady Hecate Brown's failed evangelical dream of a healthy environment where a good Christian life and enlightened working conditions would be the antidote to all the ills of city life. Her failure to supply the model village with familiar recreations, public houses, and fried fish shops caused even the most enlightened artisans to view her idealistic community as a kind of prison. The village had flourished as a middle-class enclave until, without servants or city facilities, the bourgeoisie chose the suburbs of Tudor Hamlets and Lyonne's Greene. The tram service had been discontinued, though the tracks were intact, lost beneath the encroaching weeds and brambles.

As Begg and Sinclair disembarked, the sky clouded darker and it began to rain heavily. Peering with difficulty through the ever thickening mist, Begg quickly saw that his intuition had been right.

Sinclair was the first to observe how the track had been cleared through the swampy ground leading up to the ruins. "Look, Begg. There's the shine of brass. A tram was diverted at this very spot and went up Ham Hill towards the old village. What do you make of it?"

"The best place to take a tram off the usual routes, Taffy. The emptied vehicle was sent back on its way, perhaps to divert attention from whatever dark deed was done here. Let us pray we are in time to save those poor souls—victims, no doubt, of some rogue band caring nought for the rules and habits of an old guild!"

With difficulty, they followed the line up the muddy terrain, their boots sinking and sliding in ground normally frozen hard.

As the rain let up, Ham Hill's ruins were seen bleak beneath a lowering sky. The air was unseasonably muggy; thunder rolled closer. Melted snow left pools so that the hill might have been the remains of Hereward's Romney fastness. Sinclair suppressed a shiver as a sudden chill crept up his spine. The afternoon's gloom was illuminated by a sudden sheet of lightning throwing the ruins into vivid silhouette.

"Press on, Taffy," murmured Seaton Begg, clapping his friend on his sturdy shoulder. "I sense we're not far from solving this mystery!"

"And maybe perishing as a consequence." The mordant Welshman spoke only half in jest.

Making some remark about the "dark instincts of the Celtic soul," Begg tramped on until they at last stood regarding the outskirts of the ruins, looking down at Tufnell Vale whose yellow lights offered distant reassurance.

No such friendly gas burned in the ruins of Hampstead Model Village, yet a few guttering brands lit the remaining glass in the low church chapel, said now to harbour all manner of pagan ritual and devil worship. The nearby Anglican church had been desanctified on orders from Southwark, but the ragged walls remained. Close to the church blazed three or four bonfires built from the wood of old pews and other religious furniture.

Begg and Sinclair kept to the cover of fallen walls and shrubbery. Human figures gathered around the fires.

"Vagrants, perhaps?" murmured Sinclair. "Do such people still exist?"

Signalling his friend to silence, Begg pointed to a collapsing house sheltering the bulky shapes of horses. Rough laughter and uncultured voices told Begg they had found another tramwayman gang. "Guildless outcasts, Taffy, by the cut of their coats. Rejected by every mobsmen's association from here to York."

Keeping well down, the detectives crept closer. Unlike Tom Anchovy's men, guildless tram thieves were known for their cruel savagery.

"It's been years since such a gang was seen this close to London," whispered Sinclair. "They risk life imprisonment if caught!"

Begg was unsurprised. "I knew Captain Zenith was outside Beaconsfield and suspected of several tram robberies in that region. Quickly, Taffy, drop down." He flung himself behind a broken wall. "That's the rogue himself!"

A tall, white-haired man in a black greatcoat sauntered towards one of the fires, eyes burning like rubies in the reflected light. A handsome albino with skin the colour of ivory, Zenith was an old enemy of Begg's. The two were said to be cousins who had often crossed swords.

As the two watched, Zenith approached a thin individual, as tall as himself, on the far side of the fire. It was Sinclair's turn to draw in a sharp breath. Henry Marriage, one of the missing passengers, seemed to be on friendly terms with the most notorious tram thief in Europe!

It grew darker until all the inhabitants of the ruins were mere silhouettes.

"We can't take 'em single-handed," murmured Begg. "We'd best return to the depot and telegraph to Scotland Yard."

Picking their way carefully down the hill, they had scarcely gone twenty yards before dark shadows suddenly surrounded them. They heard a horrible, muffled noise.

Moving towards them across the unnaturally damp ground, big pistols threatening, came an unsavoury circle of leering tram robbers.

"Good evening, gentlemen!" The leader doffed his cocked hat in a mocking bow. "Always pleased to welcome a few more guests to our holiday harum-scarum!" He removed the shutter from his night lamp, showing the face of their unfortunate tram driver. The leverman's hands were tied before him, and a gag had been forced into his mouth. He had been trying to warn his passengers of his own capture.

～❧ CHAPTER FOUR ❧～

The mobsmen had not reckoned with the two detectives being armed. In a flash Begg and Sinclair produced the latest repeating Webleys! "Stand, you scum," levelly declared the investigator. "You no doubt recognise this revolver which I intend to use to advantage."

Triumph draining from their decadent features, the mobsmen fell back, knowing full well the power and efficiency of the Webleys over their own antique barkers. Then a voice cut through the misty air. Sharp as a diamond, it bore the tone of a man used to obedience.

"Fire one chamber, Sir Seaton, and count yourself responsible for the death of an innocent woman."

Turning their heads, the investigators saw Captain Zenith, a bright lantern in one hand, pressing his barker against the head of a dishevelled coster girl grinning stupidly from under her raised veil, her hat at an unseemly angle.

Sinclair stifled a cry of outrage. "You fiend!" He did not let his Webley fall, nor did he disengage the safety catch. "What have you done to that poor young creature?"

"I, sir?" An almost melancholy smile played across the mobsman's pale lips. "What d'ye think I've done? Murdered her?" The light from the lantern gave his red eyes a savage sparkle.

"Drugged her!" Sinclair muttered in disgust. "You're cowards as well as kidnappers."

Captain Zenith's face clouded for a moment before resuming its habitual mask. "She's unhurt, sir. However, aggressive action on your part might alter her circumstances."

"No doubt one of the missing passengers, but where are the children?" demanded Sir Seaton.

"Safe and sound with their mother and full of mince pies," Zenith assured him.

"Then show them to me."

"I'd remind you, Sir Seaton, that you are at a disadvantage."

"And I'd remind you, Captain Zenith, that I am a servant of the Crown. Harm me or those under my protection and you'll answer to Her Majesty's justice."

"I have been escaping that justice, sir, for longer than you and I have travelled the moonbeam roads. Put that fancy barker aside and be my welcome guest." He stepped away from the giggling young woman as Begg and Sinclair reluctantly reholstered their weapons. Then, tucking the woman's somewhat limp arm into his, Captain Zenith led them back to the central fire, built just outside the ruined chapel where more of his gang and their captives could clearly be seen.

All but the wide-eyed children were in artificially good humour. Another pair of young women wore their hats on the backs of their heads. Sinclair guessed they had been well supplied with alcohol, but Begg shook his head, saying softly, "Not beer or spirits, I think, Taffy, old man. I suspect another hand in this, don't you?"

Sinclair nodded gravely. "Do we share the suspicion of who it was put Zenith up to this crime?"

"I think we do, Taffy."

Standing among the other prisoners they noticed that only the young mother showed signs of concern. Even the reverend gentleman cheerfully led the leverman, the conductor, and a youth wearing the cadet uniform of the Farringdon Watch in a rather jolly hymn.

"See how our guests enjoy their Boxing Day?" Captain Zenith offered Begg and Sinclair a somewhat cynical grin. "And all with their pocket books in place."

"Drugged with laudanum." Sinclair picked up an empty black bottle and was sniffing it, just as tall, lugubrious Henry Marriage stepped into the firelight and extended his hand. Sinclair ignored the gesture, but Begg, ever the diplomat, bowed. "Good evening, sir. Are these villains holding you to ransom?"

Marriage's hearty manner thinly disguised an evasive expression. "Not at all, sir." He stared around him somewhat helplessly.

"Or is Captain Zenith in your employ?" demanded Sinclair. "Why do you only bind our driver?"

"He'll be released at once." Captain Zenith signed for the leverman to be freed. "He offered my men violence. Whereas these other good fellows accepted our hospitality—"

"—and were drugged into doltishness."

"Please, sir, are you here to help us?" The young mother clutched imploringly at Sir Seaton's sleeve.

With his usual gentle courtesy towards the fair sex, Sir Seaton smiled reassurance. "I am indeed, madam. What charming children! Is their father here?"

"I am a widow, sir."

"My dear lady!"

"We have not been mistreated, sir."

"I should hope you have not!" interjected Henry Marriage. "I doubt if your children have ever eaten so well!"

"You have been feeding them, Mr Marriage?" Dr Sinclair offered the thin man an intense glare of inquisition.

"I returned from visiting a generous relative who gave me the hamper. It was meant for my family at home."

"Indeed, sir," said Sir Seaton. With the toe of his shoe he touched a large, open basket. Stencilled on its side were the words MARRIAGE'S OPIATES, MARRIAGE'S WHARF, LONDON E. "This is the Christmas Box, eh?"

"The same, sir."

"You were sharing it on the tram before Captain Zenith appeared?"

"He was very generous, sir." The conductor looked up from where he sat beside the fire. "I know it's against regulations, but the company generally turns a blind eye at Christmas. Of course, we didn't take any alcoholic beverage."

"Quite so. What did you enjoy from Mr Marriage's hamper?"

"Just a piece of game pie, sir. Some ginger beer. And a couple of sandwiches."

"Whereupon you reached the old Hampstead Model Village stop, broke down, and, at Mr Marriage's suggestion, continued up here, eh, conductor?"

"Such merry yule fires, sir. Who could resist 'em? It was commonly agreed, sir, even by that reverend gent, there could be no happier way of celebrating Boxing Day until rescue came." A stupid, sentimental grin crossed the conductor's long face.

"Except by you, madam, I take it?" Again Sir Seaton turned to the mother.

"I've been pained by a bit of a dicky tummy since we had the goose at my husband's brother's house. I'd rather hoped the children and me'd be home by now. But it was either come here or stay on the tram." She was close to tears. Again Begg laid a gentlemanly hand on her arm. "And Mr Marriage promised you his protection."

"He did, sir. The tramwaymen have offered us no harm. But they're a bad example, sir, and—"

"Captain Zenith and his men make no threats. They keep the traditional tramwaymen's Christmas truce." Marriage was insistent. "I offered them a handsome fee to act for our safety when the tram broke down. They helped us guide it up the old line to this spot where we could find some sort of shelter."

"How on earth did the tram find its own way back to the terminal?" Dr Sinclair was clearly not entirely convinced by this story.

"She slipped backwards, sir, once the horses were untethered," offered the conductor. "Somehow she must have reconnected to the overhead power line and continued her journey. It has been known, sir, for such things to happen."

"So I understand."

"Stranding us here, of course," explained Henry Marriage. "Well, it seems you've brought another vehicle to take everyone home, and no harm done. We are all grateful to you, Sir Seaton and Doctor Sinclair. I am prepared to stand guarantee for Captain Zenith. My honour depends upon promising safe conduct to all parties. I shall elect to stay as evidence of good faith and come morning shall board a fresh tram on the regular morning route. This will give Captain Zenith and his men time to make themselves scarce. A fair bargain, eh, Sir Seaton?"

"Very fair. And very noble of you, Mr Marriage." Speaking with a certain irony, Sir Seaton was careful not to challenge anything. They were seriously outnumbered and had many innocents to consider. Since Zenith the Albino was mixed up in this affair Begg was convinced not everything could be above board. He had several reasons to suspect Marriage's tale. Nevertheless he did not object when the tramwaymen lit the way with their lanterns to lead the happy party back down the hill. At last the passengers were safely aboard and the leverman reinstalled at his controls.

The passengers cheered as the overhead power rail sparked in the darkness. The magnificent Special hummed, lurched, and began to move forward. "A generous soul, that Mr Marriage," declared the conductor. "We'd be mighty hungry by now had he not been so free with his pies." He reacted with a muttered explanation as Dr Sinclair's eyes stared sternly into his own. "I speak only the honest truth, sir. I've done nothing against Company tradition."

"Of course you haven't, Conductor," interrupted Sir Seaton, his hand on his friend's shoulder. "You must now ensure your charges arrive safely at the terminus."

"My duty, sir." The conductor saluted, shaking off his euphoria.

The two detectives returned swiftly to the tram's boarding plate. "We have to go back, of course," said Begg.

"Absolutely, old man!"

As soon as the tram took a bend, they dropped quietly from the platform. Ankle deep in marshy ground, they moved rapidly back to the village.

"You noticed their eyes, I take it, Taffy?"

"Drugged! All but the mother and children. Something in those meat pies, eh?"

"Opium or Indian hemp. That preposterous story of a generous relative!"

"And at least two of the party were not returned to the tram."

"Two young women? Exactly!"

"No doubt they imbibed more freely from the hamper's contents than any of the others."

"Hurry, old man! Knowing Marriage's obsessions, you can guess as readily as I what the fiend intends."

The detectives rapidly regained the camp, creeping carefully up to the ruined chapel where Zenith's gang continued to make merry. Yet of the leader or Henry Marriage, there was no sign.

Drawing his Webley, Begg motioned towards the ruined Anglican church. Sinclair had already noticed lights shining through the broken stained glass. They heard voices, what might have been laughter, a stifled cry, and then a piercing scream. Caution abandoned, they rushed the building, kicking open the rotting doors.

"Oh, for the love of God!" Sinclair was almost forced backward by the horrible smell. The scene's bestial reality was unfit to be seen by anyone save the curator of Scotland Yard's Black Museum. Two young women hung in ropes above the remains of the church altar. One was bleeding from deep wounds in her lower extremities. Her blood dripped into two large copper basins placed there for the purpose. She had fainted, but her companion shrieked in terror through her gag. Henry Marriage, long razor in hand, prepared to perform the same operation upon the friend as the gloating albino placed bowls in readiness.

Marriage seemed completely deranged, but Zenith was fully alert, his face a mask of hatred as he saw Begg and Sinclair. His long white hair hanging loose to his shoulders, he snarled defiantly, lifting a copper bowl to his lips.

Levelling his pistol, Begg snapped off a single shot spinning the bowl from Zenith's hands. Sinclair darted forward and with an expert uppercut knocked Marriage to the floor. The razor fell with a clatter from the opiate merchant's hands.

Growling like a wild animal, Zenith produced his own pistol, but Begg's revolver sounded again, and Zenith's weapon went flying. Sinclair jumped up to the altar and, using Marriage's razor, severed the cords, lowering the two young women gently down as he kicked the bowls of blood clear.

Next Begg leapt forward to press the barrel of his Webley against Zenith's heart. The albino raised his hands, his ruby eyes glaring.

Knowing that his shot had probably alerted Zenith's men, Sinclair turned to face the door.

Motioning with his revolver, Begg forced Zenith to stand between them and the entrance. Henry Marriage groaned and came to his senses as the first outlaws appeared in the doorway.

"Stand back there!" The metatemporal investigator held his Webley against the albino's head. But Zenith's gang was already circling the altar.

His lips rimmed with blood, mumbling curses, Marriage climbed to his feet, his eyes staring into space.

"As you guessed, Taffy, he believes he possesses supernatural powers." Begg motioned with his pistol.

"Let's hope we are not alone, old man. We decidely need help from those who promised it . . ."

"Without them we're dead men, I agree. Have you any spare ammunition?"

"None."

Grimly Begg and Sinclair prepared for the worst. Aware of their dilemma, Zenith grinned even as Sir Seaton's pistol pressed against his head.

The investigator knew his captive too well to demand he call his men off. Whatever dark evil Zenith practised, he was no coward and would die before allowing the two detectives to escape.

Ironically Henry Marriage came to their aid. Drugged eyes rolling in his head, he lifted up his arms and ran for the door. "I am free!" he cried. "Free! Invisible, I shall climb like an eagle into the sky." His long arms flapping at his sides, he stumbled towards the entrance and, before the astonished outlaws, ran wildly into the night. Zenith laughed grimly. "He believes the spell has worked. He forgets our ritual was interrupted."

"Silence, you monster!" Sinclair covered as many outlaws as he could. Savouring their anticipated triumph they tightened the circle.

From outside came a fusilade of shots and sounds of Marriage screaming in frustrated rage. "No! No! I am invisible. I fly. You cannot—" There descended a sudden silence.

Taking advantage of this unexpected turn, Zenith broke free to join the mass of his own men. Grabbing a pistol from one of them, his red eyes blazing, he curved his pale lips in a snarling grin. "You're lost, Begg! Arming the leverman and a drugged vicar won't save you!"

Then a figure appeared in the smashed doorway. A gold-trimmed tricorne on his bewigged head, a black domino hiding his upper face, he had pushed back his huge three-caped coaching coat, two massive barkers in either beringed hand. Captain Tom Anchovy laughed as the guildless tramwaymen fell back in fear. Behind him in the fancy coats and three-cornered hats of their trade, pressed his men, contemptuous of the guildless outlaws bringing their trade into disrepute.

"Drop your arms, lads, or we'll blow you all to the hell you thoroughly deserve!" rapped Anchovy.

But Captain Zenith, using the cover of his men, disappeared through the far door.

"After him, quickly!" ordered Tom. Some mobsmen followed the Albino into the night.

Realising how outnumbered they were, the remaining outlaws gave up their pistols with little resistance, leaving Sir Seaton Begg, Doctor Sinclair, and Tom Anchovy to bind the young women's wounds and get them decently covered.

"Their hats will be waiting for them at the terminus, no doubt," said Dr Sinclair. "They owe their lives to that lost headgear."

"Indeed they do, Taffy. It was our clue that two young women were still held by Marriage and Zenith. All the others we saw still had their hats, even if worn at a rather unladylike angle!" He warmly shook hands with the tobeyman. "You turned up in the nick of time, Captain Tom. Thanks for keeping your word to help us. We remain on opposite sides of the law, but I think we share a moral purpose!"

"Probably true, sir." Captain Anchovy prepared to leave. "We'll truss those rogues thoroughly. Should we catch Zenith, he'll also be left for the peelers to pick up. Boxing Day's almost over, and we must return to our regular trade if we're to eat. Marriage's hamper out there was sadly empty of all its vitalls."

"Just as well. You'd best warn your men that those pies and sausages were poisoned with hern meat and opium. They won't die, but they'll be unable to ride for a day or two should they try any."

"I'll tell 'em at once. Good luck to ye, gentlemen!" The daring tramwayman disappeared into the night.

"That's what I saw at The Red Mill," said Sinclair. "The tiny tracks of the crested hern. I've studied the little creatures a fair bit and was surprised to find some still around London. Brought too early out of hibernation by the unseasonal weather and easily caught by Marriage while staying at the Inn. Some opiates, and his food was ready for those unsuspecting passengers."

"From what I know of his debased brand of alchemy, Taffy, hern meat is only thought efficacious if fed to female virgins first. Partaking of the flesh, or preferably your victim's freshly drawn blood, imparts great supernatural powers, including those of invisibility and flight. Luckily he proved himself a liar with that tale of his hamper being a relative's gift. It clearly came from his own warehouse."

The doctor shuddered. "Thank God we were able to stop him in time."

The two men strolled from the ruined church to see that Anchovy's band had already bound Zenith's followers. Anchovy, astride his magnificent black

Arab, saluted them as they appeared. "If I know Zenith, he'll be long gone in the direction of London, to lose himself in the twitterns of Whitechapel. No doubt our paths will cross again! As for Henry Marriage, I could have sworn my men filled him with enough lead to sink the HMS *Victory*, yet he, too, has disappeared. Perhaps his beliefs had substance, eh?" With that the gallant tramwayman doffed his tricorne in a deep bow, then turned for distant Waymering where Begg knew he lived a double life as Septimus Grouse, a Methodist parson.

Though weak from their experience, the two young victims had recovered somewhat by the time another Special arrived towing a hospital car and a prison van full of peelers. Attended by expert doctors, the women were made comfortable in the hospital car while Zenith's gang were manacled to hard benches, destined for Wormwood Flats.

Thus the tale garbled by the yellow press as "The Affair of the Hampstead Cannibals" was brought to a successful conclusion and all innocent lives saved. Enjoying their pipes the detectives relaxed in the first-class section of the tram's top deck.

"I think I'll be returning to the Red Mill as soon as possible," murmured Sinclair thoughtfully.

"You're curious to retrace the stages of the case, Taffy?"

"What's more interesting, old man, was finding those London hern tracks when all naturalists are agreed the species became extinct during the latter part of the last century. I'd like to find another specimen."

"And vivisect it?" enquired Sir Seaton in some disapproval.

"Oh, not at all. I want to see it in the wild for myself and confirm that Henry Marriage, God rest his soul wherever he may be now, did not destroy the entire species. After all, it isn't every day one discovers that part of the past can yet be recovered, however small that part might be."

With a sudden rattle the tram began to move forward. Its buzzing electric engine could not quite disguise the sound of Sir Seaton Begg's approving grunt.

The Pleasure Garden of Felipe Sagittarius

Reality, I suggested, might be merely what each one of us says it is. Does that idea make you feel lonely, Mr Cornelius?

Lobkowitz
Recollected Dialogues

~๏ CHAPTER ONE ๏~

The air was still and warm, the sun bright, and the sky blue above the ruins of Berlin as I clambered over piles of weed-covered brick and broken concrete on my way to investigate the murder of an unknown man in the garden of Police Chief Bismarck.

My name is Sam Begg, Metatemporal Investigator, and this job was going to be a tough one, I knew.

Don't ask me the location or the date. I never bother to find out things like that. They only confuse me. With me it's instinct, win or lose.

They'd given me all the information there was. The dead man had already had an autopsy. Nothing unusual about him except that he had paper disposable lungs. That pinned him down a little. The only place I knew of where they still used paper lungs was Rome. What was a Roman doing in Berlin? Why was he murdered in Police Chief Bismarck's garden? He'd been strangled, that I'd been told. It wasn't hard to strangle a man with paper lungs; it didn't take long. But who and why were harder questions to answer right then.

It was a long way across the ruins to Bismarck's place. Rubble stretched in all directions, and only here and there could you see a landmark—what was left of the Reichstag, the Brandenburg Gate, the Brechtsmuseum, and a few other places like that.

I stopped to lean on the only remaining wall of a house, took off my jacket and loosened my tie, wiped my forehead and neck with my handkerchief, and lit a cheroot. The wall gave me some shade and I felt a little cooler by the time I was ready to get going again.

As I mounted a big heap of brick on which a lot of blue weeds grew I saw the Bismarck place ahead. Built of heavy, black-veined marble, in the kind of Valhalla/Olympus mixture they went in for, it was fronted by a smooth, green lawn and backed by a garden surrounded by such a high wall I only glimpsed the leaves of some of the foliage even though I was looking down on the place. The thick Grecian columns flanking the porch were topped by a baroque facade covered in bas-reliefs showing hairy men in horned helmets killing dragons and one another apparently indiscriminately.

I picked my way down to the lawn and walked across it, then up some steps until I reached the front door. It was big and heavy, bronze I guessed, with more bas-reliefs, this time of clean-shaven characters in ornate and complicated armour with two-handed swords and riding horses. Some had lances and axes. I pulled the bell and waited.

I had plenty of time to study the pictures before one of the doors swung open and an old man in a semi-military suit, holding himself straight by an effort, raised a white eyebrow at me.

I told him my name, and he let me in to a cool, dark hall full of the same kinds of armour the men outside had been wearing. He opened a door on the right and told me to wait. The room was all iron and leather—weapons on the walls and hide-covered furniture on the carpet. Thick velvet curtains were drawn back from the window, and I stood looking out over the quiet ruins, smoked another stick, popped the butt in a green pot, and put my jacket back on.

The old man came in again and I followed him out of that room, along the hall, up one flight of the wide stairs, and into a huge, less cluttered room where I found the guy I'd come to see.

He stood in the middle of the carpet. He was wearing a heavily ornamented helmet with a spike on the top, a deep blue uniform covered in badges, gold and black epaulettes, shiny jackboots, and steel spurs. He looked about seventy and very tough. He had bushy grey eyebrows and a big, carefully combed moustache. As I came in he grunted and put one arm into a horizontal position, pointing at me.

"Herr Begg. I am Otto von Bismarck, Chief of Berlin's police."

I shook the hand. Actually it shook me, all over.

"Quite a turn up," I said. "A murder in the garden of the man who's supposed to prevent murders."

His face must have been paralyzed or something because it didn't move except when he spoke, and even then it didn't move much.

"Quite so," he said. "We were reluctant to call you in, of course. But I think this is your speciality. Devilish work."

"Maybe. Is the body still here?"

"In the kitchen. The autopsy was performed here. Paper lungs—you know about that?"

"I know. Now, if I've got it right, you heard nothing in the night—"

"Oh, yes, I did hear something—the barking of my wolfhounds. One of the servants investigated but found nothing."

"What time was this?"

"Time?"

"What did the clock say?"

"About two in the morning."

"When was the body found?"

"About ten—the gardener discovered it in the vine grove."

"Right—let's look at the body and then talk to the gardener."

He took me to the kitchen. One of the windows was opened on to a lush enclosure full of tall, brightly coloured shrubs of every possible shade. An intoxicating scent came from the garden. It made me feel horny. I turned to look at the corpse lying on a scrubbed deal table covered in a sheet.

I pulled back the sheet. The body was naked. It looked old but strong, deeply tanned. The head was big, and its most noticeable feature was the heavy grey moustache. The body wasn't what it had been. First there were the marks of strangulation around the throat, as well as swelling on wrists, forearms, and legs which seemed to indicate that the victim had also been tied up recently. The whole of the front of the torso had been opened for the autopsy and whoever had stitched it up again hadn't been too careful.

"What about clothes?" I asked the Police Chief.

Bismarck shook his head and pointed to a chair standing beside the table. "That was all we found."

There was a pair of neatly folded paper lungs, a bit the worse for wear. The trouble with disposable lungs was that while you never had to worry about smoking or any of the other causes of lung disease, the lungs had to be changed regularly. This was expensive, particularly in Rome where there was no State-controlled Lung Service as there had been in most of the European City-States until a few years before the War when the longer lasting poly-thene lung had superseded the paper one. There was also a wristwatch and a pair of red shoes with long, curling toes.

I picked up one of the shoes. Middle Eastern workmanship. I looked at the watch. It was heavy, old, tarnished, and Russian. The strap was new, pigskin, with "Made in England" stamped on it.

"I see why they called us," I said.

"There were certain anachronisms," Bismarck admitted.

"This gardener who found him, can I talk to him?"

Bismarck went to the window and called: "Felipe!"

The foliage seemed to fold back of its own volition, and a cadaverous dark-haired man came through it. He was tall, long faced, and pale. He held an elegant watering can in one hand. He was dressed in a dark green, high-collared shirt and matching trousers. I wondered if I had seen him somewhere.

We looked at one another through the window.

"This is my gardener, Felipe Sagittarius," Bismarck said.

Sagittarius bowed, his eyes amused. Bismarck didn't seem to notice.

"Can you let me see where you found the body?" I asked.

"Sure," said Sagittarius.

"I shall wait here," Bismarck told me as I went towards the kitchen door.

"Okay." I stepped into the garden and let Sagittarius show me the way. Once again the shrubs seemed to part on their own.

The scent was still thick and erotic. Most of the plants had dark, fleshy leaves and flowers of deep reds, purples, and blues. Here and there were clusters of heavy yellow and pink.

The grass I was walking on felt like it crawled under my feet, and the weird shapes of the trunks and stems of the shrubs didn't make me want to take a snooze in that garden.

"This is all your work is it, Sagittarius?" I asked.

He nodded and kept walking.

"Original," I said. "Never seen one like it before."

Sagittarius turned then and pointed a thumb behind him. "This is the place."

We were standing in a little glade almost entirely surrounded by thick vines that curled about their trellises like snakes. On the far side of the glade I could see where some of the vines had been ripped and the trellis torn. I guessed there had been a fight. I still couldn't work out why the victim had been untied before the murderer strangled him—it must have been before, or else there wouldn't have been a fight. I checked the scene, but there were no clues. Through the place where the trellis was torn I saw a small summerhouse built to represent a Chinese pavilion, all red, yellow, and black lacquer with highlights picked out in gold. It didn't fit with the architecture of the house.

"What's that?" I asked the gardener.

"Nothing," he said sulkily, evidently sorry I'd seen it.

"I'll take a look at it anyway."

He shrugged but did not offer to lead on. I moved between the trellises until I reached the pavilion. Sagittarius followed slowly. I took the short flight of wooden steps up to the verandah and tried the door. It opened. I walked in. There seemed to be only one room, a bedroom. The bed needed making, and it looked as if two people had left it in a hurry. There was a pair of nylons tucked half under the pillow and a pair of man's underpants on the floor. The sheets were very white, the furnishings very oriental and rich.

Sagittarius was standing in the doorway.

"Your place?" I said.

"No." He sounded offended. "The Police Chief's."

I grinned.

Sagittarius burst into rhapsody. "The languorous scents, the very menace of the plants, the heaviness in the air of the garden, must surely stir the blood of even the most ancient man. This is the only place he can relax. This is what I'm employed for.

"He gives me my head. I give him his pleasures. It's my pleasure garden."

"Has this," I said, pointing to the bed, "anything to do with last night?"

"He was probably here when it happened, but I . . ." Sagittarius shook his head and I wondered if there was something he'd meant to imply that I'd missed.

I saw something on the floor, stooped, and picked it up. A pendant with the initials E.B. engraved on it in Gothic script.

"Who's E.B.?" I said.

"Only the garden interests me, Herr Begg. I do not know who she is."

I looked out at the weird garden. "Why does it interest you—what's all this for? You're not doing it to his orders, are you? You're doing it for yourself."

Sagittarius smiled bleakly. "You are astute." He waved an arm at the warm foliage that seemed more reptilian than plant and more mammalian, in its own way, than either. "You know what I see out there? I see deep-sea canyons where lost submarines cruise through a silence of twilit green, threatened by the waving tentacles of predators, half-fish, half-plant, and watched by the eyes of long-dead mermen whose blood went to feed their young; where squids and rays fight in a graceful dance of death, clouds of black ink merging with clouds of red blood, drifting to the surface, sipped at by sharks in passing, where they will be seen by mariners leaning over the rails of their ships. Maddened, the mariners will fling themselves overboard to sail slowly towards those distant plant-creatures already feasting on the corpse of squid and ray. This is the world I can bring to the land—that is my ambition."

He stared at me, paused, and said: "My skull—it's like a monstrous fish bowl!"

I nipped back to the house to find Bismarck had returned to his room. He was sitting in a plush armchair, a hidden HiFi playing, of all things, a Ravel String Quartet.

"No Wagner?" I said and then: "Who's E.B.?"

"Later," he said. "My assistant will answer your questions for the moment. He should be waiting for you."

There was a car parked outside the house—a battered Volkswagen containing a neatly uniformed man of below-average height. He had a small toothbrush moustache, a stray lock of black hair falling over his forehead, black gloves on his hands which gripped a military cane in his lap. When he saw me come out he smiled, said, "Aha," and got briskly from the car to shake my hand with a slight bow.

"Adolf Hitler," he said. "Captain of Uniformed Detectives in Precinct XII. Police Chief Bismarck has put me at your service."

"Glad to hear it. Do you know much about him?"

Hitler opened the car door for me, and I got in. He went round the other side, slid into the driving seat.

"The Chief?" He shook his head. "He is somewhat remote. I do not know him well—there are several ranks between us. Usually my orders come from him indirectly. This time he chose to see me himself."

"What were they, his orders, this time?"

"Simply to help you in this investigation."

"There isn't much to investigate. You're completely loyal to your chief I take it?"

"Of course." Hitler seemed honestly puzzled. He started the car and we drove down the drive and out along a flat, white road, surmounted on both sides by great heaps of overgrown rubble.

"The murdered man had paper lungs, eh?" he said.

"Yes. Guess he must have come from Rome. He looked a bit like an Italian."

"Or a Jew, eh?"

"I don't think so. What made you think that?"

"The Russian watch, the Oriental shoes—the nose. That was a big nose he had. And they still have paper lungs in Moscow, you know."

His logic seemed a bit off-beat to me but I let it pass. We turned a corner and entered a residential section where a lot of buildings were still standing. I noticed that one of them had a bar in its cellar. "How about a drink?" I said.

"Here?" He seemed surprised, or maybe nervous.

"Why not?"

So he stopped the car, and we went down the steps into the bar. A girl was singing. She was a plumpish brunette with a small, good voice. She was singing in English, and I caught the chorus:

"Nobody's grievin' for Steven,
And Stevie ain't grievin' no more,
For Steve took his life in a prison cell,
And Johnny took a new whore."

It was *Christine*, the latest hit in England. We ordered beers from the bartender. He seemed to know Hitler well because he laughed and slapped him on the shoulder and didn't charge us for the beer. Hitler seemed embarrassed.

"Who was that?" I asked.

"Oh, his name is Weill. I know him slightly."

"More than slightly, it looks like."

Hitler seemed unhappy and undid his uniform jacket, tilted his cap back on his head, and tried unsuccessfully to push up the stray lock of hair. He looked a sad little man, and I felt that maybe my habit of asking questions was out of line here. I drank my beer and watched the singer. Hitler kept his back to her, but I noticed she was looking at him.

"What do you know about this Sagittarius?" I asked.

Hitler shrugged. "Very little. His name, of course, is an invention."

Weill turned up again behind the bar and asked us if we wanted more beer. We said we didn't.

"Sagittarius?" Weill spoke up brightly. "Are you talking about that crank Klosterheim?"

"He's a crank, is he?" I said. The name rang a distant bell.

"That's not fair, Kurt," Hitler said. "He's a brilliant man, a biologist—"

"Klosterheim was thrown out of his job because he was insane!"

"That is unkind, Kurt," Hitler said reprovingly. "He was investigating the potential sentience of plant life. A perfectly reasonable line of scientific enquiry."

From the corner of the room someone laughed jeeringly. It was a shaggy-haired old man sitting by himself with a glass of schnapps on the little table in front of him.

Weill pointed at him. "Ask Albert. He knows about science."

Hitler pursed his lips and looked at the floor, "He's just an embittered old mathematics teacher—he's jealous of Felipe," he said quietly, so that the old man wouldn't hear.

"Who is he?" I asked Weill.

"Albert? A really brilliant man. He has never had the recognition he deserves. Do you want to meet him?"

But the shaggy man was leaving. He waved a hand at Hitler and Weill. "Kurt, Captain Hitler—good day."

"Good day, Doctor Einstein." Hitler turned to me. "Where would you like to go now?"

"A tour of the places that sell jewelry, I guess," I said, fingering the pendant in my pocket. "I may be on the wrong track altogether, but it's the only track I can find at the moment."

We toured the jewelers. By nightfall we were nowhere nearer finding who had owned the thing. I'd just have to get the truth out of Bismarck the next day, though I knew it wouldn't be easy. He wouldn't like answering personal questions. Hitler dropped me off at the Precinct House where a cell had been converted into a bedroom for me.

I sat on the hard bed smoking and brooding. I was just about to get undressed and go to sleep when I started to think about the bar we'd been in earlier. I was sure someone there could help me. On impulse I left the cell and went out into the deserted street. It was still very hot, and the sky was full of heavy clouds. Looked like a storm was due.

I got a cab back to the bar. It was still open.

Weill wasn't serving there now. He was playing the piano-accordion for the same girl singer I'd seen earlier. He nodded to me as I came in. I leant on the bar and ordered a beer from the barman.

When the number was over, Weill unstrapped his accordion and joined me. The girl followed him.

"Adolf not with you?" he said.

"He went home. He's a good friend of yours, is he?"

"Oh, we met years ago in Mirenburg. He's a nice man, you know. He should never have become a policeman. He's too mild. I doubt he'll ever find his Grail now."

"That's the impression I got. Why did he ever join in the first place?"

Weill smiled and shook his head. He was a short, thin man, wearing heavy glasses. He had a large, sensitive mouth. "Sense of duty, perhaps. He has a great sense of duty. He is very religious, too—a devout Catholic. I think that weighs on him. You know these converts, they accept nothing, are torn by their consciences. I never yet met a happy Catholic convert."

"He seems to have a thing about Jews."

Weill frowned. "What sort of thing? I've never really noticed. Many of his friends are Jews. I am, and Klosterheim.

"Sagittarius is a friend of his?"

"Oh, more an acquaintance I should think. I've seen them together a couple of times."

It began to thunder outside. Then it started to rain.

Weill walked towards the door and pulled down the blind. Through the noise of the storm I heard another sound, a strange, metallic grinding. A crunching.

"What's that?" I called. Weill shook his head and walked back towards the bar. The place was empty now. "I'm going to have a look," I said.

I went to the door, opened it, and climbed the steps.

Marching across the ruins, illuminated by rapid flashes of gunfire, I saw a gigantic metal monster, as big as a tall building. Supported on four telescopic legs, it lumbered at right angles to the street. From its huge body and head the snouts of guns stuck out in all directions. Lightning sometimes struck it, and it made an ear-shattering bell-like clang, paused to fire upwards at the source of the lightning, and marched on.

I ran down the steps and flung open the door. Weill was tidying up the bar. I described what I'd seen.

"What is it, Weill?"

The short man shook his head. "I don't know. At a guess it is something Berlin's conquerors left behind. A land leviathan?"

"It looked as if it was made here . . ."

"Perhaps it was. After all, who conquered Berlin—?"

A woman screamed from a back room, high and brief.

Weill dropped a glass and ran towards the room. I followed.

He opened a door. The room was homely. A table covered by a thick, dark cloth, laid with salt and pepper, knives and forks, a piano near the window, a girl lying on the floor.

"Eva!" Weill gasped, kneeling beside the body.

I gave the room another once-over. Standing on a small coffee table was a plant. It looked at first rather like a cactus of unpleasantly mottled green, though the top curved so that it resembled a snake about to strike. An eyeless, noseless snake—with a mouth. There was a mouth. It opened as I approached. There were teeth in the mouth—or rather thorns arranged the way teeth are. One thorn seemed to be missing near the front. I backed away from the plant and inspected the corpse. I found the thorn in her wrist. I left it there.

"She is dead," Weill said softly, standing up and looking around. "How?"

"She was bitten by that plant," I said.

"Plant . . . ? I must call the police."

"That wouldn't be wise at this stage maybe," I said as I left. I knew where I was going. Bismarck's house. And the pleasure garden of Felipe Sagittarius.

It took me time to find a cab, and I was soaked through when I did. I told the cabby to step on it.

I had the taxi stop before we got to the house, paid it off, and walked across the lawns. I didn't bother to ring the doorbell. I let myself in by the window, using my glasscutter.

I heard voices coming from upstairs. I followed the sound until I located it—Bismarck's study. I inched the door open.

Hitler was there. He had a gun pointed at Otto von Bismarck who was still in full uniform. They both looked pale. Hitler's hand was shaking, and Bismarck was moaning slightly. Bismarck stopped moaning to say pleadingly, "I wasn't blackmailing Eva Braun, you fool—she liked me."

Hitler laughed curtly, half hysterically. "Liked you—a fat old man."

"She liked fat old men."

"She wasn't that kind of girl."

"Who told you this, anyway?"

"The investigator told me some. And Weill rang me half an hour ago to tell me some more—also that Eva had been killed. I thought Sagittarius was my friend. I was wrong. He is your hired assassin. Well, tonight I intend to do my own killing."

"Captain Hitler—I am your superior officer!"

The gun wavered as Bismarck's voice recovered some of its authority. I realized that the HiFi had been playing quietly all the time. Curiously it was Bartok's Fifth String Quartet.

Bismarck moved his hand. "You are completely mistaken. That man you hired to follow Eva here last night—he was Eva's ex-lover!"

Hitler's lip trembled.

"You knew," said Bismarck.

"I suspected it."

"You also knew the dangers of the garden, because Felipe had told you about them. The vines killed him as he sneaked towards the summer house."

The gun steadied. Bismarck looked scared.

He pointed at Hitler. "You killed him—not I!" he screamed. "You sent him to his death. You killed Djugashvili—out of jealousy. You hoped he would kill me and Eva first. You were too frightened, too weak, to confront any of us openly!"

Hitler shouted wordlessly, put both hands to the gun, and pulled the trigger several times. Some of the shots went wide, but one hit Bismarck in his Iron Cross, pierced it, and got him in the heart. He fell backwards. As he did so his uniform ripped apart and his helmet fell off. I ran into the room and took the gun from Hitler who was crying. I checked that Bismarck was dead. I saw what had caused the uniform to rip open. He had been wearing a corset—one of the bullets must have cut the cord. It was a heavy corset and had a lot to hold in.

I felt sorry for Hitler. I helped him sit down as he sobbed. He looked small and wretched.

"What have I killed?" he stuttered. "What have I killed?"

"Did Bismarck send that plant to Eva Braun to silence her? Was I getting too close?"

Hitler nodded, snorted, and started to cry again.

I looked towards the door. A man hesitated there.

I put the gun on the mantelpiece.

It was Sagittarius.

He nodded to me.

"Hitler's just shot Bismarck," I explained.

"So it appears." He touched his thin lips.

"Bismarck had you send Eva Braun that plant, is that so?" I said.

"Yes. A beautiful cross between a common cactus, a Venus Flytrap, and a rose—the venom was curare, of course."

Hitler got up and walked from the room. We watched him leave. He was still sniffling.

"Where are you going?" I asked.

"To get some air," I heard him say as he went down the stairs.

"The repression of sexual desires," said Sagittarius seating himself in an armchair and resting his feet comfortably on Bismarck's corpse. "It is the cause of so much trouble. If only the passions that lie beneath the surface, the desires that are locked in the mind, could be allowed to range free, what a better place the world would be."

"Maybe," I said.

"Are you going to make any arrests, Herr Begg?"

"It's my job to file a report on my investigation, not to make arrests," I said.

"Will there be any repercussions over this business?"

I laughed. "There are always repercussions," I told him.

From the garden came a peculiar barking noise.

"What's that?" I asked. "The wolfhounds?"

Sagittarius giggled. "No, no—the dog-plant, I fear."

I ran out of the room and down the stairs until I reached the kitchen. The sheet-covered corpse was still lying on the table. I was going to open the door onto the garden when I stopped and pressed my face to the window instead.

The whole garden was moving in what appeared to be an agitated dance. Foliage threshed about and, even with the door closed, the strange scent was unbearable.

I thought I saw a figure struggling with some thick-boled shrubs. I heard a growling noise, a tearing sound, a scream, and a long drawn-out groan.

Suddenly the garden was motionless.

I turned. Sagittarius stood behind me. His hands were folded on his chest. His eyes stared down at the floor.

"It seems your dog-plant got him," I said. "Herr Klosterheim."

"He knew me—he knew the garden." He ignored my challenge.

"Suicide maybe?"

"Very likely." Sagittarius unfolded his hands and looked up at me. "I liked him, you know. He was something of a protégé. If you had not inter-fered none of this might have happened. He might have gone far with me to guide him. We could have found the cup."

"You'll have other protégés," I said.

"Let us hope so." His voice was cold as the stars.

The sky outside gradually began to lighten. The rain was now only a drizzle falling on the thirsty leaves of the plants.

"Are you going to stay here?" I asked him.

"Yes—I have the garden to work on. Bismarck's servants will look after me."

"I guess they will," I said.

Once again I'd gotten to keep the Cup, but I told myself this was the last time I played the game. I wanted to go home. I went back up the stairs and I walked away from that house into a cold and desolate dawn. I tried to light my last Black Cat and failed. Then I threw the damp cigarette into the rubble, turned up the collar of my coat, and began to make my way slowly across the ruins.

The Affair of Le Bassin des Hivers

~@ CHAPTER ONE @~

Le Bassin des Hivers

U ntil the late part of the last century, the area known as Les Hivers was
notorious for its poverty, its narrow, filthy streets, and the extraordinary
number of crimes of passion recorded there. This district lay directly behind
the famous Cirque d'Hiver, the winter circus, home to performing troupes
who generally toured through the spring and summer months. Residents
complained of the roaring of lions and tigers or the trumpeting of elephants
at night, but the authorities were slow to act, given the nature of this part of
the 11th arrondissement whose inhabitants were not exactly influential.

The great canal, which brought produce to most of Paris, branched off
from the Canal Saint Martin just below the Circus itself, to begin its journey
underground. For many bargees, what they termed Le Bassin des Hivers was
the end of their voyage, and here they would rest before returning to their
home ports with whatever goods they had purchased or traded. Surrounding
the great basin leaned a number of wooden quays and jetties, together with
warehouses and high-ceilinged halls where business had always been done in
gaslight or the semidarkness created by huge arches and locks dividing the
upper and the lower canal systems. The banks rose thirty meters or more,
made of ancient stone, much of it reused from Roman times, backing onto
tall, windowless depositories built of tottering brick and timber. The sun
could gain no access here, and at night the quays and markets were lit by gas
or naphtha and only occasionally by electricity. Beside the cobbled canal
paths flourished the cafés, brothels, and cheap rooming houses, as well as the

famous Bargees' Mission and Church of Our Lady of the Waterways, operated since the ninth century by the pious and incorruptible White Friars. Like Alsatia, that area of London also administered by the Carmelites, it formed a secure sanctuary for all but habitual murderers.

The bargees not continuing under the city to the coast, and even to Britain, concluded their voyages here, having brought their cargoes from Nantes, Lyon, or Marseille. Others came from the Low Countries, Scandinavia, and Prussia, while those barge folk regarded as the cream of their race had sailed waterways connecting the French capital with Moscow, Istanbul, or the Italian Republics. The English bargees, with their heavy, red sailed, oceangoing boats, came to sell their own goods, mostly Sheffield steel and pottery, and buy French wine and cheese for which there was always a healthy market in their chilly nation chronically starved of food and drink fit for human consumption. It was common for altercations and fights to break out between the various nationalities, and more than one would end with a mortal knife wound.

And so for centuries few respectable Parisians ever ventured into Les Hivers and those who did so rarely returned in their original condition. Even the police patrolled the serpentine streets by wagon or, armed with carbines, in threes and fours. They dared not venture far into the system of underground waterways known collectively as the Styx. Taxi drivers, unless offered a substantial commission, would not go into Les Hivers at all but would drop passengers off in the Boulevard du Temple close to the permanent hippodrome, always covered in vivid posters in summer or winter. The drivers claimed that their automobiles' batteries could not be recharged in that primitive place.

Only as the barge trade slowly gave way to more rapid commercial traffic, such as the electric railways and mighty aerial freighters, which began to cross the whole of Europe and even as far as America, Africa, and the Orient, did the area become settled by the sons and daughters of the middle classes, by writers and artists, by well-to-do North Africans, Vietnamese, homosexuals, and others who found the rest of Paris either too expensive or too unwelcoming. And, as these things will go, the friends of the pioneering bohemians came quickly to realise that the district was no longer as dangerous as its reputation suggested. They could sell their apartments in more expensive districts and buy something much cheaper in Les Hivers. Warehouses were converted into homes and shops, and the quays and jetties began to house quaint restaurants and coffee houses. Some of the least stable buildings were torn down to admit sunlight.

By the 1990s the transformation was complete, and few of the original inhabitants could afford to live there any longer. The district, now positively fashionable, became the place we know today, full of bookshops, little cinemas, art suppliers, expensive bistros, cafés, and exclusive hotels. The animals are housed where they will not disturb the residents and customers.

By the time Michel Houlebecq moved there in 1996, the transformation was complete. He declared the area "a meeting place of deep realities and metaphysical resonances." Though a few barge people still brought their goods to Les Hivers, these were unloaded onto trucks or supplied a *marché biologique* to rival that of Boulevard Raspail, and only the very desperate still plied the dark, subterranean waterways for which no adequate maps had ever existed. The barge folk continued to be as clannish as always. Their secrets were passed down from one family member to another.

When he was a lowly detective sergeant, Commissaire Lapointe lived on the Avenue Parmentier where he came to know the alleys and twitters of the neighborhood. He developed relationships with many of the settled bargees and their kin and did more than one favor to a waterman accused unjustly of a crime. They respected Lapointe, even if they did not love him.

A heavyset man in a dark Raglan overcoat and an English cap, Lapointe was at once saturnine and avuncular. Lighting a Cuban cheroot, he descended from the footplate of his heavy police car, its motors humming at rest. Turning up his collar against the morning chill, he looked with some melancholy at the boutiques and restaurants now crowding the old wharfs. "Paris changes too rapidly," he announced to his long-suffering young assistant, the sharp-featured LeBec, who had only recently joined the special department. "She has all the grace and stateliness of an aristocratic whore, yet these stones, as our friend de Certau has pointed out, are full of dark stories, an unsavory past."

Lapointe had become fascinated by psychogeography, the brainchild of Guy DeBord, who developed the philosophy of "flaneurism" or the art of *dérive*. DeBord and his followers had it that all great cities were the sum of their past and that the past was never far away, no matter what clever cosmetics were used to hide it. They had nothing but contempt for the electric trams, trains, and cars which bore the busy Parisians about the city. Only by walking, by "drifting," could one appreciate and absorb the history inhaled with every breath, mixing living flesh with the dust of one's ancestors. Commissaire Lapointe, of course, had a tendency to support these ideas, as did many of the older members of the *Sûreté du Temps Perdu* and their colleagues abroad. This was especially true in London, where Lapointe's famous opposite number, "Sir Seaton Begg," chief metatemporal investigator for the Home Office, headed the legendary White-hall Time Center, whose very existence was denied by Parliament, just as the Republic refused to admit any knowledge of the Quai d'Orsay's STP.

LeBec accepted these musings as he always did, keeping his own counsel. He had too much respect to dismiss his chief's words but was also too dedicated a modern to make such opinions his own.

Reluctantly Lapointe began to move along the freshly paved quay until he reached the entrance to a narrow canyon between two of the former warehouses. Rue Mendoza was no different from scores of similar alleys, save that a pale blue STP van stood outside one of its entrances, the red light on its roof turning in slow, voluptuous arcs while uniformed officers questioned the inhabitants of the great warren which had housed grain but now was the residence of publicity directors, television producers, and miscellanous media people, all of whom were demanding to know why they could not go about their business.

Behind him on the canal, Lapointe could see a faint mist rising from the water, and he heard a dozen radios and Vs, all tuned to the morning news programmes. So far, at least, the press had not yet got hold of this story. He stubbed out his cigar and put it back in his case, following the uniformed man into the house. He told LeBec to remain outside for a minute and question the angry residents before continuing upstairs. There were no elevators in this particular building and Lapointe was forced to climb several storeys until at last he came to a landing where a pale-faced young man, still in his pyjamas covered by a blue check dressing gown, stood with his back to the green and cream wall smoking a long, thin Nat Sherman cigarette, one of the white Virginia variety. He transferred the cigarette from right to left and shook hands with Lapointe as he introduced himself.

"Bonjour, M'sieu. I am Sébastien Gris."

"Commissaire Lapointe of the Sûreté. What's all this about a fancy dress party and a dead girl?"

Gris opened his mouth, but there was no air in his lungs. His thin features trembled and his pale blue eyes filled with helpless fury. He could not speak. He drew a deep breath. "Monsieur, I telephoned the moment I found her. I have touched nothing, I promise."

Lapointe grunted. He looked down at a pretty blonde girl, her fair skin waxy in the artificial light, who lay sprawled in the man's hallway, a meter or so from the entrance to his tiny kitchen filling with steam from a forgotten kettle. Lapointe stepped over the body and went to turn off the gas. Slowly the steam dissipated. He removed a large paisley handkerchief from his pocket and mopped at his head and neck. He sighed. "No name? No identity? No papers of any kind?"

The uniformed man confirmed this. "Just what you see, Monsieur le Commissaire."

Lapointe leaned and touched her face. He took something on his finger and inspected it carefully. "Arsenic powder," he said, "and almost certainly cochineal for rouge." He was growing depressed. "I've only seen this once before." He recognized the work on her dress. It was authentic. Though unusually beautiful for the period and with an unblemished face, she was as certainly an inhabitant of the early nineteenth century as he was of the twenty-first, and as sure as he was alive, she was dead, murdered by a neat cut across her throat. "A true beauty and no doubt famous in her age. Murdered and disposed of by an expert."

"You have my absolute assurances, Monsieur, that her body was here when I got up this morning. Someone has done this, surely, to implicate me. It cannot be a joke."

Lapointe nodded gravely. "I fear, Monsieur Gris, that your presence in this building had little or nothing to do with the appearance of a corpse outside your kitchen." The young man became instantly relieved and began to babble a sequence of theories, forcing Lapointe to raise his hand as he dropped to one knee to inspect something clutched in the corpse's right fist. He frowned and checked the fingernails of the left fingers in which some coarse brown fibers had caught. The young man continued to talk, and Lapointe became thoughtful and impatient at the same time, rising to his feet. "If you please, Monsieur. It is our job to determine how she came to die here and, if possible, identify her murderer. You, I regret, will have to remain nearby while I question the others. Have you the means to telephone your place of work?"

The young man nodded and crossed over to a wall bearing a fashionably modeled telephone. He gave the operator a number. As he was speaking, LeBec came in to join his chief. He shuddered when he saw the corpse. He knew at once why their department had been called in. "She's 1820 or perhaps '25," he murmured. "What's that in her hand? A rosary? An expensive gold crucifix, too? Poor child. Was she killed here or there?"

"By the look of the blood it was there," responded his chief. "But whoever brought her body here is still amongst us, I am almost certain. He turned the crucifix over to look at the back. All he read there were the initials "J.C." "Perhaps also her murderer." With an inclination of his massive head, he indicated where the bloodstains told a story of the girl being dragged and searched. "Did they assume her to be a witch of some sort? A familiar story. Her clothes suggest wealth. Yet she wears too much makeup for a girl of her age from a good family. Was she an adept or the daughter of an adept, maybe? What if she made her murderers a gateway into wherever they thought they were going, and they killed her, either to be certain she told no others or as some sort of bizarre sacrifice? Yet why would she be clutching such an expensive rosary? And what about those fibers? Were they disguised? You know how they think, LeBec, as well as I do." He watched as his assistant took an instrument from an inside pocket and ran it over the girl's head and neck. Straightening himself, LeBec studied his readings, nodding occasionally as his instincts were confirmed.

The commisioner was giving close attention to the series of bloody marks leading away from the corpse to the front door of the apartment. Again he noted those initials on the back of the crucifix. "My God!" he murmured. "But why . . . ?"

CHAPTER TWO

Monsieur Zenith: A Brief History

"**I** suspect our murderer had good reason to dispose of the corpse in this way," declared Lapointe. "My guess is that her face and body were both too well known for her to be simply dropped in the Seine, while the murderer did not wish to be observed moving her through the streets of Paris, either because he himself was also highly recognizable or because he had no easy way of doing what he needed to do. And no alibi. So, if not one himself, he called in an expert, no doubt a person already known to him."

"An expert? You mean such people understood about metatemporal tran-science in the 1820s?"

"Generally speaking, of course, very few of our ancestors understood such things. Even fewer than today. We are not talking of time-travel, which as we all know, is impossible, but movement from one universe to another where one era has developed at a slower rate in relation to ours. Needless to say, we are not discussing our own past but a time approximating our own present. That's why most of our cases take us to periods equivalent to our own twentieth or early twenty-first century. So we are dealing here with a remote scale, far removed from our own. Another reason for our murderer to put as many alternative scales between ours and theirs."

Lapointe was discussing the worlds of the multiverse, separated one from another by mass rather than time. Each world was of enormously larger or smaller scale to the next, enabling all the alternate universes which made up the great multiverse to coexist, one invisible to the other for reasons of size. Not until the great French scientist Benoit Mandelbrot developed these theories ($Z = z^2 + c$) was it possible for certain adepts to increase or decrease their own mass and cross from one of these worlds to the other. Mandelbrot effectively provided us with maps of our own brains, plans of the multiverse. This in turn led to the setting up of secret government agencies designed to create policies and departments whose function was to deal with the new realities.

Now almost every major nation had some equivalent to the STP in some version of its own twenty-first century, apart from the Confederation, which had largely succeeded in refusing to enter that century in any significant sense and was forced to rely on foreign agents to cope with the problems arising from situations with their roots in the twenty-first century.

"But you are convinced, chief, that the murderer is French?"

"If not French, then they have lived in France for many years."

Habitually unused to questioning his superior's instinctive judgements, LeBec accepted this.

As their electromobile sped them back to the Quai d'Orsay, Lapointe mused on the problem. "I need to find someone who has an idea of all the metatemporals who come and go in Paris. Only one springs to mind and that is Monsieur Zenith, the Albino. You'll recall we have worked together once or twice before. As soon as I get back to the office, I will put through a call to Whitehall. If anyone knows where Zenith is, it will be Sexton Blake."

Sexton Blake was the real name of the detective famously fictionalized as Sir Seaton Begg and Lapointe's opposite number in London.

"I did not realize Monsieur Zenith was any longer amongst us," declared LeBec.

"There is no guarantee that he is. I can only hope. I understood that he had made his home in Paris. Blake will confirm where I can find him."

"I thought, chief, that he was in earlier days wanted by the police of several countries."

"Quite so. On our plane his last encounter as a criminal with Blake was during the London Blitz. He and his old antagonist fought it out on a cliff house whose foundations were weak. The fictional version of the case has been recorded as *The Affair of the Bronze Basilisk*. Zenith's body was lost in the ruins of the house and never recovered, but we now know that he returned to Jugo-Slavia where he fought with Tito's guerillas against the Nazis, was captured by the Gestapo before he could smoke the famous cyanide cigarette he always kept in his case, and was found half dead by the British when they liberated the infamous Milosevic Fortress in Belgrade, HQ of the Gestapo in the region. For his various services on behalf of the allied war effort, Zenith was given a full pardon by the authorities, and in his final meeting with his old adversary Sexton Blake, both men made a bargain: Blake would allow no more stories of Zenith to be published as part of his own memoirs, and Zenith would not publish his memoirs until fifty years after that meeting which was in August 26, 1946. Both men have been exposed to the same effects which conferred longevity upon them, almost by accident. That fifty years has now, of course, passed."

"And Monsieur Zenith?" asked LeBec as the car hummed smoothly under the arches into the square leading to their offices. "What has happened to him?"

"He has become a kind of gentleman adventurer, working as often with the authorities as against them and spending much of his time tracking down ex-Nazis, especially those with stolen wealth, which he either returns in whole to their owners or, if it so pleases him, pays himself a ten percent 'commission.' He sometimes works with my old friend Blake. His adventures may take him across parallel universes, but he still keeps up with his old acquaintances from the criminal underworld, mostly through a famous London thieves' warren known as 'Smith's Kitchen' which now has concessions in Paris, Rome, and New York. If anyone has heard a hint of the business here, it will be Zenith."

"How will Mr Blake know how to contact him, chief?"

Lapointe smiled to himself. "Oh, I think Blake will have a fair idea."

～✿ CHAPTER THREE ❀～

Familiar Names

A broken rosary, a silver crucifix bearing the initials "J.C.," a few coarse, brown fibers, some photographs of the corpse seen earlier at Les Hivers. One by one, Commissaire Lapointe laid the things before him on the bright, white tablecloth. He was sitting in a fashionable café, L'Albertine, situated in the Arcades de l'Opéra, whose windows looked into a square in which a beautiful ornamental fountain played. Outside Paris's *haut-monde* strolled back and forth, conversing, inspecting the windows of the expensive shops, occasionally entering to make purchases. Across from him, sipping alternately at a small coffee cup and a glass of yellow-green absinthe, sat a most extraordinary individual. His skin was pale as alabaster. His hair, including his eyebrows, was the color of milk, and his gleaming, sardonic eyes resembled the finest rubies. Dressed unusually for the age, the albino wore perfectly cut morning dress. A grey silk hat, evidently his, shared a shelf near the cash register with Lapointe's wide-brimmed straw.

"I am grateful, Monsieur, that you found time to see me," murmured Lapointe, understanding the value the albino placed on good manners. "I was hoping these objects would mean more to you than they do to me. Evidently belonging to a priest or a nun . . ."

"Of high rank," agreed Zenith continuing to look at the photographs of the victim.

"We also found several long black hairs and traces of heavy red lipstick of fairly recent manufacture."

"No nun wore that," mused Zenith. "Which suggests her murderess was disguised as a nun. In which case, of course, she is still unlikely to have worn lip-rouge. It was not the young woman's?"

"Hers was from an earlier age." Lapointe had already explained the circumstances in which the corpse was discovered, as well as his guess at the time and date when she was murdered.

"So we can assume there were at least two people involved in killing her, one of whom at least had knowledge of the multiverse and how to gain access to other worlds."

"And at least one of them could still be here. Those footprints told us that part of the story. Some effort had been made to wrest the rosary from her fingers after she had arrived in Les Hivers."

"The man . . . shall we assume him to be a priest?" Monsieur Zenith raised the rosary as if to kiss it, but then sniffed it instead. "J.C.? Some reference perhaps to the Society of Jesus?"

"Possibly. Which might lead us to assume the Inquisition to be at work?"

"I will see what I can discover for you, Monsieur Lapointe. As for the poor victim . . ." Zenith offered his old acquaintance a slight shrug.

"I believe I have a way of discovering her identity also, assuming she was not what we used to call a 'virtuous' girl," said Lapointe. I have already checked the police records for that period, and no mention is made of a society disappearance that was not subsequently solved. Therefore, by the quality of her clothes, the fairness of her skin, condition of her hair, not to mention her extraordinary beauty, we must assume her to be either of foreign birth or some kind of courtesan. The cut of her clothes suggests the latter to me. There is, in that case, only one place to look for her. I must inspect our copy of De Buzet."

Zenith raised an alabaster eyebrow. "You have a copy of the legendary Carte Bleue?"

"One of the two known to exist. The property of the Quai des Orfèvres for almost two hundred years. Of little value, of course, in the general way. But now . . . it might just lead us to our victim, if not to her murderers."

Monsieur Zenith extinguished his Turkish cigarette and rose to leave. "I will do what I can to trace this assumed cleric, and if you can discover a reasonable likeness in La Carte Bleue, we shall perhaps meet here again tomorrow morning?"

"Until then," declared Lapointe, standing to shake hands. He watched with mixed feelings as the albino collected his hat and stick at the door and strolled into the sunlit square, for all the world a flaneur from a previous century.

Later that same day, wearing impeccable evening dress as was his unvarying habit, Monsieur Zenith made his way to a certain unprepossessing address in the Marais where he admitted himself with a key, entering through a door of peeling green paint into a foyer whose interior window slid open and a pair of yellow, bloodshot eyes regarded him suspiciously. Zenith gave a name and a number and, as he passed through the second door, pulled on a black domino which, of course, did nothing to disguise his appearance but was a convention of the establishment. Once within, he gave his hat and cloak to a bowing receptionist and found himself in those parts of the catacombs made into a great dining room known to the aristocrats of the criminal underworld as La Cuisine de Smith. Here that fraternity could exist unhindered and, while eating a passable dinner, could listen to an orchestra consisting of a violinist, a guitarist, double-bassist, an accordionist, and a pianist. If they so wished they could also dance the exotic tango of Argentina or the Apache of Paris herself.

Zenith took a table in an alcove under a low stone ceiling that was centuries old. He blew out the large votive candle which was his only light. He ordered his usual absinthe and from his cigarette case removed a slender oval, which he placed between his lips and lit. The rich sweetness of Kashmiri opium poured from his nostrils as he exhaled the smoke, and his eyes became heavily lidded. Watching the dancers, all at once he became aware of a presence at his table and a slender woman, whose domino only enhanced her dark beauty, an oval face framed by a perfectly cut "pageboy" style. She laid a hand lightly on his shoulder and smiled.

"Will you dance, old friend?" she asked.

Although she was known to the world as Una Persson, Countess von Bek, Zenith thought of her by another name. He rejoiced inwardly at his good fortune. She was exactly whom he had hoped to meet here. He rose and bowed, then gracefully escorted her to the door where they joined in the rhythms of The Entropy Tango, that strange composition actually written for one of Countess Una's closest friends. In England she had enjoyed a successful career on the music hall stage. Here she was best known as a daring adventuress.

Arranging their wonderful bodies in the figures of the tango, the two carried on a murmured conversation. When the final chords rose to subtle crescendo, Zenith had the knowledge he sought.

At his invitation Countess Una joined him, the candle was relit, and they ordered from the menu. This was to prove dangerous for, moments after they began to eat, a muffled shot stilled the orchestra, and Zenith noted with some interest that a large-calibre bullet had penetrated the plaster just behind his left shoulder. The bullet had flattened oddly, enough to tell him that it was made of an unusual alloy. Countess Una recognized it, too. It was she who blew out the candle so that they no longer made an easy target.

They spoke almost in chorus.

"Vera Pym!"

Who else but that ruthless mistress of Paris's most notorious gang would ignore Smith's rules of sanctuary, respected even by the police?

But why had she suddenly determined to destroy the albino?

Zenith frowned. Could he know more than he realised?

~◉ CHAPTER FOUR ◉~

Fitting the Pieces

Commissaire Lapointe was unsurprised by Zenith's information when they met at L'Albertine the next morning. Vera Pym (believed to be her real name) was the acknowledged leader of a gang which had in its time had several apparent leaders. Only Pym, however, had remained in control of *Les Vampyres* throughout their long career. She was one of a small group capable, to one degree or another, of moving between the worlds and living for centuries. The rank and file of her gang, for all their sinister name, had no such qualities. Some did not even realize she was their leader, for she generally put her man of the moment in that position. Occasionally she changed her name, though generally it remained a simple anagram of her gang's. And she had many disguises. Few were absolutely sure what she looked like or, indeed, if she was always the same person. Several times she had been captured, yet she had always been able to escape.

"She has been a thorn in the side of the authorities for well over a century," agreed Lapointe. "And, of course, she is one of the few we can suspect in this case."

"What's more," added Zenith, "she has recently been seen in the company of a man of the cloth. An Abbé by all accounts."

"My God!" Lapointe passed a photocopied picture across the table. "Tell me what you make of that!"

Frowning, the albino examined the picture. "Not much, I'm afraid. Is she . . . ?"

"The likeness is remarkably similar to our victim. Her name was Sarah Gobseck, a Jewess better known in her day as La Torpille."

"A surprisingly unfeminine sobriquet."

"I agree. But at that time a torpedo was something which lay in the water, half-hidden by the waves, until hit by a ship, whereupon it would explode and as likely as not sink the ship. She is most famous from Balzac's *History of the Courtesans*."

"Ah!" Zenith sat back, drawing on his cigarette. "So that's our Abbé! Carlos Herrera!"

"Exactly. Vautrin himself. Which would explain the initials on the rosary. So he is here now with Madame Pym. Which also explains anomalies in his career as reported by Balzac. Vautrin is Jacques Collin, the master criminal, who vanished from the historical records at about the time our 'Torpedo' became an inconvenient embarrassment to more than one gentleman. Suicide was suspected, I know. But now we have the truth."

"No doubt Collin also vanished into the twenty-first century, since Balzac becomes increasingly vague concerning his identity or his exploits and appears to have resorted to unlikely fictions to explain him. He knew nothing of La Pym, of course!"

"But this does nothing to tell us of their whereabouts," mused Zenith.

"Nor," added Lapointe, "how they can be brought to justice."

For some moments Zenith was lost in thought, then he glanced at his watch and frowned. "Perhaps you will permit me, Monsieur le Commissaire, to solve that particular problem."

Lapointe became instantly uncomfortable. "I assure you, Monsieur Zenith, that while I appreciate all your help, this is ultimately a police matter. I would remind you that you are already risking your life. La Pym has marked you as her next victim."

"A fact, Monsieur Lapointe, that I greatly resent. Because of a promise I made to a certain great Englishman, I regret to say I have been forced to suffer the existence of a bourgeois professional, almost a tradesman, and no longer pursue the life I once relished. However, in this case a certain personal element has entered the equation. I feel obliged to satisfy my honor and perhaps avenge the death of that beautiful young creature who, through no fault of her own, was forced into a profession for which she had only abhorence and which resulted, at least according to de Balzac's history, in an unholy, early, and wholly undeserved death."

"My dear Monsieur Zenith, if I may make so bold, this still remains a matter for the judiciary."

"But you are helpless, I think you will agree, certainly in the matter of Collin. He will evade you, as no doubt also will La Pym."

"If so, then we will continue to hunt for them until we can arrest them and prove their guilt or innocence in a court of law."

The albino bowed from where he sat. "So be it." With that he got to his feet and, making a polite gesture, bade the policeman au revoir.

Commissaire Lapointe immediately made his way back to the Quai d'Orsay where LeBec awaited him. He read at once the concern in his superior's face.

"What's up, chief?"

Lapointe was in poor humor and in no mood to explain, but he knew he owed it to LeBec to say something. "I'm pretty sure that Zenith has an idea of our murderers' whereabouts and intends to take the law into his own hands. He is convinced that he knows who they are and how to punish them. We must find him and follow him and do all we can to thwart him!"

"But, chief, if he can deliver justice where we cannot . . . ?"

"Then all our civilization stands for nothing, LeBec. Already the Confederates and the British have adopted the language of the blood feud in their foreign affairs, demanding eyes for eyes and teeth for teeth which is nothing more or less than a reversion to the most primitive form of law available to our ancestors. France cannot follow the Anglo-Saxons down that road, and I will do all in my power to make sure she does not!"

"And yet . . ."

"LeBec, for twenty centuries we have steadily improved civilization until our complex system of justice, allowing for subtle interpretation, for context, for motive, and so on, has become paramount. It is the law I live to serve. Zenith, for all that he behaves with courage and honour, would defy justice, just as he used to, and I will have no part in it. Though I lack his resources and knowledge, even, perhaps, his courage, I must stop him. In the name of the Law."

Understanding at last, LeBec nodded gravely. "Very well, chief, but what are we to do?"

"Our best," declared Lapointe gravely. "I suspect that Countess von Bek, your own distant cousin, is still helping him in this. For that reason, I put a man to follow her. If we are lucky she will lead us to Zenith. And Zenith, I sincerely hope, will lead us to the murderers, to Vautrin and Vera Pym, while there is still a chance of our apprehending them."

"Where are they going, chief? Do you know?"

"My guess is that since they failed to kill Zenith last night, they will attempt to return from whence they came. But how they will make that attempt remains a mystery to me."

~◉ CHAPTER FIVE ◉~

Zenith's Resolution

Una Persson's car had been seen heading up the Boulevard Voltaire towards the Boulevard du Temple carrying at least two passengers, so it was for the Marais that the policemen headed in their own Citroen ECXVI, perhaps the fastest car in France, powered by three enormous supercharged batteries. The sleek, black machine delivered them outside the Cirque d'Hiver within minutes, but from there they had to run towards the canal and down the steps to the great basin, by now, at twilight, alive with dancing neon and neurotic music. There at last Lapointe caught a glimpse of his quarry and pointed.

Zenith, as was appropriate, wore white tie and tails and carried a slender silver-tipped ebony cane, an astonishing sight to LeBec who had never seen him thus. "My God, chief, we are pursuing Fred Astaire and Ginger Rogers!" He smiled.

The Commissaire found no humor in the situation. "This could be dangerous business, lad. There was never any profit in making that man one's enemy. He was once the most dangerous thief in Europe, and Europe is lucky that he gave his word to his old friend to forsake his life of crime or he would still be causing us considerable grief!"

Suitably chastened LeBec panted. "What is he? Some kind of vampire?"

"Only in legends. And not in any way associated with Vera Pym and her gang." Lapointe continued to push through the crowd as the evening grew darker. "At least I have some idea now where he is heading. There must have been a gateway created by the murderers . . ."

Crossing the old wooden bridge over the basin, they saw what had brought the crowd here. It was a huge black barge of the kind once used in the canal folk's funerals, two decks high. "It came up out of there not ten minutes ago!" said an underdressed young woman wearing garish face paint. "It just—just appeared, messieurs!"

Lapointe stared into the mysterious maw of the underground canal. "So that's where they've been hiding. A veritable water maze," he muttered. "Hurry, LeBec, for the love of God!"

At last they had forced a passage through the crowds, back to the tall looming house in rue Mendoza where the corpse of Sarah Gobseck had been discovered. As Lapointe had guessed, the two ahead of them had abandoned their own car and were hurrying towards the entrance of Number Fifteen into which they swiftly disappeared.

By the time Lapointe and his assistant reached the door, it was locked and bolted. Much time was wasted as they attempted to rouse the residents and gain access.

From the very top of the building, they could hear a strange, single note, as of an organ, which began to drown almost all other sound and made communication difficult. As they neared the fifth floor, they became aware of a violent, pulsing brilliance filling the stairwell above. It seemed to pour through the skylight and have its origins on the roof. The air itself had an unnatural smell of vanilla and ozone which reminded Lapointe irrationally of the corniche at Nice, where as a boy he had holidayed with his family.

Next an unnatural pressure began to exert itself on the men, as if gravity had somehow tripled in intensity. They moved sluggishly with enormous effort up to the final landing where Monsieur Gris, an expression of terror on his features, was attempting to descend the stairs. Behind him a ladder had been pulled down from the ceiling and gave access to an open door in the roof.

Lapointe and LeBec eventually struggled up the ladder to the roof. There amongst the old chimneys and sloping leads stood four people. A vicious looking woman whose beauty was marred by her rodent snarl and a tonsured priest whom Lapointe immediately identified as Vautrin, otherwise known as Jacques Collin but here disguised as the Abbé Carlos Herrera! Confronting Vautrin and his coconspiratator, Vera Pym, were Zenith the Albino and the Countess Una von Bek. All were armed, Vautrin with a rapier and Pym with a modern automatic pistol. Zenith carried his ebony sword-stick while Countess von Bek pointed a Smith and Wesson .45 revolver at the snarling leader of the Vampires.

And, if this scene were not dramatic enough, there yawned behind Pym and Vautrin a strange, swirling gap in the very fabric of time and space which mumbled and cried and moved with a nervous bubbling intensity.

"Sacred Heaven!" murmured Lapointe. "That is how they got here and that is how they intend to leave. They have ripped a hole through the multiverse. This is not a gateway in the usual sense. It is as if someone had taken a sledgehammer to the supporting walls of Saint Peter's! Who knows what appalling damage they have created!"

Then suddenly Vautrin lunged, his long, slender blade driving for Zenith's heart. But the Albino's reflexes were as fast as always. Dodging the feint, he drew his infamous rapier of black, vibrating steel which sang a song of its own. Mysterious scarlet runes ran up and down its length as if alive. He replied to Vautrin's thrust with one of his own.

Parrying, Vautrin began to laugh, a hideous obscenity of sound which somehow blended with that awful light pouring through the rift in multiversal space their crude methods had created. "Your powers of deduction remain superb, Zenith, even if your taste in friends is not. She was indeed 'La Torpille.' I thought I had driven her to self-destruction, but she failed me in the end. I struck her down, as you and the others have guessed, and then, to make sure the body was never discovered and seen to be murdered, I employed the services of Madame Vera Pym here, my old colleague."

Now Lapointe had drawn his revolver and was levelling it. "Stop, Monsieur Vautrin. In the name of the Republic! In the name of the Law! Stop and put down your weapon. On your own admission, I arrest you for the murder of Mademoiselle Sarah Gobseck!"

Again Vautrin voiced that terrible laugh. "Monsieur Zenith, Commissaire Lapointe, your mental qualities are impressive, and I know I face two wonderful opponents, but you will not, I assure you, stop my escape. The multiverse herself will not permit it. Put up your weapons! You cannot kill me any more than I can kill you!"

Perhaps goaded by this, Zenith struck again, not once but twice, that black streak of ruby-coloured runes licking first at Vautrin's heart and then, as she raised her pistol to fire, at Vera Pym's.

The woman also began to laugh with Vautrin. Together their hideous voices created a resonance with the pulsing light and held the gateway open for them. Vera Pym was triumphant. "You see," she shouted, "we are indestructible! You cannot take our lives in this universe, nor shall you be able to pursue us where we go!"

She then stepped backwards into the howling vortex and vanished. In a matter of seconds, Vautrin, still smiling, followed her.

For a moment there was silence. Then came a noise, like a huge beast breathing. The roof was lit only by the full moon and the stars. Lapointe felt the oppressive weight disappear from him and knew vast relief that circumstances had refused to make Zenith a murderer and Countess Una his accomplice, for then he would have been obliged to arrest them both.

"We will find them," he promised as the snoring vortex dwindled and disappeared. "But if we do not, I expect they will find us. Have no doubt, we shall be waiting for them." He raised exhausted eyes to look upon a bleak, emotionless albino. "And you, Monsieur, are you satisfied you cannot be revenged on the likes of Vautrin?"

"Oh, I fancy I have taken from him something he valued more than life," said the albino, sheathing his black rapier with an air of finality. He shared a thin, secret smile with the Countess von Bek. "Now, if you'll forgive me, Monsieur le Commissaire, I will continue about my business while the night is young. We were planning to go dancing." And, offering his arm to Countess Una, he walked casually down the stairs and out of sight.

"What on earth did he mean?" LeBec wondered aloud.

Commissaire Lapointe was shaking his head like a man waking from a doze. He had heard about that black and crimson sword cane and believed he might have witnessed an action far more terrible, far more threatening to the civilization he valued, than any he had previously imagined.

"God help him," he whispered, half to himself, "and God help those from whom he steals . . ."

The Flaneur des Arcades de l'Opera

In the Luxembourg Gardens

In all the many cases investigated by Sir Seaton Begg of the Home Office Metatemporal Investigative Agency, one of the most curious concerned his cooperation with his opposite number, Commissaire Lapointe of the Sureté du Temps Perdu, involving not only the albino gentleman connected to a royal house whom we call "Monsieur Zenith," but members of an infamous terrorist gang, a long-dead enemy of Begg's German cousins and the well-known adventuress Mrs Una Persson. As Begg's friend, the pathologist Dr "Taffy" Sinclair, remarked, "for a while it seemed that Chaos, in all its unchained wildness, had been let loose through every region of our vast and complex multiverse, so that even now we cannot be certain whether it was contained or whether we are merely experiencing a moment of relative harmony in a howling cacaphony . . ."

"I cannot tell you, my old friend, how delighted I am that you should come over at such short notice."

Lapointe, his assistant LeBec, Taffy, and Begg were wandering through the pale gold autumn light of the Luxembourg Gardens. The chestnut trees were shedding dark reds and yellows, and the flower beds were full of beauty on the verge of succumbing to winter. Lapointe had thought it expedient for them to talk in the open air where there was less chance of being overheard.

"The train? Was it comfortable?"

In his light tweed sports jacket, white shirt, and well-pressed flannels,

Lapointe had a bulky, stiff-necked, slightly professorial air, with a great wave of grey hair untidily arranged over his pale forehead. His deep, green eyes, angular features, and heavy body gave him the air of a large amiable dinosaur. Begg knew his opposite number had one of the sharpest minds on the Continent. Single-handedly Lapointe had captured the ex–police inspector turned crook: George Marsden Plummer (alias "Maigret" in France) who had once been Lapointe's chief. Lapointe had also been the one to bring "Fantomas" to book at last. Together he and Begg had tracked down "Jock Collyn," otherwise known as The Master Mummer, and been instrumental in his lingering to this day on Devil's Island.

Inspector LeBec, on the other hand, had no spectacular record but was much admired at the Quai des Orfevriers for his methodology and his coolness under pressure. Small and dark, he seemed permanently and privately amused. He wore a buttoned-up three-piece grey suit and what was evidently an English school tie.

The two Home Office men had come from London via the recently opened Subchannel Excavation whose roads and railway lines now connected the two nations, a material addition to the decades-old Entente Cordiale, an alliance which had been cemented by the signing of a European-wide Mutual Cooperation Pact, which, with the Universal Civil Rights Act, united all the Great Powers, including the Confederated Forty-seven States of America, in one mighty alliance sharing common laws and goals.

"Perfectly, thank you," said Begg, speaking excellent French. Lapointe had put the STP's private express at his disposal. The journey had taken less than an hour and a half from London to Paris. "I must say, Lapointe, that you French chaps have your priorities well in hand—rapid and comfortable transport and excellent food among them. We had a superb lunch en route."

The French detective acknowledged this compliment with a small, self-deprecating shrug.

Taffy, taller than the others, murmured his own discreet appreciation.

"I gather, Dr Sinclair, that you are recently back from the Republic of Texas?" Lapointe courteously acknowledged the pathologist, whose expertise was internationally famous.

"Indeed." Sinclair removed his wide panama and wiped his glistening head with a large Voysey-patterned Liberty's handkerchief, which seemed an uncharacteristic part of his otherwise muted wardrobe. Save for his taste in haberdashery, no one would have guessed that during his time at Oxford he had been a leading light in the post-PreRaphaelite revival and that women had swooned over his massive head of hair and melancholy features almost as much as they had over his poetry. Like his friend and colleague, he wore a cream-coloured linen suit, but whereas Begg's tie was a rather flamboyant bow, Sinclair's neck was adorned by his old school colours. Indeed his tie was identical to LeBec's. The two had been contemporaries at Blackfriars School and later had attended the Sorbonne before LeBec, eldest son of a somewhat infamous Aquilonian house, entered the service of the Quai D'Orsay and Sinclair, after a spell in the army, decided to follow his father into medicine and the civil service.

"You are familiar with the shopping arcades which radiate off the Place de l'Opera?" asked Lapointe once they were strolling down a broad avenue of chestnut trees towards the gardens' rue Guynemer entrance. "And you are aware, I am sure, of the reputation the area has at night, where assignations of the heart are pursued, and men and women of a certain inclination are said to come together."

"I have read something of the place," said Begg, while Taffy nodded gravely.

"These arcades are the most complex in Paris, of course, and extend into and beneath the surrounding buildings, in turn becoming a warren of corridors and suites of chambers connected to the catacombs. They have never been fully mapped. It is said that some poor devils have been lost there for eternity, cursed to wander forever beneath the city."

Begg smiled. "I am familiar with Smith's Kitchen in London, which is similarly configured. I know the stories of the arcades, yes. How fanciful they are, I have yet to judge. I know, too, that they were spared destruction by Haussmann, when he was building the boulevards of Paris for Louis Napoleon, because the emperor himself wished to preserve his own somewhat lavish pied-de-terre where he maintained the notorious Comtesse de Gavray."

"Exactly, my friend. Whose favours he was said to share with Balzac the Younger. I gather there was some scandal. Didn't Balzac denounce her as a German spy?"

"In 1876. Yes. It was the end of her career. She fled to Berlin and finished her days in penury. Strangely this present case has echoes of that one."

As he reached the little glass and wrought-iron café across from the Theatre du Marionettes, Lapointe paused. "The coffee here isn't too bad, and I see there is a table just over there where we are unlikely to be disturbed."

With the acquiescence of the others, Lapointe let them seat themselves at the dark green metal table and signalled for a *serviteur*, who came immediately, recognising a regular customer. A brief exchange followed. Typically, the Englishmen ordered café crème, and the Frenchmen took theirs espresso. They sat in silence for a little while, admiring the merry-go-round with its vividly painted horses rising and falling in comforting regularity, circling to the tune of a complex steam-driven fairground calliope, as excited little boys and girls waved to waiting parents. The puppet theatre was yet to open and many of the children, Begg knew, would disappear into its darkness soon enough to witness the traditional bloody escapades of Guignol which had entertained French children for the past century or more.

It delighted Begg to see that the same diversions which he had enjoyed as a boy were equally pleasing to this, the first generation of the new century. He was always grateful that his father's diplomatic work had allowed him to make a home in the French capital. For him London and Paris made a natural marriage, if not exactly of opposites, then of complementary personalities. Both had powerful public images and a thousand secrets, not all of them by any means sinister.

Commisioner Lapointe leaned forward so that his voice could only be heard by the other three men at the table. "You have no doubt already reached the conclusion, my friends, that this business concerns the ongoing problems we have in Germany. While the insurgency is generally under control, Hitler's terrorists continue to trouble the German government, and our friends in the Reichstag have asked us for help. In the main we have done our best to remain uninvolved with internal German politics. After defeating Hitler and driving him out of Poland, we were quickly able to support a new democratic government and withdraw our troops to this side of the Rhine. However—" Lapointe shrugged, slowly stirring his coffee.

"Röhm and his Freikorps?" murmured Begg.

"Precisely. They are relatively few, of course. But Röhm's insurgents continue to do considerable damage. They have attacked Wehrmacht barracks, civilian institutions, and even targets outside the country. They have set off bombs in public places and continue to violate synagogues and Jewish cemetaries. While Hitler remains at large, insurgent morale remains high and their plans ambitious. Disaffected petites-bourgeousie for the most part, who had hoped to succeed in war where they had failed in peace. Well, gentlemen, we have reason to believe they are planning an ambitious attack outside Germany's borders. This attack, we think, is aimed at creating a large number of civilian casualties, probably Jewish. And we are fairly certain that it will occur in France, probably in Paris."

"And how can we be of assistance?" asked Begg, clearly puzzled by being asked to engage in what, on the surface, appeared to be primarily an internal matter for the French government.

"In two words, my old friend—" Lapointe glanced around before dropping his voice even lower "—*Monsieur Zenith* . . ."

Now the British investigator understood. He sat back in his chair, his face suddenly grave. From his pocket he took his ancient briar and a tobacco pouch. He began to fill the pipe with dark shag. Taffy Sinclair, too, was frowning. A profound silence surrounded the four men. At last Inspector LeBec spoke. "He is known to be in Paris. Indeed, he has been here for some time. A familiar figure in the Opera arcades. Since his pardon, he has exposed himself quite openly, yet, whenever our people attempted to speak to him, *pouf!* He is gone like smoke."

"Eventually, it became clear to us that we would be better engaged in keeping watch on him," continued Lapointe. "For some months he has continued the same habits. Every morning between eleven and one he appears in the Passage D'Iappe wearing perfect morning dress. He takes his coffee at L'Albertine. He reads his newspaper: *Le Figaro*, usually, but sometimes the *New York Herald Tribune*. He strolls. He makes a small purchase or two. He enters a bookshop and inspects a few volumes. He has even been known to visit Larnier's Waxworks. Occasionally, he buys a book, usually a classic of some kind. Then at lunchtime he either strolls towards the Quartier Latin, taking the Pont St-Michel, where he eats lunch at Lipp's, or he enters one of the more shadowy branches of the arcades and—vanishes! Sometimes he can be seen again in the afternoon making his way to the Louvre, where he inspects a different exhibit each day, though he seems to favour Da Vinci's *Portrait of a Young Jew in Female Dress*. Then he returns to the arcades and, yes, he disappears again."

"He speaks to no one?"

"Oh, he passes the time of day with any number of persons. He is politeness itself, especially where a lady is concerned. He has conversed with more than one of our own people, usually realising immediately who they are. He is the very model of a gentlemanly *flaneur*, whiling away his hours in what some would call a desultory way. He buys his cigarettes at Sullivan's and his newspaper from the same kiosk at the southeastern corner of the arcades. He carries a cane in ebony and silver. His gloves are always that perfect shade of lavender, matching his cravat. His coat is cut just so, his hat sits at just such an angle, and in his buttonhole always the same crimson rosebud emphasising those blood red eyes of his. Women, of course, are fascinated by him. Yet, with a recent exception, he keeps no regular engagements with anyone, though he enjoys a little flirtation over an aperitif, perhaps. He tips well and is much liked by the staff wherever he takes refreshment. Sometimes a Lagonda limousine calls for him at the northwest entrance. We have been able to trace the car to the general area of Clichy, but all we know is that it is driven by a Japanese chauffeur and is garaged in rue Clement in the name of a Monsieur Amano. There its batteries are recharged. Everything is in order. The Lagonda has not left Paris since we have been observing it."

"And as far as you know neither has Monsieur Zenith?"

"Exactly."

"Where does he go at night?" Dr Sinclair wanted to know.

"That's the thing, old man," said LeBec in English, "we simply can't find out!"

"It is as if he becomes invisible from the evening hours until mid-morning," added Lapointe. "Then, suddenly, he appears in the Opera Arcades, perfectly dressed and poised, as ever. Even if we had a cause to arrest him, which we have not, he would still evade us. Indeed if he had not been seen in the company of a suspected Nazi agent, we would not devote so much interest to him. He is a decorated war hero, after all, leading a Polish electric cavalry brigade during the recent conflict. But sadly his actions suggest that he is helping organise whatever Nazi plot is about to be unleashed on honest civilians. His name has come up more than once in various coded messages we have intercepted. Sometimes he is merely Monsieur Z, sometimes 'Zenith,' and sometimes 'Zodiac.' All versions of his own given name, of course. There is no doubt at all that he is Count Rudolf Zoran von Bek, descendant of the infamous 'Crimson Eyes' who terrorised the people of Mirenburg and London in the course of the last century. He renounced his title as hereditary ruler of Wäldenstein. So as for Hitler's intention to restore Zenith as puppet monarch there, had his plans for the conquest of Europe been successful, it is surely nonsense!"

"He has never regretted giving up his title," mused Sir Seaton. From his mouth now issued alarming quantities of dark smoke as he fired up his old pipe. "I am still curious as to why he moved his base from London to Paris. He was even rumoured to have been seen recently in Berlin. It is as if he were fascinated by our friend Herr Hitler. This is not the first time he and that gentlemen have been linked in various incarnations across the multiverse."

"Perhaps he agrees with Hitler's ideas?" ventured Lapointe. But Begg shook his head.

"They are scarcely 'ideas.' They are the opinions of beerhall braggart of the kind commonly found throughout the world. They emerge to fill a vacuum. They might appeal to an uneducated and unemployed labourer, a dispossessed shopkeeper or disenchanted professional soldier like Röhm—even some brainless and inbred titled fool. But Zenith is none of those things. He is both well educated and of superior intelligence. His only weakness is his thirst for danger, for the thrill which fills the veins with pounding blood and which takes one's mind off the dullness of the day to day." Begg knew exactly what moved his old adversary. The expression on Dr Sinclair's face suggested that he thought the metatemporal investigator's remark might well have been a self-description. Begg continued, "He would only ally himself with such a creature if it somehow suited his own schemes. Years ago after he was rescued from secret police headquarters where he had been imprisoned and tortured for his resistance to the dictator, he gave me his solemn promise that he was renouncing his old ways and from then on would only steal from the thieves, as it were, and contribute most of his gains to excellent causes, some of which would founder completely if he didn't help. And the Polish military will tell you how he equipped that electric tank division from his own pocket!"

"So you think he is planning a job in Paris?" asked the commissioner. He allowed a small smile to flicker across his face. "After all, we are not short of the undeserving rich . . ."

"Perhaps. Or he could be diverting himself here while all the time what he is doing at night is the important thing. Eh?" From under his lowering, sardonic brow, Sir Seaton returned Lapointe's smile. "Might he be making himself so public that all our attention is drawn to his flaneurism, and we ignore his true activities?"

"What do you suggest? We need to know details of Hitler's plans soon, Sir Seaton. We must anticipate and counter whatever terror the Nazi insurgents intend to unleash."

"Naturally you must. What else can you tell me?"

"Only that the adventuress Mrs Una Persson recently took rooms above the arcades shortly after I contacted you. For the last three days she has been seen in the gardens walking her two cats, one grey and one black Oriental shorthair. She is a known associate of Monsieur Zenith."

"Of him and others," agreed Begg, his eyes narrowing in an expression of reminiscence. "And does she have a female companion, perhaps? A Miss Cornelius?"

"Not as far as we know."

Sinclair seemed surprised. His eyes darted from Lapointe to Begg and then to LeBec, who shrugged.

"Mrs Persson has been seen talking to Zenith," LeBec offered. "Yesterday she had lunch with him at L'Albertine. We had a lip reader eating at a nearby table. Zenith mentioned Hitler and Röhm. He might have spoken of an explosive charge in Paris. Unfortunately we did not learn where. She said that she had investigated a site where a bomb would create the most damage. So certain of those among our superiors are now convinced they are working together for the Nazi insurgents."

Lapointe interrupted rapidly. "Of course, I find that impossible to believe." He shrugged. "But I, as do we all, have certain bosses owing their jobs more to their connections than their native abilities, who insist on believing Zenith and Mrs Persson are in league with Hitler and his underground army. It could be, perhaps, that they are working for themselves and that they have plans which Hitler's activities will facilitate. My guess is that some treasure is involved, for it is not Zenith's habit to dabble in civilian politics. At least as far as I know. Not so, of course, Mrs Persson. Is there a way you could find out any more, Sir Seaton? Something I could take to my superiors which will put me onto the real business Zenith has in Paris? Whatever that may be."

Sir Seaton finished his café crème, smiling out at a group of little boys and girls running with fixed attention towards the pleasure of the carousel.

"I could ask him," he said.

✙ THE SECOND CHAPTER ✙

A Conversation at L'Albertine

Inevitably Seaton Begg met his albino cousin close to the noon hour in the Arcades de l'Opera which branched, eight galleries, off a central court containing a paved piazza and an elaborate fountain. He appeared almost by magic, smiling courteously and lifting his hat in greeting. Impeccably well-mannered, Zenith, of course, was incapable of ignoring him.

"*Bonjour, cher cousin!*" The albino raised his own tall grey hat. "What a pleasure to come upon you like this! We have a great deal to talk about since our last meeting. Perhaps you would be good enough to take a cup of coffee with me at L'Albertine?"

After they dispensed with their hats and ordered, Count Zenith leaned back in his chair and moved his ebony cane in an elegant, economic gesture in the direction of a beautiful young woman, wearing a long, military-style black coat and with a helmet of raven black hair, walking two cats in the sunny gardens at the centre of the arcades. He gave no indication that he was already acquainted with the woman who was, of course, Mrs Una Persson. "Has anyone, I wonder, ever really tried to imagine what it must be like to have the mind of a beast, even a domesticated beast, like one of those exquisite cats? I think to enter such a brain, however small, would be to go utterly mad, don't you, Sir Seaton?"

"Quite." The Englishman smiled up at a pretty waitress (for which L'Albertine in the morning was famous) and thanked her as she laid out the coffee things. "I have heard of certain experiments in which a beast's brain has been exchanged with that of a human being, but I don't believe they have ever been successful. Though," and in this he was far more direct than was his usual habit, "some say that Adolf Hitler, the deposed Chancellor of Germany, succeeded and that he did indeed go quite mad as a result. Certainly his insolent folly in attacking three great Empires at once would indicate the theory perhaps has some substance!"

Only by the slightest movement of an eyebrow did Zenith indicate his surprise at Begg's raising this subject. He said nothing for a moment before mentioning how the Russo-Polish empire was already at the point of collapse. His own Middle-European seat remained part of that sphere of influence, as Begg knew, and the fact was considered a source of some distress to the albino.

"As one who showed such courage on their side during the war, you cannot think Hitler should have been encouraged to attack the 'alliance of eagles'?" Begg offered. "The other Great Powers have since made an oath to protect the Slavic empire. Perhaps you feel that we have not been more resolute in tracking down the Hitler gang? I cannot believe you share their views."

"My dear Begg, the deposed Chancellor was a barrack room lawyer supported by a frustrated military bully, a plump bore with aristocratic pretension, and a third-rate broadcasting journalist!" References to Röhm, Göring, and Goebbels, whose popular radio programme was thought to have helped Hitler to power. "It was a matter of duty for anyone of taste to frustrate his ambitions. He was warned often enough by the Duma, the Assembly, and your Parliament. His refusal to sign the articles of confederation was the last straw. He should have been stopped then, before he was ever allowed to marshall his land leviathans and aerial battleships. As it was, it should have taken three days, not a year, to defeat him. And now we have the current situation where he and his riff-raff remain at large, doubtless somewhere in Bavaria, and far too many of our armed forces, as well as those of Germany herself, are engaged in putting a stop to his Freikorps' activities. I understand that some fools in the French foreign service think I yearn to 'free' my ancestral lands from the Pan-Slavic yoke, but believe me I have no such dream. If I were to deceive myself that the people were free under my family's reign, I would deserve the contempt of every realist on the planet. And if some self-esteeming coxcombs on the Quai D'Orsay continue to believe I would ally myself with degenerate opportunists, I shall, in my own time, seek them out and require them to repeat their presumptions."

Beg permitted himself a small smile of acquiescence. He had needed only this statement to confirm his understanding. But what was Zenith doing here in Paris keeping such a strange, yet regular schedule? He knew that there was little chance of the albino offering him an explanation. All he had done was rule out the theory, as his French opposite number had hoped, of certain underadmired civil servants at the Quai d'Orsay. He regretted that he was not on terms of such intimacy with Mrs Persson. Although unlikely, she could be allying herself with the Hitler gang to further her own schemes.

Of course Zenith had said nothing of any collaboration between himself and the Englishwoman, though it was probably not the first time he and she had worked together. Zenith required a great deal of money with which to maintain his lifestyle and finance his favoured causes. He employed at least six Japanese servants of uncommon loyalty and proficiency and maintained several houses in the major cities of Europe and the Côte d'Azur. Though he had received an amnesty from the European Alliance after the war, he remained wanted by the police in certain countries, especially the American Confederation, yet lived elegantly in such insouciant openness that he had only occasionally been captured.

The secret of Zenith's great success was that he understood the psychology of his opponents marginally better than they understood his. Thus his penchant for openness and his willingness to depend entirely on his own quick wits should he ever be in danger. One day, Begg hoped, that cool intelligence would be employed entirely on the side of the law. He remained convinced of Zenith's highly developed sense of honour, which meant the albino never lied to those he himself respected.

Moreover, Zenith was equally hated and feared by the criminal classes. That ebony stick of his hid a slender sword remarkable in that it was black and carved with certain peculiar scarlet markings which gave the appearance of moving whenever the blade was unsheathed.

In the old days Begg had pursued Zenith across the multiverse more than once and knew that sometimes the sword became an altogether larger weapon, sometimes carried in an instrument case. Zenith was a skilled musician, as expert in the classical cello and violin as he was with the popular guitar. Begg knew also that more than once Zenith's opponents had been found dead, drained in some terrible way not only of blood but of their very life force. Underworld legend suggested that Zenith was a kind of vampire, drawing his considerable physical power from the souls of his enemies.

At that moment any casual customer of the salon would have seen one elegant man of the world in amiable conversation with another. An observer might have noted that both seemed to be taking an admiring interest in the tall woman walking, *à la* Colette, her two Oriental cats in the noon sunlight sparkling through the waters of the central fountain where classical marble merfolk paid homage to a Neptune whose trident was green with verdigris. The spraying water formed a blur of rainbow colour giving the woman an almost unearthly appearance as she passed by. She stood for a while staring thoughtfully into the middle distance seemingly utterly oblivious of the two men.

Begg smiled to himself, well aware that this was Mrs Persson's characteristic way of taking stock of those she believed were watching her. It had the effect of disconcerting any observer and causing them to turn their gaze away. Even though she aroused no such response in Begg or Zenith, whom she recognised, nonetheless it seemed even to them that somehow she stepped through the shimmering wash of colour and, with her cats, disappeared.

"You are acquainted, I know, with Mrs Persson." Begg lowered his voice. "The Quai d'Orsay, if not the Quai des Orfevriers, are convinced that she works for the German insurgency. I would be surprised if it's true. I thought her nature too romantic to let her fall in with such a gang."

"Mrs Persson rarely confides in me." Monsieur Zenith raised one finger as a signal for the waiter to bring him a drink. "Will you join me, Begg? Is it too early for an Armagnac?"

When the detective acquiesced, Zenith raised a second finger and made a small gesture. The waiter nodded. Zenith watched with approval as the *serviteur* mixed his absinthe and placed two specially formed pieces of sugar in the saucer, while Begg received a generous measure of St-Aubyn. It was rarely his habit to drink his favourite Special Reserve before lunch, but he was unusually anxious to remain on agreeable terms with his old opponent. Zenith appeared to live chiefly on Turkish ovals and absinthe.

"Would you permit me, cousin, to ask you a rather direct question?" he enquired after a couple of appreciative sips.

"How could I refuse?" A smile crossed Zenith's handsome lips. Clearly this approach amused him, and Begg knew he desired amusement almost as much as he required action to relieve his ennui.

"I have to assume that your business in Paris at present has something to do with the present situation in Germany. I am also curious to know what Mrs Persson's association with the Germans might mean."

"Any confidence Mrs Persson chooses to share with me must remain just that." Zenith's voice sharpened a little. "Naturally the British and French are in haste to conclude their present problems with Colonel Hitler, but, while I wish them well, you must know—"

"Of course." Begg regretted his directness. He suspected he had offended his cousin whose sense of decorum was if anything somewhat exaggerated. But there was no retreat now. "I suppose I am asking your help. There is some suggestion that many innocent lives are at stake."

"My dear Begg, why should you and I care if a few bourgeois more or less are gone from central Paris by next Sunday." Monsieur Zenith finished his absinthe. He removed a large, crisp note from his slender case, laid it on the table, and stood up. "And now, if you will forgive me, I have some business which cannot wait."

Begg rose, trying to frame some kind of apology or even protestation but for once was at a loss. With his usual litheness and speed, Zenith slipped his hat from the shelf and with a perfunctory bow strolled towards the exit. Cursing himself for his uncharacteristic impatience, Begg watched his relation depart.

Only as he took up his own broad-brimmed hat did he allow, small smile to appear on his face while under his breath he offered a heartfelt "Merci beaucoup."

⤶ THE THIRD CHAPTER ⤏

Into the Labyrinth

ommissaire Lapointe had set his men in waiting for M. Zenith, and the albino was followed once again, and once again, as his old colleague was bound to admit to Begg, they had lost him. Mrs Persson, too, was gone. The four metatemporal detectives met that afternoon in Lapointe's rather grand offices overlooking the Seine.

"She was last seen visiting Caron's print shop in that section of the arcades known as La Galerie de l'Horloge. But she was never seen emerging. Two of our fellows entered on a pretext just as old Caron was closing for lunch. The shop is small. It has long been suspected as a place of illegal assignations concerning the Bourse and the arms trade. There is an even smaller room behind it. Neither Mrs Perssson nor the trio of men were to be found. My chaps did, however, discover a good excuse for making a further visit to Caron's. He also specialises, it appears, in a particularly unsavoury form of pornography in which Nazi insurgents are portrayed in acts of torture or worse with their victims. The photographs are almost certainly authentic. Caron made an error. He omitted to hide the photographs in his office when our men entered. So although they pretended to notice nothing, it will be possible for us to stage a raid, ostensibly by that of the regular vice department, to see what else we can discover. Would you and Dr Sinclair care to accompany us?"

"I would be unable to resist such an invitation," said Begg. Sinclair assented by lowering his magnificent head.

"I think you are right, old friend, in your interpretation of Monsieur Zenith's communication," added Lapointe. "Not only will Hitler's plot be realised in a crowded part of Paris, it will occur before next Sunday."

"So he suggested. But whether Mrs Persson is party to this plot, we still do not know. The sooner we can question her, I think, the better."

"Precisely!" Lapointe inspected his watch. "Come, gentlemen. A powerful car awaits us! Her batteries are charged and ready!"

So it was that the four men accompanied by two uniformed sergeants arrived at the Galerie de l'Horloge with its magnificent glass, wrought-iron roofs and ornate gas lamps, its rows of small shops on either side. They crowded into M Caron's little establishment carrying a search warrant on the excuse that he was known to be selling forbidden material.

Begg felt almost sorry for the short, plump, grey-haired print seller, who shivered in terror at the understanding he faced possible arrest. When, however, the material, which was the excuse for the raid, was revealed, Begg's sympathy dissipated. These were almost certainly pictures taken from the infamous Stadelheim fortress where prisoners were tortured, humiliated, and subjected to unmentionable sexual horrors. Caron swore that he was not responsible for the material being in his office. "It was the woman, I assure you, gentleman. The English woman. She knows—she . . ." And the little man broke down weeping.

It did not take long to elicit from the print seller the secret of Mrs Persson's ability to vanish. Behind a large cabinet of prints, he revealed another door with steps leading down into dank darkness which echoed as if into the infinite cosmos. "She—she insisted, messieurs. She knew my shop had once been a gate into the labyrinth. It is by no means the only one leading from the arcades. As I am sure you are aware, the labyrinth has long served as a sanctuary for those who do not wish to be apprehended for a variety of reasons. I wanted nothing to do with it, thus the cabinet pushed against the wall, but the Englishwoman—she knew what was hidden. She demanded to be shown the gate." Again he began to weep. "She knew about my—little business. She threatened to expose me. The photographs. I was greedy. I should have known not to trust such degenerates."

Commissaire Lapointe was counting the large denomination banknotes he had discovered in the old man's safe. "Degenerates who were apparently helping to make you rich, m'sieu! We also know about your arms brokering." He replaced the money in the safe and locked it, pocketing the key. "Have you told us everything? Have the passages been used by members of the German 'underground'? Is it they who gave you the photographs? In exchange for guns?"

"I don't know who they were. They appeared in this room one day, having pushed aside the cabinet. It's true they had come to know of me through my interest in perfectly legal discontinued ordnance. They supplied the photographs in return for using the door occasionally. They were foreign civilians, they assured me. They spoke poor French, but I could not recognise the accents. As for the woman, she came and went only by day. She occasionally used my premises out of normal hours. I never saw her with anyone else. She was never below for very long. This is, I promise you, the longest she has ever been d-down there . . ." With a shudder he turned his back on the mysterious doorway.

"Well," Lapointe decided, "we shall have to wait for her, I think. Meanwhile, m'sieu, you will be charged with distributing pornography. Take him away."

After the terrified proprietor had been led off still snivelling, the metatemporal detectives replaced the door and cabinet exactly as they had discovered it and settled down to await Mrs Persson's return. But the afternoon turned to evening, hours after the print seller would have closed his shop, and still she made no appearance.

Eventually LeBec was dispatched to Mrs Persson's apartments and soon returned to report that they were unoccupied save for two somewhat hungry and outraged Siamese cats. "I fed them and cleaned their litter, of course, but . . ." He shrugged.

This news brought a look of concern to Begg's aquiline features. "I think I know Mrs Persson pretty well. She would not desert her cats, especially without making arrangements to have them fed. She has not only broken her usual habits, but perhaps not willingly."

"My God, Begg! Do you mean she has been captured by whoever it was she has been seeing in the labyrinth? Murdered. By Zenith, perhaps? Could he be playing a double game?"

"Possibly, old man. Instinct tells me that if she is not found soon, she will be in no condition to help us with our enquiries."

"Maybe her paymasters have turned against her? Or Zenith has betrayed her?" Lapointe drew a deep breath of air.

"Monsieur le Commissaire, time is in all likelihood running out for Mrs Persson, if she still lives. We could be further away than we thought from discovering which public place is under threat. And we have, if Monsieur Zenith told me what I think, only three more days at most before they strike! Come on, gentlemen! Help me shift his cabinet."

The doorway once again revealed, Begg took a small but powerful electric lantern from his overcoat pocket. With a serviceable Webley .45 revolver in his other hand, he led the way down into the echoing darkness. The two sergeants were left behind to guard the entrance.

From somewhere below came a slow, rhythmic, tuneful booming, as of some great clock. Familiar to three of the detectives, the sound caused in each man a thrill of horror. For a second Begg hesitated. Then he continued down the long flight of stone steps which revealed, by the marks in the mould which grew inches thick upon them, recent useage.

Only LeBec had never before heard the thrumming sound. "What on earth is it?" he enquired of Sinclair.

The pathologist drew his brows together, clearly wondering if he should reply. Then he spoke rapidly and quietly: "Well, firstly, old man, it is not exactly *of* our earth. It is what we, who have travelled frequently between the worlds, sometimes refer to as the Cosmic Regulator. Others know it as the Grand Balance. I have heard it more than once but have never seen it. There are many conflicting descriptions. Perhaps every person who has seen it has imposed their own image upon it. The Regulator is said to lie at the very centre of the multiverse, if the multiverse can be said to possess a centre."

"Have you ever known anyone who has seen it?" whispered LeBec, wiping cold sweat from his brow. He had only recently been transferred to the STP.

Sinclair nodded. "I believe both Begg and Lapointe have set eyes on it, but even they, articulate as they are, have never described it. It is often represented in mythological iconography as a kind of scale, with one side representing Chaos and the other Law, but no one knows its true form, if it has one."

"Law and Chaos? Are those not Zoroastrian conceptions. The forces which war for control of the world?"

"So far no one has ever gained power over the Balance, but should someone eventually succeed it will mean the end of Time but not of consciousness. If Chaos or Law controls existence, we shall all *continue to live at the exact moment prior to the extinction of everything*. For eternity! Or so the theory goes. But there will always be madmen to challenge that conception, to believe that by controlling the Cosmic Balance they can exert their *own* desired reality upon the multiverse. Heaven help us if Hitler and his lunatics have in mind such an attempt!"

Only half comprehending this idea, LeBec firmed his shoulders and continued to follow Begg's thin ray of light down into the sonorous darkness.

∼◉ THE FOURTH CHAPTER ◉∼

The Roads between the Worlds

As they reached the bottom of the steps, they found themselves on uneven flagstones peering through a series of vaults supported by ancient pillars.

"No doubt," suggested Sinclair, "these are your famous Parisian catacombs?"

"Possibly. I am not familiar with every aspect of them." LeBec peered into the rustling darkness.

The strange, distant booming continued. Was the noise mechanical or natural? Lapointe and Begg both cocked their heads to listen. The echoes resounding through the vaults made it almost impossible to determine their source. At one moment Sinclair thought it might be water, at another, some sort of engine. But he was also of a disposition to discount his own metaphysical speculation.

The vaults seemed endless, and their darkness sucked the light from Begg's lantern, yet the detective continued to lead the way as if he had some idea where an exit might be.

"The arcades above us are a maze," remarked Lapointe, "which to some degree duplicate this second maze below."

"Remarkable," murmured Begg. "I had some idea of what to expect but did not realize we were so close to the Regulator. This is not the first time I have used such a gate myself to move between one reality and another. But I have never before felt so near the centre. What about you, Lapointe?"

"I must admit I have heard it before only as a very distant echo," replied the Frenchman. "Until now I have used mechanical means to negotiate the spaces between realities. We are issued with Roburian speedshells by the department. Naturally, old friend, I knew that you had not always taken advantage of such vehicles . . ."

"One learns," the detective muttered to himself. "One learns." His progress seemed erratic and without logic as he moved backwards and forwards, then side to side, keeping the sound constant at a certain distance, treading a trail which only he could perceive.

Suddenly a silvery light appeared ahead.

"Can it be possible that the Arcades de l'Opera lead directly to the roads between the worlds?"

Hearing this, Sinclair gave an involuntary shudder.

Above them the great arches grew taller and taller until they were impossibly high, no longer structures of human architecture but part of a natural vault which had become one with the night itself.

All four men gasped and stopped in their tracks as Begg's lantern revealed a long, twisting pathway which seemed to vanish into infinity. Above them, as well as below them, were myriad paths, crossing and recrossing. And on some could be distinguished tiny figures, not all of them human, walking back and forth along the causeways.

When Sir Seaton Begg turned to address his fellow detectives his eyes were glistening with tears.

"Gentlemen," he whispered, dousing the lantern, "I believe we have discovered the roads between the worlds!"

Their eyes soon became accustomed to the light which emanated from the moonbeam roads themselves. Paths stretched in every possible direction. The legendary trails which led to all possible planes of the multiverse.

"I have dreamed of this discovery," said Begg. "On occasion I have glimpsed these roads as I passed from one aspect of reality to another, but I never suspected I would ever discover access to them, particularly by accident. Just think: the gateway has existed in Paris since the beginning of time, their patterns perhaps unconsciously imitated by the architects who designed the city above. Our mythologies and folktales have hinted at this, of course, through sensational tales. Yet they hardly prepare one for the reality. Is this Zenith's and Mrs Persson's secret, do you think?"

"And is it also Hitler's?" asked Lapointe grimly. "Are his ambitions greater than we ever expected?"

Dwarfed by the vast network of moonbeam roads, the detectives were frozen in their uncertainty. There were no maps, no evident routes to follow. They had made an extraordinary discovery!

"At least it is no longer a mystery as to how Zenith was able to evade our men. And Mrs Persson also. How long have they known of this route?" LeBec wondered.

Begg shook his head slowly. "I believe Mrs Persson has probably been using these roads for a very long time. Yet it is my guess that she did not come this far voluntarily."

"How on earth can you make that supposition, Begg?" enquired Lapointe.

"Her cats," said Begg. "I know she would never have left her cats unattended. She would have brought them with her, or she would have made arrangements for them to be looked after. No, gentlemen, if she was not faced with an overwhelming emergency, I believe Mrs Persson was lured down here and then made a prisoner."

"By Zenith?"

"Possibly."

"If not by Zenith, then by whom?"

"By Hitler. Or one of his people." Begg placed his foot firmly upon the road which led away into the darkness. There seemed nothing below them but more roads on which the tiny wayfarers came and went.

"How do you know she came this way, old man?" Taffy Sinclair wished to know.

"I have only instinct, Taffy. An instinct honed, I might say, by a lifetime spent travelling between the worlds."

And steadily, still unseen, came the booming of that unearthly balance.

~◈ THE FIFTH CHAPTER ◈~
An Unexpected Newcomer

With the familiar world far behind them, Begg and his fellow detectives were by now crossing a long, sinuous path from which gleamed a faint silvery light.

"What surprises me," said Lapointe, "is why so few people have reported finding this entrance to the moonbeam roads."

"I suspect because it is not always open," Begg speculated. "If Mrs Persson came this way and was abducted, perhaps she opened the gate but had no time to close it. My guess is that Hitler's men, with whom she was clearly involved in some way, stumbled on the road and bribed Caron, who had already sold them arms, with those filthy photographs. No doubt they also paid M. Caron to let them know when she next planned to use his shop. Your men said they saw others enter the shop and not emerge, eh?"

"Three of them. Isn't it possible Mrs Persson unwittingly lead them here?"

"Impossible to say, Lapointe. I am hoping that question will shortly be solved!"

"But how do you know we are even on the right road?"

Begg pointed downward. Stretching ahead of them the others now detected the faintest of glowing pale traces, like ghostly drops of blood.

"What is it?" Lapointe wanted to know.

"I believe those frauds of mystics like to call it ectoplasm," said Begg, "but I prefer to think of it as the traces left by each human soul as it passes through the world—or, in this case, between them. Only those 'old souls' like Mrs Persson, who has moved for so long between planes and has developed a form of longevity we might call immortality, leave such clear traces." His smile was grim. "We are still on her trail."

Only when he looked back, did Taffy Sinclair see, not unexpectedly, similar phosphorescent traces running behind them. And he knew for certain who had left those.

After walking a bit further, when the booming of the balance seemed closer, Sinclair realised they had left the moonbeam roads and were once again passing through a more earthly sequence of vaulted chambers. Still the electric lamp was in Begg's left hand. And still his right hand gripped his service revolver. Was it his imagination, the Home Office pathologist asked himself, or was there something familiar about the smell of the air? Was it pine trees? Impossible!

"Where are we?" enquired Lapointe in a whisper.

"If I am not mistaken, my old friend," answered the Englishman, "we are somewhere in the Bavarian mountains. Probably near a place called Berchtesgaden. Either that, or my nose deceives me!"

"So we were right!" LeBec exclaimed. "Mrs Persson *is* working for the German insurgents!"

"That, Inspector LeBec," responded Begg, "remains to be determined."

Soon the ground began to slope upward, and they heard voices loud enough to drown out the chiming balance. Unmistakeably speaking German, the loudest of them had a distinct Austrian accent.

Sir Seaton doused his lamp but did not return his revolver to his pocket.

The unseen Austrian's voice rose with excitement. "Victory is in our grasp, my friends. Our army is passing through the Eagle Gate as we speak, to assemble in the Great Siegfried Cavern, where they await our signal. Those degenerate fools thought they had defeated us, reduced us to a mere rabble. But they did not reckon with our heritage, the ancient Nordic secrets locked deep within our Bavarian homeland. The Hollow Earth theory has been proven a scientific fact. You have done well, Frau Persson, leading us to this road. We should have been sad if you were to become the subject of the next set of pictures sold in Herr Caron's shop. By next Saturday the course of history will be changed forever. We shall strike a blow against the Jewish race from which it will never recover. And if you continue to cooperate, you shall witness my becoming world leader, master of time and space. You will make a fitting consorte. Together we shall rule the universe!"

They heard only a faint reply. But the Austrian, evidently Colonel Hitler, continued his monologue unchecked. He hardly understood the nature of his own situation, so blinded was he by petty dreams of power and banal notions of his own superiority. A typical megalomaniac. Yet why on earth would a woman of Una Persson's intelligence and integrity lend herself to such evil folly?

Using the ancient columns as cover, the four crept closer. In a circle of light stood the figures of a short fat man, a squat military type with a hideously disfigured face, another with gaunt, skeletal features and a black medical boot. To one side of these stood a tall, lugubrious-looking individual and another man of medium height with a short, dark "Charlie Chaplin" moustache and a lock of greasy hair falling over one eye. They were recognised immediately from their "Wanted" posters. Here was the entire über-heirarchy of the Hitler gang.

The four detectives drew their revolvers and advanced. This was their chance to capture all the leaders of the German insurgency.

Mrs Persson, seated at ease on a chair to one side of the main group, was the first to notice them.

"Raise your hands!" Begg barked in German, motioning with his Webley. "You are all under arrest."

"Thunder and lightning!" The tall man, whom they recognised as Captain Hess, one of Hitler's closest coconspirators, made a movement to his belt. But Lapointe crossed quickly and placed his hand on the man's arm.

Colonel Hitler glowered, his tiny blue eyes points of almost insane rage. "How did you—?"

"Cross from one plane of the multiverse to another? The same way Mrs Persson did. Indeed, she led us to you . . ."

"But only a few of us knew the secret!" Herman Goering, the fat Nazi, looked rapidly from face to face. "Zenith swore—"

"So Zenith is in league with you!" Lapointe looked almost disappointed. "Well, he, too, will be arrested in good time."

"But I am surprised, Mrs Persson, that you should associate yourself with such scum. Enemies of all that is civilised . . ." Begg shook his head.

Una Persson stood up. Her beautiful face was an icy mask and her eyes showed no expression. "Ah, Sir Seaton." Her voice mocked him. "So you are, like so many of your kind, the sole arbiter of what is civilised."

"Englishman, *we* are the ones who will save everything valuable in civilization!" The gaunt man with the medical boot was Herr Goebbels, the journalist. "Without Germany there would be no civilisation. No music, no art, no poetry. All that is best in your own country is the creation of the Nordic soul. All that threatens you, from without and within, is also Jewish. By saving Europe from the Jews, we shall establish a new Golden Age across our Continent. Even the Slavs will welcome this renaissance and willingly join in. Soon we shall be able to manipulate the very stuff of Creation."

Unthinking, a furious Taffy Sinclair took a step closer to the crazed creature. "I find you unconvincing, Colonel Hitler. You would establish this new civilisation by blowing up innocents and throwing the whole of our world into turmoil?"

The hideously scarred Captain Erich Röhm laughed in Sinclair's face. "Only through blood and iron will Europe be cleansed. I am a soldier. I know nothing but the art of battle. And even I understand how the Jews continue to corrupt political and cultural life! Martin Luther warned us. So, too, have a succession of popes and bishops. Not only do Jews refuse the true messiah, they wish to wipe all trace of Jesus Christ from the world! Once the warriors of Europe rose up to save Christendom from destruction. Now we rise again to mount our great crusade against the sons of Abraham. By working against us, gentlemen, you are making a terrible mistake. Join us! The Holy Grail itself will soon be in our hands. He who holds the Grail controls the Balance and therefore the universe itself!"

"You are as mad as I understood you to be, messieurs." Lapointe drew a set of handcuffs from his overcoat pocket and advanced towards the glowering Hitler. "Now, if you will kindly—"

A shot rang out from the shadows, and the revolver went spinning from Lapointe's grasp. Another shot and LeBec clutched his right shoulder. Blood began to seep through his fingers.

"Drop your weapons!" Came a cold commanding voice. "Drop them or you shall all die immediately."

And strolling out into the circle of light came a tall, stiff-backed man dressed in perfect evening clothes and wearing a black domino obscuring the upper half of his face. In his right hand was a smoking 9 mm Sabatini automatic.

Begg recognised him immediately. "So it was true," he murmured. "I have been guilty of underestimating you, mein herr. I knew that if Monsieur

Zenith was not helping this gang, it had to be someone equally knowledge-able in the ways of the multiverse."

The newcomer's thin lips formed a mocking smile of triumph. "You had thought me defeated, Sir Seaton, in the matter of the Corsican Collar. Then your life was saved by my old enemy, your cousin, who calls himself Zenith. But you knew I would return to continue with my quest."

Lowering his revolver, Begg turned at once to Colonel Hitler. "Believe me, if you think to link your interests with this creature's you are mistaken. He will betray you as he has betrayed every other man, woman, or spirit whom he has persuaded to act with him. You might know him by another name, but I can tell you his real identity, for he is the master of lies. He is Hieronymous Klosterheim. Some believe him a fallen angel expelled from Hell itself, but I know that he was once a member of the Society of Jesus before he was expelled from that order and excommunicated by the pope himself."

"*Klosterheim!*" Captain Goering's plump features shook with amusement. "What nonsense! This is Herr Johan Cornelius. You would have us believe that we have linked our fortunes with a figure from folklore—the infamous Gaynor the Damned!"

"As he is called in the opera," said Begg quietly, "but Wagner took cer-tain liberties with the old legends, as before him did Milton."

Lapointe, Sinclair, and the pale, wounded LeBec all looked at him as if he were mad. They knew the stories from the opera of the enemy of Parsifal, who had sought the Grail and found it, only to be cursed with eternal damna-tion, to wander the earth until the end of time for the crime of attempting to drink Christ's very blood.

"Drop your weapons, gentlemen, or this time I shoot your colleague in his heart and not his shoulder," was Klosterheim's icy response.

The Nazi colonel himself was now staring a little nervously at the masked man, wondering whether any bargain he might have made with him could possibly still be to his advantage.

Then Mrs Persson stepped out of the circle and joined Klosterheim, standing close beside him, making it clear she was the fiend's ally.

"It's said that promise of the Grail's power will corrupt even the noblest of human creatures," declared Begg. "Had I realised exactly what we were up against, my friends, I would never have led you here! This will be forever on my conscience."

"Fear not, Sir Seaton," came Klosterheim's hollow, terrible voice. "You will not have to suffer for very much longer. Meanwhile I shall be obliged if you will drop your weapons at your feet."

And as their revolvers clattered down, he uttered a mirthless laugh which echoed endlessly through the vaulted chambers and chilled the blood of all who heard it.

∽❦ THE SIXTH CHAPTER ❦∽

The Ultimate Power

Begg felt physically sick standing with his hands raised watching the Nazi gangster gloat over his reversal. He had underestimated not only Hitler and Company but everyone he had opposed. He had been foolish to assume that he alone, save for Mrs Persson and Monsieur Zenith, knew the secret of the moonbeam roads. He had wanted too badly to trust that pair. Cursing himself for not anticipating his old enemy Klosterheim's ambitions, he refused to believe he might have been forgiven. Almost everyone believed Klosterheim to have met his end in Mirenburg a decade or more earlier. Not that Begg himself had been there to witness the evil eternal's demise. None other than Zenith had given him the information.

From his earliest appearance as a Satanic angel expelled from Hell in the myths and legends of the seventeeth century, Klosterheim had been said to die more than once. But his antipathy to Begg's family, or at least the German side of the family, the von Beks, was well known. He had survived one apparent death after another through the years, remaining alive for two reasons only: to kill all who carried the blood of his old enemy, Ulrich von Bek, and to lay his hands upon the Holy Grail and thus control, in his understanding, the very nature of reality. Yet here he was in alliance with Una Persson, Countess von Bek!

Begg had narrowly escaped terrible death at the hands of this near-immortal before, and now there seemed there was no hope of escape at all.

Klosterheim's sunken sockets hid eyes which burned within like the unquenched flames of hell. He pocketed his revolver as the triumphant Nazis trained their own weapons on the detectives. Then the masked man bent and placed his thin lips upon those of Mrs Persson. Begg was astonished. Klosterheim had never shown warmth, let alone passion, for any creature, least of all a woman. And Mrs Persson smiled admiringly back at the cadaverous devil with whom she had cast her lot. Colonel Hitler meanwhile glowered jealously, clearly furious that the woman had collaborated with him because Klosterheim had instructed her to do so. Noting all these connections, Begg now believed himself thoroughly outwitted. Was it possible that Zenith was also part of this unholy alliance?

"I cannot believe this of you, Mrs Persson!" exclaimed Taffy, still shocked and clearly unable to accept this turn of events. Like his colleagues, save the wounded LeBec, his hands were now firmly tied behind his back by Herr Hess. It was just possible that a tear gleamed in his eye. "How can any decent Englishwoman possibly ally herself with such riff-raff?"

"Oh, I think you'll find it's quite commonly done, Mr Sinclair." Mrs Persson seemed partially drunk as she leaned against the gaunt skeleton who was not only her ally but apparently also her master, perhaps even her paramour. "We women are silly creatures, eh, thoroughly addicted to powerful men? There's a larger interest here which I'm sure you'll appreciate. Very few of us are privileged to know one of Satan's very own angels . . ."

Sinclair, his mouth set in a hard, disapproving line, was frozen in horror, completely incapable of a response.

The Nazis began to herd their captives back towards the moonbeam roads.

"We await only Count Zenith," chuckled Captain Goering, "and our plan will be complete. On Saturday, the *Hindenburg* brings the Jewish Palestinian deputation from America to Munich. They intend to discuss an obscenity with Comrade von Hugenberg, chairman of the Munich Supreme Soviet—the establishment of a new Jewish state in the Bavarian lake district!

Can you imgine a worse insult to our Christian community? But it will never take place. Our man Zenith will introduce a bomb on board while the *Hindenburg* refuels overnight at the Eiffel Tower in Paris. He will take the Star of Judea as his payment. The Jews intend to use that priceless emerald as down-payment for the land they buy from the treacherous Bavarian soviet. The *Hindenburg* will blow up, and the French will be blamed for their sabotage. A wedge is thereby driven between the various allies. Jews, Frenchmen, and Bavarian communists will all be implicated by the British and Americans. Chaos will ensue. Meanwhile, we will be prepared, as soon as news of the *Hindenburg*'s destruction comes through, to announce a new National Socialist Bavarian state. The Freikorps will already have passed through the Eagle Gate and be crossing the moonbeam roads into the Arcades of the Opera, a stone's throw from the Arc de Triomphe. We shall announce our victory there. Our guns will by that time command the whole of Paris. Germans will rise to our victorious standard, and this time the British and French will find it impossible to subdue us. Paris will already be hostage to our cannon!"

"But this is madness!" gasped Lapointe. "All you will succeed in doing is harming hundreds of innocent people. You *will* be defeated again. Your logic is entirely flawed, Captain Goering."

"Nonsense. You are addressing the cream of the Nazi elite!" barked Herr Goebbels. "Our plan is flawless!"

"Has Herr Klosterheim talked you into this?" asked LeBec through gritted teeth. His wound had, for the moment, stopped bleeding. He assured his friends that it was only a superficial flesh wound. Slowly the group came to a halt at the very edge of the silvery road through the multiverse.

"We have perfected this plan together with Herr Klosterheim's involvement," said Hess, his strange eyes shifting back and forth from one member of the group to the other. "By Sunday Europe will have accepted the reality of a new Germany. We are already certain that many Frenchmen as well as English aristocrats will flock to our standard!"

"Klosterheim uses you for his own purposes," said Begg quietly. "He has beguiled you, as he has beguiled so many others. He has no interest in reviving Nazi Germany or, indeed, doing anything but gaining control of the Cosmic Balance. Mrs Persson. You know this to be true!"

"I have no reason to disbelieve him, Sir Seaton." With a giggle the adventuress turned away.

Once again they could hear the rhythmic booming as of a great drum. Some shivered at the sound, waiting at the beginning of the moonbeam roads. Motioning again with their pistols, the Nazis forced Begg and Co to move ahead. Each second they moved closer to the noise of the great regulator. And the vision of the multiverse grew more vivid, the roads more vivid and detailed.

The detectives gasped. Once again on every side of them, the distance was filled with glowing silvery roads, twisting in all directions, forming an extraordinary labyrinth. Unconscious of the drama being played between the Nazis and their enemies, travellers walked between a million realities.

"Where are they going, Begg?" muttered Doctor Sinclair.

Klosterheim read the bewilderment in Taffy's eyes. "Do not fear, doctor. You will soon have the whole of eternity to contemplate this puzzle. Now, move on! There are still more wonders to greet you . . ."

LeBec groaned, feeling himself weakening. He was the only one of the prisoners not to be bound. His injured arm hung limp at his side, and he staunched the blood from his wounded shoulder with his right hand. He seemed dazed, unable to accept the actuality of these events. He looked up through the swirling, scintillating colour which filled the great ether, the shimmering lines of light cutting between them, the distant figures, the immense beauty of it all, then back at the grotesquely grinning uniformed men training their Lugers on the captured detectives.

Behind them, having removed the black diamond mask he affected, Klosterheim stood stock still. He had wrapped his great cloak around him, as if against a chill, though the temperature was moderate. Within his head cold eyes shifted from face to face, displaying no expression, no empathy, no sense of humanity.

To Begg's certain knowledge, the former priest was virtually indestructible. Like Zenith, like Mrs Persson herself, he was an eternal, one of those whose longevity was considerably greater than that of an ordinary human being. He was accustomed to life in the semi-infinite. Some said they sustained their long lives by dreaming a thousand years for every day of their ordinary existence and that what we witnessed of them were dream projections rather than the actual person. That most of them lived *forever* was, in Begg's opinion, debatable. Yet those who had encountered Klosterheim over the centuries had come to believe the tale of his being one of Satan's favourite accomplices until the time when Satan himself sought reconciliation with their former lord. Then, it was said, Klosterheim had turned against Satan, too. As he perceived it, he had been betrayed by the two mightiest masters in his universe. For all his well-hidden spirituality, Begg was not a man to accept superstition or supernatural explanation but he certainly entertained the truth in the stories as he stared back at Klosterheim. Begg's own face was expressionless as he considered ways and means of turning the tables on their captors.

Step by remorseless step they moved along the opaque, silvery causeway towards the sonorous booming until at last the road ended abruptly, upon the edge of the void, its silver falling away like mist. For the first time a smile crossed Klosterheim's thin, bloodless lips. And he looked down.

Begg was the first to follow his gaze.

The detective's immediate instinct was to step back. There below them, its blade pointing down into the dancing, obscuring mist, he could see the shape of a gigantic black sword fashioned to resemble a balance, with a cup depending from either arm. Within the metal of the black blade scarlet characters writhed and twisted, the gleaming bejeweled cups moved slowly as they measured the weight of the world's pain. Multicoloured strands of ectoplasm swirled from the bowls. Begg knew instinctively in his soul that once again he did indeed look upon the legendary Cosmic Balance which regulated the entire multiverse, weighing Law and Chaos, good and evil, truth and falsehood, life and death, love and hate, maintaining the equilibrium, and therefore the existence, of all created matter.

Through the great voice of the Balance Klosterheim's cold tones amplified clearly. "If the multiverse has a centre, it is here. I have sought it for many years and across many universes. And you, gentlemen, will have the privilege of seeing it briefly before you die. Indeed," and now he chuckled to himself, "you will *always* see it before you die . . ."

Lapointe interrupted. "You are a dangerous fool, M'sieu Klosterheim, if you believe you can control that symbol of eternal justice. Only God Almighty has the way of altering the scales maintaining the balance beween

Law and Chaos. What you see is doubtless only one manifestation of the Cosmic Balance. Can you *control* a symbol?"

"Perhaps not," answered the sweet, calm voice of Mrs Persson. She had turned up the collar of her coat. Framed by her helmet of dark hair, her beautiful, pale, oval face shone with the reflected light of the great scale. Her indigo eyes sparkled with excitement. "But one who gives power to the symbol can sometimes control what it controls . . ."

With an expression of disgust Lapointe turned away.

Hitler, Hess, Göring, Röhm, and Goebbels had all crowded to the verge of the road to stare down at the great Balance. "All we need now is to set into that hilt the Star of Judea," said the Nazi colonel.

"Which you will not receive until Saturday, as I understand it," said Begg, genuinely puzzled. "Tomorrow?"

Hitler became suddenly alert. He turned brown, questioning eyes to Klosterheim.

"I brought you here where Time has no end and no beginning, merely to show you why and for what you will die," declared Klosterheim. "A small offering to the Gods of Chaos who will soon be serving *my* cause."

"But what is the chief price you pay for their compliance?" Begg enquired coolly. "The souls of four mortals could hardly be enough."

"Oh, they are scarcely ordinary mortals. Their crimes have resonated across the entire multiverse. Their souls have far greater weight than yours, Sir Seaton, certainly in that respect. Yet will the Balance accept them? We still await the one who brings us the Star of Judea. The *Hindenburg* docked an hour ago and now stands ready at Eiffel's great mooring mast." Klosterheim's cold voice was amused. "With that great and ancient jewel, I make my true offering and in return shall have control of the Balance."

"How could a mere jewel—any jewel—have value here?" demanded Doctor Sinclair, his eyes half mad with what they had seen.

"The Star of Judea is of immense value to the Lords of Chaos, Taffy," murmured Begg. "They will hugely reward any being who brings it to them, and it will even *seem* to give that being control of the Cosmic Balance. Meanwhile . . ." He noted an opportunity and gestured, drawing the Nazis' attention away from his friends . . .

A revolver suddenly jerked upward in LeBec's left hand. Begg had anticipated this and had been deliberately distracting their captors, giving LeBec time to act. The Frenchman's eyes were a mixture of contempt and pain. "You poor, unimaginative brutes could not imagine one of us owning a second weapon. Throw up your hands and drop your guns, gentlemen."

The startled Germans swung round, staring into the barrel of LeBec's serviceable Hachette .38. They looked from him to Klosterheim to Mrs Persson. Only the woman found some amusement in this reversal, yet she did not move either to comply or to resist.

At LeBec's demand, Captain Hess drew his elaborate, ornamental dagger from the scabbard at his belt and cut the ropes binding the metatemporal detectives. Hess's deep-set eyes were dreamy, as if he believed himself the victim of an hallucination. Constantly his gaze returned to the great scintillating scales adjusting gently in constant balance, their movement continuing to create the deep booming, the heartbeat of the multiverse.

Klosterheim snarled. "Do you think you can defeat my plans now merely by turning the tables on my servants?" And without warning, arms outstretched, he rushed at Hess and pushed the startled Nazi to the edge of the moonbeam road. Before the detectives could reach him, he shoved again, and this time Hess's awkward arms flailed as he fought to keep his balance. He reached towards Klosterheim, yelling something unintelligible, and then fell backwards.

They all watched him drop, spinning and waving, like a scarecrow, falling, falling, down towards the Balance, passing the swaying beam until he hung frozen in the pulsing light rising from one of the cups. They heard him scream, a high-pitched and terrible noise, and when he had disappeared momentarily into the light, the cup suddenly flared scarlet.

Klosterheim stepped to the edge and watched with an air of satisfaction. "A sign of my good faith, I hope."

Colonel Hitler swore in German. "You bastard! You killed him. You killed my closest friend!"

Klosterheim shrugged. "It is perhaps disputable that he's actually dead, but my master needs blood and souls." He shrugged then. "The Grail—"

"That thing is not the Grail!" growled Röhm. "There cannot be *two* grails!"

Now Klosterheim smiled openly. "Not in *your* mythology, perhaps. But one cup holds the stuff of Chaos, the other holds the stuff of Law. That is what regulates the multiverse. Combined they become the Balance, but remain in constant conflict."

Still cursing Klosterheim, the Nazi colonel reached down and picked up his fallen Luger. In one movement he pointed and pulled the trigger, firing shot after shot into the mocking figure. Again came that cold, humourless chuckle, as Klosterheim spread his arms and looked down at his unwounded body. "I am not so easily killed, you see, Colonel Hitler. How can you take away the soul of a man who does not have one?"

Still Una Persson did not move. She seemed to be waiting for something, perhaps to watch the opposed groups destroy one another. Yet enigmatic amusement continued to glow in her indigo eyes.

Only when Röhm retrieved his own automatic pistol and pointed it at her did her expression change. Begg was sure, eternal though she might be, that she was not invulnerable.

"*Arioch! Arioch! Aid me now!*" called Klosterheim in that leaden voice which seemed to deaden the air it filled.

◂◉ THE SEVENTH CHAPTER ◉▸

Old Souls

Begg knew he could not kill Klosterheim easily and that the Nazis would soon return their attention to the detectives. He raised his Webley and, taking careful aim, shot Röhm between the eyes. The captain's expression changed from anger to surprise, and then he, too, lost his footing and fell, his body spinning rapidly downwards then stopping suddenly, as if in the grip of some powerful magnetic force which held him spread-eagled and screaming silently in space above the Balance.

Another shot. This time it was Lapointe who sent Captain Goering into the void to hang in the air immediately above the cup which held the weight of Chaos.

"No!" cried Una Persson suddenly. "No! Don't kill them! Not yet! You don't know what you're doing. There is a plan—"

But Begg had no choice, for the malevolent clubfooted Goebbels screamed something about betrayal and turned his gun on her. The Webley's bullet found its target in Goebbels's heart, and another Nazi went down, whirling and shrieking and coming to a sudden halt when embraced by the light from the cup, which now boiled with smokey scarlet and black fumes.

"Sir Seaton!" cried Mrs Persson. "No more shooting, I beg you! Don't you realise you're aiding Klosterheim. Their souls are already pledged to Chaos. *They* are the blood sacrifice they intended to make of you. One last action and he can use them to destroy everything. Everything!"

Begg was confused. He kept his Webley levelled at the remaining Nazi, the slavering, terrified Hitler who whispered in his lisping Austrian: "She's right. Nothing but harm will come from killing me."

"Then get down on your knees and lock your hands above your head," snapped Begg. Slowly, with every part of his body trembling, Hitler obeyed. Taffy Sinclair knew his old friend well enough to understand that Begg accepted that he had, inadvertently, done Klosterheim's work. The beat of the balance had changed subtly. Now it was as if they heard a distant wildfire, like the crackling and snapping of burning timber.

Una Persson came to stand beside Begg. He stepped backward quickly as if she threatened him, but her expression was one of mixed anger and fear. "I did not believe you could follow me," she said. "Oh, Seaton, your courage is now likely to lose us the fight—even perhaps destroy the multiverse! Do you understand what this means?"

The massive, swordlike balance, its cups swaying and groaning, continued to beat and pulse. The light around its hilt was a golden halo surrounding dull metal of a blackness greater than the void. From somewhere below Begg thought he heard the rattle of distant laughter.

Klosterheim's voice joined in the laughter. It was the bleakest, most desolate sound Sir Seaton Begg had ever experienced. He lowered his gun and looked helplessly from Mrs Persson, to Klosterheim, to the kneeling, gibbering Hitler, and to his friends.

"By Jupiter!" he whispered as realisation dawned. "Oh, my good Lord! What have I done?"

The booming of the great balance had now taken on yet another different, arythmic note. Under its deep, masculine throb, Begg thought he could hear the thin screams of the Nazis. The gulf surrounding the not-dead men now boiled vigorously with blood and black smoke.

"We would have mastered creation and moulded it in our desired image until the end of time," wept Hitler. Begg did not care that the sobbing man now lowered his hands and buried his face in them. "Klosterheim! That was what you promised me!"

"Like you, my friend, I have made many promises in my long career." Klosterheim's toneless voice betrayed no emotion. "And like you, Colonel Hitler, I have broken many promises. I helped you and your followers because it suited me. Now you have failed me and it no longer suits. Your actions brought my enemies to me, and we have reached this pass. Only the blood and souls of your colleagues will compensate for your clumsiness." He turned to the metatemporal detective. "My master has his initial sacrifices, thanks to you, Sir Seaton. Now he will come to my aid, as he promised . . ."

Begg could not disguise his own self-disgust. He was about to speak when a new voice, light and mocking, sounded from out of the scarlet mist behind them. He recognised the voice at once.

"Oh, do not count on Lord Arioch turning up just yet, Herr Klosterheim." The newcomer's tone held a kind of courage which could belong, Begg knew, only to one man. He looked in surprise back down the road which had brought them here. Strolling towards them, swinging his cane, for all the world as if he were still the insouciant flaneur of the Arcades de l'Opera in full evening dress, including a silk-lined cape and a silk hat, came Monsieur Zenith. "Good evening, gentlemen." He lifted his top hat. "Mrs Persson. This is not quite the scene I imagined I would find. Where are Herr Hitler's friends?"

"I fear they have become at least a potential blood offering to whatever demon of Chaos Heironymous Klosterheim obeys," replied Begg in chastened tones. "I believe I have made the greatest mistake of my life. Can it possibly be reversed, cousin?"

The elegant boulevardier paused and selected one of his opium cigarettes from his slender, silver case. He lit it with an equally elegant silver Dunhill. "I must be truthful with you, Sir Seaton. I am not sure. Theoretically, if Chaos or Law achieves total ascendancy, then Time stops. Like those fellows down there, we shall be frozen forever at the moment before our deaths. Scarcely a palatable fate."

"Indeed." Begg looked around him and then at the great balance below. "What is this gem they said you'd steal?"

"It is already stolen." Zenith smiled to himself. "That is what brought me here. I possessed it before the ship ever left Jerusalem. Their perception of time remains, as ever, very crude. The gem emits both light and vibrations and acts as a kind of compass. Madame Persson, understood this, I believe? It was what we discussed before the situation grew less controllable. My objective remains the Da Vinci in the Louvre, which I expected to possess by now. They have absolutely no right to it, you know. I had not reckoned, however, on Herr Klosterheim's involvement. The rules of this game seem to be constantly changing. I underestimated its nature. Madame Persson suggested . . ."

"I regret that I misled you a little, old friend." Mrs Persson still stood close to the expressionless Klosterheim. "Self-interest sometimes demands a fresh strategy. A new reality."

"The Nazis continue to be useful," said Klosterheim. "Whether their souls go to Chaos or their bodies serve my cause matters not. Like all women, Mrs Persson understands where her loyalties are best placed."

"Great Heavens, man! Does life have no value to you?" Taffy Sinclair broke away from his fellow investigators and strode towards the cadaverous creature. "How on earth can you allow such infamy?"

Klosterheim's dreadful laughter echoed into the void. "You speak to one who has defied both God and Lucifer and now stands ready to challenge their mastery of reality itself. I am not the first to try. But I shall be the first to succeed."

"Such confidence is reassuring in these uncertain times." Zenith seemed amused. "I envy you, Herr Klosterheim. When do you expect my lord Arioch?"

"He will arrive imminently. He gave his word." Klosterheim turned those hollow eyes on the albino. "He shares my impatience as well as my ambition."

"Some would say he is already with us." Monsieur Zenith motioned with his sword stick. Klosterheim's eyes followed its direction as if he thought Zenith pointed out the powerful Chaos Lord, but he saw nothing but the Balance below and four bodies suspended above one of the cups, an instant from being absorbed into the cause of Entropy.

Behind Begg, Commissaire Lapointe was forcing Hitler to his feet and handcuffing him. "It is my duty, gentlemen, to get this fellow back to the authorities in Berlin. As to the rest of the matter, I fear it is far beyond my competence. So if you will permit me . . ." He began rapidly to push the whimpering insurgent colonel ahead of him, followed by his wounded assistant whose expression was one of regret and embarrassment. "Duty demands," said LeBec.

"Of course," agreed Begg, "I have no objection. Were the situation a little less complicated, I would be with you. Can you find your own way back?"

"I think so. With good fortune we will meet again in Paris very shortly."

"You may count on it, Commissionaire." Monsieur Zenith bowed and again raised his hat. "I will take the most conscientious care of your colleague."

Herr Klosterheim however was having none of this. "I cannot permit *any* of you to leave. Not now. Your souls are the price of my success." When LeBec's pistol was again aimed at his chest he let out an explosive guffaw. "Oh, fire away, my dear policeman. Have you any idea how many times I have been killed by the likes of you. Your lives are mine, just as these others belong to me. All are promised to my patron . . ."

"My dear Klosterheim," drawled Zenith, "are you truly so ignorant of the change in your situation that you believe you can threaten these good officers and stop them performing their duty? I believe the clinical term for your condition is 'denial.' You no longer possess any power to speak of." And, smiling, he pressed a silver stud in his ebony cane and swiftly withdrew the slender blade.

The sword now in Zenith's hand was actually darker than the ebony which had contained it. Along its slim length writhed bloody scarlet characters, the runes of some long-forgotten lexicon. Sinclair turned to question Begg and to his astonishment saw his colleague laughing and holding his Webley so loosely in his hand that it threatened to fall into the void.

"Aha!" exclaimed Begg, almost in delight. "Here is your sought-for demonic aid, my dear Klosterheim! What a jest! What a jest!" He stepped back as his cousin advanced holding before him the thrumming épée now crying with its own voice. Bewildered at last, Klosterheim looked from Mrs Persson to Zenith to the sword.

"Mrs Persson, you assured me . . ."

"I told you that the black broadsword you call Stormbringer was no longer in Monsieur Zenith's possession. I said nothing of any other blade perhaps bearing similar characteristics, which he finds convenient to carry in a more modern form under a different name." The Englishwoman grinned like a lioness who had just made a kill. "You must know, Herr Klosterheim, that just as the wielder of the sword takes many guises, so does the sword itself. And even the creature which inhabits the sword has more than one identity!"

She stepped aside as Klosterheim began to back away from the advancing albino. "I shall not be threatened, Monsieur! Arioch! Lord Arioch of the Seven Darks! Aid me, I beg thee. Arioch, thou promised me . . ."

"Lord Arioch's promises are of a practical and volatile nature, also," declared Zenith, the slender sword still pointed at Klosterheim's throat. "It surprises me that you did not consider this when laying out your equation for this particular adventure."

"But you forget, monsieur. That blade and your master feed on souls as well as blood." Klosterheim's smile was bitterly sardonic. "Nein?" With a quavering laugh, somehow even more disgusting than any of his previous expressions, he folded his arms and challenged Zenith to stab him.

If anything, the albino's smile stilled the onlookers' blood more than the other eternal's laughter. Without hesitation, Monsieur Zenith lunged forward in an elegant fencer's position, and his delicate, black blade took Klosterheim in the throat.

For a second the ex-priest continued to laugh . . . and then his eyes widened. He clutched at his neck, at the shivering blade . . . He gasped. He groaned. He staggered backwards towards the very edge of the moonbeam road and hung there, swaying, as blood bubbled from the wound Zenith had made. "Nein!" he said again, this time with fear. "Nein!"

He realised suddenly where he stood and attempted to regain his balance, but it was too late. His deep-set eyes burned with terror, lighting his cadaverous head with an unholy fire. Begg and the others were uncertain what emotion they witnessed, but they all agreed that it *was* emotion.

"How can this be?" Klosterheim spoke in the old, Hoch Deutsch German of his youth. "How—?"

"You forgot, Herr Klosterheim." With a lithe, reverse movement Zenith resheathed the black blade. "My sword is capable of conferring souls as well as stealing them." He stepped forward again, his hand light on Klosterheim's chest, as with two fingers he tipped him gently off into the void above the pulsing Balance. "And only a creature with a human soul, no matter how corrupt, can enjoy that moment of forever, poised between eternity and oblivion, which comes with the end of everything. Meanwhile, I send you to consider that thought for as long as you shall last. Which is, of course, until the end of time."

Klosterheim fell backwards screaming and joined the others whose distant bodies hung in the void, like flies in a web, conscious and frozen in the instant before their deaths.

Monsieur Zenith turned with a bow. Reaching out, he kissed Mrs Persson's hand. "Well played, madam. Our plan was almost foiled by these good-hearted fellows." He inclined his head towards Begg and Sinclair.

"You two had planned all this?" Sinclair found himself torn between rage and relief. "All of it?"

"Most of it," declared Mrs Persson, advancing towards the famous pathologist. "Really, Doctor Sinclair, we had no intention of deceiving you or your colleagues. Neither did I expect to be detained by them, so very likely you saved my life by arriving when you did. But from then on, I thought it the best strategy to pretend to ally myself with Klosterheim, at least until Monsieur Zenith made his somewhat belated appearance. We really did not know you would have either the powers of deduction or the sheer courage to reach this place. Then, when you did turn up, I for one was rather baffled. Everything Monsieur Zenith and myself had worked out was threatened." She drew a deep breath. "Happily, as you see——"

"Klosterheim, for all his evil, does not deserve such a fate," declared Begg gravely. "And neither do those others."

"Oh, I assure you, dear cousin, they *do indeed* deserve everything." Zenith looked down into the void to where the great Balance still swayed. "And this affair is probably not yet over, though your part is certainly done." And with a casual flick of his wrist, he threw his swordstick after the man on whom he had just conferred both life and a kind of death. He turned to guide the rest of the party back in the direction from which they had come. "Quickly. The thing that is my sword is not so easily defeated in its ambitions."

Begg hesitated, demurring as Zenith's face became a mask of urgency. "Hurry man! Hurry! If you value your soul!"

From somewhere below there now sounded a voice more terrifying than anything they had yet heard and blossoming upwards they saw a huge, bloody black cloud rising, roiling forward like a wave, which Begg knew must soon engulf them. The noise became deafening, bringing bile to their throats. With some alacrity Begg obeyed his cousin. Grabbing Doctor Sinclair's arm, he turned and ran, the Frenchmen, their prisoner, Mrs Persson, and Zenith the Albino immediately behind him.

As in a powerful earthquake, the moonbeam road quivered and trembled beneath their feet. They ran on, knowing that not only their lives but their eternal souls would be the price of any further hesitation . . .

. . . Until suddenly a deep calm settled over them and a silvery whiteness sprang up ahead, forming a kind of wall. They were once again in the catacombs they had seemingly left behind millenia before.

Monsieur Zenith straightened his silk hat. "I shall miss that cane," he said. "But I know the exact place I can buy another in the Galerie d'Baromètre. Come, Mrs Persson, gentlemen. Shall we return to the Arcades de l'Opera? I think we have a rather extraordinary adventure to celebrate."

Epilogue

His shoulder thoroughly bandaged, LeBec joined the four men and one woman who shared an outside table at L'Albertine the following day. He was received with a round of muted applause and a great sense of celebration as the hero of the hour. "Without you, my dear LeBec, we should perhaps even now be enjoying the fate of our Nazi antagonists. As it is, the arrest of Colonel Hitler took the wind out of the Freikorps insurgents, who were indeed massing to enter the tunnel into Paris. The *Hindenburg* made a successful mooring at the Eiffel Tower and spent a tranquil night there. The Star of Judea was returned, and even now negotiations to found a new Jewish homeland in Bavaria are proceeding. It is fully expected that the exodus to Southern Germany will begin some time towards the end of next year!" Seaton Begg clapped his French colleague on his good shoulder and ordered him an Armagnac.

The autumn sun was rising high in a golden sky, and the great fountain in the centre of the arcade spread dark blue and green sheets of water over the verdigris, marble, and tile of the statuary. There was a tranquil, leisurely quality to the day which Begg agreed he had not experienced for some time. The capture of Hitler and his men had created a general euphoria.

"Illusion though it might be, my friends," said Commissaire Lapointe softly, "it seems to me that our world is about to embark upon a new era of peace and prosperity. Call me optimistic, if you will, but I believe our defeat of the Nazi gang achieved something lasting. Do you follow my meaning, Sir Seaton?"

Begg permitted himself a small smile. "We can only hope you are right, my dear commissioner. But you are of another opinion, I think, Taffy?"

Doctor Sinclair did his best to make light of his own thoughts. "It was that Balance," he said. "Something going on down there terrified me. And the manner of Klosterheim's death—well, I still have difficulty sleeping when I think about it." He glanced shyly at Monsieur Zenith who leaned back, taking a long puff on his Turkish oval.

"I am sorry you were forced to witness that, Doctor Sinclair. If I had had any other choice, of course I would not have conducted matters in that way. But Klosterheim was the force behind Hitler and his men. He has lived for a very long time. Some will tell you he counselled Martin Luther. Others say he was the angel who stood with Duke Arioch at Lucifer's right hand during the great war in heaven. Having no soul, he was almost impossible to destroy. Thus only by conferring a soul upon him could I kill him. Or, at least, I hope I killed him . . ."

"But I think what is concerning my old friend, Sinclair," interrupted LeBec, "is a very important question."

"Which is?" Zenith seemed genuinely puzzled.

"Taffy and I have both wondered about it." Begg leaned forward to address his cousin. "Our question would be—where did that soul come from? Whose did you use? You can surely see why we would be curious . . ."

"Aha!" Monsieur Zenith turned, laughing, to Mrs Persson, who clearly knew the answer. She leaned down and petted her two Orientals, who lay, perfectly behaved, at her feet. "I think I will leave that explanation to you, Mrs Persson."

The exquisitely beautiful adventuress reached for her glass of absinthe. "It was the last soul the sword drank on another plane than this one, n'est-ce pas? It has been many years, if I am not mistaken, since you have unsheathed that particular weapon on this particular plane, eh, Monsieur Zenith?"

"Oh, many. I suppose, my friends, I will let you into a secret I have kept for rather a long time. While I have in the course of the past two thousand years sired children and indeed founded a dynasty which is familiar to anyone who knows the history of the province of Wäldenstein and her capital Mirenburg, I am not truly of this world or indeed this universe. It is fair to say that I have, in the way some of you will know, been dreaming myself. I have another body, as solid as this one, which, as I speak lays on a 'dream couch' in a city more ancient than the world it inhabits." He paused in sympathy as he observed their expressions.

"The civilisation to which I belong is neither truly human nor of this universe. Its rulers are men and women capable of manipulating the forces of nature and, if you like, super-nature to serve their own ends. People sometimes call them sorcerers. They learn all manner of arcane wisdom by making use of their dream couches, sleeping sometimes for thousands of years while experiencing other lives. Upon waking, they forget most of the dreams save for the skills they employ to rule their world. I am one of those sorcerous aristocrats. The island where I dwell is called, as far as I can pronounce it in your language, Melniboné. We are not natives of its world, either, but were driven to inhabit it during a terrible upheaval which ultimately forced us to become the cruel rulers of another planet.

"The demonic archangel Arioch, upon whom Klosterheim called to aid him, is our people's patron. Both your Bible and the poet Milton mention him. On occasions he inhabits the black blade you saw me use. On other occasions the sword contains the souls of those its wielder has killed. Some parts of those souls are transferred to whoever uses the blade. Other parts go to placate Arioch. When Satan attempted, hundreds of years ago, to be reconciled with God, neither Klosterheim nor Arioch accepted it and have, across many planes of the multiverse, sought not only the destruction of God himself, but also of Satan, or whatever manifestations of his forces exist here."

"You have still not explained whose soul Klosterheim's body drank," pointed out Sinclair.

"Why, the last soul it took," said Monsieur Zenith in some surprise. "I thought that is what you understood."

"And whose was that—?"

Monsieur Zenith rose swiftly and elegantly and kissed Mrs Persson's hand before moving towards the shelf where he had placed his silk hat and gloves. "You must forgive me, gentlemen. I have some unfinished business nearby."

Instinctively Commissionaire Lapointe was on his feet as if to apprehend him but then caught himself and sat down again quickly.

Sir Seaton Begg, with dawning comprehension, laid his hand on his old friend's arm, but Taffy Sinclair was insistent. "Whose, Monsieur Zenith? Whose?"

Zenith the Albino slipped gracefully from the table and in a moment seemed to disappear, merging with the sunlit spray of the fountain.

"But whose . . . ?" Sinclair turned a baffled glance at Mrs Persson who had lifted her two cats into her lap and was stroking them gently. "Do you know?"

She inclined her head, raised her perfectly shaped eyebrows, and looked intimately at Sir Seaton Begg whose nod was scarcely perceptible.

"It was his own, of course."

About the Author

MICHAEL MOORCOCK is a British writer and musician living in Texas, France, and Spain. The author of many literary novels and stories in practically every genre, he has won and been short-listed for many awards including the Nebula, World Fantasy, Hugo, August Derleth, Booker, Whitbread, Guardian Fiction Prize, and others. As a member of the prog-rock band Hawkwind he won a platinum disc. As editor of *New Worlds* he received an Arts Council of Great Britain award and a BSFA award. His journalism appears regularly in the *Guardian*, the *Daily Telegraph*, the *New Statesman*, and the *Spectator*. He has been compared, among others, to Balzac, Dumas, Dickens, James Joyce, Ian Fleming, J. R. R.Tolkien, and Robert E. Howard.

Visit Michael Moorcock online at www.multiverse.org.